THE 13TH KEY

Sarah Fisher

Book One in the Dragonscale series

A catalogue record for this book is available from the National Library of Australia

Disclaimer
This is a work of fiction. Names, characters, places, incidents and events, other than those clearly in the public domain, are fictitious and any resemblance to actual persons, living or dead, is entirely coincidental.

To my mother, Judith and my dearest friend, Maree, who read every word of every draft

Acknowledgements

I am eternally grateful to my parents, Ray and Judith; and my brothers, Cameron and Daniel for their support and encouragement.

I am indebted to spirit-sister, Maree for her love and guidance, and to Angus for believing in me.

Thanks also go to Patrice and Kirsty for their editorial and design expertise, and to Lucy for amazing artwork.

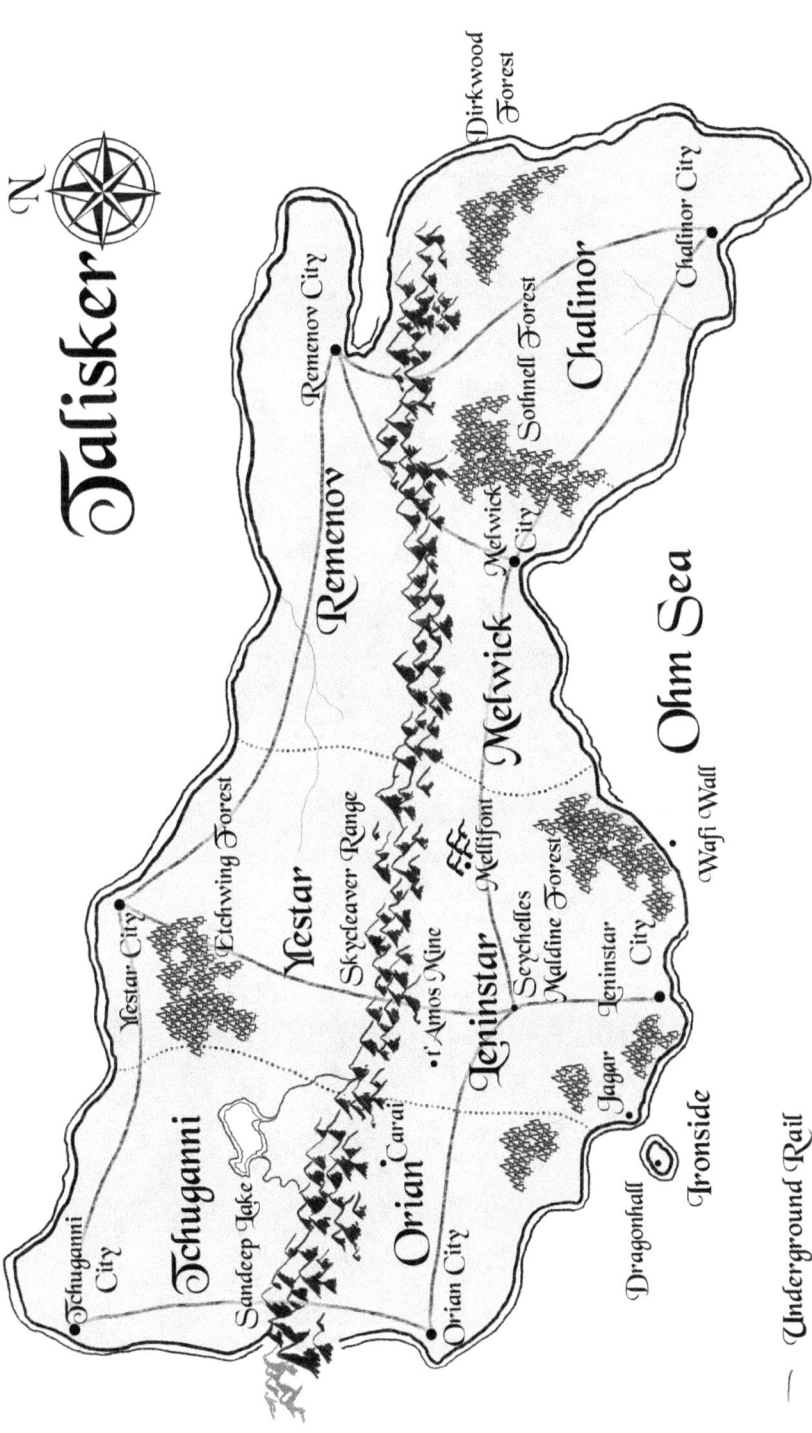

Chapter 1

Noah could feel her teacher's disapproving gaze boring into her. Nothing new. She refocused her eyes, if not her attention, on the summaries scrawled across the whiteboard. *Romeo and Juliet*. Aside from the costumes, the film didn't interest her. She'd faithfully copied all the costuming notes into her book, supplementing them with full colour sketches, but had disregarded everything else.

As Noah set about putting the finishing touches on her artwork, she prayed for the promised storm. All the windows of the ground floor classroom had been pushed out to their limits – Regi Alston had almost fallen out the one nearest to him in his quest to snare some fresh air – but the breeze never came. The fans twirled uselessly on the ceiling, barely stirring the cloud of perfume and body odour that dogged the English class.

Noah looked up when Mr Brennan arrived at her desk. Experience had taught her that ignoring him would not make him go away. He raised his hands to speak.

'If this were an art and design course you would be achieving fantastic grades, Noah,' he signed, 'but this is *not* art and design. It is English. You are going to fail if you don't broaden your knowledge of the genre.'

Noah's face burned. While few of her fellow students understood sign language, they all knew when she was being told off.

'Pass or fail, I'm out of here at the end of the year,' Noah signed back.

'You think failing senior is going to get you a good job?'

When Noah didn't answer, Mr Brennan pointed to her drawings.

'Do you really think you're just going to walk out of here and become a world-famous fashion designer?'

Noah nodded.

The teacher's eyes narrowed. 'I suggest you talk to your maths tutor about the likelihood of *that* happening. You're destined for the streets if you don't pick up your act, young lady. Quite frankly I'm surprised at you. I'd have thought you'd want to make something of yourself – become someone your parents would've been proud of.'

Noah held his gaze, inhaled slowly and pressed her palms onto the desk. She would not be baited. Not this time. Long moments passed before Mr Brennan broke the impasse.

'I'll call your aunt this afternoon to discuss your lack of effort in this subject,' he signed before turning his back on her.

You do that, she thought as a hand closed over hers. Noah looked at the girl beside her.

'Ignore him,' Libby signed, rolling her eyes. 'He's a jerk.'

'Oh, I know it,' Noah replied.

'Just don't let him get to you. He's wrong.'

'About?'

'You. Your parents would already be proud of who you are.'

Noah felt her angst melt away. 'Thanks.'

She took the girl's hand and gave it a gentle squeeze. Libby was one of the few students at Sayle South High who knew how to sign, and the gregarious drama student enjoyed signing with someone other than her annoying little brother. Noah was just thankful for someone friendly and bubbly to talk to.

'You can have my notes to copy if you need them,' Libby offered.

'Thanks,' Noah signed. 'I might just take you up on that.'

Noah looped her dark ponytail into a knot to keep it out of her way and went back to her artwork. The notes would wait a bit longer. As she added more detail to the bodice of Juliet's dress, a tingling sensation in her ears distracted her. It wasn't painful but it was … gone now. She took a deep breath then exhaled but the feeling returned, stronger this time. Noah sat up straight in her chair. Mr Brennan, who was sitting at his desk writing a note in his diary, was distracted by her sudden movement. He looked up and glared at her – as did the cat that was perched next to him.

Where did that come from? Noah wondered. As she studied the feline she was increasingly worried that the answer to her question might be "not from Earth". The cat was about the size of a domestic pet but it had the distinctive markings of a tiger. Perhaps the science department had been miniaturising African cats in the lab and one had escaped. Noah shook her head. Though Sayle South boasted the best technology the twenty-first century had to offer, high school science students were more likely to blow things up than create things.

Noah looked around the room. The other students were dutifully writing in their English books – some were probably even writing the notes from the board – while Mr Brennan continued glaring at her. No one else appeared to notice the cat. Noah closed her eyes and counted to five before opening them again. The cat was still on the desk but it wasn't sitting now. It sauntered across the desk in front of Mr Brennan, its tail trailing across the teacher's top lip, giving him a stripy moustache. Reflexively, Noah rubbed her nose.

Mr Brennan went back to writing in his diary while the feline stopped to sniff the whiteboard markers on his desk. It recoiled violently and swatted at one of the pens with a testing paw. Noah had long believed that teachers' pens were implements of torture and if this animal could sense their inherent evil, she might have to reassess her dislike of cats. After a few more swipes, it lost interest in the pens and jumped onto Mr Brennan's head. He didn't react. Noah gaped as the cat balanced easily on the greasy dome. She watched its mouth move and she noticed that as it did, the strange sensation in her ears started again.

Weird.

The cat closed its mouth and the sensation stopped.

Very weird.

Noah shivered. Imaginary cats should not make her feel this way. *Must be the perfumes in here,* she thought. *I'm hallucinating.*

When Mr Brennan stood up, the cat jumped lightly onto the desk again. Noah continued to stare at the feline as her classmates packed up their belongings.

Libby tapped her on the shoulder and signed, 'Bell's gone.'

Noah looked up. 'Yeah thanks. I'm almost done. I'll see you tomorrow.'

'Okay,' Libby signed. 'Don't stay too long. Storm's coming.'

As the classroom emptied, the creature leapt from the teacher's table onto one of the student desks in the front row. Like a frog negotiating lily pads on a pond, it jumped from desk to desk until it got to Noah's. Leaning as far back in her chair as she could, Noah studied the apparition. It clearly wasn't a miniaturised tiger. The proportions were all wrong. Tigers – even the cubs – were powerfully built with large heads and paws but this specimen was delicate. The striking markings lent its lean frame undeserved credibility while its mesmerising orange eyes blazed beneath its pointed ears. A slender tail waved cobra-like behind it.

The cat studied her too when, without warning, its hackles went up and its tail exploded into something that would have been perfect to dust her dressing table. It bared its teeth at her and Noah clamped her hands over her ears.

From deep in her brain a word floated to the surface.

Hearing.

What?

You can hear the cat, her brain said.

Hear the cat? That's ridiculous, she thought. *I'm deaf. I can't hear.*

You can *hear,* her brain insisted.

Not keen on arguing with her own brain, Noah acted quickly to set things straight. *Okay Brain, there are only two problems with your theory. If we ignore the first one for a moment – the rather obvious one about me being deaf – we get to the second problem, which relates to the cat not being real. Surely a person can't hear something that doesn't exist.*

Her brain was not dissuaded.

Why not? You're seeing something that doesn't exist, apparently.

Noah had to admit that her brain had a point. She stared at the cat that didn't exist and frowned. Again, the feline bared its teeth and Noah clutched at her head.

Her brain was back.

If you can't hear, then why have you got your hands over your ears?

It was a good question but one that she set aside as she fumbled to get her pencils packed away. Hugging her satchel to her chest, Noah threaded her way between the desks, picking up speed at the doorway. She ignored Mr Brennan's scowl as he locked the classroom, and she scooted down the hallway and out the front door of the English block.

Noah looked to the sky. Dark clouds were building but the storm was still a little way off. With luck, she'd make it to the city before the downpour. When she was clear of the school gate, she pulled her mother's ring from the fob pocket of her school shorts and slipped it on her middle finger. A glance at the silver dragon coiled protectively around the large oval sapphire brought her parents' faces to mind. *I'll make something of myself,* she promised. *I may not become an English professor but I'll be something.*

The train station was swarming with storm-shy commuters when she arrived. People crammed under the awnings in anticipation of the impending deluge. Noah checked the board. Three minutes until the next city-bound service. She took a spot in the open, confident the rain would hold off. When the train arrived, Noah waited until the initial surge of passengers subsided before she boarded. The carriage air-conditioning was performing admirably despite the crowding and was a welcome reprieve from the day's oppressive humidity. She stood by the door and passed the fifteen-minute ride by watching the lightning show over the mountains to the west of Sayle.

Instead of changing trains at Grand Central and going home to the inevitable argument with Aunt Polly about her English assignment, Noah headed for her favourite fabric boutique. Bibs & Bobs was only four blocks away but the heavy foot traffic at this time of day made the journey slow going.

Holding her satchel in front of her to manoeuvre through the throng more easily, she angled to the left of the footpath, aiming for the newsstand up ahead. The latest edition of *Sayle Chic* was out today with the full list of upcoming fashion shows. She took a copy of the free weekly without breaking stride. Later she'd pour through the magazine to choose which shows to attend. Every night in Sayle scores of events took place in ballrooms and basements across the city. Established designers competed with up-and-coming artists while die-hard wannabes clamoured for recognition as well. Noah's stomach tightened in anticipation. She needed to choose the best events to show her designs and assess the quality of her competition.

By the time she reached Bibs & Bobs, her cotton blouse was plastered to her skin. She looked up and caught a large raindrop in the eye for her trouble. Noah wiped her face, thankful that the rain had held off as long as it had, and pushed open the door. Once inside, she tucked her copy of *Sayle Chic* inside her satchel and slung her bag over her shoulder.

The site which housed Bibs & Bobs was once an Olympic swimming facility. Whoever thought that a swimming pool in a prime, inner-city position was a good idea had been mistaken. It was a spectacular flop but it did make for a unique shop layout. The water was gone and the pool was now filled with rolls of fabric, cards of lace, spools of ribbon, tubes of buttons, reels of thread and drawers stuffed with pattern templates. Where the stadium seating had been, elevated walkways allowed customers access to rooms containing a plethora of other sewing paraphernalia – mannequins, sewing machines, overlockers, cutting machines – as well as studios for hire.

Noah headed for one of the service rooms on the Level 2 walkway. In fancy script on the glass door was one word – Alterations.

The petite young woman behind the counter looked up and smiled when Noah entered.

'Raining yet?' Jemima Chase signed as she made her way around the counter towards Noah.

Noah nodded and signed back, 'Just started.'

'How was school?'

Noah rolled her eyes. 'The same. Can we talk about something else?'

'Of course,' Chase signed. 'Have you finalised your collection yet?'

'Almost.'

'You're a terrible liar,' Chase signed. 'Noah Chord, I swear to God, I'm going to strangle you with this'—she whipped her tape measure from its customary place around her neck and dangled it in front of Noah's face—'if you don't get organised.'

Though small, Chase was not to be messed with. Her diminutive stature and plain looks were in sharp contrast to the personality that lurked within. Jemima Chase was imaginative, intelligent and headstrong. This young woman didn't wait for life to come to her. She went out and hunted it down.

Noah wrung her hands before signing, 'I can't decide.'

Chase frowned and hung the tape measure back around her neck to free her hands. 'Save the woe-is-me artistic crap for someone else,' she signed. 'The show is only two months away. You have to decide.'

'It's such a big decision.'

'Duh! That's why you've got to make it,' Chase signed. 'This is the Junior Design State Titles, Noah. You need this one if you want to get to the Nationals.'

'I know.'

'So decide. You can kiss the Nationals goodbye if you can't even pull a collection together for the State Titles.'

'Yeah, I know.'

Chase's eyes narrowed. 'I'll get my mother down here.'

Noah shook her head. 'I'll decide. I promise. Can you help me?'

'As luck would have it, I can. Let's go out the back.' Chase gestured for Noah to follow.

Inside the utility room Noah noted the full rack of "finished" alterations on one side of the doorway and then the empty rack of "to do" alterations on the other side. Chase's workspace was neat and functional, being organised was in her nature. It meant she had no trouble meeting her mother's high standards of efficiency at Bibs & Bobs. Though some people quailed at the thought of working for one of Sayle's most successful CEOs – Noah counted herself amongst them – Chase loved it. To her there was nothing better than having her mother as her boss.

Noah glanced at the compendium on the small table in the corner – Chase's other job. The leather case was her mobile office. On top of her sewing work, Chase had probably added a few chapters to her novel today too. Noah wished she could be as productive as her friend.

Chase pointed to the empty workbench. 'Spread them out. I'll choose,' she signed.

Taking her much-loved folio from her bag, Noah laid it on the bench. After cleaning her hands with a wet-wipe, she pulled out a wad of papers and spread them out. Chase walked around the bench, studying each drawing in turn.

'They are all fabulous,' she signed at last. 'I can see why you're having trouble deciding.'

Noah tried to smother a triumphant smile but failed.

'Lose the cat-who-got-the-cream look, Noah. Smug doesn't suit you,' Chase signed.

'I've got a story about a cat that you might enjoy,' Noah signed.

'Yep, in a minute …'

Chase selected seven sketches and slid them into a plastic sleeve. She put them on top of her compendium and turned back to Noah. 'Teen Street collection,' she signed. 'I'll draw up the patterns for you tomorrow.'

With an equal mix of envy and relief, Noah signed, 'Thanks. I owe you.'

'Yes, you do. How about that cat story and we'll call it quits?'

'Deal,' Noah signed.

Chase helped her re-pack the remaining sketches. Just because the drawings hadn't made the cut today didn't mean they wouldn't be useful someday.

Noah started to explain about the miniature tiger but hadn't got far when Chase stopped her.

'I need my tablet.'

Out of necessity, the story was on hold until Chase retrieved her device from her compendium. When she was ready to watch again, she nodded. By the end of the tale, Chase had interrupted four times to make notes.

'Weird, huh?' Noah signed when she was finished.

'For you, yes,' Chase replied. 'For me …' she shrugged.

Noah smiled. Chase had told her many times that weirdness was relative. For someone like Jemima Chase, whose life revolved around fantasy fiction, a deaf girl hallucinating about hearing an imaginary cat was something to be celebrated.

Noah checked her watch. The later she was home, the worse the argument with Aunt Polly would be.

'Better go,' she signed.

'Do let me know if the cat comes back,' Chase replied with a wink.

'Yeah, right.'

Chapter 2

Noah stormed out of the house leaving her Aunt Polly inside ranting to herself. At least, she assumed her aunt was still ranting. Being deaf made it impossible to be sure but her legal guardian was unlikely to be deterred from an argument by something as trivial as her opponent leaving the room. The confrontation had been even worse than Noah imagined. The storm, which had delayed the trains for over an hour, hadn't helped her cause. Despite the fact that there were still two hours of daylight left courtesy of Summer Light Time, Aunt Polly had deemed it unacceptable for Noah to arrive home at "such an hour".

As she ran down the back steps, Raven scampered around the side of the small suburban house. It was a ritual. The Alsatian knew that the back-door slamming was his cue to join his mistress. Noah shoved the back gate open and Raven darted through ahead of her. In spite of her anger, she marvelled at her dog's agility. At sixteen, he still acted like a puppy. He'd been with her since she was a baby; the only member of her immediate family still alive.

Noah followed Raven through the gate to the nature reserve that backed on to Aunt Polly's house. Tracts of forest this close to the city were rare but as she wound her way through the gums that stood as ghostly sentinels, she was grateful for this one. Its future was uncertain in the face of Sayle's exploding population but for now it stood, fresh and inviting in the wake of the afternoon's downpour. Inhaling deeply of the scent of eucalypts as she walked, Noah tried to calm her mind. She soon reached the small creek where she liked to meditate and sat down heavily on a lichen-ridden rock. Raven flopped at her feet.

'That woman is impossible,' she signed to him.

Although he was a dog, Noah was convinced that he could understand her. She continued her silent tirade.

'She just doesn't get it! Fashion is *not* a waste of time and I *don't* need to understand the finer points of Shakespeare to succeed in life.'

Raven sat up and put his shaggy head in her lap, panting happily. Noah scratched his ears. His fur was silky smooth, which was more than could be said for his breath. She managed a smile.

'What have you been eating?' she signed. 'Your breath comes straight from Satan's behind!'

The words were barely out of her hands, when it happened again. The tingling sensation in her ears that she'd felt earlier was back. She twisted around on her rocky seat to find the striped cat sitting on the ground not far behind her. Next to the cat was a young man in a smart black suit. She leapt to her feet as Raven jumped between them. Noah shivered. If her dog could see them too, her hallucination theory was on shaky ground.

The young man raised his hands quickly and began signing. 'Do not be alarmed,' he signed. 'We mean you no harm.'

Despite the balmy evening, Noah shivered again. The tingling sensation in her ears returned when the young man's lips moved.

'Who are you?' Noah signed back warily. 'And is that suit a Maladine?'

If he was surprised by her second question he didn't show it.

'My name is Emir,' he signed, 'and yes, the suit is a Maladine.'

Noah nodded. She'd thought as much. Maladines were unmistakable.

'And this is Brinn,' he added.

Brinn nonchalantly groomed her face with her paw despite intense scrutiny from Raven, who loved cats – as a snack.

'We met earlier,' Noah signed. 'That's a weird-looking cat.'

Emir nodded. 'A keen observation, Miss Chord,' he signed. 'There is much that is unusual about that cat and it goes far beyond her looks.'

After everything that had happened today, Noah was not surprised that the man knew her name. She should have been concerned at being accosted by a strange man in an isolated place but the cat had not hurt her this afternoon and the man had impeccable taste in clothes. The cut of his suit convinced her to give him a chance.

'What do you want?' she signed.

His lips moved as he signed. 'Can you hear me speaking?'

Noah's stomach tightened. 'I don't know if I can hear or not. I don't know what hearing is.'

Emir nodded. 'You're experiencing something more than just seeing us though, aren't you?'

Noah nodded. The more his lips moved, the more she could analyse the sensation in her ears. It was more than just tingling. The tingling had … variations.

'Say something longer,' she signed.

The young man continued to sign as he spoke. 'My name is Emir Delorian. I come from a world called Talisker. I have come to Earth on behalf of my master, Major Sachin, to ask for your help.'

Noah stared at Emir and then signed, 'Again?'

Emir did as Noah asked, speaking and signing his words. His hand-signing was very precise but he needed to work on his facial expressions. He was too serious.

Struggling to put her thoughts into words, Noah signed, 'I can feel something in my ears but it's difficult to describe. It's like a tingling but the … level of it changes.'

'Sounds,' Emir offered. 'You're hearing sounds.'

Noah frowned. Sounds. People had tried to explain the concept of sounds to her over the years. As Noah grappled with her thoughts, she was distracted by the cat. Brinn stood up and stretched extravagantly before walking a few paces and sitting down right under Raven's nose. Mimicking the feline, Raven sat too. Noah squeezed her eyes shut and then opened them again. Raven still sat calmly in front of Brinn.

'What is going on?' Noah signed.

'They're communicating,' Emir said.

'Can you hear them?' Noah signed.

Emir shook his head.

Noah remembered what Emir had said about Brinn. *There is much that is unusual about that cat and it goes far beyond her looks.* Unsettled, Noah stepped forward to stand beside Raven.

To Emir, she signed, 'If I am hearing sounds, why is it that I can hear you and the cat, but not anyone else?'

'The explanation has to do with frequencies – sound waves – but it isn't an explanation I can give you. That is best left to Major Sachin.'

'Where is he?'

Before Emir could answer, the cat made sounds.

'Brinn wants to see your birthmark,' Emir signed.

Noah stared at him. '*The cat talks?*' she signed.

'When the mood takes her, yes.'

'And she wants to see my birthmark?' Noah signed.

'Yes.'

Thinking that the conversation was taking a turn for the creepy, Noah signed, 'Does that usually work for you?'

'Does what work for me?'

'Your little routine,' Noah signed. 'Accosting women in isolated places and using a cute cat to have them reveal parts of their body to you.'

'It's not a routine,' Emir signed. 'If I turn around will you show Brinn?'

'Is it a girl cat?'

Emir nodded.

'Okay,' Noah signed.

Emir turned away and Noah lifted the hem of her school blouse and pulled at the waistband of her shorts to reveal the crescent-shaped mark near her right hip. Brinn nodded and made a sound.

'Is she happy?' Noah signed when Emir turned back to face her.

'She's satisfied with the birthmark,' he signed.

'Fantastic,' Noah signed. 'Perhaps you should tell me what you want.'

'Certainly,' Emir signed. 'As I said before, we come from a world called Talisker and it is in grave peril. Major Sachin requests your help to save our world.'

'Where is this place?' Noah signed. 'I've never heard of it.'

'Talisker is far from here in terms of distance and time,' Emir signed, 'but easy to get to if you know how.'

With a quick glance at Raven to make sure he was okay, Noah signed, 'How many people know about this place?'

'Very few people here on Earth know that Talisker exists,' Emir signed, 'and we'd like to keep it that way. But we need your help to ensure that it *continues* to exist. There is a great evil that stalks our world – if it is not stopped, our world will be destroyed.'

'What great evil?' Noah signed, thinking of Chase. She could picture her friend salivating over this exchange. 'Some kind of monster or something?'

'*We* think he's a monster,' Emir signed, 'but technically he's human. Here, you'd probably call him a wizard.'

'A wizard? This is starting to sound like a fantasy novel,' she signed.

Emir's brow furrowed slightly. 'Talisker is *not* a fantasy world. It is real,' he signed.

'Sorry, I didn't mean to be rude,' Noah signed. In Chase's absence, Noah did her best to think like her friend. 'So you want me to come to your world because you want me to save it?' she signed.

Emir nodded. 'Yes.'

'Why me?'

'There's a prophecy ...'

Noah couldn't stop her eyebrows. They went up despite her best intentions.

Emir started again. 'There's a prophecy that you are going to save Talisker from destruction.'

'Right,' Noah signed. 'And how am I going to do that?'

'You're going to find the 13th key. And when you do, you will use it to save the world.'

'Okay. If I'm looking for the 13th key, can I assume that there are twelve other keys that don't work?'

'Something like that,' Emir conceded.

'Finding one key on a whole planet sounds tricky. How am I supposed to find this key? Do you know what it looks like?'

'No.'

'No?'

'No.'

Noah stared at the young man. Throughout their conversation his expression had barely changed. Aside from frowning once or twice his face was a mask.

'So let me get this straight,' Noah signed. 'You want me to go to a world I've never heard of, to find a key that you know nothing about, to save you from an evil wizard who will probably turn me into a toad the minute I arrive?'

The cat made a sound.

'Is the cat talking again?' Noah asked.

Emir nodded.

'What did she say?'

'I'm not repeating it,' Emir signed. 'And I didn't say I knew *nothing* about the key. I know it's a musical instrument.'

'How can a musical instrument be a key? What kind of lock does it open?'

'That's not really my area of expertise. Major Sachin is the best person to explain that.'

Noah frowned. 'Maybe this Major Sachin should have come here instead of you. Let's try this question. What makes you think I'm the one you need? I'm deaf you know, so musical instruments – not really my thing.'

Emir nodded. 'Three things. You wear an Academy ring, you have a crescent birthmark and you're on the same frequency as us.'

Noah looked at her ring then at Emir. 'This was my mother's ring.'

'It is a Taliskeran ring,' he signed.

Noah's stomach tightened. 'Maybe it's just like rings you have,' she suggested.

'It's a Taliskeran ring,' he repeated.

Now convinced she was hallucinating, Noah signed, 'If you're from another world – why are you wearing a Maladine suit?'

Again, the young man did not bat an eyelid. 'It was a gift from my master,' he signed.

'Where did he get it from?'

'He has contacts here.'

'Contacts?' Noah signed. 'I thought you said not many people knew about Talisker.'

'They don't,' Emir confirmed. 'My master is very … influential. Will you come?'

One thing was clear. If she did go to this Talisker place, she wasn't going to have any fun. Emir hadn't cracked a smile. He made the cat look like good company.

'How would we get there?'

'We know the way,' Emir signed. 'If you choose to come, we will show you the way.'

'It's a big decision,' she signed. 'Can I sleep on it?'

'Of course,' Emir replied. 'Be here at midday tomorrow if you decide to come.'

Sounds came from the cat again and Emir retrieved a small parcel from the breast pocket of his jacket. He handed it to Noah. She held her breath as she unwrapped the brown paper and found a piece of folded material inside. An intricate paisley pattern roamed delicately over the fabric but unlike most of the paisley fabrics Noah had seen, this one had been embroidered, not printed.

The moment she touched it she not only felt it with her fingers, but she felt it in her ears too. It wasn't as strong as the sounds from Emir and Brinn but it was definitely there. She lifted a corner of the fabric from the paper, waving it gently to reveal its true shape. A scarf. Noah draped it around her neck. She folded the brown paper and tucked it in the pocket of her shorts, leaving her hands free again.

'I think I can hear the fabric too,' she signed. 'How is that possible?'

'Music is the basis of our world,' Emir said. 'Everything that exists is made of music.'

'This is from your world?' Noah asked.

Emir nodded. 'Take it. Go home now and get some rest. We hope to see you tomorrow.'

♪♫

Noah let the back-door slam shut behind her to herald her return. She went straight to her bedroom, confident that her aunt would leave her in peace until morning. She grabbed her phone to message Chase.

Cat returned! Can u meet me @ café in the morning?

Noah watched the screen, awaiting her friend's reply. The response came quickly.

0800?

Sounds good. Maybe going away for a few days …

Where?

Talisker. Heard of it?

No. If I can clear a few days with the boss, would you like company?

Sure thing! Pack light.

Roger that! C u then.

As she had expected, the lure of adventure was something Chase couldn't resist. Noah smiled. This was crazy. She put her phone on her bedside table and lay down on her bed, though she knew sleep would be impossible. Thoughts of Talisker scurried through her mind. She looked at her mother's ring. *Her* ring now. The dragon's wings spread either side of the sapphire that made its body. Emir had called it an Academy ring. How could her mother have gotten a ring from Talisker? Noah's stomach tightened again. And what of *hearing* and the scarf? The Junior Design State Titles were two months away. Her collection would definitely have an edge if she could source materials from another world.

Her aunt, school and English assignments aside, there was still one major problem. She wasn't sure it was real. It couldn't be real. Noah stared at the scarf that hung over the bedpost. *If that's there in the morning,* she thought, *I'll go to Talisker.* If the scarf wasn't there, she'd know it was all a dream and she'd go to school as normal. Or maybe she'd make an appointment with a psychiatrist instead.

Chapter 3

The Billy Goat Cafe was doing a steady trade when Noah arrived. She had half an hour before Chase was due to join her so she ordered a coffee and found a booth in the back. A young waiter appeared with a cloth to wipe down the table as Noah sat down.

'Thank you,' she signed.

He smiled and winked at her before attending to the table. Once he'd wiped and dried the table, Noah pulled her English folder out of her satchel and fished out a pen. She opened the folder and started writing, hoping that she looked like a high school senior cramming for an exam and not a high school senior planning to truant for the day and travel to another world.

Noah had stuck to her usual morning routine. She'd dressed for school and Aunt Polly had dropped her at the train station on her way to work. Noah had boarded the train but gone only six stops before disembarking. Now she just needed Chase to arrive. Then Noah could explain the past evening's events to her and show her the scarf before returning home to collect her bag and Raven. It was then a short walk to the forest to meet up with Emir and Brinn.

While she waited for Chase, she penned a note to her aunt. She and Aunt Polly didn't always see eye-to-eye but her aunt had taken her in after her parents' deaths and kept her fed and clothed. Noah knew that her aunt had always tried to do what she thought was right for her.

She just wished their ideas of what was "right" were the same, but they weren't and that meant conflict, which had been particularly bad of late. Even so, Noah didn't feel right about simply disappearing. She would at least do her aunt the courtesy of letting her know that she'd gone of her own accord and that she hadn't been abducted.

Dear Aunt Polly,

I have gone away. I'm not sure exactly where I'm going or how long I'll be. Chase is with me – I'll be fine. I know you will be angry and I am sorry about that but I need some space just now.

See you when I get back,

Noah

She tore the page out of her book and folded it neatly before placing the note in an envelope. Chase arrived just as Noah was writing her aunt's name on the back.

'You're early,' Noah signed.

'So are you,' Chase replied. 'Are you okay? What's going on? Tell me everything.'

Chase's face was a mix of concern and poorly concealed anticipation. Noah grimaced at her friend, suddenly feeling foolish about the story she was about to tell.

'You're probably not going to believe this ...' Noah began.

Chase rolled her eyes and opened her compendium. 'Look who you're talking to.'

'You're going to take notes.' It wasn't a question.

Chase nodded as she switched on her tablet. 'Standard operating procedure when someone starts a story with "you're probably not going to believe this". You know that.'

Noah nodded. 'Yes, I know that.'

Noah told Chase about Emir and Brinn, about the alleged prophecy on Talisker and her apparent role in it. And even after Noah had shown her the paisley scarf, Chase's page was still blank.

'You didn't write anything,' Noah pointed out.

Chase shook her head as if fighting her way out of a daze and looked down at her screen. Noah tapped on the table to get her attention. Chase looked up at her.

'Well?' Noah signed. 'What do you think of the scarf?'

'Very nice,' Chase answered absently.

Noah frowned. She'd hoped for a more enthusiastic response. All of a sudden Chase jumped in her seat, which made Noah jump as well. Chase looked at her watch.

'We've got a few hours before the deadline but we should get moving. We don't want to be late.'

Noah looked at her ring before signing, 'So you think this *is* possible? That we can actually *go* to this place?'

'I don't know but I'm certainly not going to die wondering! I'm just going to call Mum to let her know where we're going. She's got someone to cover my work while I'm gone but she'll be *very* interested to hear where I'm going!'

Noah sighed as Chase dialled her mother's number. She knew that Chase would faithfully repeat the story to her mother and that she would be nearly as excited as her daughter at the prospect of travelling to another world. Chase's mother, while a shrewd and down-to-earth businesswoman, always indulged her daughter's love of the fantastic.

'What did she say?' Noah asked when Chase hung up.

Chase grinned. 'She said have fun and bring back some samples.'

♪♫

Emir, now dressed in black cargo pants and a long-sleeved blue shirt, was waiting when Noah, Raven and Chase arrived but Brinn was nowhere to be seen.

'Who is this?' Emir signed to Noah.

'This is my dearest friend,' she signed back, 'Jemima Chase.'

Emir frowned. 'This was not part of our arrangement.'

'She's my best friend and I want her to come,' Noah signed.

Chase was more like a sister than a friend. After Noah had moved to Sayle following her parents' deaths, Chase had taught her to sew and learned sign language so she could talk to her.

Emir considered her words. 'Are you deaf?' he signed to Chase.

Chase shook her head.

Noah watched as he spoke to Chase without signing. Like yesterday, Noah felt the sensation inside her head. Hearing. Chase said something in return.

Emir looked at Chase. 'We have a job to do,' he signed for Noah's benefit. 'How could you help us get that job done?'

'Just a second,' Chase signed. She opened her compendium and took out her tablet. Once she'd opened the appropriate document, she handed the screen to Emir. 'Feel free to scroll through my resume. I haven't updated it in a little while but you'll certainly get a feel for my skills.'

He looked at the screen and then at Chase.

Noah waved at him to get his attention. She signed, 'You don't have these on Talisker?'

He shook his head.

Noah swiped her finger across the screen to show him how it worked. One arched eyebrow was all the reaction she got from him. He spent a few moments reading each screen before handing the device back to Chase.

'Essentially, you're a seamstress and a fantasy writer,' Emir signed.

Chase tucked the tablet back in her compendium. 'I prefer fiction-eer,' she signed back, 'but yes – I write stuff and I sew stuff.'

'I don't see how that's going to help us,' he signed.

Noah interrupted. 'We both go or neither of us goes,' she signed pointedly.

Raven came to sit at his mistress's side and nuzzled at her hand.

'*None* of us goes,' Noah corrected herself. 'Not me, not Chase, not Raven.'

'Alright,' Emir signed after a moment's thought. 'We'll all go. Major Sachin can sort it out when we get there.'

Brinn chose that moment to reappear. Out of the corner of her eye, Noah saw Chase flinch at the cat's unexpected arrival. Raven bounded over to the striped feline and danced around her excitedly. Noah shook her head, unable to fathom her dog's behaviour.

The cat made sounds that Noah didn't understand. Emir translated in signs. 'Why are you coming?'

'I'm coming to find your 13th key and save your world,' she signed to Brinn. 'Just like you asked.'

Emir dutifully signed what the cat said next.

'She didn't ask *what* you are coming to do. She asked you *why* you're coming.'

Noah stared at the cat. The cat stared back.

'What difference does it make?' Noah signed.

'It doesn't make any difference,' Emir signed on Brinn's behalf.

'If it doesn't make any difference, then why does she want to know?'

'She says she already knows.'

'Then why is she asking?' Noah signed, exasperated.

'Because she wants to hear *you* say it. She has a bet with someone back home.'

'A *bet*?' Noah took a deep breath to calm herself. 'Okay, I'm curious to *hear* more. I don't know why I'd be able to hear on your world when I can't hear on my own world. But the fact that I can hear you makes me believe that it's possible.'

'And …'

'*And*,' Noah continued, 'I'm intrigued by the scarf you gave me. The fabric is unlike anything I've ever seen or felt. If I can find something unique on your world, it might just give me an edge for the show.'

'Show?' Emir signed.

'A fashion show,' Noah signed. 'Actually it's the Junior Design State Titles. It's not for a couple of months yet but I still need to work on my collection. I couldn't bring much with me,' she signed, eyeing her overnight bag, 'but I'm thinking I can still work on my garments, in between looking for keys and saving the world, of course.'

'A fashion show?' Emir repeated.

Noah nodded.

'A fashion show is more important than saving our world from destruction?' Emir signed.

'Don't say it like that,' Noah signed testily. 'You make it sound terrible.'

'Well, how else can I say it?'

'It's not *more* important. I would just like to do both.'

Chase butted in. She signed, 'Does the cat have her answer? Can we go now?'

Brinn nodded.

Emir signed, 'Now we can go. We need to find a tree.'

Noah signed, 'Couldn't you have gone before you came?'

Emir looked at her. 'You're so funny you'd make a cat laugh.'

Noah glanced at Brinn, who looked less than amused.

'Well, not that cat, obviously,' he said. 'She's got even less of a sense of humour than most cats.'

'So, this tree you're after. I don't suppose it's just any old tree, is it?' Noah signed.

'No.'

'Okay, lead the way then.'

Chase retrieved her camera from her bag before setting off. They walked among the towering smooth-barked eucalypts for over an hour before coming to a small stream where Raven stopped to drink. While they waited, Noah signed to Chase.

'I wouldn't have thought the forest extended this far. I've been out here heaps of times but none of this looks familiar.'

Chase patted her camera. 'I'm cataloguing as we go. The forest is definitely getting denser – more ironbarks here. I love their rough bark and the way the dark sap bleeds down their trunks. Hang on ... I just need to get a snap of that rock over there ... I'll be back in a jiffy.'

Noah smiled to herself. Only Chase could *need* a photo of a rock. She walked over to Emir. 'How much further?' she signed.

'It's not far from here,' he replied.

When they set off again they'd walked for only a few minutes before Emir called a halt. Noah looked around her. 'Where's the tree? I thought you said we were looking for a special tree.'

Emir pointed.

'Is that it?' Noah signed.

'Problem?' he asked.

'Well, could you really call that a tree?'

To Noah it looked like a pencil that had been mauled by a rabid poodle.

'Let me guess,' Emir signed, 'not tall enough?'

'I suppose I was expecting something … a little taller.'

'And I suppose you also expected leaves of gold and a trunk that glowed silver?'

'It would have been a nice touch, don't you think?'

Emir frowned. 'A little gauche, I would say.'

Chase touched Noah's arm. 'It's usually best if magical trees aren't too spectacular,' she signed. 'The more obvious they are, the more attention they get.'

Noah glanced at the tree again. 'Well, that one should be quite safe, I think.'

Noah watched as Brinn sauntered towards the tree. When Brinn reached the trunk, she vanished.

Neat trick, Noah thought. Raven needed no coaxing; here was a tree he obviously hadn't marked yet. He ran over, but didn't even get time to lift his leg and … *whoomp* … he was gone too.

Noah stared at where Raven had been. There was now no question that she was going. Wherever her dog had gone, she was going. She looked at Chase who was already on her way.

'Awesome,' she signed before she too disappeared.

Noah looked at Emir.

'After you,' he signed.

Noah had taken only a few steps when she started to hear it. It was music. She didn't know how she knew it was music, but she knew. It flooded through her mind, through her veins, through every muscle in her trembling body. Walking became more difficult. There were probably only half a dozen more steps to go but it seemed impossible that she'd make it. She took another step. And then, another. Though her leg muscles protested, Noah made it to the tree.

The music continued to course through her as she collapsed against the trunk. Though reedy, the tree was surprisingly resistant to her weight. The music filled her lungs, making breathing almost impossible. Why hadn't she just vanished like the others? Why was she stuck here against the tree, gasping for air? She felt Emir grab her shoulders as consciousness deserted her.

♪♫

Noah's eyes were slow to adjust to the cave's dim light. She thought she should probably sit up and was seriously contemplating doing just that when a warm wet tongue on her face gave her the extra motivation she needed. Raven. She hugged her Alsatian tightly, burying her face in his shaggy fur, until a tap on her shoulder distracted her.

It was Chase. 'Glad you finally made it,' she signed. 'Welcome to Talisker.'

Noah looked around her. The cave would have made a comfortable lounge room if it had had some furniture. At least the fire in the pit gave the chamber a warm glow.

Noah heard Emir's voice. She turned. His long-sleeved shirt was gone, replaced with a blue vest with a flute insignia embroidered across the front. Heavily tattooed and muscled arms protruded from his vest and a long sword was strapped to his back. He stood beside a young boy.

Noah studied the youngster. He looked about eight years old – a sickly waif, she decided. Pale skin hung over his small-boned frame. His short brown hair was clean but lacklustre and his eyes were lemur-like with dark rings around them. He wore the same style of black cargo pants as Emir but with many more pockets.

'Noah,' Emir signed. 'This is Major Sachin.'

'He's a major?' Noah signed. 'A major of what?'

'A Major of the Academy,' Emir signed. 'He is one of the twelve Majors. Major Sachin has mastered one of the twelve keys – the flute – which he will use now to correct your hearing.'

'How's he going to do that?' she asked.

'Major Sachin is going to perform a very complex tonic on you.'

'A what?'

'A tonic,' he repeated. 'It's what you would call a spell.'

'What sort of spell?'

The cat made sounds.

'What did she say?' Noah asked.

Emir smoothed his already smooth vest before replying. 'Brinn said that Major Sachin is going to perform a complex series of connections in your mind. He will be using his key – the flute – to achieve this miraculous feat. Using music, he will make associations between the imprints of word signs that already exist in your brain and the sounds of each of those words.'

Noah looked at the cat and then back at Emir. 'It didn't sound like she said that much.'

'She paraphrases,' he acknowledged glibly.

On Earth, Emir would make a great used-car salesman, Noah thought.

'So all these connections and associations, what's the point?' she signed.

Sachin and Brinn exchanged sounds. Noah ignored them, confident she didn't want to know what they were saying. The sounds had an uncomplimentary ring to them. She patiently awaited Emir's reply.

'It means, Noah, that you'll be able to understand words by sound. You won't have to have them signed to you.'

Noah started to tingle all over as she absorbed what Emir had said.

'How long will it take?' she signed.

'Several hours,' Emir replied. 'It depends on how many words you know.'

Noah looked at Sachin. 'Are you sure you're qualified to do this? You look … quite young.'

'I have the relevant training,' he signed. 'Age is irrelevant.'

Noah stared at him. 'Not to me.'

'I'm eleven,' Sachin signed.

From a pocket that could not possibly have contained such a thing, Sachin produced an old silver flute.

'Wow!' Noah signed. 'How'd you do that?'

Emir signed, 'Perhaps we could save explanations for later, Noah. Things will be much easier when we can *talk* to you rather than signing everything.'

'That flute looks pretty battered,' Noah signed. 'Are you sure this will work?'

Emir nodded. 'The key is very old and it's had many owners. It has played a big part in shaping the history of Talisker. Now – lie down and relax, Noah. We need to get started.'

Noah did as she was told and Raven came to lie at her side while Chase rummaged through her bag for her tablet. When Sachin started to play, Noah felt the music flowing through her, and she wanted to cry. Music, beautiful music. Every note seemed to touch her soul. But without warning, a prickling sensation invaded her head. It quickly escalated, as if an army of spiny ants was marching through her brain, scouring every neuron. Noah instinctively clenched her teeth and fists.

'Relax.'

It was Emir. She understood that word. It was working!

She tried to relax but it was difficult. With his flute, Sachin sifted through her mind for every word she knew so he could imprint a series of sounds alongside it. How a pre-adolescent boy with a battered flute could perform such an act was beyond Noah. She focused on her breathing and on the notes Sachin played as a way to distract herself from the irritating sensation of the spell.

Noah lost track of the time. She pictured herself floating through space, counting the stars as she passed them. The spell went on. Hours could have been minutes and minutes could have been hours – it was impossible for Noah to tell.

Finally, it was done.

'Sit up, Noah.'

Noah gasped, opened her eyes and sat up.

Without signing, Emir said, 'How do you feel?'

Noah smiled until she thought her face would split in two. 'Fabulous,' she signed excitedly. 'This is going to be *fantastic*.'

She'd never dreamed of being able to hear, let alone understand spoken words. Doctors had always told her there was nothing they could do for her. She was profoundly deaf. She'd never hear anything. Then another thought occurred to her.

'Have you got a spell that would help me talk?' she signed.

'There is indeed a *tonic* that would achieve that,' Emir said without signing, 'but it is more complicated and takes much longer. That is for another time.'

'Noah!' Chase said.

Noah turned to look at her friend, whose eyes were wide with excitement.

'I can *hear* you,' Noah signed. 'I so wish I could talk to you too.'

'We'll work on it,' Chase promised.

Raven barked and Noah smiled. 'Is *that* what you sound like!' she signed to him.

Raven barked again and Noah shook her head. It was strange to think that he'd been doing that for sixteen years without her being able to appreciate it.

Sachin said, 'Noah. There is much I need to tell you. Can we get started?'

Eager to hear more, Noah signed, 'Yes.'

'Good,' Sachin said. 'We have a two-day ride to Mellifont, so we'll talk on the way. The horses are outside. Let's get going.'

'Two days?' Noah signed. 'Shouldn't we start looking for the 13th key straight away?'

The boy's cheeks flushed red. 'I said we're going to Mellifont and that's where we're going. I know what I'm doing.'

Emir put a hand on Sachin's shoulder.

'The Major will tell you his plan on the way, Noah,' Emir said. 'As Sachin said, there is much you need to know. We will spend this time bringing you up to speed.'

'The way she interrupts all the time,' Brinn said, 'you might need more than two days, Major.'

Sachin frowned. 'Do you think we should leave the horses and just walk to Mellifont?'

Swishing her striped tail, Brinn replied, 'I'm sure the horses would like that.'

'We'll see you in Mellifont in two days,' Emir said to the cat.

To the girls, Sachin said, 'Grab your bags. We need to get going so we can start the first lesson.'

'The first *lesson*,' Chase said, tucking her tablet under her arm as she slung her pack over her shoulder. 'I can't wait! What's it on?'

'The first lesson,' Sachin said, 'is on Noah Chord.'

Chapter 4

Sachin had refused to give away anything more about his lesson until the party was in motion. A few hours of daylight remained and he was keen to make good progress before stopping for their evening meal. Noah and Chase rode either side of the boy Major while Emir brought up the rear. Raven bounded around in a frantic display of sniffing and marking. The grasses and low shrubs on the undulating landscape were all new to him and the Alsatian had a job ahead of him to catalogue all the vegetation and not fall too far behind.

'Are you ready for your first lesson, Noah?' Sachin asked.

Unwilling to let go of the reins, Noah nodded her acquiescence rather than signing.

Sachin took a deep breath. 'Some of this will not be easy for you to hear,' he said, 'but it is all true. The first thing you must know is that you are part Taliskeran – on your mother's side of the family.'

Noah stared at him as he opened a pocket on his trousers and pulled out a folded piece of paper. He held it out towards her but Noah shook her head. Clenching the reins even tighter, she nodded her head towards Chase. Sachin passed the paper to her.

Dropping the reins, Chase took the paper solemnly and unfolded it. She read aloud. 'Isla Doris Dexter born 37.02.3-9823 in Welshire Province, Leninstar State.'

Noah's stomach churned. The date was strange but the name wasn't. Isla Doris Dexter. Her mother's name. Looping the reins around her wrists and taking care not to exaggerate her hand movements and startle the horse, Noah signed, 'That can't be right. My mother would have told me.'

'I'm sure she meant to,' Sachin said. The boy looked at her ring and then at her. 'That ring – is an Academy ring. It's been in your family for over six hundred years. One of your distant ancestors was a Major at the Academy. She was custodian of the violin key for nearly sixty years. The ring has been passed down through the generations of your family ever since.'

Noah shook her head. 'That can't be right,' she signed.

'It *is* right,' Sachin said. 'And your birthmark is another clue. You have a crescent on your abdomen?'

Noah nodded.

Sachin said, 'It's not actually a birthmark. It's a birth*brand* – it was put on you after you were born – after you were born here on Talisker. It is the mark of the Dragonsbane.'

'The what?' Chase asked.

'The Dragonsbane,' Sachin said.

'And what's that?' Chase pressed.

'Later, I will explain what the Dragonsbane does but for now, what you need to know is that it is an esteemed position here on Talisker and bearing the mark is a big deal.'

'Who branded me?' Noah signed.

'A seer,' Sachin replied.

'I don't believe it,' Noah signed. 'It sounds ridiculous.'

'I can imagine how it sounds, Noah,' Sachin said, 'but it's true. Did Emir tell you that everything on Talisker is made of music?'

Thinking of the scarf Emir had given her, Noah nodded.

Sachin continued, 'Noah, you're one of those things. You have a musical signature – I can read it – and it tells me you're 'made' here.' He pointed to Chase. 'Chase doesn't have it, but *you* do. You're on the same frequency as us. You *are* Taliskeran.'

Rings, brands, musical signatures ... Noah fought to make sense of it.

'So that's why I could hear Brinn and Emir on Earth – and why I can hear everything here?' Noah signed. 'Because the frequencies match?'

'Partly,' Sachin said, 'but it's actually more complicated than that. There was some kind of spell on you—'

'I didn't think you had spells here,' Chase interrupted. 'Don't you call them tonics?'

Sachin said, 'What *we* do – and when I say "we", I mean the musicians at the Academy in Mellifont – is manipulate the music of this world using tonics. Whatever was on Noah wasn't our work. My best guess is that it was applied by the Descera – any ancient civilisation that pre-dated humans on Talisker. Let's call it a *charm* rather than a spell.'

'How can an extinct species put a charm on someone?' Chase asked.

'I didn't say they were extinct,' Sachin said, 'and I really hope they're not. The Descera made the twelve keys that we have. If we can find the Descera, I believe we can find the 13th key.'

'You *hope* they're not?' Noah signed. 'When was the last time anyone saw one?'

'There are occasional sightings reported but they're generally not taken seriously,' Sachin conceded. 'But leaving that aside,' he continued, 'this is what I think. Noah, you were born here. A seer branded you here. Your parents knew the brand was significant but then the Descera showed up. My guess is that the Descera thought you were at risk and instructed your parents to take you to Earth – your father's home world – to keep you safe. The charm they put on you would protect your hearing until you returned.'

'At risk from what? Why would my hearing need protecting?' Noah signed.

'The Dragonsbane needs exceptionally good hearing,' Sachin said.

Before Noah could ask her next question, Sachin cocked his head and reined in his horse. Noah and Chase stopped too.

'I'll be back soon,' he said. 'Wait here.'

The Major nudged his horse into motion again and headed north at a trot over a small hill. Emir steered his horse to fill the gap where Sachin had been.

'Where's he going?' Noah asked.

'I don't know,' Emir said. 'The Major has sensed something that needs correcting. He'll be back soon.'

'I have a question,' Chase said.

'Yes?' Emir replied.

'How could Noah hear you and Brinn on Earth if there was a Desceran charm on her?'

'That would be Brinn's doing,' Emir said.

'How can a cat do that?' Noah signed.

'Well, you know how you can train dogs, but you can't train cats?' he said.

Noah nodded.

'That's because cats refuse to follow rules.'

Noah nodded again. Just one of the reasons she preferred dogs to cats.

'Well, *this* particular cat,' Emir said, 'refuses to follow *any* rules. Brinn defies all rules, even rules of nature. I have no idea how she does it.'

Noah watched Raven as he trotted between the shrubs and strappy grasses and wished she felt as carefree as he looked. On impulse, she twisted in the saddle to dismount.

'Noah?' Chase said.

Noah turned. 'Need a minute,' she signed.

Raven raced towards her and nuzzled her hands with his wet nose. She knelt down and stroked his dark fur. 'I'm glad you're here,' she signed to him.

Hearing footsteps behind her, Noah turned.

'Want more company?' Chase asked.

'If all that's true,' Noah signed, 'why didn't they tell me?'

Chase put her arm around her friend. 'Noah, you were *six* when your parents died. I'm sure they were going to tell you.'

'They could have written it down somewhere. Instead, I had to hear it from a ... strange kid.'

'It's certainly not ideal,' Chase said. 'I'd never have written it that way.'

'Chase, I'm not a character,' Noah protested. 'I'm a person! And this is serious.'

'Yes, it is,' Chase agreed. 'So what are you going to do about it? What would your mum and dad have expected you to do about it?'

Noah flinched. 'I don't know,' she signed. 'I haven't had much of a chance to think about it yet, have I?'

She pictured her parents' faces. They'd been gone for ten years now. She remembered waiting outside the school gate for them to come and pick her up one Friday afternoon. Noah had been excited about the skiing weekend they'd had planned. Her mother had picked her father up from work early so they'd be at school when Noah finished for the day. But they'd never arrived. A man running a red light had seen to that.

An unsettling feeling crept through Noah. In light of what Sachin had told her, she felt that she didn't really know who her mother was. That's assuming he'd told her the truth. Was Sachin telling the truth? What reason would he have to lie?

'I need more information,' she signed to Chase before walking back to where Emir waited.

Noah glanced at her mother's ring and then looked up at Emir. 'What do they do at the Academy?' she signed.

Chase appeared at Noah's side as Emir dismounted.

'Essentially, they channel the music of our world for the good of Talisker. The adepts, as they are called, use musical instruments to manipulate the dragonsong – Talisker's natural rhythms and melodies – to heal living things or to regulate discord in the environment. We call this raiki and we use tonics to do it.'

'Like using spells to do magic,' Chase said.

'Yes,' Emir said, 'but there is a difference. Adepts do not perform magic. Magic utilises power from *living* things and spells that rely on magic corrupt the fabric of Talisker's dragonsong. Our tonics use non-living amplifiers which is in keeping with the natural order. Adepts perform raiki using tonics. Wizards perform magic using spells.'

'What are amplifiers?' Noah signed.

Emir said, 'Both magic and raiki channel dragonsong. The difference is in the way it is channelled – the amplifier. In magic, the spells are amplified by living things – blood from human or animal sacrifices. In raiki, non-living things act as amplifiers – gems, stones, and shells for example. Adepts' instruments are modified to include these amplifiers. Music is performed by common people for entertainment. Raiki requires instruments with amplifiers.'

As Noah digested the information, Sachin re-joined them. Mud clung to his trouser legs from the knees down and his cheeks were flushed red. Two rabbits were tied to the pommel of his saddle.

Emir eyed the rabbits. 'They'll make a tasty stew tonight. Good hunting, Major.'

'They better be good,' Sachin replied testily. 'Look at what they did to my trousers.'

'Your trousers will be fine, Major,' Emir said calmly.

Sachin scowled.

'And what about the keys?' Chase asked.

'What?' Sachin said.

Emir said, 'We were discussing raiki and amplifiers in your absence.'

'Oh,' Sachin said. 'The twelve keys use the most powerful amplifier on Talisker – firestone – also called dragonscale. To you it would look like opal.'

'Dragonsong, dragonscale, dragonsbane – you talk a lot about dragons here,' Chase said. 'Will we see one soon?'

Sachin shook his head. 'There are no living dragons here anymore. That is a story for tonight's campfire.'

'What are the twelve keys?' Noah signed.

'Well, the flute, obviously,' Sachin answered, 'and then there is the clarinet, bagpipes, lyre, violin, harp, bugle, trombone, tuba, drums, bells, and xylophone.'

Chase wrung her hands.

'What's wrong?' Noah signed.

'I've got so much work to do to record all this backstory,' she said. 'I hope I can remember it all when we stop tonight.'

Chapter 5

Noah watched as Chase scrambled to capture her first Taliskeran sunset on camera. As the sun winked its last rays of pink and gold across the smudges of grey cloud Noah thought about her mother. *How could I not know she was an alien?* Noah thought. *How could I not know I'm* part *alien?*

When Chase had finished taking photographs, she came to sit beside Noah.

'I know this is a huge shock for you,' Chase said, putting her hand on Noah's knee, 'but it's really pretty awesome. I can't believe my best friend is an alien. That's fantastic.'

'*Part* alien,' Noah corrected her.

'Which part?' Chase asked.

'What?'

'Which is your alien part?'

Was this a trick question?

'My Taliskeran side,' Noah signed cautiously.

'Interesting,' Chase said.

'What do you mean?'

'*Well,* if you were born here, on Talisker,' Chase said, 'then technically you're Taliskeran so the Earth part you got from your dad is actually the alien part.'

Noah stared at her. 'If you were trying to make me feel better,' she signed, 'you've failed.'

As twilight swept the sunset away, Chase said, 'Do you want to try talking?'

Thankful for a distraction from her ancestral crisis, Noah nodded eagerly.

'Alright,' Chase said, 'but you need a quick lesson in phonics first.'

'Phonics?'

'Speech sounds,' Chase clarified.

Although it sounded like an English lesson was on its way, Noah found herself excited at the prospect. Chase used a stick to write Noah's name in the dirt. N – O – AH.

'Your name has three sounds,' Chase said, pointing with the stick to each part as she said it, 'N – O – AH. You try.'

Noah did try but it didn't sound anything like the way Chase had said it.

'If you've never used your vocal cords, it's going to take time, Noah,' she said. 'You need to train your muscles first.'

Chase wrote her own name in the dirt and sounded it out. Noah's version sounded more like "Jace" than "Chase" but she was pleased with that. Noah took the stick and wrote Raven's name in the dirt. Chase modelled the sounds for her.

'That one's harder,' Noah signed after several attempts.

Chase smiled. 'I'm surprised he's not over here. The number of times I've said his name – he'd usually come running.'

'He's otherwise occupied,' Noah signed. 'He's "helping" Emir with the rabbit stew.'

'How about you go and check on them,' Chase suggested. 'I just want to get a few notes down before dinner. We'll have plenty of time in the saddle tomorrow to work on your speech.'

'Cool,' Noah signed.

Noah strolled over to the fire. Emir and Raven looked up as she arrived but Sachin sat, apparently mesmerised by the flames.

'Can I help?' she signed.

Raven barked and Noah smiled. She liked that sound.

'You could taste this,' Emir said, passing her a spoon.

Noah crouched in front of the cooking pot where the murky broth bubbled away ferociously. She dipped the spoon in and waited a moment for it to cool before putting it anywhere near her lips. Given its appearance, her expectations weren't high but she was pleasantly surprised.

Noah nodded her approval and put the spoon down so she could sign again. 'Tasty.'

'Thank you,' Emir said as he continued stirring the broth to stop it sticking to the bottom of the pot.

'I'm hungry,' Sachin said.

Noah's eyes nearly popped out of her head.

'I'm sure you are, young Master,' Emir replied evenly. 'You've worked very hard today.'

In the moment's silence that followed, Noah marvelled at the dynamics of this unusual relationship. The "young Master", while obviously a talented adept, also had the ability to be petulance personified while Emir, whose role seemed to encompass everything from nanny to personal assistant, was seemingly unflappable. *No wonder Emir's so dour,* Noah thought. *I would be too if I had to deal with someone like that all day every day.*

Sachin stood up, hands on hips, staring at the young man who was pretending to inspect his stew. Eventually, the Major got the hint.

'May I have some stew now, please?' he asked.

'Certainly, Major,' Emir replied. 'You bring me your bowl and I will fill it for you.'

Once everyone had a bowl of stew and all the stumps around the campfire were occupied, Sachin gave thanks. Noah noticed that Raven had gulped his down before the blessing was finished.

'It's amazing he didn't burn his throat,' Chase said in wonder.

'I took a portion out for him earlier so it would be cool by the time we were ready to eat,' Emir said.

'Ah, good thinking,' Chase replied. 'This is very tasty, by the way. My compliments to the chef.'

Emir accepted her compliment without smiling. 'Thank you.'

Noah balanced her bowl on her lap, watching the fire as she ate. While the evening wasn't especially cold, the fire was inviting. Noah loved campfires. Memories of camping trips with her parents, toasting marshmallows over the coals, filled her mind. Tonight though, was something new. Sound. That was something about fires she hadn't understood. The flames had always entranced her, the warmth calmed her – but the sound added a new dimension.

When everyone had had their fill, Emir collected the bowls.

'Are you feeling refreshed after your dinner?' he said to Sachin.

'Yes.'

Emir nodded. 'Perhaps now is a good time for a history lesson then,' he suggested.

'Yes,' Sachin agreed.

'Wait!' Chase said, leaping up from her log seat. 'I need my notebook.'

Chase had been distressed to find that Talisker did not have electricity so there was no way to charge her tablet. She'd had to resort to the old technology – pen and paper.

Sachin glared at Chase but said nothing.

When Chase returned, he said, 'Are you ready now? Can we get started?'

'That'd be tops,' Chase said, settling herself back on the log.

'Talisker is actually built on the bones of an ancient dragon,' Sachin began. 'Millions and millions of years ago, the Great God – Elani – was busy creating many beautiful worlds across the galaxies. Elani had a brother, Jong, who was equally powerful, but destructive. Jong rode through the galaxy in his brother's wake on his trusty steed – the great dragon Xan – destroying worlds as they encountered them.

'At one time, Elani came across Xan while she was sleeping. As Jong was nowhere in sight, Elani disguised himself as his brother and tricked Xan into riding with him. He created a world for her that was the most beautiful and exotic that he'd ever made. For the first time, she saw the beauty of creation and was instantly sorry for the destruction she had caused. Then she was angry and decided to eat her evil lord. Elani threw off his disguise in time to save his life.

'Xan vowed there and then to find the destructive Jong and kill him. When she found him, there was a great battle in the heavens. God and dragon battled. Xan did finally eat the evil Jong but he was not dead. Xan was wounded and begged Elani for help to contain Jong. To honour her and to contain his wicked brother, Elani built a world around them. Talisker. Our world. The dragon is not dead; she sleeps. Elani soothed her with music – his dragonsong. It is the music that sustains her sleep and therefore, sustains our world. Still, she sleeps. The dragon's heart still beats, her blood still flows in the earth and the universe is safe from Jong.'

'Nice,' Chase murmured as she wrote furiously in her journal. 'A very tidy creation story. So this dragonsong is like a lullaby then?' she added.

'Yes,' Sachin agreed.

'I know a lullaby is what mother's sing to babies to put them to sleep,' Noah signed, 'but I've never heard one.'

'I'll sing you one later,' Chase promised.

'I think I'll survive without it,' Noah signed.

Sachin continued his explanation. 'The firestone I told you about earlier is what sets the twelve keys apart from other instruments. Firestone is dragonscale – little pieces of Xan's scales.'

'Cool,' Chase said. 'So that's dragonsong and dragonscale … what about the Dragonsbane?'

Sachin said, 'The Dragonsbane is what it sounds like. The Dragon's bane. The person who is ultimately responsible for making sure Xan continues her slumber.'

'How?'

'I'm getting to that,' Sachin said. 'So Emir told you that we adepts use our instruments to maintain the integrity of the dragonsong. Our focus is on the physical world but there is another piece of the puzzle. The spiritual world also requires monitoring.'

'And that's what the Dragonsbane does?' Noah guessed.

Sachin shook his head. 'No. The spiritual world is the responsibility of the High Priestess. She oversees the Order of Elani and is charged with upholding the Score.'

'Score?' Chase asked, still scribbling feverishly.

'People on your world would probably call it a bible,' Emir continued. 'It's a set of instructions that are aimed at promoting harmony between people. Disharmony between people will unravel the natural order – and therefore, music – of our world and hence wake the dragon.'

'So let me see if I have this straight,' Noah signed. 'You adepts look after the dragonsong which is the music of the physical world. If something goes wrong, you use tonics to fix it so the dragon stays sleeping. And the High Priestess looks after the Score so that everyone plays nicely and doesn't wake the dragon with their fussing and fighting.'

'That is a reasonable summary,' Sachin confirmed.

'Does the High Priestess have a key?' Chase asked.

'No,' Sachin said.

'Right,' Chase said.

'Now the Dragonsbane is our direct link to Xan,' Sachin continued. 'She – our current Dragonsbane is a she – checks in to see that everything is actually working. She resides in Ironside, in the ancient temple of Dragonhall. There she enjoys a life of seclusion and deep contemplation, solitude and focus as she monitors the music of the deep world where the bones of the dragon lie.'

'She makes sure that what you guys are doing is working,' Noah concluded.

'Exactly,' Sachin said.

For a few moments all that could be heard was the crackling of the new log that Emir had just added to the fire and the trickling creek behind them.

Noah rubbed the mark on her abdomen then signed, 'And that's what I'm supposed to do?'

'One day,' Sachin said. 'Yes.'

Noah wondered if Mr Brennan would consider that a worthy career but she quickly pushed the thought aside.

'But in the meantime,' Noah signed, 'I'm supposed to find the 13th key and save the world?'

'With our help, yes,' Sachin said.

Noah frowned. 'So how am I supposed to find this key?'

Emir cut in. 'I think you have enough information for one day, Noah. I suggest you take some rest and we'll tell you more tomorrow.'

♪♫

'Noah, wake up,' Chase said.

Noah sat bolt upright. She wasn't used to being woken by the sound of her name – or any sound for that matter. Instantly aware of her surroundings, she looked at Chase. Noah put her hand to her eyes to shield them from the torchlight.

'Emir and Sachin have just gone to investigate a fire over the other side of the creek,' Chase whispered. 'We should follow.'

'Why are you talking so quietly?' Noah signed. 'If they've gone, there is no one here to hear you.'

Chase sighed. 'It's called whispering, Noah. You have a lot to learn about *mood*,' she said. 'By whispering I am creating a sense of anticipation and excitement in the scene. If I'd just *said* "we should follow", the reader wouldn't appreciate that we are about to do something bold and daring.'

'What reader?' Noah asked. 'No one is reading this. This isn't a book. We're *real people* in a real ...'

Noah trailed off as she thought about what she was just about to say. She *was* certain that she was a real person but she didn't have quite the same confidence in the reality of the place.

'Well, even if it's not a real place, we're still real people doing real things and no one is reading this,' Noah finished.

'They might be one day,' her friend said, grinning.

'Just make sure you change the names,' Noah signed. 'You know how much these people want to keep Talisker a secret.'

She extricated herself from her sleeping bag and slipped out of the tent to find Raven sitting guard. He barked once. Chase put her fingers to her lips.

'Shhh, boy,' she said. 'Don't give us away.'

She turned to Noah. 'Do you need to change before we go?'

Noah looked down at her night-dress. She'd feel no embarrassment at being seen in it. She'd designed it herself and it was both comfortable and fashionable.

'No. I'm ready,' she signed.

The flames were on the other side of the creek. It didn't appear to be a large fire and Noah wondered what had started it. The ground was dry and the sky clear. There was no storm, so that ruled out a lightning strike. Was someone camping nearby?

The light from the three moons was sufficient for the girls to find their way without the torch. They followed Raven who was bounding along through the sparse undergrowth. When they reached the creek, Noah could see Emir and Sachin on the other side.

'It seems quite localised,' Chase said.

'Do you think it's safe for us to go closer?' Noah signed.

Chase nodded. 'Emir and Sachin wouldn't be over there if it wasn't safe.'

Noah hitched up her night-dress before wading into the creek. The water was cold but clear. In the moonlight Noah could see the rocks on the bottom. The creek wasn't deep but Noah still chose her path carefully, sticking to the larger, elevated rocks. There was no point getting more wet than necessary.

Once on the far bank of the creek, the girls crept up behind Emir and Sachin.

'You should come and see this,' Emir said without turning around.

Noah looked at Chase who smiled back like a mischievous imp who'd been caught with her hand in the lolly jar.

Noah saw that it was no random fire. It certainly wasn't a campfire that had escaped its boundary in search of more wood. In fact, this fire did not feast on wood at all.

'Are those stones that are burning?' Noah signed.

'Rocks,' Emir corrected.

'So you burn rocks here?'

'Not usually, no,' he replied flatly. 'We burn wood, just like you do on Earth.'

There had been a wood fire at the campsite, Noah remembered. Then she saw something that made her mouth dry. There was a pattern in the rocks. They had been specially placed. Specially placed and then set alight.

Noah Chord beware.

'That's not very nice,' Chase said.

Noah agreed. 'Who would do that?' she signed.

'We will discuss such things after this unnatural fire is out,' Emir replied.

Sachin put his flute to his lips. He closed his eyes as his fingers moved frenetically over the keys. Almost instantly, the flames danced a little slower. Noah watched as the fire bowed to the Major's will. After a few minutes, only smoke remained. Noah watched as Sachin knelt beside the first rock at the bottom of the "N".

'What's he doing now?' Chase asked.

'He is calming the rocks.'

'They look pretty calm to me,' Noah signed dubiously.

'It has to do with the flow of music. Rocks, like everything on Talisker, are made of music. That fire was unnatural and so disrupts the music of the rocks. Sachin is trying to restore their natural flow of music.'

Noah waited patiently while Sachin performed his raiki. She looked at the still-smoking rocks again. *Noah Chord beware.* Twirling her ring around on her finger, she wondered what her mother would have made of all this.

'Who would do this?' Chase asked. 'Who even knows that Noah is here?'

'The Dragonsbane,' Emir answered.

Noah looked around in panic.

'Relax, Noah. The Dragonsbane is not here,' Emir said. 'She is powerful and her reach is long. She is more than capable of such a thing without leaving Ironside.'

'Then why?' Noah signed.

'The "why" is obvious. She sees you as a threat.'

'Surely such an act is counterproductive,' Chase put in.

'What do you mean?' Emir asked.

Chase's eyes blazed with excitement. 'You said that the fire was unnatural and that Sachin now has to realign the natural music of the rocks.'

'That's right,' Emir said.

'So why would the Dragonsbane risk it?'

'Risk what?'

'Upsetting the natural order of things,' Chase said. 'Surely by messing with the dragonsong, she risks waking Xan herself.'

'Disturbing a few rocks isn't enough to wake the dragon,' Emir said.

'I still wouldn't have thought it was a good idea for someone in her position to be setting rocks on fire,' Chase said.

'The Dragonsbane's job is to protect the world as a whole but not necessarily the individual things in it,' Emir explained.

'Still,' Chase continued, 'setting things on fire just to protect your own position doesn't seem right.'

Emir considered her words as the Major finished up his work. 'When I said that the Dragonsbane saw Noah as a threat, I didn't mean that she saw her as a threat to her position,' he said. 'The Dragonsbane is above such things. Her priority is to ensure Xan stays sleeping. If she sees Noah as a threat it probably means that she thinks Noah might wake the dragon.'

Having finished his work, Sachin joined them. 'This is good,' he said.

'*Good?*' Noah signed. 'How?'

Cradling his flute in his arms, he said, 'The Dragonsbane has sensed your arrival. For her to send a message like this tells me that she knows your potential.'

'But what do I need to *beware* of?' Noah signed.

'At the moment,' Sachin said, 'everything.'

Chapter 6

Sachin was keen to reach Mellifont by nightfall so the party broke camp before sunrise. Chase spent the first hour on horseback drilling Noah on vocal exercises, having her repeat sounds and sequences of sounds. Noah was not only glad for the practice but pleased to have a distraction from the riding itself. Noah didn't dislike horses, she just didn't love riding them.

'Okay. Enough!' Sachin cried. '*I* need a break from this racket. Time for another history lesson.'

'Okay,' Noah said.

'Great job, Noah,' Chase said. 'That was perfect.'

Noah smiled. 'Yes, it was,' she added.

Chase clapped enthusiastically at her friend's progress. 'You'll have this speaking thing down in no time.'

'*Anyway,*' Sachin said. 'As I was saying … history lesson.'

'Go for it,' Noah said.

Sachin rolled his eyes. 'We have told you that Talisker is in grave danger and that there is a prophecy about the 13th key being needed to save us. The prophecy goes like this … *The thirteenth key the world shall need, for evil to be brought to heel – One of two, the Dragon's bane must rise; and the music wield.*'

'That's it?' Noah signed, giving her tired vocal cords a rest.

'That's it,' Sachin said.

'I don't see how that applies to me,' she signed. 'What's the "one of two" thing about?'

Sachin took a deep breath. 'Many adepts are searching for the 13th key,' he said, 'but there is one that bears the same mark you do. The mark of the Dragonsbane. His name is Dr Grainger and he is Doctor of raiki at the Academy – one rank down from Major.'

'So he's next in line for a key, were one to become available,' Emir added.

'Knows his stuff then,' Chase said.

'Yes,' Sachin said. 'He is skilled and well-regarded in Mellifont.'

'So you think it's between him and Noah to find the key and use it to save Talisker?'

Sachin nodded. Noah frowned. 'Hardly seems like a fair fight,' she signed. 'You expect me to *find* a musical instrument, type unknown and then learn how to *play* it – better than a doctor of raiki? And then somehow, I'm to take the Dragonsbane's job from her – before Dr Grainger does – and *then* save the world?'

Sachin looked at Emir. 'She's definitely not as stupid as Brinn said she was.'

'That's not polite, Major,' Emir said.

Noah felt the heat rising in her cheeks. She didn't come here to be insulted by a kid and a cat. She took a deep breath and reminded herself what she did come here for – the chance to hear and to source fabrics for her collection for the State Titles. And now, Noah had another reason to stay – to find out more about her family tree.

'Perhaps you could tell us more about the great evil you face,' Chase suggested, trying to steer the conversation in a more constructive direction.

'The great evil comes to us in the form of Orville Kurz,' Sachin said.

'So Orville Kurz is a wizard?' Chase asked.

'Yes,' Sachin said. 'He and his disciples will use blood magic on such a scale as to destroy the fabric of our world.'

'Do they use wands?' Noah signed.

'Sorry?' Sachin said.

'When they're doing magic, do they use wands?' she signed.

Chase slapped her with her notebook as Sachin frowned.

Noah was surprised. She wouldn't have thought Chase could reach her from horseback. 'What was that for?' she signed.

'Noah,' Chase said, 'no self-respecting wielder of magic would ever use a wand. It's so clichéd; it's awful.'

'I've read heaps of stories about wizards using wands,' Noah signed.

'*Bad* stories,' Chase said.

'Well, you could have just told me,' Noah signed. 'You didn't have to slap me.'

'I'm sorry,' Chase said. 'I didn't mean to hurt you. I was just shocked, I guess.'

Emir joined the conversation. 'Orville has King Tambian of Leninstar on his side. He is Tambian's chief adviser and he has convinced the king that raiki is from the dark ages and that blood magic is the way of the future. Orville's vision is to implement an electricity network, powered by blood magic.'

'An electricity network?' Noah signed. 'How does he even know about electricity?'

Emir said, 'Orville's been to Earth.'

'So Orville's been to Earth,' Noah signed, '*you've* been to Earth'— she pointed to Emir and then looked to Sachin—'and I suppose you've had a visit too?'

'Guilty,' Sachin said.

Chase said, 'Emir, I thought you said that not many Earthlings knew of Talisker and that you wanted to keep it that way. How do you expect to keep it a secret with all this travel backwards and forwards?'

'Strict regulations are in place for travel between Talisker and Earth,' Sachin said. 'Each state keeps a register of travel tickets so they can keep track of the comings and goings.'

'We didn't get tickets,' Noah signed.

'As a Major of the Academy, I am exempt from the protocols,' Sachin said. 'I need only record details of our travel – and yours – in the Academy register. Anyway, back to Orville's electricity network. Emir?'

'Orville has convinced King Tambian to construct a network of underground wires to service Leninstar City – the capital of Leninstar

State. While we have the materials here to construct the network, we don't have any clean fuels to power an electricity grid. Orville's plan is to power it using blood,' Emir said.

'Sounds gruesome,' Chase said.

'Power from the people, for the people,' Sachin said.

'Excuse me?' Chase said.

'That's Orville's slogan,' Emir said. 'His justification for blood magic.'

'Surely that's going to take a lot of blood,' Noah signed. 'Where's it all going to come from?'

Sachin said, '*That* is the problem. Orville says it will all be by way of donation. But we know better. We believe that entire populations in towns across Leninstar are already being slaughtered to build up the blood stocks he needs.'

Noah shuddered. 'Whole towns don't disappear without anyone noticing,' she signed. 'If Orville is doing this, how is he getting away with it?'

'Most of the official reports say that the recent explosion in goblin numbers is to blame. They say that goblins are running rampant because the adepts are not doing their job.'

'What job is that?' Chase asked.

'Goblin management. Part of our role in maintaining the order of the natural world is to control goblin populations.'

Emir spoke up. 'Orville is blaming us for the disappearances to divert suspicion from himself,' he said.

'Correct,' Sachin said. 'But some reports have gone even further. Not content to suggest that we are simply standing idly by while goblins run wild, they say that we are *breeding* goblins specifically to decimate these towns as a way to discredit blood magic.'

'That's twisted,' Chase said. 'If the adepts have protected life on this world for millennia, do people really believe they'd do that?'

'When it comes from the king's news service, people believe it,' Sachin said.

Noah thought for a moment. 'So Orville using blood magic like this is going to destroy Talisker and you need me to find the 13th key to stop him?'

'Yes,' Sachin said. 'Using blood magic on such a scale will corrupt the dragonsong and destroy Talisker – we need the 13th key to stop him.'

'So what's the plan?' Noah signed. 'How do we find it?'

'We need to go to Mellifont first,' Sachin explained, 'so I can register you as the candidate for our House – the House of Wind. There are four Houses at the Academy – Wind, Brass, Strings, and Percussion – and the keys are divided up with three in each. The flute, clarinet and bagpipes are in Wind; the bugle, trombone and tuba are in Brass; the lyre, violin and harp in Strings and the bells, drums and xylophone in Percussion. Each House has the opportunity to put forward a candidate to use the 13th key when it's found. The House of Brass is putting forward Dr Grainger and I will put your name forward for the House of Wind.'

'There are no others?' Chase asked.

Sachin shook his head. 'Many are *looking* for the 13th key,' he said, 'but only *one* can use it – one of two, in fact.'

'So we don't have to find it?' Noah signed.

'Not necessarily,' Emir said. 'It would be best if we did though. Many who are looking for the 13th key are in it for the wrong reasons. Orville and his cronies want to get their hands on it and then there are all the bounty hunters who are after it to make a quid by selling it to the highest bidder.'

Noah considered what he'd said. 'I don't play any musical instruments,' Noah signed. 'Having been deaf my whole life, they weren't really an option.

'Let's not worry about that today,' Sachin said, taking his flute out of his pocket.

'How do you do that?' Chase asked. 'There is no way that flute should fit in that pocket.'

'Raiki,' Sachin said. 'These trousers are standard issue to all adepts at the Academy. They were invented by Major Anok. He found a way to use dragonsong to miniaturise objects so they fit into pockets in the trousers. When the fabric is made, a special tonic is woven into it, which gives the trousers their special power. I think the best thing though is that new pockets appear as you need them – when you first get the trousers, there are no pockets on them.'

While Chase scribbled in her notebook, Noah stared at the Major's trousers. Tantalising ideas about commissioning special fabrics for the State Titles raced around her mind.

Sachin handed his flute to Noah. 'Hold this,' he said.

When she cradled it in her hands, her fingers started tingling.

'Do you feel anything?' Sachin asked.

Noah nodded.

'Good. Now close your eyes and listen to it closely.'

Juggling the flute to free her hands, she signed, 'I just told you I can't play it.'

'I'm not asking you to play it,' he replied. 'When I say listen to it, I want you to feel the music in it. I want you to describe what you feel or hear when you hold it.'

Noah closed her eyes, tried to concentrate. After a few moments the tingling in her fingers stopped and she thought she heard a voice, very faint, soft and sweet. Colours swirled in her mind, randomly at first but then a strange figure emerged from the chaos. Human in form she was diminutive and impossibly pale. Her eyes were alien though – large, round and black. She sat on a low stool in the centre of an underground chamber. Twelve arched doorways had been carved out of the wall that encircled the expansive, polished onyx floor.

A flute, like the one Noah held now, lay in the girl's lap. She stroked it with tapered fingers, chanting softly to herself. It was her voice that Noah could hear. She was singing. Noah couldn't understand the words but she sensed the power in them. As the song continued Noah felt hot. Without opening her eyes, she took one hand off the flute to loosen the scarf around her neck. As Noah put her hand back on the flute the girl appeared to look directly at her. 'Ti'ashi,' she cried. Instantly lava streamed into the cavern through the archways.

Noah could feel her whole body heating up as the lava filled her mind but she was powerless to stop it. The girl appeared not to notice the lava. Even as it ran over her feet, she did not react. Noah cried out as her own feet burned and she opened her eyes.

Leaning over from his horse, Sachin took the flute from her grasp.

'Tell me what happened,' Sachin said.

Feeling the heat dissipate, Noah told him about the girl and the lava.

'The Descera,' he said. 'That is good.'

Chapter 7

The party reached Mellifont late in the afternoon. Noah wished she could have seen it from above. Orange and black striped domes towered above her as they rode into the ancient city. The massive beehive-like structures sprouted inexplicably from the surrounding grasslands. As they entered a narrow gorge – one of hundreds that snaked throughout the range – the group had to advance in single file.

Noah could feel the weight of stone around her. According to Sachin, the city had been fashioned by the Descera using the twelve keys that the Academy now held in trust. She listened intently. Stones crunched under the hooves of their horses. Insects hidden in the low scrub chorused as they passed. The evening breeze whistled through the gorge alongside them – but she couldn't hear any sounds from inside.

'Not far from here,' Sachin said.

'I'm glad about that,' Chase said, smiling ruefully. 'My backside wasn't meant for the saddle.'

'Same here,' Noah managed to say.

She had made progress with her speech. Sachin had done what he could with his flute to massage her vocal cords into action but she still had work to do.

Turning a corner, they came to a dead end. A metal door blocked their path. Sachin, at the front of the small procession, pulled his flute from his pocket and played a few notes. The door slid silently aside.

Raven darted through first, with Sachin, Noah and Chase behind him. Emir brought up the tail.

Inside was like a spring dawn. Noah shielded her eyes with her hands.

'Where are the lights?' Chase asked.

'The light comes from the rock,' Emir explained.

'But the rock is orange and black,' Chase said. 'How is the light so white?'

'Dragonsong,' Sachin said. 'Believe it or not, rocks are full of light. We use raiki to extract the light from the rock. We use raiki for everything here. This is the City of the Adepts. Everyone here is trained in raiki.'

'Cool,' Noah said surveying the entryway.

The music the Descera had woven here had not only exposed the natural beauty of the rock, but enhanced it. The ceiling hovered about ten metres overhead. Noah walked over to the wall, placing her hand on the stone. It was cool but it made her fingers tingle. She pulled her hand away and inspected her fingers.

'Feel something?' Sachin asked.

Noah nodded, signing the word "tingling".

'Talisker's music is strong here. You can feel its vibrations.'

Chase, who had dismounted before Noah and was currently preoccupied with a series of stretching exercises, put her hand on the wall.

'I don't feel anything,' she said.

'You won't,' Sachin replied. 'You're not on the same frequency.'

Before Chase could ask any more questions, a man, who looked like a sack of flour with arms and legs, waddled through the archway on the opposite side of the chamber.

'Welcome back Major Sachin, Emir,' the flour-sack man said, clutching a clipboard in one pudgy hand and saluting officiously with the other. 'And this must be—'

He stopped abruptly when he saw the two girls.

'No one said anything about *two* visitors,' he said, scrutinising his clipboard. 'I have only one band to issue.'

While flour-sack man fussed over his clipboard, clearly vexed by not having been informed of the extra arrival, Sachin walked to stand next to Noah.

'Professor Alan,' Sachin said, 'this is Noah Chord.'

Alan took a dramatic breath and composed himself.

'Professor Alan at your service,' he said, extending his hand. 'You can call me Al.'

Noah smiled as he shook her hand vigorously.

'Noah can hear but she can't speak,' Sachin said.

'Oh. Right,' Alan said.

Emir stepped forward. 'Alan,' he said, 'you can let go of Noah's hand now.'

Reluctantly, Alan released her hand. 'Of course, of course,' he said.

'Did you have something for Noah?' Sachin prompted.

'Oh yes!' Alan said, reaching into one of the pockets on his trousers. 'In the sheer excitement of the occasion I nearly forgot ...'

He felt around in his pocket for a moment and then frowned.

'I was sure it was in that pocket,' he said. 'Must be this one,' he added, chuckling.

'When he laughs, it sounds like a wet fart,' Noah signed to Emir as Alan continued to fish in his pockets.

Emir nodded. 'He's trying to be ingratiating.'

'It's not working,' Noah replied.

'I know.'

Noah looked sideways at Emir. 'You don't like him very much, do you,' she signed.

'Nonsense,' Emir signed back. 'Of course I like him.'

Noah raised an eyebrow.

Sachin, who'd been watching the exchange, signed, 'Emir does like him – in a target practice kind of way.'

Noah stared as Emir chastised his young charge. Oblivious to the exchange, Alan gave a triumphant cry. 'Found it!'

He held a circular, black object in his hand. On closer inspection Noah could see it was a bracelet of some kind.

'One standard issue House of Wind wristband,' he said. 'Serial number 235971-ax, and issued on this day to Noah Chord. Please sign next to the crosses,' he added, shoving the clipboard and a pen in her direction.

Noah scrawled her signature on the paper and Alan handed her the wristband. It was huge. Maybe if she hoisted it up over her elbow and never straightened her arm, she might have some chance of retaining it. But failing that, she didn't know how she'd keep it on.

'You won't lose it,' Alan said smugly. 'Just pop it on.'

Noah did as she was told and when she slipped it over her hand, it fitted snugly onto her slim wrist.

'Just like magic,' Alan said.

'And not a wand in sight,' Sachin added.

Noah ignored him, intent on inspecting her wristband. It was about as wide as her finger and had the appearance of black stone, polished to an eye-watering gloss. Inlaid into the stone was a silver flute – a miniature copy of Sachin's key.

'Happy with the fit?' Alan asked.

Noah nodded.

'Good,' he said. 'It would have been a thundering nuisance to have to issue you a different one. You wouldn't believe the paperwork!'

Noah looked around the group. 'So I'm officially part of the club then?' she signed.

'It's not a club,' Sachin said, frowning.

'I'm going to have to learn how you do that sign language,' Alan said. 'I feel like I'm missing out.'

Brinn chose that moment to reappear.

'So Alan,' she purred, 'have you officially met the reason you owe me another fleece cocoon?'

Raven raced to be by the cat's side. He lay down next to her, tongue lolling in adoration. Noah rolled her eyes, as perplexed by her dog's behaviour as she was by Brinn's statement.

Alan reached into one of the many pockets on his trousers and pulled out a knitted object.

'Is that a teapot cosy?' Noah signed.

'It's a cat bed,' Sachin said.

'A fleece cocoon,' Brinn corrected as Alan placed the knitted dome on the floor. 'It has a lovely cushioned base with a knitted cover to keep a cat toasty warm on cold winter nights. This one looks particularly nice.'

Noah watched Brinn walk around the knitted bed before slinking in through the slit at the front. The cat turned herself around and settled down with her head in the opening.

'Delightful,' Brinn said. 'Just delightful.'

'Do you like the colours?' Alan asked. 'I know how much you like greens and browns.'

The cat snuggled her cheek against the base. 'It's fabulous ... and a pleasure doing business with you again, Alan,' she said. 'And thank you too, Noah. I couldn't have done it without you.'

'What do you mean?' Noah signed.

'We had a wager,' Brinn said. 'Alan thought you'd come to Talisker because you wanted to save the world. *I* said you'd come for the fabric.'

Noah remembered Brinn asking her why she'd decided to come to Talisker and a bet being mentioned.

Noah shrugged an apology to Alan.

Alan smiled. 'It's okay. I lose on purpose – to humour her,' he said, winking. 'Keeps her on side.'

Noah didn't know if he was just saying that to make her feel better or not but she signed, 'What kind of wool is that?'

Chase translated for Alan. 'Noah wants to know what kind of wool that is.'

'The finest llama wool in Talisker,' Alan gushed, stowing his clipboard and pen in one of his pockets. 'It is soft and luxurious but also incredibly durable.'

'And you knitted that?' Noah signed.

Once Chase had translated, Alan beamed. 'Indeed I did! Knitting is one of my many hobbies. Do you knit?'

Noah shook her head.

'I could show you sometime,' he enthused. 'It's wonderfully rewarding and also very therapeutic.'

Brinn said, 'I agree. This is certainly a just reward for me and *very* therapeutic.'

♪♫

'I can't believe you're still in the bath, Noah,' Chase said. 'The ceremony starts in half an hour.'

From the doorway of the bathroom, Chase tapped her watch to emphasise her point.

'This is awesome,' Noah signed before ducking her head under the water again.

Noah loved their accommodation. She'd happily have given up Sachin's ceremony to stay and work on her collection for the State Titles. The carved wooden table that occupied the wall to the right of the entranceway was already covered with her sketches. Like the entrance chamber, the interior lighting was courtesy of the walls and while the king-size bed looked inviting, it was the bath that preoccupied her at present.

The rear wall of the en suite was a sheet of water. Emir had explained how water was pumped up through a series of massive square pipes in the multi-storey dome. Once it reached the top it cascaded down the outside of the shafts, which formed the bathroom wall in each apartment. It meant that there was a small gap between the floor and the wall so that unused water could flow back to the reservoir to be pumped back up again.

When water was required for a bath, one had simply to pull a lever which diverted the water into the tub. The temperature was regulated by raiki. By adjusting another set of levers, the dragonsong in the rock was altered to either heat or cool the water. Once water had been used, the grey water was carried away through another set of pipes to be purified before being returned to the reservoir again. It was ingenious.

Noah had been in the bath, alternating between soaking and scrubbing, for the past half an hour and she wasn't done yet. There was still a raspberry juice astringent to put through her hair. Noah popped her head up to see Chase still standing in the doorway.

'Noah, hurry up,' Chase said.

'I have to wash my hair,' she signed back.

Chase sighed as Noah ducked her head under the water.

'Do you like the black trousers?' Chase asked when she reappeared.

Noah looked at her as she massaged the raspberry astringent into her scalp. At length, she signed, 'They look functional.'

'They're actually very comfortable,' Chase said.

They weren't terrible, Noah decided but they certainly weren't stylish. She'd been left a pair on her bed too and she knew she was expected to wear them. Everyone she'd passed on her way to the room had been wearing the uniform trousers teamed with a blue vest. Emir had given Noah a House of Wind vest to wear to the ceremony too.

Noah ducked her head under the water again to rinse her hair. It felt so good to be clean again. After two days riding, she'd been fearful that she'd never rid herself of the grit she'd accumulated on the road. When she resurfaced, Chase was standing over her, towel in hand.

'Out,' she demanded.

Noah snatched the towel and gave her friend a baleful stare. It was hard to sign her protest while holding a towel to protect her modesty. She wished she could speak so she could give Chase the telling-off she richly deserved. The writer turned her back and walked into the adjoining room as Noah climbed out of the tub.

'I should have brought more journals with me,' Chase lamented as Noah joined her in the bedroom. 'I've almost filled one already. This place is fabulous but I hate to say it – it would be better with electricity so I could recharge my tablet. This story is easily going to be my best ever.'

Chase burbled on about her latest work while Noah slipped into her trousers.

'I've already decided to dedicate it to you, Noah,' she said.

'Sounds great,' Noah signed before donning her vest.

'Great? Is that it?'

Noah stopped. 'I would be deeply honoured if you dedicated your story to me,' she signed.

Chase beamed and abruptly changed the subject. 'So what do you think of Emir?' she asked.

'He takes himself way too seriously,' she signed. 'And I reckon it's a bit weird that someone his age is so subservient to a little kid.'

Chase's brow furrowed. 'That "little kid" – as you put it – is an incredibly talented and revered adept, Noah. You might do well to remember that.'

'He might be more convincing if he had a wand,' Noah signed.

Chase, knowing her friend was baiting her, picked up a rolled up pair of socks from Noah's bag and threw them at her. 'Troglodyte,' she said.

Noah caught the socks easily and threw them back. 'I hope this presentation doesn't take too long,' she signed.

'You nervous?' Chase asked.

'A little,' Noah admitted. 'Sachin hasn't told me what I'm supposed to do.'

'Maybe he doesn't really know,' Chase suggested. 'It's probably not every day a Major has to endorse a candidate for the 13th key.'

'Probably not,' Noah agreed.

'Well, at least Dr Grainger won't be there,' Chase said. 'That's got to be a bonus.'

'I guess,' Noah signed.

Chapter 8

Sachin led Noah and Chase behind the stage of an immense auditorium. From the wings, Noah could see hundreds of people filing in and taking their seats.

'Wait here,' Sachin said, 'Emir will be back shortly. He will tell you when to come on stage.'

Without waiting for a response, he walked away.

'Sachin must be *really* nervous,' Chase said. 'He's very edgy.'

Go on stage? Noah thought. *In front of all those people?*

By the time Emir finally arrived, Noah was livid. 'You knew about this?' she signed. 'You knew he was going to drag me out on stage in front of all those people?'

Emir nodded.

'And when were you going to tell me?' Noah demanded.

A pillar of calm, Emir said, 'When the time was right.'

'And when was that?'

'Is now good for you?'

Noah glared at him. 'What am I supposed to do out there?' she signed.

'Make them love you,' he said. 'The Major is going to endorse you as a candidate for the 13th key. It would be most helpful if they approved of you.'

'And if they don't?'

'The Major will endorse you nonetheless but it would be good for morale if the majority of the House of Wind supported him.'

'Who would risk his displeasure by opposing him?' Chase asked.

Emir shrugged. 'There are many here who believe they have what it takes to use the key. For some it will be difficult to accept that someone from outside the House is the preferred candidate.'

Now about ready to blow a fuse, Noah signed, 'Well, that's just—'

Chase grabbed her arm. 'Calm down,' she whispered in her ear. 'Treat it like a fashion show. Use it as practice. Go out there and play the crowd.'

Noah took a deep breath.

'Okay,' Emir said, 'I will be out on stage with Major Sachin. The Major will brief the assembly on recent developments and then introduce you as his candidate for the 13th key. Alan will wait here with you to prompt you if necessary.'

At the mention of his name, Alan appeared.

'Noah,' he schmoozed. 'Lovely to see you again.'

Noah thought it was anything but lovely to see him again but she kept her thoughts to herself.

Emir continued his instructions. 'A selection of adepts will play a composition that's been written in your honour.'

'A song?'

'Yes, a song.'

'For me?'

'The song was composed in honour of the successful candidate, which is you,' Emir confirmed.

'How many instruments will there be?' Noah signed.

'About fifty,' Emir answered.

'How many people will be out there?'

'About three thousand. It is a full assembly of the House of Wind. Majors Dolon and Maggie will be there also. They hold the other two woodwind keys – Major Dolon has the bagpipes and Major Maggie has the clarinet.'

'Right,' Noah said.

'Ready?' Emir said.

Noah looked around, desperate for a way to stall proceedings. 'How did the cat get out of this?' she asked.

'Technically, Brinn is not a member of the House so she is not required to attend,' Emir answered.

'Technically, I'm not a member of the House either,' Noah signed.

Emir pointed to her wristband. 'Technically you *are* a member of the House.'

'Damn it,' she said aloud.

Emir frowned. 'I hope you're not going to use that language on stage.' He turned to Chase. 'Could you not have taught her something more befitting her role?'

Chase at least had the good grace to look chastened.

'Okay, people,' Emir said, 'show time.'

He walked onto the stage. Noah still did not dare look out into the auditorium but she heard the hush descend as Emir walked out.

'Good evening everyone,' he began. 'Welcome and thank you for coming. I shan't waste any time. I'll hand straight over to Major Sachin.'

The rapturous applause and cheering that greeted the boy Major as he strode onto the stage from the opposite wing went on for well over a minute. Noah peered out from behind a heavy silver curtain, stunned. When Sachin started to speak, the crowd hung on his every word.

'Bizarre,' Noah said to no one in particular.

Alan, who was the most qualified "no one in particular" in the immediate vicinity, responded.

'They love him,' he said.

Noah reverted to signing, 'But he's just a kid. Surely all this adulation will give him a massive head.'

Chase interpreted for Alan.

'Emir will see to it that that doesn't happen,' Alan said. 'He has a real knack for keeping the Major ... grounded.'

'Well, if he's able to do that, I know who *I* think is the greater magician of the two of them, and it's not the Major,' Noah signed.

As Sachin continued his briefing, Chase gave Noah a few tips on winning over a crowd.

'Remember to smile,' she said. 'And wave – but only use one hand at a time. Waving with two hands makes you look conceited.'

Noah nodded. 'One hand. Got it. Anything else?' she signed.

'Don't fold your arms and don't put your hands in your pockets.'

'Okay.'

'And a slight bow of your head wouldn't go astray either,' Chase added.

'Who am I supposed to bow to?' Noah asked.

'First to the Major and then to the crowd.'

Chase turned her head towards the stage. 'Did Sachin just say Orville will be here tomorrow?' she asked.

Alan nodded.

'No wonder the Major was so testy when he dropped us off here,' Chase mused.

Noah had put the Major's mood down to his natural petulance but she kept her thoughts to herself. Orville's arrival was bad news.

'Speaking of magic and music and stuff,' Alan said ingratiatingly, 'I wondered if you might spare me some time at some stage to talk about the music of numbers?'

'Mmm?' Noah said absently as she tried to listen to what Sachin was saying.

'I mean I know you'll be very busy hunting for the 13th key and everything,' he gushed, 'but I could really use your expertise in my research.'

Noah looked at him, confused. *Expertise? Research?*

Mistaking her confusion for interest, he said, 'As you've probably heard, I am employed here chiefly as an auditor but I have recently received a grant to explore the music and magic of numbers.'

'Numbers?' she said, trying to repeat the last word she'd heard.

'Oh yes. Fascinating topic. People think accounting and numbers are dull but they couldn't be more wrong. I have a theory that the world is actually built upon, and dependent on, numbers. Pretty radical stuff. We've known for a long time that the world is made of music, but we don't understand the structure. My theory is that it is *numbers* that underpin music and hence gives music its structure. It's a theory that—'

'Please give your warmest House of Wind welcome,' she heard Sachin say, 'to Noah Chord.'

'I'm on,' she said, interrupting the jabbering auditor. So much for him giving her the cue to go on.

'Good luck,' Chase whispered.

There was cheering again, though not as wild this time, as Noah walked across the stage to stand beside Sachin. She opened her mouth to speak and the hall went instantly silent. 'Hello and thank you,' she croaked, before her throat seized up.

Emir came to her rescue. 'Miss Chord has a case of laryngitis,' he said. 'She really needs to rest her voice.'

Sachin stepped forward. 'I present Noah Chord as a candidate for the 13th key.'

Several moments' silence followed his introduction before Major Dolon spoke.

'Major Sachin,' Dolon said, adjusting his bagpipes under his arm, 'tell us why we should support your endorsement.'

Sachin nodded, 'She wears an Academy ring and she bears the mark of the Dragonsbane.'

A murmur rippled through the assembly.

'Is there more?' Major Maggie asked. 'Does she have training?'

'Noah has no training in raiki,' Sachin said, 'but she's been chosen by the Descera. There was a charm on her. The Descera have marked her for this job.'

'The Descera?' Dolon said. 'Are you sure?'

'I'm sure,' Sachin replied calmly.

Noah's stomach gurgled. She hoped that no one else in the hall could hear it.

Major Maggie said, 'Noah, can you contact the Descera?'

'On account of Noah's ... laryngitis, allow me to speak on her behalf,' Sachin said. 'She has had a vision of the Descera. It is my belief that she can contact them and get the information we need to find the 13th key.'

A smattering of applause started at the back of the hall. Noah held her breath as the noise swelled. Remembering what Chase had said, Noah bowed her head towards Sachin and then to the audience.

'Though Dr Grainger is clearly more qualified,' Major Dolon said, 'we accept your endorsement of Miss Chord.'

Sachin bowed to his fellow Majors and the cheering began. When the noise eventually subsided, Emir said, 'Adepts ready?'

Players stood in their place in the crowd. The song started with one solitary instrument. A piccolo. Gradually more and more wind instruments joined in. Noah could hear each of them as they joined. The variety of instruments surprised her and they all blended to make an enchanting melody.

It captivated Noah. She stood completely still, letting the music dance all around her. But as the song wore on, something changed. The music wasn't just swirling around her. It seemed to be going *through* her. First a note here and there but then more followed. Still more slipped under her guard and she started to swoon. The song marched on, building feverishly towards its climax.

Noah watched as Sachin raised his flute to his lips. As he began to play, her vision blurred and she felt herself falling.

The last thing Noah heard was a scream. Hers.

♪♫

'What do you mean "sort of dead"?' Chase demanded. 'How does that work?'

From the ceiling of Sachin's private quarters, Noah watched the strange scene unfold. Her body lay on the bed. The fact she could see herself suggested that she was having one of those out-of-body experiences people talked about. While Raven lay at her feet, Chase sat at her side, holding one of her hands. Sachin stood on the other side of the bed with Emir beside him.

'It means she's kind of dead,' Sachin said.

Noah watched as Chase shook her head in disbelief.

'Kind of dead? That doesn't make sense. A person is either *dead* or *not dead.* There are no in-betweens. It's like being unique, or white, or round. Things can't be *rather* unique or *very* white or *sort of* round. These things are absolute. There are no degrees of uniqueness, whiteness or roundness. Things are unique or they are not, white or not, round or not. Being dead is the same. You are either dead or not dead.'

Sachin, perhaps ignorant of the futility of arguing with a writer about the subtleties of word usage, said, 'On *your* world maybe but not on *this* world. Your rules do not mean much here.'

'They're not my rules,' Chase argued. 'They're just *the* rules. How did she get to be *sort of* dead anyway?'

'I did it,' he said.

'How?' Chase said.

Sachin pulled his flute from his pocket. 'Using raiki,' he said. 'I've separated her soul from her body.'

Raven sat up on his haunches and growled. Emir moved to put himself between the Alsatian and the young Major.

'Why would you do that?' Chase asked, incredulous.

'To protect her,' Sachin answered.

Noah hoped that Chase would demand an explanation as to how *sort of* killing her was supposed to protect her.

Chase obliged. 'How do you figure that?' she asked.

'Orville is going to be here in the morning,' he said. 'We need him to think that Noah is dead. If he does, she is safe. We don't need Orville breathing down our necks.'

'So where is her soul now?' Chase asked.

Sachin looked up, right at Noah, and pointed. Everyone else looked too. Raven barked.

'I don't see anything,' Chase said.

'Most people won't,' Sachin said, 'and that's what we're counting on. It's not so much seeing as sensing. I can sense her. So can Raven.'

Chase frowned. 'Doesn't that mean everyone here with raiki training would be able to sense her too?' she asked.

Sachin shook his head. 'Even with training you need to be specifically looking for a particular thing. It's actually a musical signature we listen for. Everyone has a unique signature.'

I'm just a soul floating around up here, Noah thought. *How strange.* Even stranger perhaps was the fact that Chase wasn't recording all this in her journal. Concern obviously overrode her writer's instincts.

'So what do we do now?' Chase asked.

'Get some sleep,' Sachin said. 'We've got a big day tomorrow.'

'I'm staying here,' Chase declared.

'Fine,' Sachin said.

Chase climbed onto the bed next to Noah's body as Raven reclaimed his spot. It's not like they needed to compete for space. The boy's bed was enormous.

'Are you going to swap them now?' Emir asked.

Sachin nodded. He climbed onto the bed and took Noah's hand.

'What are you doing?' Chase asked.

'Swapping wristbands,' he said as he eased the black band off Noah's limp wrist.

'Why?'

'Because.'

'Because is a *conjunction*, not a reason,' Chase said.

The boy glared at her. 'Because I want to,' he said.

'Alan will be beside himself if he finds out. Think of the serial numbers.'

'*If* he finds out, I'll smooth it over with him,' Sachin said as he took off his own bracelet. 'I am the boss, you know.'

What do I do? Noah thought.

'Stay close,' Sachin answered.

'What?' Chase said.

'I'm talking to Noah,' he said.

Chase looked around. 'She's talking to you?'

'Jemima, be quiet,' Emir said.

With visible effort, Chase did as she was told.

'Noah,' Sachin said, 'you need to stay close to your body. After Orville leaves tomorrow, I will put you back together again. But you need to stay close. The longer your soul is out of your body the more dangerous it is.'

Why?

'There is a chance that your soul will forget it had a body. If you drift off too far, your body will die and I won't be able to put you back together. I want you to come down and sit on this rug.'

The Major pointed to the black woollen rug at the end of his bed.

I like it up here.

'Now,' he said, pointing again.

'Please do what he says, Noah,' Chase said.

Even disembodied, Noah found it was possible to sigh. She floated down to the rug. As she settled herself, Raven leapt off the bed to join her. Sachin nodded.

'Stay with Raven. He will help you remember what to do. Everyone else,' he said, 'bedtime!'

If the assembled adults thought there was anything odd about a child giving bedtime instructions, no one said. Chase lay down and closed her eyes as Sachin climbed onto the bed and lay on the other side of Noah's body. Emir went to sleep in the adjoining room.

Noah didn't feel sleepy. Perhaps souls didn't sleep. Maybe people only slept because their bodies needed rest. Noah was restless but remembered what Sachin had said. She needed to stay close.

♪♫

'We need to get going,' Sachin announced.

Where? Noah asked.

'To Elani's Chamber,' Sachin said. 'That is where the meeting of the Four Houses will be held. There are preparations to be made before Orville arrives. We must hurry.'

'Is Noah going to be okay?' Chase asked.

'Yes,' Sachin said. 'Emir, get her body.'

Emir didn't move.

'Oh, for crying out loud,' Sachin whined. 'Please. *Please* get her body.'

'Good manners cost nothing,' Emir said, before bowing his head and going to do his master's bidding.

Noah floated after Emir to check on what he was doing with her body. A gurney sat beside the bed where Noah's body lay.

Gently, she thought.

Emir didn't react. Even if he could have sensed her, Noah suspected that he would have taken advantage of the opportunity to ignore her. She watched as he slid his arms under her shoulders and knees. In one seemingly effortless move, he lifted her off the bed, turned and lay her on the gurney. She floated closer. It was strange to look down on herself. Her skin looked greyer this morning. It sagged over her bones like a painter's worn drop sheet.

Emir ducked into the adjoining room and returned quickly with a folded cloth. Like a waiter dressing a table in a restaurant, he unfurled the black sheet and let it settle over her. He then pushed the gurney back into the living area where the others were waiting.

'Ready,' he said.

Sachin nodded. 'Let's go.'

Pushing the gurney, Emir fell in behind Sachin while Chase and Raven brought up the rear. When they reached the outer precinct of the great chamber, Sachin gave his instructions. 'Emir, take the body to my dressing room ... *please*. Take Raven with you. No, Noah—,' he hissed, 'you stay here.'

I thought you said I had to stay close.

'I need you to see and hear what happens in the chamber this morning. You're going to watch from the back. At some point, your body is going to be brought into the chamber – so we can prove to Orville that you're "dead". When your body leaves again, you need to go with it.'

And then you'll put me back together?

'And then, when the meeting is adjourned, I'll put you back together again.'

Can Raven stay with me?

Sachin shook his head. 'No animals in the chamber. Raven and Brinn will stay in my dressing room.'

'What about me?' Chase asked.

'You will watch as a member of the audience,' Sachin said. 'Emir will show you where to sit.'

Chase was clearly unhappy but didn't argue.

Emir pushed the gurney and called for Raven to follow. The dog ignored him, instead staying put in front of Noah's spirit. Brinn called Raven's name. He whimpered but didn't move.

Go, protect, Noah thought.

With that, Raven loped off after Emir and Brinn.

'Come on, Noah,' Sachin said. 'I'll show you where you need to be.'

Chapter 9

Noah floated in front of a gold curtain at the top of Elani's Chamber. She was tucked behind the very top row of stadium style seating in the great hall. From her vantage point, she watched the arrival of Mellifont's adepts. She noticed that everyone wore the same black cargo pants. Only the colours of the vests and the embroidered patterns on the front of them changed. As adepts from the different Houses scurried here and there, the chamber became a giant kaleidoscope. A hum of tense antici-pation reverberated around the chamber.

Dominating the centre of the hall, a gigantic slab of marble rested on a scattered assortment of other rocks. Only the surface of the table had been polished and the mottled greens and browns on the exposed sides reminded Noah of a mossy creek bed. Pieces of quartz embedded in the slab glinted and winked in the light of the chamber, giving the illu-sion of running water. Even to someone who was sort of dead, the stone seemed to be alive. Seemed to breathe.

Twelve thrones encircled the irregular-shaped stone table. Each throne featured a carving of a musical instrument. Noah could see Sachin's seat from her hiding place. The intricately carved flute on the head of the throne was instantly recognisable.

The chamber was filling rapidly now. Noah tried to estimate the seating capacity by comparing it to the auditorium she'd been in last night in the House of Wind. Emir had told her that one held three thousand. This one was easily five times that size.

At no signal that Noah could discern, the assembly fell quiet. The twelve Majors filed into their seats. After a minute's silence, the Major sitting under the clarinet insignia stood up. Major Maggie's short, mostly silver curls framed a face not only wrinkled with age but with worry.

'Welcome everyone, to Elani's great chamber,' Major Maggie said. 'May his spirit and his dragonsong preserve us today and always.'

'May his spirit and his dragonsong preserve us today and always,' the assembly intoned.

'We will need the dragonsong today,' she continued, 'King Tambian and his henchman, Orville Kurz, are on our doorstep.'

Intense booing echoed around the chamber and Major Maggie stood patiently waiting for order to be restored.

When quiet returned, she said, 'Our purpose has not changed. We must find the 13th key, and quickly. Orville's plan to eradicate raiki and supplant it with blood magic gathers force. Should he succeed, the world as we know it will end. If he disbands the Academy, who will keep vigil over the dragonsong? If we are outlaws, how will we maintain order in our world? If we cannot preserve the Elani's work, Xan will wake. The prophecy *must* be fulfilled.'

The assembly murmured its agreement.

'But before the king arrives,' Major Maggie continued, 'I need to share some bad news.' She looked around the assembly. 'Last night, Major Sachin presented a candidate for the 13th key to the House of Wind. Her name was Noah Chord. This morning we were to present her to you, to stand alongside Dr Grainger, in our quest to fulfil the prophecy of the 13th key. It is with great sadness however, that I report of Miss Chord's passing during the night.'

A moment's silence was followed by a communal gasp. Someone wailed. Others joined in as all the Majors bowed their heads.

Maggie said, 'At this stage we don't know—'

The doors at the back of Elani's Chamber opened.

'All rise, in the name of the king,' cried a voice from the threshold.

A soldier in full livery strode into the chamber first. *He looks important,* Noah thought. An old man in flowing robes and a crown followed him. *He looks more important.* A young man in a tailored blue suit walked behind the king. As a dozen soldiers brought up the rear, the only sound in the chamber was the synchronised footsteps of the king's retinue.

When the king reached the stage, the Majors bowed.

King Tambian nodded then turned to the assembly. 'Be seated,' he said.

Running his hand over his white beard, the king looked around the chamber at the assembled adepts. 'I have fond memories of Mellifont,' he began, 'but unfortunately, I don't think I'll be adding to those fond memories today. I don't come with glad tidings. I am here today, not just as King of Leninstar but as an authorised emissary of the Sovereign States Alliance. The kings of the seven states of Talisker are united on the issue I am addressing today.' He turned to the man in the blue suit. 'Papers please, Orville.'

That's Orville? Noah thought.

Orville did not look at all as Noah had expected. He was, in fact, rather easy on the eye and looked only to be in his early twenties. A certain lack of height was compensated for to some degree by a hairstyle that reached for the heavens. Either there was a lot of product in that hair or he was blessed with naturally wilful locks. A mole just above his lip probably made the morning shaving ritual problematic but it did make him look rather dashing.

Orville reached into the breast pocket of his jacket, pulled out a wad of papers and handed it to the king.

King Tambian said, 'These papers contain a decree of the Sovereign States Alliance in relation to the 13th key.'

The assembled adepts murmured.

'We know of your prophecy,' the king continued, 'and I am here to tell you that you are wrong. Our electricity network in Leninstar is not the great evil you believe it to be. It is the envy of all the other states. They are watching us closely – and learning. One day, all the states of Talisker will have electricity. Leninstar is pioneering this new technology and we will all be better off for it. *All* of us – including you here in Mellifont.'

Major Maggie stepped forward. 'We don't believe electricity is evil,' she said. 'We believe blood magic is evil. Using blood magic to power this network will destroy this world. As we have said before, firestone is what you should be using.'

'But we have no firestone,' Tambian countered, 'unless you know something that we don't?'

'We continue to search,' Maggie said, 'but have not been successful so far.'

'So the only firestone we have, is inside the twelve keys,' Tambian said. 'Not enough to sustain a nationwide network long term.'

Sachin spoke up. 'Then the network must wait,' he said.

Tambian shook his head. 'The network will go ahead. We will flick the switch at the Solstice Festival and Leninstar will have the benefit of electricity. And as your opposition to our plans is still obvious, let me explain the Alliance's decree. If the 13th key *is* found, it will be turned over to the Alliance. And if any of the existing twelve keys are used in any way that will compromise Leninstar's network, they too will be turned over to the Alliance.'

'That is outrageous,' Maggie declared. 'Our job is to protect this world. How can we do that without the keys?'

'I would remind you Major Maggie, I would remind *all of you,*' Tambian said with a sweeping arm gesture, 'that you do not *own* the keys. You hold them in trust. Your job is to use them for the good of Talisker, not to protect your own interests here in Mellifont.'

The crowd booed. Maggie held up her hand for silence.

'We *do* act for the good of Talisker,' Maggie said. 'Widespread use of blood magic will destroy this world. Why can you not see that?'

The king gestured to Orville, who stepped forward.

'Blood magic poses no danger to Talisker,' Orville said. 'Blood is a natural part of our world. We are creating a sustainable network – it is the right way to go – power *from* the people, *for* the people.'

Sachin joined the conversation. 'Blood *is* a natural part of our world,' he agreed, 'but used in this way, it will corrupt the dragonsong. Arsenic is a natural part of this world too but we need to be careful how we use it. If we eat it, for instance, we will die. Just because something is natural, doesn't mean we can use it for everything.'

Orville smiled. 'Clinging to the old ways will do you no good, Major Sachin,' he said. 'People are seeing the light – literally. Taliskerans are growing tired of the elitism here at the Academy. You cling to the technology of the dark ages to protect your positions. People will not stand for this anymore. If you will not move with the rest of us, you will be left behind.'

'And what will you do with the 13th key?' Sachin asked.

'You have it?' said Tambian.

'Not yet,' Sachin replied, 'but what would you do with it?'

'Keep it safe,' Orville said. 'Perhaps you could enlighten the king as to your progress in finding this key?'

As Noah watched she began to wonder why she was here. It was mildly entertaining but she was losing interest. She had a vague recollection of waiting for something. Sachin had told her to wait for something. But what was it? Maybe she should watch a bit longer and see if she remembered what it was.

A wiry man in the front row stood up. He wore an orange vest with a bugle embroidered on the front. His grey eyes were sharp and clear and his salt and pepper hair had been wrestled into a knot at the base of his skull. Well, most of it had been. A few wily wisps had sprung free and waved defiantly whenever he moved his head.

'I am Dr Grainger,' he announced. 'I am the candidate who will use the 13th key.'

The 13th key, Noah thought. *I'm supposed to do something about that, aren't I?*

Orville raised an eyebrow. 'Use the 13th key?' he asked. 'Did you not hear what the king just said?'

'I heard,' Dr Grainger confirmed.

'Well, Dr Grainger,' the king said, 'thank you for identifying yourself. At least we know who we need to keep our eye on.'

'The prophecy says one of two,' Orville said. 'Either there is another candidate in the wind or your prophecy is on shaky ground?'

Another candidate in the wind? Noah wished she still had eyebrows so she could raise them at Orville's remark. He couldn't possibly know she was floating around up here. Could he?

'The prophecy is fine,' Major Maggie said.

'So there is another candidate?' Orville pressed.

Maggie looked at Sachin. 'There was,' she said. 'There *was* another candidate.'

'And?' King Tambian said.

'She's dead,' Sachin said.

'Dead?' Orville said. 'How dead?'

'Pretty dead,' Sachin replied.

Orville's eyes narrowed as he walked across the floor to stand in front of Sachin. He squatted down in front of the boy.

'This is no time to be funny,' he said, leaning in closer to Sachin. 'Dead is dead. We all know that. How did your candidate come to be dead? That is the question.'

Sachin didn't back away but stared into Orville's eyes, giving his reply.

'All I can tell you is that she collapsed … and then died.'

'When did this happen?' Orville asked.

'Last night.'

'What is your candidate's name?' Orville asked.

'Her name *was* Noah Chord,' Sachin replied, emphasising the past tense verb.

'*Her* name was Noah? Noah is a girl?'

'Was a girl, yes.'

'Funny name for a girl,' he said. 'Where is her body now?'

'In my dressing room,' Sachin said.

'You will get it,' Orville said.

There was a stunned silence in Elani's Chamber. No one moved.

'Did you not hear him?' King Tambian said. 'Retrieve her body.'

The silence endured as six soldiers escorted the boy Major out through the main doors of the hall. For the time Sachin was gone, the adepts murmured amongst themselves. Only when the soldiers returned, bearing Noah's lifeless body, did they cease their chattering.

Orville and the king stood side by side as Noah's body was wheeled next to the bench. Orville threw back the black cloth.

From her hiding place, Noah caught a glimpse of her body on the gurney. It was only a brief glimpse but enough for her to remember why she was there. This was what Sachin had told her to wait for. When her body left the chamber again, she was to follow it. Then Sachin would reconnect her body and soul. Then, she'd wring his little neck.

'It's a girl,' Orville noted. 'Definitely dead.'

'Major Sachin,' Tambian said, 'you will tell us the circumstances that led to this girl's death.'

Sachin recounted his story, in excruciating detail, from when Noah had arrived on Talisker.

'Why would you think someone from Earth would be a candidate for the 13th key?' Orville asked.

Before Sachin could answer, the king said, 'I don't believe you. People don't die from laryngitis. I think you killed her.'

'Did not!' Sachin said.

'Based on the evidence we've just heard,' King Tambian continued, 'I contend that you, Major Sachin, killed Miss Chord. You said yourself that she collapsed and died as you joined in the musical composition that was – and I quote – "written specifically for her".'

'Why would he do that?' Emir demanded from the sidelines.

'Yes,' Sachin said. 'Why would I do that? Why would I go to all the trouble of bringing Miss Chord here and then knocking her off as soon as she got here?'

'Ah,' Orville said, 'but you didn't kill her as soon as she got here did you? You said you rode with her for two days before you arrived back in Mellifont. Perhaps in that time, you realised she wasn't the one who was going to find your precious 13th key. That being the case, you would have no need for her. It would be easier to kill her than to return her to her home world. And furthermore,' he added, 'you chose to commit this heinous deed in such a public manner to deflect suspicion. Your adoring followers might never have suspected a thing but you should never underestimate us, Major. We are not blinded by your black magic.

This case will just add further weight to the calls for raiki to be banished from Talisker.'

'Our magic is pure,' Sachin argued. 'It is the magic of our world. The world is made of music and raiki uses that music to maintain life and the land. It is your *blood* magic that is an abomination.'

'So you say,' Orville replied.

'Well, it seems to me,' King Tambian said, 'you have a case to answer, Major Sachin. You will be detained until your trial.'

The crowd rose to their feet as one and there was a resounding *schwing* as the king's soldiers drew their swords. There was instant quiet.

Two soldiers shackled the boy.

'Remember the decree of the Alliance,' King Tambian said as he handed the wad of papers to Major Maggie. 'If you find the 13th key, you turn it over to the Alliance.'

As quickly as it had come, the king's retinue was gone.

Noah slipped out from behind the gold curtain. It was getting increasingly difficult to see the dais with so many bodies in motion. She floated up a little to see where her body was. It would be easy to just float on over the crowd to see what was going on but Sachin had told her to stay out of sight.

She saw Emir pushing through the crush of people milling around her body. Maggie too was making a beeline for her. Chase already had Noah's body in her grasp but others from the House of Wind were clamouring to take it. Their beloved Major had been taken away and Noah, his hope for saving the world from the evils that Orville had in store, was something precious.

Without warning, Raven darted through the doors. He unleashed a frenzy of barking before hurtling down the aisle towards the dais. Raven ran, snarling and growling. People scattered like butterflies in a hurricane. Even the knot of people around Noah's body untangled and dispersed. Only Emir and Maggie stood firm. Emir took Noah's body from Chase as Raven reached him.

Dismissing the gurney, Emir cradled Noah's body. With Raven in the lead and Maggie bringing up the rear, Emir made a hasty exit from the chamber as mob mentality set in. A throng of people harassed the small group despite Raven's vicious snarling. The initial shock had passed. He was only one dog; there were hundreds of them.

With no regard for the consequences, Noah flew down over the crowd and slipped through the doors just ahead of the others.

'Lock the doors!' Emir yelled at Maggie, who was agile for her age.

Wondering if she could be put back together again, Noah followed Emir who raced after Raven. Behind them, Maggie barricaded the door and then gave chase. Raven darted through a narrow crack in the wall. It was a tight fit but within a few metres it led to a small room. A very small room. He whined softly as everyone crammed in.

'They won't find us here,' Maggie said, referring to the mob who'd have broken through the barricaded doors by now.

'Jemima, hold her,' Emir said as he shoved Noah's body into the writer's arms.

'There's not even enough room in here to lie her down,' Chase said.

'I'm glad you didn't say that there wasn't enough room in here to swing a cat,' Brinn said as she sauntered in.

'I hope you're going to do more than just take up space in here, cat,' Emir said.

Brinn's only answer was a swish of her striped tail.

Chase manipulated her friend's body into position against her own. Noah's head lolled to one side.

'Major Maggie,' Emir said. 'Can you undo Sachin's tonic?'

'I will try,' she said, taking her clarinet from a pocket. She started to play a slow, haunting melody. Noah listened, watching her body for signs of life.

'Noah, move over and face your body,' Brinn instructed. 'There will be a point in the tonic shortly when you need to re-enter your body.'

'You'll tell me when?'

'If you can't figure it out for yourself – yes.'

Noah listened as Maggie continued to play but kept half an eye on the cat. Raven whimpered. Noah floated forward, ready to re-join her body.

'Is it working?' Chase asked.

Emir didn't answer. Raven whimpered more loudly and then started barking as Maggie's playing became more frantic. Noah battled against her skin. It was strange that the body she'd grown up in and taken care of was now closed to her. She'd been out of it too long. It did not remember life.

And then there was a noise that defied description. Noah looked at the cat who was inspecting her claws.

'*CAT!*' Emir yelled. 'Don't *EVER* do that again.'

'What?' Brinn replied innocently.

'You know exactly what,' he replied, pointing to the claw marks on the wall. 'You know how excruciating that noise is for us.'

'But it worked.'

Everyone looked at Noah.

'What the—' Chase said.

'It shocks the soul into flight and the body, momentarily stimulated by the sound, is able to reabsorb the spirit,' Brinn explained. 'Sometimes you adepts really overcomplicate things. Keep it simple, I say.'

Emir frowned.

'You can thank—' Brinn didn't get to finish her smug retort. When Noah launched herself at Emir, the cat high-tailed it out of the small compartment – hackles up.

'What is wrong with you people?' Noah demanded as she locked her hands around his throat. 'Why did you bring me here?'

In such close quarters Emir had no time to react and no room to manoeuvre. It was left to Chase and Maggie to wrestle Noah off him.

'She doesn't seem any worse for wear from being dead,' Emir said as he twisted Noah's arms up behind her back. Noah tried to lash out with her legs but with such limited room for a backswing, it was sadly ineffective.

'She can talk!' Chase whispered.

Noah continued her tirade, oblivious to the miracle that allowed her to do so, 'Let me go!' she yelled. 'Take me home. You people are all crazy.'

'Calm down, Noah,' Emir said. 'You're overreacting.'

'*Overreacting?*' she said. 'You bring me here to *save* you but you kill me before I even get started! Good riddance to Sachin, I say. I'm glad the king has taken him. I hope he rots in jail.'

'He saved your skin,' Brinn reminded her from the doorway. 'It could be you heading off to jail right now.'

Noah glowered at her, remembering once more why she was a dog person.

'Noah,' Chase said, 'you can talk.'

Noah stopped, dumbfounded. 'How is that possible?' she whispered.

'That would be me,' Brinn said. 'I did that too.'

'If I let go of your arms, will you be calm?' Emir asked.

Dazed by the realisation that she'd been speaking, Noah nodded. Emir released his grip.

'I can talk,' she said, testing her vocal cords. She looked at Brinn. 'How is it that you can do that in an instant but Sachin said it would take ages for him to do?'

'She doesn't obey rules,' Emir said. '*Any* rules.'

'Well,' Noah said. 'Thank you.'

'You're welcome,' Brinn said. 'Now if you'll excuse me, I'm leaving before I have to endure the consequences of my actions.'

Major Maggie smiled.

'What's so funny?' Noah asked.

'Nothing,' Maggie replied.

Blood pounded in Noah's temples. Sachin hadn't asked her permission or even warned her about what he was up to. Killing her, even half killing her, was too big a risk to take. She was alive again now though. And she was off Orville's radar.

'I suppose you intend rescuing Sachin,' Noah said.

'Of course,' Emir replied.

'Well, let's go then,' she said.

If they did manage to rescue him, Noah would take great pleasure in giving him a piece of her mind.

Chapter 10

After six days' hard riding, Noah was relieved to reach their destination. Though she chafed at how little progress she'd made on her collection since her arrival on Talisker, Emir had promised her that she could go fabric shopping once they'd liberated Sachin from the king's jail. In the cool pre-dawn, Noah swilled down the last of her tea.

'Let's get this show on the road,' she said.

Emir looked at Chase. 'Once again, thanks,' he said.

'You're welcome,' Chase replied.

Noah had enjoyed practising her speaking and Chase had been very accommodating in enhancing her grasp of the vernacular, much to Emir's displeasure.

'Does everyone remember what they have to do?' Emir asked.

'Yes,' Noah said. 'We've been over the plan a million times. Let's just do it already.'

Emir wasn't finished with his preparations yet. 'Noah, do you remember what's *not* part of the plan?'

'Yes,' Noah replied. 'For the hundredth time, I promise not to strangle him when I find him.'

'Good,' he said.

His tone made Noah's blood boil but before she could say anything Brinn appeared.

'Where did you come from?' Noah asked.

'I have just come from where I was before,' the cat replied. 'I can't believe you aren't ready.'

'We would be if it weren't for Mr Pedantic here,' Noah said, cocking her thumb towards Emir.

'Don't just stand there telling me about it,' Brinn said. 'Get this camp packed up.'

Noah pushed to her feet and dusted off her pants. She'd stuck with the standard issue cargo pants that she'd been given. Everything she needed was stashed in a pocket somewhere. Even her precious sketch pads and pencils were safely stored in pockets. When she was in need of another pocket, one magically appeared. Even more surprising was the fact that the size of the object being stored didn't need to match the size of the pocket. Noah had her sleeping roll in one pocket, her tent in another. She rinsed her crockery and cutlery in the nearby stream and stashed those away as well. Once stored inside a pocket, the items were weightless.

'Ready?' Brinn said.

Noah and Emir nodded.

'Do I have to wait here?' Chase said. 'I'd really like to help.'

'You will be helping,' Emir said. 'You and Alan will be guarding the horses.'

Chase sighed. 'Guarding the horses? Really?'

'It's an important job, Jemima,' Emir said. 'We're going to need them. It's a long way back to Leninstar.'

Chase reached into a pocket and pulled out her digital voice recorder. Handing it to Noah, she said, 'Pretty please?'

Noah took the device, keen to do her friend a favour since she'd be left behind with Alan.

'Sure,' Noah said.

'Remember what I said about the forest?' Emir said.

'Yeah, it's spooky,' Noah said. 'I get it. Let's go.'

Noah nodded to Brinn who took the lead. With Raven at her side, Noah followed the cat who strolled nonchalantly between the giant fir trees. Emir walked behind her. As Noah passed the trees she sensed their disquiet. She listened more carefully, testing their music. It was complex and discordant. It didn't feel right. She was left with an impression that the trees were holding their breaths, waiting. Waiting to see what would happen to the small party in their midst. They didn't see many living creatures in this place. Things happened to living creatures here. Bad things. The trees didn't like witnessing the bad things but they had no choice. They were stuck here.

'How far is it to the entrance of the jail?' Noah asked.

'Not far,' Brinn answered.

'Are we likely to find any trouble between now and then?'

The cat hissed. 'The more you yabber, the more likely it is.'

Noah stopped talking. This forest was part of the reason this location had been chosen for the jail site. It was a natural barrier. No guards patrolled here. They didn't need to. The forest took care of any escapees that made it this far. Noah wanted to run, to get out of the forest as quickly as possible but Brinn was setting the pace. The feline meandered here and there, occasionally stopping to sniff a plant or piece of bark. As repugnant as the cat could be, Noah trusted that she'd get them through the forest. If she set this pace, there was a reason for it. Noah took a deep breath, forced herself to be calm. Raven stuck by her side. He didn't like the forest either.

The forest ended a stone's throw from the Wafi Wall – a cliff that plunged into the Ohm Sea. From this point on the coastline, the sheer cliff stretched for a kilometre in both directions. The barren strip of ground between the forest and the cliff's edge bore testament to the fact that even the trees quailed at the prospect of looking over the edge.

Somewhere under their feet, Sachin languished in a cell. The jail had been carved out of the rock of the cliff rather than being built above ground. The only evidence that anything existed here was a padlocked trapdoor on the bare ground. Emir made short work of the padlock with a couple of slender metal spikes.

Emir was first to climb down the ladder with Brinn under one arm. Raven jumped down. Noah climbed down quickly. After her experience of the forest, she was glad to be inside, even if it was a maximum-security jail.

Brinn led the way down the narrow corridor. Whereas the stone corridors in Mellifont sparkled with rich, vibrant colour, the stone here was cold and unyielding. It sapped the warmth from Noah's body as she walked along the dimly lit passageways. On the left and right they passed silent steel doors. Occasionally, another corridor branched off perpendicular to the one on which they travelled. If a guard were to come along, there was nowhere to hide. At last they came to a set of stairs.

'Where do these stairs go?' Noah whispered.

'Down,' Brinn replied testily. 'Now be quiet.'

Noah did as she was told – not because she wanted to but because her mouth was getting drier by the second. The silent procession continued. As they walked Noah noticed that her wrist felt warmer. It was her wristband – Sachin's wristband actually. She remembered that he'd swapped them after he'd half killed her.

'Brinn,' she whispered.

The cat whipped around, vexed, her dark stripes blurring momentarily with the speed of her movement.

'What?'

'This bracelet is starting to burn my wrist.'

Brinn cocked her head slightly, her eyes narrowing. 'Good,' she said. 'Means we're close.'

Brinn turned her back on Noah's discomfort and slinked off. It was not far to the end of the corridor where they were forced to turn left if they wanted to continue. The cat stuck a cautious nose around the corner while Noah and Raven waited at a respectable distance. Noah watched the feline's tail.

'Trouble?'

The banded tail stiffened and tripled in width as every hair went horizontal. An unmistakable order for silence. Noah considered the idea that a cat's tail was infinitely more expressive than its face but in light of the situation at hand, decided against airing her thoughts.

At length, Brinn turned around.

'How's the wristband?'

'Almost unbearable,' Noah said.

Brinn nodded, 'Right. I believe Sachin's cell is halfway down this block. Fifteen cells down to be precise.'

'How can you tell that from the wristband?' Noah asked.

'I can't,' the cat admitted. 'But there are two guards standing outside a cell down there and I'm betting that's the one Sachin is in.'

'Two guards?' said Noah, crestfallen. 'How are we supposed to get passed them?'

Brinn thought for a moment. 'I don't suppose my cute kitty routine will work on them,' she said.

'You have a cute kitty routine?' Noah asked dubiously.

Brinn didn't answer Noah's question directly.

'Maybe I'll just go the feral cat—'

But before she could finish, Raven bolted. All barking and black fur, he darted around the corner and down the corridor. Noah chased him with Brinn and Emir behind her. As they approached, the guards set their position across the corridor, swords at the ready. Raven's barking reverberated off the stone. It was deafening but Noah was focused on her wrist. The burning was excruciating now. She wanted to scream as she felt her skin blistering under the bracelet.

As Raven skittered to a halt just out of sword range of the guards, one of them broke rank and ran away down the corridor.

'I'll get help,' he yelled to his companion as he disappeared into the gloom.

'I'll be back,' Emir said as he ran after the guard.

The remaining guard grunted but didn't take his eyes off the Alsatian who was now snarling and baring his teeth. The guard held his ground. Clearly, he wasn't going to do anything rash. Noah knew that the longer Raven stood and barked without attacking, the more confident the guard would become that he would not attack at all. And the longer this went on, the more time it gave the reinforcements to arrive. Aside from that, Noah didn't know how long it would be until the bracelet burned through her wrist. She needed to get Sachin out now. If anyone could stop the burning, it would be him.

Raven feinted. The guard did not hesitate. He lunged at the dog, committing all his weight behind his sword. Raven dodged. The guard overextended and his sword sheered across the stone floor, sending sparks flying. Raven sank his teeth into the guard's leg. The guard cried out in pain as he twisted, trying to use the pommel of his sword to bludgeon the dog.

Noah jumped on the guard's back. 'Get him!' she yelled at Brinn. 'Go for his jugular.'

Though Brinn's expression barely altered, she managed a look of disdain.

'I think not,' she replied. 'That's just unsanitary.'

A retort about licking one's own bottom was on Noah's lips but a flash of silver got her attention – a key on the guard's belt. As the guard took another shot at Raven, Noah kicked at his wrist with all her might. Her foot connected sweetly and sent the sword clattering along the floor. She was about to reach for the key when the guard grabbed her ankle and sent her sprawling. Blood filled her mouth but the pain of her bitten tongue was nothing compared to her wrist. She was sure she smelled burning flesh.

Kicking out, she tried in vain to win free of the guard's vice-like grip. She twisted, saw Raven release his grip and then bite down on the back of the man's other leg. It distracted him long enough for Noah to scramble away. She almost crawled right over Brinn in the process. The cat had the key in her mouth. Noah hadn't seen her retrieve it but obviously in all the kerfuffle she'd managed to swipe it. Noah put out her hand and the cat dropped the key into it. She went quickly to the door.

'Hurry!' came a voice from behind the door.

'Yeah, yeah – keep your hair on,' Noah called back, fumbling with the key.

Once lined up, the key slid in easily and turned without protest. The door swung open to reveal a surprisingly well-lit room. After roaming the dingy corridors, Noah was momentarily blinded by the intense light coming in through the window in the far wall. She put her arm up to shield her eyes, blinking away tears.

'Give me your hand,' Sachin said.

Noah reached out to him. Small hands closed around her burning wrist. Almost instantly there was relief.

'Get the sword, quickly,' he ordered.

Grateful that the pain in her wrist was abating, Noah grabbed the sword. Raven still harassed the guard so she was able to retrieve it uncontested.

'Put it on the bed,' Sachin ordered.

'You're welcome,' Noah replied, her gratitude for the pain relief waning as her annoyance at the Major's snippy orders grew.

Leaving Raven to harry the guard, Noah picked up the heavy sword and carried it inside the cell, placing it on the bed.

'There is something very wrong with that sword,' she said.

'Blood magic,' Sachin said. 'Brinn will have to fix that. I have to go.'

'Go? Go where?' Noah demanded.

'There is someone else here I need to rescue. I'll meet you at the edge of the forest. And when I get there, I want that guard and his sword with you.'

'*What?*' Noah said.

'I don't have time to explain,' he snapped. 'Just get the guard and the sword and go.'

'Take the guard with us? Are you crazy?'

'There is no time to argue,' he said. 'More guards are on their way.'

Sachin turned to Brinn. 'You know what to do,' he said.

The cat nodded once and Sachin was gone.

Noah heard him call to his assistant as he ran down the corridor. '*Emir! With me!*'

Left alone with a cat and a dog and an order to take the injured guard with them, Noah stood in the doorway of the cell considering her options. Brinn was behind her, walking around the sword on the bed. As Raven stood over the semi-conscious guard in the corridor, blood dripped from his muzzle. Noah grimaced at the sight. That her lovable Alsatian could inflict such wounds unsettled her.

'Sit up, soldier!' she demanded.

The guard raised his head slowly and glared at her.

'Needs a haircut, wouldn't you say?' Brinn commented as she brushed passed Noah's leg.

Noah frowned. 'I don't think that's his biggest problem at the moment,' she said.

'Who are you talking to?' the man asked, trying to sit up.

Noah looked at Brinn who at that moment looked every bit the stupid animal she should be.

'Never mind,' Noah said.

The man's eyes narrowed. 'The cat talks?'

'Don't be ridiculous,' Noah snorted. 'Can you hear her talking?'

The guard didn't answer.

'I need to know his name,' Brinn said.

'What's your name, soldier?' Noah asked.

'Who's asking?' he said.

Noah made a big show of turning around to her right and then turning around to her left and then squarely facing the soldier again.

'I don't see anyone else here, so I guess that it would be *me*, asking.'

The man glared at her and spat. 'Why should I tell you?'

'Because I will have my dog bite you again if you don't,' Noah replied.

He shrugged. 'Do your worst.'

Before she could utter another word, there was a roaring sound outside. Noah turned to face the window on the far side of the cell. Now that her eyes had adjusted to the light she found that there was no window, it was actually a doorway. No door, no bars – just an open doorway. From where she stood, she could see the ocean. Sachin had had a cell with a view.

'What's with that?' she said.

'They don't need bars,' Brinn said. 'Climbing is impossible and jumping means certain death. And then there are the grom.'

'What's a grom?' Noah asked.

'What's coming to get you,' the guard answered.

Noah turned to look at him. His triumphant look gave her a squeamish feeling. She ran to the doorway. A very unsavoury creature was climbing up the cliff face.

'They have the body of an eel and the head of a crocodile,' the soldier called. 'Their webbed feet have suckers on them so they can climb up the rock face. The smaller ones are about three metres long and prisoners are part of their diet.'

The grom was still about a hundred metres below her but by looking out the doorway she'd given the creature a target. It was coming for her.

'Get up,' she said to the soldier. 'We're going.'

'I can't. I'm injured.'

'Get up.'

'Give me my sword,' he said.

'No sword for him until the blood spell is broken,' Brinn said. 'I need his name to break it.'

'No sword.'

'I need it,' the guard said. 'I need a crutch.'

'No sword,' Noah said, 'until I get your name.'

He stared at her, his eyes full of hate. 'Ardis,' he said at last.

'Stall him, Noah,' Brinn said as she fussed around the sword. 'I need a minute.'

Alien notes cascaded through Noah's head as Brinn went to work on the sword. The vibrations seemed to amplify as they coursed through her body. Every nerve screamed. She looked at Brinn who was sitting on the bed next to Ardis's sword. The cat sat unmoving, staring at the sword. With no visible instrument, Brinn was making the most terrible music. Despite the pain coursing through her, Noah found some muscles that would do her bidding. She sprang at Ardis, sending him sprawling on the floor. He howled in pain but it bought Brinn more time.

'I need that sword!' he insisted. 'Groms are not to be trifled with.'

'Nearly there,' Brinn muttered with another flurry of notes.

Raven's barking intensified. The grom was getting closer.

Noah saw Ardis roll over and inch closer to the sword. She had to stop him but even injured, he would overpower her if he got hold of her. She kicked at his head.

Raven growled and Noah looked towards the ocean. A warty snout filled the open doorway. It was easily as wide as Noah's shoulders and it opened its mouth to reveal stubby teeth. Ardis was now on his knees and close to wresting his sword from the bed but Noah's attention turned to her dog's plight. He was going to be the grom's entrée. Brinn would have to fend for herself.

The grom's head filled the doorway. Its jaws snapped at the Alsatian but missed as the canine jumped nimbly out of the way. Noah crawled forwards. The jaws opened wide – almost wide enough for Noah to walk in upright – and the stench that rushed out made her gag.

The music stopped and the pain coursing through Noah's body eased marginally. She grabbed her dog and despite him weighing almost as much as she did, she hurled him out of the creature's path. Ardis had the sword but Brinn launched herself at the soldier's face. Raven landed on Ardis, knocking him to the ground. The sword clattered loudly on the floor.

Noah dodged one snap of the grom's powerful jaws. It now had one foot inside the cell. If it got all the way in, there would be no room for anything else. She grabbed the sole wooden chair in the cell and thrust it deep into the gaping mouth. The grom shook its ugly head to dislodge the unwanted snack while Noah looked for something else to arm herself with. With both its forelegs now inside, she took two steps back, tripping over Raven as she did so.

She hit the floor, twisting quickly to avoid yet another snap of the dangerous jaws. The music restarted and intense pain shot through Noah's body once again. Such was her pain, she couldn't tell whether the beast had got her or not.

'Give me that sword!' Ardis demanded.

Raven barked and growled at the guard, buying Brinn a couple of extra seconds.

'Hurry!' Noah pleaded.

They were all on top of each other now but Noah was still the one the grom would eat first.

'Done!' Brinn said, grabbing the pommel of the sword in her teeth and dragging it towards Noah.

Noah grabbed the sword and thrust it into the grom's eye. The creature roared in pain. Noah heaved out the sword and thrust again, aiming for its neck. Inky blood spurted over her but she held the sword tightly, pushing and twisting to inflict maximum damage. The grom collapsed, its breathing laboured. Noah pulled the sword out and waved it in front of the guard.

'Want your sword?' she said. 'Come and get it.'

Without waiting for a response, she raced out of the cell.

Chapter 11

'*Noah!*' Emir called.

As Raven and Brinn flew passed her, Noah turned to see Emir, Sachin and a woman hurtling down the long corridor towards her. She waited for them to arrive.

'Where's—' Sachin started.

Before the young Major could finish his sentence, Ardis crawled into the doorway, the bites on his legs and buttocks inhibiting his ability to stand.

'Ah,' the boy said.

'Could do with your help here,' Noah said to Emir, inclining her head towards the injured guard.

Emir offered his sword to the lady behind him. 'Would you mind, m'lady?' he asked.

The woman accepted it with a quick nod of her head. She was finely built but she held Emir's sword like a seasoned warrior. An auburn braid trailed over her shoulder and hung down below the corded belt that cinched the lilac robe she wore. While her milky skin was youthful, her eyes looked to have seen many summers.

'You're coming with us,' Emir said to the guard. 'How you do that, depends on you. Either you can let me help you or I'll knock you out and drag you. The choice is yours.'

'Over my dead body,' Ardis said, still on his hands and knees.

Turning to the lady, Sachin asked, 'He's definitely the one?'

'May I see his sword?' she answered.

Noah held out the sword that she'd used to dispose of the grom.

'Thank you, Noah,' she said, leaning in to inspect the weapon more closely. 'My name is Montana, by the way.'

'Nice to meet you, Montana,' Noah said, thinking that now probably wasn't the ideal time for introductions.

'It's the right sword,' Montana declared. She turned her attention to the guard. 'How did you come by this sword, soldier?'

Ardis looked up at her through his straggly black locks. 'High Priestess?'

Montana nodded sharply.

He stared at her wide-eyed for a moment before bowing his head.

'That sword belonged to my father,' he said.

'Then you must be Ardis,' she said. 'Your father spoke of you often. Will you take your father's place in my army?'

He held her gaze for a long moment. 'I'll come,' he said. 'But I'll need help.'

Emir pulled him up off the floor, ducking his head under the injured man's arm. Being of similar height meant Emir was able to support Ardis's weight rather than having to carry him.

Montana raised Emir's sword. 'I'll lead.'

She set off after Raven who was waiting halfway down the corridor. He danced around, whining but not barking while Brinn sat licking her paw. When Raven saw the party moving again he raced off. Noah prayed that he didn't get too far ahead. If a squad of guards came around the corner he'd be a sitting duck.

'*There! Get them!*'

The voice came from behind Noah. She turned. Six guards.

'*Run!*' she yelled.

'My sword,' Ardis panted. 'Give me my sword.'

'Do it, Noah,' Montana said. 'Quickly.'

Noah was hesitant to hand over Ardis's sword. His sudden change of heart unnerved her.

'Noah, give him the sword,' Montana repeated.

Emir said, 'Go back to the surface. We'll take care of these guards. Go now!'

Without another word, the High Priestess grabbed Sachin's wrist and started running. Against her better judgement, Noah handed over the sword before following. The trio raced after Raven, letting him lead the way back to the ladder.

Brinn flew past them on her way back to help Emir with the guards. When Raven turned to follow the cat, Noah slapped him on the rump.

'Brinn will be fine, Raven,' she said. 'Let's get the Major out of here.'

They ran through the dim corridors without encountering any other guards. Raven was first up the ladder.

'Agile dog,' Montana said. 'You're next, Major.'

Sachin scrambled up the rungs.

'Noah, go.'

Noah climbed with the distinct impression that people didn't defy the High Priestess very often. Once outside, Montana squatted beside the open trapdoor.

'Let's see how long it takes them,' she said.

'Thirty million years,' Sachin declared.

'Forty,' Montana countered, accepting the wager.

Noah frowned as the pair counted. Raven nuzzled her hand.

'One million years, two million years, three million years, four million years ...'

Noah watched on as they continued. She was obviously the only one who wasn't convinced the others would make it at all. The count reached thirty with no sign of Emir or Ardis.

'Thirty-one million years, thirty-two million years, thirty-three million years ...'

Sachin started jumping up and down, willing his assistant to come in time.

'... Thirty-four million years, thirty-five million years, thirty-six million years ...'

'Bugger,' Sachin said.

Montana raised an eyebrow but kept counting.

'... Thirty-seven million years, thirty-eight million years—'

Raven barked twice.

'They're here!' Montana said.

Ardis was first on the ladder. As his legs were of limited use, he used his arms to drag himself up. Noah and Montana each grabbed one of his hands as he reached the top and pulled him out onto the barren ground. Emir emerged last, slamming the trapdoor down and sitting on top of it while he refastened the padlock.

'Ready?' he asked once he was finished.

'Just a minute,' Montana said. 'The Major owes me five dinah.'

The boy looked down at the grey trousers he wore. 'Don't have any,' he said. 'They took my trousers. Emir?'

Emir slipped his hand inside one of his pockets and pulled out a handful of coins. He counted out five into Montana's hand.

'Settled?'

'Yes, thank you.'

'Do I want to know what you were betting on?' Emir asked.

'No,' she said, smiling.

'Fine. Can we go now?' he asked.

'Just one more thing,' Montana said, her levity evaporating. 'Before we enter the forest, I need to know we're all on the same side. There are many dangers in there. We don't need to take any more in with us.'

She looked pointedly at Ardis. 'Are you really with us?'

Noah watched as the man studied his weapon.

'I want to know what the cat did to my sword,' Ardis said.

Brinn. Noah looked around. Brinn was nowhere to be seen. 'Where does that cat disappear to?' she said.

'Wherever she needs to be,' Sachin replied. In response to Ardis, he said, 'The cat removed a blood spell from your sword.'

'What kind of blood spell?' he asked.

Montana answered his question with a question. 'How have you been feeling lately?'

He looked thoughtful. After a few moments he said, 'Angry.'

'Hateful? Vengeful?' she offered.

Ardis looked down. 'Yes, m'lady.'

'It is nothing to be ashamed of,' Montana said. 'Soldiers are not immune to magic. You could not have known. But your sword is clean now and you are free of its influence. What I need to know is – will you leave us here or will you take your father's place in my army?'

Ardis held up his sword and stared at it intently. Turning his gaze to the High Priestess he said, 'I would like to come but my injuries will slow you down.'

'I can help with that,' Sachin said, taking his flute from a pocket on Emir's trousers.

'That is that, then,' Montana said. 'Sachin, play.'

As Sachin played his flute to help Ardis, Noah was pretty sure that the situation could have been rectified with a wand and a couple of well-chosen magic words. Every story she'd ever heard that had magic in it had involved a wand. There must be something in that. Scorned as she had been the last time she'd mentioned a wand though, she decided against bringing it up again.

Noah decided to focus on the job at hand and moved to stand next to Emir.

'Why does the High Priestess have an army?' she asked.

Emir looked at her, confused.

'Well, she's religious, isn't she?' Noah said. 'Why would she have soldiers? Soldiers kill people. Surely a priestess couldn't condone that.'

'Montana travels extensively,' Emir said, 'and she encounters many dangers in her travels. Goblins and bandits are constant threats.'

'But an army?' Noah said.

'Only a relatively small contingent travels with her but soldiers are stationed all over Talisker, on standby so to speak.'

'I see,' she said.

Hand on her sword hilt, Montana said, 'Ardis, can you walk?'

'I can,' he replied.

'Okay, we need to go,' Montana announced. 'The sooner we get through the forest, the better.'

Emir and Sachin nodded. Raven barked.

'Follow me,' Sachin said. 'Single file. Emir at the end.'

The Major turned and marched into the forest. Montana motioned for Noah to follow him. Raven slunk along at her side while the others fell in behind. Noah felt vulnerable the second she passed the tree line and found herself wishing the cat was with them. As revolting as she could be, Brinn knew things about this world. She'd know what to do, even if only to save her own fur. Noah had never really contemplated evil before but the forest scared her.

In her peripheral vision Noah saw shapes moving between the trees but she didn't dare turn her head to look. The dismal light under the canopy made it difficult to see and she struggled to watch where she was going. The slimy leaf litter was treacherous, hiding uneven ground. Creatures jabbered in the undergrowth; Raven whimpered at her side. Noah put a reassuring hand on his head, scratching his ear as a dread wind whipped around the tree trunks howling in apparent annoyance at not having an unimpeded path. Without warning a figure appeared in front of Sachin. Emir raced up from the end of the line and installed himself between the Major and the tall, hairless creature.

'Goblins,' Ardis hissed. 'I hate goblins.'

'Cover the rear,' Emir said to him, his voice flat.

Noah wondered what it would take for Emir to show any emotion. Since she'd arrived here his demeanour had barely changed. His manner was consistent to the point of robotic.

The goblin was a head taller than Emir but wiry and it wore only a loincloth. Pointed, lopsided ears hung from its bean-shaped head while its nose looked to have been smeared across its face. Flared nostrils longed for symmetry and the creature's teeth, like its talons, were thick and pointy. It levelled its sword at Emir and bared its teeth. A cordon of goblins sprang up from the undergrowth, surrounding the small party. A growl rumbled in Raven's throat.

The goblins advanced. Emir readied his sword. Montana herded Noah closer to Sachin.

'Stay close,' she said.

Raven was doing his bit to be menacing.

'I need to help Raven,' Noah said.

Montana shook her head. 'He doesn't need your help, Noah. You're more likely to get in the way.'

Ignoring the High Priestess, Noah lurched forward as the head goblin swung his sword at Emir's neck. Emir ducked and then sprang at the creature, ramming his shoulder into its abdomen. It fell back and landed hard on the ground, losing its sword in the process. In one motion, Emir dispatched the goblin and then shoved Noah back near Sachin and Montana.

'Stay,' he said, pointing the tip of his sword at her. 'That's an order.'

Noah glared at him. 'I don't take orders from you,' she said. 'You're not *my* nanny.'

Again, his expression and tone remained level. 'You have no weapon. Stay out of the way.'

He turned his back on her and engaged another goblin. If he hadn't been otherwise occupied, Noah thought she would have thrown something at him. His arrogance was galling.

'Major,' Montana said. 'Ardis – can you help him?'

Noah followed Montana's line of sight. She was looking at Ardis. He was struggling.

Sachin played.

'This'd better work,' Montana said. 'Emir is good but I don't think he'll hold off all these goblins by himself.'

Noah counted two dozen armed goblins. Not great odds against two swords and a set of canine fangs. Emir and Ardis were remarkably effective though. Fighting almost back to back meant a concentrated battle zone. Even though there were considerably more goblins, they had to queue for the opportunity to fight.

When there were only two goblins left, Noah was ready to breathe a sigh of relief – but she missed her chance. The ground started to rumble.

Sachin stopped playing. 'At Emir's signal, run,' he said before putting his flute back to his lips.

A discordant, staccato melody sprang from his instrument. The rumbling underfoot became trembling. An earthquake, Noah thought.

'Hold …' Emir cautioned.

Noah grabbed Raven's collar, afraid he might take off prematurely. She had no idea why they had to wait. Seconds dragged by. Noah's feet started to get hot. The ground was not simply moving underfoot, it was melting. Noah jumped from foot to foot as the ground got hotter. Raven's barking became more frenzied.

At an almost imperceptible nod from Sachin, Emir gave the cue.

'Run!'

Noah took off, urging Raven as she did so. Strangely though, as soon as she started to run, she felt as though she were in a dream. Her feet didn't feel like they were hitting the ground; she didn't feel like she was moving forwards. She tried to scream, but couldn't. Panic set in when she realised she couldn't see anyone else.

Montana's voice cut through her panic.

'Keep running, Noah! Just run. Sachin's music will do the rest.'

The melody penetrated her. As she ran she tested it. It was helping her. She understood that much. Noah pushed herself even harder. Suddenly, without warning, the forest was behind her. Noah stumbled and fell, landing on her hands and knees. She looked up, but one look at the sky made her wish she was back in the forest. A seething, roiling mass of thick, black cloud churned overhead.

'Is everyone here?' Emir said.

'All here,' Montana confirmed. 'Now we need to find cover.'

'Noah!'

Noah spun around to see Chase running towards her. Alan was doing his best to keep up but was lagging.

'Glad you're back,' Chase said, hugging her tightly.

'Glad to be back,' Noah replied.

Chase pointed to the rocky overhang behind them. 'We need to get under cover before the storm.'

'I've seen a green tinge to storm clouds before,' Noah said, 'but never red.'

'It's a fire storm,' Alan said, panting heavily. 'Instead of hailing ice, it hails rocks and lava.'

'How does that work?' Noah asked. 'It's cold in the upper atmosphere; the water vapour in the clouds is supposed to condense and turn to ice. Having lava in the sky doesn't make sense.'

'This isn't Earth remember,' Chase said.

'There are caves,' Alan said, 'just over that ridge. We can shelter there … if we make it.'

A smouldering rock the size of Noah's fist slammed into the ground just in front of them. It was crusted black on the outside but cracks in its crust showed the molten lava within.

The horse closest reared and whinnied in fright.

'Go!' Sachin ordered as more stones fell. *'Go!'*

Raven took off as Noah clambered onto her horse. She watched Chase struggle onto her skittish gelding as Sachin raced for the mount they'd brought for him.

'Montana! Take my horse,' Emir said as he wrestled Ardis onto the pack animal.

'But—'

'I'll ride with Sachin,' Emir called. 'GO!'

Noah dug her heels into her mare's sides and the horse raced after Raven. It was a long way to go dodging missiles from the sky. The only thing in their favour was that it was now all downhill.

Raven let out a yelp of pain.

'No!' Noah cried.

She jumped from her horse and ran to her injured canine who was frantically licking a nasty burn. In one motion Noah lifted him to his feet and gave him a solid whack on the rump.

'Come on, Raven,' she urged. 'Race you to the cave.'

'Noah! What are you doing?' Chase cried.

Pumping her arms as fast as she could, she said, 'Running! What does it look like I'm doing?'

Hot rocks slammed down all around her, but Noah kept her eyes on Raven. When they finally reached the cave, she collapsed on the floor beside her Alsatian.

'Noah,' Chase said, throwing her arms around her. 'Please don't do that again.'

Unable to find enough breath to talk, Noah just nodded.

Once everyone was inside the cave, the real show started.

Montana stood at the entrance, looking out at the storm. 'Mesmerising, isn't it?' she said.

Noah wasn't watching the storm. She inspected Raven's burn. Alan squatted beside her.

'I can heal that burn,' he said.

'What's your current rank, Alan?' Montana asked.

Puffing out his already puffy chest, Alan said, 'I am a professor of raiki – certainly qualified to deal with superficial burns.'

Montana smiled. 'Congratulations,' she said.

'And if all goes to plan,' Alan continued, 'I'll be a *doctor* by the end of the year. Can you believe it? Me! A doctor! Sometimes I just have to pinch myself.'

'You certainly are doing well for yourself,' the High Priestess said.

Noah interrupted. 'Any time you want to start on Raven's burn would be great ...'

'Oh! Of course, of course,' Alan gushed, reaching into one of his pockets and extracting his instrument.

'What do you call that?' Noah asked.

'It's a bass recorder,' he said.

'It's beautifully carved.'

Alan nodded. 'As luck would have it, I have the right slider on for the job – amethyst is perfect for soothing burns. You'll notice this—'

'How about heal first, explain later?' Noah suggested.

'Oh yeah. Sure thing,' he said. 'Chase, we're going to need a little room here.'

'Oh,' Chase said, 'sure thing. I'll just ... wait with the others.'

'That'd be great,' Alan said, as Chase walked towards Sachin. To Noah, he said, 'Close your eyes and listen to the music.'

Noah did as he said and nestled herself beside Raven. He whined softly as he turned his head to lick her face.

'Lie still, Raven,' she said, running her hand down his side. 'We'll have that burn sorted shortly.'

Alan put the recorder to his lips. He closed his eyes and started to play. Noah closed her eyes too and concentrated on Raven. She found that by listening, she could feel the heat in his burned flesh. Not the pain of the burn but the heat trapped in it. Alan's melody released the heat, gave it an avenue of escape. It was slow going and took almost an hour to complete the tonic. When the music stopped, Noah opened her eyes.

'Thank you,' she said. 'It's strange to me that you can use music like that.'

'Manipulating the dragonsong is the greatest privilege on Talisker,' he said. In a conspiratorial whisper, he added, 'I can't wait until you find the 13th key. *That* is going to be amazing – just amazing!'

'*If* I find it,' Noah said.

'You're going to find it,' Alan said confidently. 'We're all here to help.'

As Raven snored quietly, Noah said, 'Well, thanks, Alan.'

'You're most welcome,' he said as he got to his feet. 'If you'll excuse me now, I'll go and see what assistance I can be to Sachin.'

Noah glanced over to where the young boy was leaning over Ardis's still form. Montana was helping him. Noah imagined Sachin was doing what Alan had just done on Raven, but on a bigger scale. While Raven's burn had been deep it had only affected the skin. Ardis had significant wounds. Deep lacerations and torn muscle needed repair. Each fibre had to be sewn back together with music. Not only that, the risk of infection was high. It would take several more hours, Noah guessed. Perhaps with Alan's help, it might get done more quickly.

Chase walked over to Noah and squatted down beside her. Giving Raven a friendly scratch, she said, 'How's he doing?'

'He'll be fine,' Noah replied. 'How's the storm?'

'Petering out. Emir says we'll have to wait a while after it finishes though before we can leave. There's a sea of hot rocks out there and apparently they stay hot for a long time.' Taking a notebook from her bag, Chase said, 'So since we've got some time on our hands, tell me about Montana and Ardis.'

Noah recounted the morning's jail break as Chase scrawled notes in her book.

When Noah finished, Chase sighed. 'I wish I'd been with you.'

'Well, you'll be joining me on my next big adventure,' Noah said.

'And that would be?'

'Shopping in Leninstar. I'm finally going to be able to buy some fabrics for my collection.'

Chapter 12

Noah patted her mare's neck as the company made their way to Leninstar. They'd been lucky none of the horses had been injured in the firestorm. Sachin had given his mount to Montana and he now rode with Emir. Ardis nursed his injuries aboard the pack animal.

Dropping back to ride alongside Noah, Montana said, 'Your friend is intense.'

'She means well,' Noah said.

Montana smiled. 'I don't doubt that but still … I'm worried about Ardis.'

Now that Chase had finished grilling the High Priestess, she'd moved on to Montana's newest recruit. It would still be a couple of days before they reached Leninstar and it was likely that Ardis would have to endure Chase's interrogation for much of the remainder of the trip.

'He's tough,' Noah said, thinking of the wounds he'd sustained just yesterday.

'Yes,' Montana agreed. 'He is.'

While Ardis was tough, Noah was still sceptical about his loyalty. That probably had something to do with the fact that he'd tried to run a sword through her, she reasoned. She needed to quiz the High Priestess.

'How do you know he can be trusted?' she asked at last.

'I guess I don't know for sure,' Montana admitted, 'but he comes from a long line of Elani warriors. Pride in one's heritage is important to these men. It is unlikely he would put a blemish on his family's name.'

'Oh,' was all Noah said.

'There is something else on your mind?'

Again, Noah was searching for the right words. She wasn't a religious person herself but she didn't want to cause offence.

'I don't really get that a Priestess commands an army,' she said at last. 'It seems a bit ... contradictory.'

Montana nodded. 'I understand what you're saying, but the men and women of my army fight only to uphold the Score.'

'You have women in your army?'

'Of course.'

Noah tried to remember what Emir had told her about the Score. 'And the Score – it's like a bible, isn't it?'

'Yes,' she said. 'It promotes harmony between people, and harmony between us and our environment.'

'So everyone should be nice to each other and look after the place,' Noah said.

'That's basically it,' Montana said.

Noah thought for a moment. 'But surely having soldiers who kill people doesn't fit with the Score.'

'I hear you,' she said. 'And while it is lamentable that people die, it is also unavoidable. Sometimes people's actions leave us no choice.'

'For example?'

'Gangs of bandits raiding villages,' Montana said, absently stroking her mount's neck as she spoke. 'Our goal is to use appropriate force to protect people and property. We do only what is required. If drawing a few swords is enough to scare bandits away, then that's what we do. If they are aggressive though, my soldiers will fight.'

'And that works?'

'It is not perfect,' she admitted. 'Nothing is.'

'I guess you'd be out of a job if things were perfect,' Noah said.

Montana laughed. 'I hadn't thought of it quite like that.'

'Have you been doing this job long?'

'Over three hundred years,' Montana said.

Noah stared. 'Three hundred years?' she echoed. 'How can that be? You don't look that old.'

The High Priestess smiled. 'You're too kind. I am actually close to eight hundred years old. My mother is human but my father is an elf.'

'An elf? There are elves here?'

'Not on this land. They live in the Outland. There isn't supposed to be any mixing of the bloodlines, so I was banished since I am not a true elf.'

'So you have no family here?'

'That's right.'

'So you're like an orphan.'

'I guess so.'

Noah nodded. 'I know how you feel then.'

The pair rode in silence for a while. Noah watched Raven as he trotted along beside her. Despite the burn he'd sustained from the hot rock, he was travelling well. Alan's tonic had worked.

'I could probably ask Chase this question. But given that she's otherwise occupied,' Noah said, 'can I ask what landed the High Priestess in jail?'

'The short answer is Orville.'

'What's he got against you?'

'I support the adepts and the Academy,' she said.

'Surely he can't lock you up for that,' Noah said.

'True,' Montana replied, 'but apparently he can have me incarcerated for treason.'

'Treason? As in crimes against the Crown?'

'Yes. That one. I had a few things to say about the blood magic policies that Orville proposed.'

'Like?'

'I said his ideas were most likely cooked up in a cow's colon.'

Noah's mouth dropped open. 'You said *that*?'

Clearly happy with Noah's reaction, Montana laughed. 'Pretty much,' she said, pulling herself together. 'I suggested that forces loyal to the Crown were behind all these mysterious disappearances of late. Orville, and by extension the king, weren't happy with that.'

'You think they are slaughtering whole populations of towns?'

'I don't think all of them are being slaughtered,' she said. 'I think some of them are being kept for breeding purposes.'

'Breeding purposes?'

'I believe Orville is breeding people to use for future blood stocks.'

Noah's stomach turned over. 'That's a bit gruesome.'

'More than a "bit",' Montana said.

'What I don't get,' Noah said, 'is how Orville has convinced anyone to support his plan. If raiki has been around for thousands of years, and has worked, why change? And why change to something that is going to require people to bleed?'

'If only more people here asked themselves those questions,' she said. 'Anyway, Orville's official marketing campaign is very slick. He's covered a number of angles. Firstly, only people over the age of fifteen are allowed to donate blood and then only a litre a month at an approved collection centre. Orville claims that donating blood in this way not only has numerous health benefits but will also boost employment – people will be needed to run the collection centres.'

'Right,' Noah said.

'But the big prize,' Montana continued, 'is that the blood will fuel an integrated power grid. "Power from the people, for the people" is his slogan.'

'Power from the people, for the people,' Noah echoed. 'It is catchy.'

'So is the flu,' Montana said, 'but that doesn't mean it's a good thing. The energy angle is a powerful one,' she continued. 'It is clean, sustainable and it creates employment. On top of that, people who donate blood will be entitled to rebates on their utility bills.'

'It sounds too good to be true,' Noah said. 'Surely they anticipate people trying to rort the system by donating more than they should – by means fair or foul.'

'Apparently there will be fines for excess donations,' Montana said.

'You don't believe that?'

'There is no way they're going to get anything like the volume of blood they need by the methods they're suggesting. Behind the scenes, Orville and his minions will be harvesting blood by other means – kidnapping, breeding … not to mention emptying the prisons.'

'On the surface, it sounds pretty appealing,' Noah ventured.

'That's the problem,' Montana said. 'We're really up against it. Orville is an undeniably charismatic figure. He's got a slick, detailed and appealing plan. And on top of that he deflects attention from his own devious activities by attributing them to his enemies.'

'Blaming the adepts for all these people disappearing.'

'Exactly.'

Noah had already accepted the idea that Orville was dangerous, but now she had an appreciation for how clever he was. They would have to be careful when they got to Leninstar. The king's city would be crawling with his loyal supporters – not a safe place for high profile prison escapees like the Major and High Priestess.

♪♫

Alan placed brightly-coloured drinks on the table in front of the two girls. 'A successful shopping trip should be celebrated.'

'I should say so,' Noah said as she scooped the glass off the table. 'I really need this drink. The markets were fabulous but all those bodies crammed in there made it really hot.'

Alan drained his glass in one go. *That explains why he's so chubby,* Noah thought.

Though his unquenchable enthusiasm for *every*thing was irritating, Alan was a better candidate for shopping guide than Emir. Sachin's choice of chaperone had surprised Noah though. She was sure Emir's humourless, autocratic style would have been the Major's first choice. *Alan probably drives Sachin nuts too,* Noah thought. *If Alan's annoying me, he's out of the Major's hair.*

Chase eyed the multitude of bags and parcels. 'Even between the three of us, I don't know how we're going to get all that stuff back to the boarding house.'

'Ye of little faith,' Noah chided. 'Where there's a will, there's a way.'

Noah took a long sip of her blue drink which tasted like a mixture of pear and mandarin juice.

'I can't wait to get back and get started,' she said. 'I have the materials, the ideas and a model. Now I just need the time.'

'Who's your model?' Alan asked.

Chase squirmed. 'You're lucky I love you as much as I do,' she said. 'Just promise me you won't make me wear more stuff like this.'

She pointed to her current ensemble.

'I don't know what you're complaining about,' Noah said. 'That dress looks great on you.'

Chase poked out her tongue. Mrs Sloane at the boarding house had given both girls something "fitting" to wear to the markets. Clearly their House garb was going to attract all the wrong kind of attention in Leninstar. Chase was openly uncomfortable with the length, or lack thereof, of the dress and even less enamoured of the colours it boasted. For her part, Noah loved her dress. Not in the least bit squeamish about short hemlines, she had at once fallen in love with the checked purple number.

'And anyway, it won't kill you to try on a few dresses,' Noah admonished. 'They won't hurt you, not even a little.'

'Not unless you stab me with one of those pins,' Chase retorted.

'Nonsense. I won't stab you. I had a great teacher and years of practice. My mannequin at home hasn't complained once.'

Chase rolled her eyes.

A commotion at the counter drew Noah's attention. A young man stood amongst the pastries and scrolls, much to the consternation of the tavern owner. Silvya, who looked like a mouldy dumpling and grew hair in places where women shouldn't grow hair, was attempting to dislodge him with the biggest rolling pin Noah had ever seen. The man deftly avoided her blows as he delivered the daily news.

'Today's news is brought to you by Helga's Hair. Be a cut above the rest.'

Whack. Silvya bounced a scone along the counter but the herald was unfazed.

'Leading today's bulletin is the death of Valada—'

A murmur swelled around the tavern.

'—fancy that—'

'—the king's tailor, who'd have thought—'

'—such a shame—'

'—heard from Janice that he was poorly—'

Whack. Another scone gone. The herald sidestepped and continued.

'King Tambian's tailor, and long-time friend, passed away in his sleep last night. His elegant designs are credited with restoring a sense of majesty to the royal wardrobe. After Jime, whose range of robes did little to inspire, Valada was seen as a breath of fresh air. Sometimes controversial, always colourful, Valada will be remembered fondly by all. A state funeral will be held in his honour at a date to be announced later in the week. The question of who'll be his successor will be answered by way of a fashion fair at this year's Summer Solstice Festival. Interested persons are invited to obtain an application form from the palace.'

Noah raised an eyebrow.

'I know what you're thinking, Noah,' Alan said. 'And the answer is no.'

'I'm designing a collection anyway; a couple more outfits would be no trouble.'

Alan folded his pudgy arms across his chest. 'No.'

Whack. Whack. The herald shuffled his papers, skipped over the rolling pin and started on his next article without missing a beat.

'The number of escapees from yesterday's jailbreak is set to pass one hundred. This extraordinarily high number is due to Major Sachin and his use of black magic.'

Noah studied Alan's face. Despite the wildly exaggerated numbers, he showed no reaction to the herald's remarks.

'The High Priestess Montana is also among the escapees. They are considered extremely dangerous and should not be approached under any circumstances. Anyone with information about them should contact the sheriff's office immediately.'

'Maybe we should get back to the boarding house?' Noah whispered to Alan.

He shook his head. 'Enjoy your drink,' he said. 'Moving now would be a mistake.'

She could see his point.

Whack. Whack. Whack. Whack. The herald was now performing a jig to avoid having his toes smashed.

'He's very good at dodging that rolling pin,' Chase said.

'He should be,' Alan replied. 'This is a daily event.'

The herald went on to speak of mysterious disappearances around the city.

Someone tapped Noah on the shoulder. Startled, she spun in her seat.

An old man at an adjacent table wagged his finger at her. 'It's an outrage, don't you know,' he said.

'What's an outrage?' Noah said.

'All these disappearances,' he replied, waving his nearly depleted glass of ale around to emphasise his point. 'It's been going on for months now.'

'Oh, yes,' said Noah. 'Terrible indeed.'

'It's those adepts and their black magic.'

'Oh Harold, leave the poor girl alone,' the woman beside him said. 'She doesn't want to hear your drunken ramblings. Come to that, I don't want to hear your drunken ramblings either but I guess *I* don't have any choice,' she continued in her whiny voice. 'Don't know why I married you in the first place. Should have listened to my mother, bless her soul. She said you'd amount to nothing. I should've—'

'Oh, shut up woman,' the man replied. 'You've got a voice that could open a can, I swear it. And these disappearances, they're serious business I tell you. Those Academy monsters, they're *murdering* people. Murdering, I say. These people that are disappearing, they are supporters of the king's new order. These people, these *patriots*, support the king's push for blood magic. The adepts want them silenced so they can continue using their vile black magic.'

'Blood magic, black magic, blah, blah, blah,' his wife said. 'It's all magic, who cares what colour it is?'

Instead of answering his wife, he directed his answer to Noah.

'Blood magic is the way forward, mark my words,' he said, draining the last of his ale. 'Magic from the people, for the people! It's only natural.'

'I'll keep that in mind,' Noah said.

The man's wife was on her feet.

'Come on Harold,' she said in her parrot-like screech. 'Time to go.'

The man tottered along behind his wife who was still bemoaning the fact that she'd married him.

'I think it's time we left too,' Alan said.

♪♫

'Just for the record, let it be noted that I said that this was a bad idea,' Alan said.

Noah smiled. 'Duly noted.'

They'd dropped the fruits of their shopping trip back at the boarding house. Mrs Sloane had wanted to charge them extra to store such a large quantity of supplies but after intense haggling she'd accepted the promise of an original garment from Noah, made from a fabric of her choice. Chase remained at the boarding house to protect the supplies from Mrs Sloane and to keep Raven company while Noah had sneaked out to snaffle an application form from the palace. Alan had caught up with her at the palace gates. He'd done his best to convince her to leave but Noah was having none of it. This was too good an opportunity to pass up.

As she waited in the drawing room for the steward to arrive with a form, she watched Alan who sat nervously on an opulently covered chaise lounge. She shared his tension but mostly she was excited. Already she pictured her designs swishing down the catwalk at the Summer Solstice Festival.

The steward strode into the room.

'This is the form you will need to complete,' he said officiously.

'Thank you,' Noah said. 'You won't be sorry.'

The steward snorted. 'Quite frankly I couldn't care less,' he said. 'While you are possibly one of the least nauseating little vultures I have had to deal with today, I would still like to spend as little time with you as possible. Just fill out the form quickly.'

He raked his gaze over her outfit.

'I hope that is not what you'd consider an appropriate ensemble at this time.'

Noah frowned. 'What time is it?'

The steward lifted a disapproving eyebrow.

'A time of grieving?' he said. 'Remember the tailor? The reason you are here? A revered man has just died and you've forgotten already?'

Noah had been impetuous but as she sat before the steward, her cheeks burning, it dawned on her just how rash she'd been in coming here. She hadn't considered that her outfit would be inappropriate for the occasion. The fact that it was a great outfit had been enough for her. She hadn't shown respect to the man whose shoes she sought to fill. Noah was just about to start filling in her paperwork when the ornately carved door swung open to reveal the king's adviser.

'Well, well, well,' Orville said. 'Who do we have here?'

Noah's heart sank as the steward said, 'Yet another repellent little hyena who is salivating over the thought of replacing the king's esteemed designer, sir,' the steward answered.

Orville smiled. 'Thank you Smythe, I'll take care of this one.'

'As you wish, sir,' he replied as he passed the paperwork to Orville.

Orville turned his gaze to Noah. This was the worst-case scenario that Alan had warned her about. The palace was a big, busy place; Noah had thought she could sneak in and out without Orville noticing.

'The last time I saw you, you were dead I think,' Orville said. Oddly, he didn't seem surprised. He might have been discussing the weather, such was the indifference in his voice. He looked her up and down, 'You seem to have made a remarkable recovery.'

She felt like he was undressing her in his mind. He certainly wasn't a textbook master criminal, Noah thought.

'Turns out it was just laryngitis,' she said.

'Right,' Orville said as he seated himself behind the marble desk. 'Let's have a look at this application form, shall we? Name. Noah Chord.'

He wrote her name with a flourish of his pen. Leaning back to survey his work, he said, 'Noah's a funny name for a girl, isn't it?'

'To some perhaps,' Noah replied evenly, and then added, 'wasn't that mole above your lip on the *right* side of your face last time I saw you?'

'You were dead,' he said. 'What would you know?'

'Hit a nerve there I think,' Noah muttered to Alan.

'What was that?' Orville demanded.

'Nothing,' Noah replied innocently.

'Address,' Orville said, going back to the form. 'The Academy, Mellifont. How would you describe your current occupation, Noah?' he asked. 'Unemployed?'

Knowing that that was not going to look good on her application, she said, 'Student. Student of the Arts.'

'Qualifications?'

'No formal qualifications,' she admitted.

'Referees?'

Noah looked at Alan. Alan nodded and gestured for the form and pen, which Orville slid across the table.

As Alan filled out his details, Noah asked, 'Is that a ballpoint pen?'

'Yes.'

'I didn't think you'd have ballpoint pens here. Where are they manufactured?' she asked.

'Earth,' Orville replied. 'We *import* certain things, if you will.'

'Contraband,' Alan coughed.

'*Imports*,' Orville reiterated. 'Okay,' he continued. 'Only one more section to go. For applicants under the age of 18, the signature of a parent or guardian is required.'

Before Noah's heart even had time to sink, Alan was reaching for the form again. She smiled gratefully at him.

'Done,' Alan said. 'Right, Noah, let's go.'

'Don't be too hasty there—' Orville made a big show of reading the name from the form, 'Professor Alan. Noah herself still needs to sign the form for it to be valid. It would be such a shame if her application was invalidated due to a simple clerical error, wouldn't you say?'

Orville pushed the form in Noah's direction. She signed hastily. She shared Alan's desire to be out of the palace and away from Orville.

The king's adviser swept up the application and leaned back in his chair, reviewing the form with obvious relish.

'Always a good idea to do a final check,' he muttered as he read.

Alan's tension was growing by the second, Noah could feel it. Orville took his time, reading the form thoroughly.

'A shame,' he said when he reached the bottom of the form, 'a real shame that your parents aren't here to sign your form. I'm sure they'd have been very proud.'

Noah flinched.

'You're surprised I know you're an orphan?' he asked.

Noah said nothing.

'You're the spitting image of your mother, I must say.'

Noah couldn't help herself. 'You *knew* my mother?' she said.

'Oh yes,' he replied. 'I remember Isla well.'

'You don't have to listen to this, Noah,' Alan interjected. 'This man is not to be trusted. We'd best be going.'

Noah was torn. She trusted Alan and her gut told her that Orville was not a person she should spend too much time with. But if he knew her mother, she certainly wanted to hear more about that.

'How do you know my mother?' she demanded.

'Tut, tut, so impatient,' Orville said. 'Your friend here is wrong on one count – I *can* be trusted. He is right, however, about your need to leave now. There are people in this palace who think that you should be detained and the longer you stay, the greater the risk that they will organise themselves to do just that.'

'What possible reason could you have to detain her?' Alan said.

'It is not I who wishes to detain her,' Orville said, smiling as he rose from his chair. 'But there are others who would be interested to learn why one who was dead, is now alive. There has been black magic at work, no doubt. Perhaps she is a zombie? In any case, there are those in the palace who would want to investigate this phenomenon.'

'And you aren't one of those people?' Noah asked.

'Actually no,' he replied, walking around the desk to stand before her. 'I am more interested in the 13th key.'

'Why?'

'It is a black power, and it must be destroyed,' Orville said simply.

'It will save our world,' Alan challenged.

'It will destroy this world,' Orville countered.

At that moment, the sound of many footsteps and raised voices intruded on the conversation.

Alan grabbed Noah's wrist. 'We must go now!'

Orville took her other elbow, put his mouth to her ear.

'Bring me the 13th key and I'll tell you about your mother,' he whispered to her. With that, he let go. 'Leave now,' he ordered.

Chapter 13

'You did *WHAT*?' Sachin squealed.

Emir's face looked like a thunderstorm.

'Are you *insane*?' Sachin said, continuing his rant. 'Do you know how much trouble I went to, to make Orville think you were dead? Did it occur to you, for even a moment, that there was a good reason for it?'

Noah didn't answer straight away. She stared at her hands, folded in her lap. 'I understand that you're upset,' she said.

'*UPSET*?' Sachin cried, his face almost purple. 'Don't even speak to me! I don't want to hear anything come out of your mouth. You are so stupid I can't find words to describe it. You are reckless beyond imagining and thoughtless beyond belief.'

He turned on Alan then.

'And you,' he said, 'not only let her *go*, but escorted her? I expect her to be stupid,' he said, pointing at Noah, 'but I relied on *you* to protect her. What made you think that it was a good idea? Please explain to me why, after all I've done to hide her, you delivered her to the one person I am trying to hide her from.'

'He didn't exactly escort me,' Noah said, daring a sideways glance at Sachin.

'I thought I told you not to speak,' he yelled.

Out of the corner of her eye, Noah saw Emir put his hands on Sachin's shoulders. With visible effort, the boy took a deep breath. Noah tried again.

'When I told Alan my plan, he locked Chase and me in the bedroom and told me to work on my collection. I climbed out the window and left Chase to make some noise in the room. Apparently Alan got suspicious when he didn't hear any talking. By the time he caught up to me, I was already inside the palace gates. I didn't think I'd run into Orville,' she added.

'You just didn't think!' Sachin said. 'You're so dumb, you're dangerous. You're a danger to yourself and to the rest of us.'

As much as she despised being told off by someone younger than her, even more galling was the knowledge that she deserved it. And to make matters worse, she'd gotten Alan into trouble as well. Though incredibly annoying, he'd been good to her and she'd repaid him by deceiving and compromising him. She dropped her head again, letting her loose, dark locks fall and hide her face.

'Professor Alan, come with me,' Sachin said.

The boy stomped to the door and wrenched it open. Alan followed sheepishly. The door slammed shut but Noah didn't look up. She knew Emir was still in the room. With Chase, Montana and Raven in the bedroom upstairs, Noah was alone with him. She almost didn't dare to breathe. Minutes dragged by and rather than being a relief, it served only to heighten her anxiety. She found herself wishing that he'd either yell at her or leave. She heard wood scraping against wood. Emir was moving furniture. Without lifting her head, Noah could see a chair being placed before her. Emir installed himself in it. Still he said nothing.

'Do you want to know why I did it?' she whispered at length.

'No,' he said. 'I want to know what Orville said to you.'

Surprised, Noah looked up.

'He wants the 13th key. He says it needs to be destroyed before it destroys your world.'

Emir considered her response.

'He thinks you might find it. That's why you're still free,' he mused.

'Why does he think this key will destroy the world, but you guys think it will save the world? How can there be such totally different ideas about the same thing?'

'It's a source of power, Noah. It can be used for good, or ill. Think of nuclear power on Earth. It can be a source of clean energy. That's good. But it can also be used to make nuclear weapons. Bad. It depends on how it's used. What else did he say?'

'He said he can be trusted.'

Emir frowned. 'Trusted, huh? Trusted to do what, I wonder ...'

'Can I ask a dumb question?'

'Undoubtedly.'

'What makes you think Orville wants to destroy Talisker? What does he gain? Where will he live?'

'So the last question is the dumb question, I take it? There are plenty of other worlds to live on – Earth for starters. What makes us think he wants to destroy Talisker? Because he wants to get rid of raiki and replace it with blood magic. Our world is based on music, and magic that has its power based in music fits the natural order of things. Using blood as a source of power for magic upsets the laws of nature. Used widely enough it will not only upset the laws of nature, it will shatter them completely.'

'So it's like a piece of fabric,' Noah said, trying to put the concept in terms she could understand. 'If you start pulling threads out of your weave, you weaken the fabric. The more you pull out, the weaker it gets until eventually you've got nothing left.'

Emir nodded. 'Maybe you're not quite as stupid as my master supposes,' he said. 'Did Orville say anything else?'

'He said he knew my mother,' she blurted, regretting it immediately. She hadn't intended to share that information.

'Did he now?'

'You don't believe it?'

Emir shrugged. 'It doesn't matter what I believe. Do you believe it?'

Noah didn't know if she believed Orville or if she just wanted to. Any connection to her mother, no matter how tenuous, drew her.

'I don't know if I believe him or not,' she said finally, 'but I think it's better if I don't believe him.'

Emir nodded but said nothing.

Noah had a sudden thought. 'Did *you* know my mother?' she asked.

He looked at her, unflinching. 'No.'

Noah waited for him to say something more. After several long moments of silence, Noah said, 'You're a cold fish, you know that?'

Whatever Emir might have said was lost when the door opened again. Ardis strode into the room. A testament to Sachin's healing abilities, two days after being savagely mauled by Raven, Ardis was moving freely. He pushed back the hood of his cloak, revealing fresh facial tattoos.

'No prizes for guessing where you've been,' Noah said, wondering how a trip to the tattoo parlour could be a priority at a time like this.

'These tattoos are the official mark of Elani warriors,' he declared as he sat at the table.

Thinking of Montana's fugitive status, Noah said, 'You think that's a good thing to be advertising at the moment?'

'For now her soldiers are free to go about their business,' Ardis said, 'but I did keep my hood up on the way back.'

The door opened again.

'Is it safe to come in?' Chase asked hesitantly.

'Safe-ish,' Noah said.

Chase took one look at Ardis and crossed the room to stand in front of him. He bowed his head. Was he embarrassed? Surely not. He'd been quite proud of his new look a few seconds ago. Chase stood patiently for a full six seconds, waiting for him to look up. When she could endure it no longer, she placed her notebook and pen on the table and reached out and put her fingertips under his bearded chin. She lifted his head gently. When their eyes met, he smiled tenderly.

Noah blinked in disbelief. Was this really the same man who'd tried to kill her? It had taken a ferocious attack by Raven and the appearance of a grom to stop him, and here he was smiling warmly at Chase.

'Would you mind if I sketched your tattoos?' Chase asked sweetly.

'That would be fine,' Ardis answered.

Noah thought she might be sick.

As Ardis posed and Chase picked up her sketchpad, Noah sidled over next to Emir.

'What's going on with those two?' she whispered.

'They're lovesick,' Emir said matter-of-factly.

'When did that happen?'

Emir looked at her like she'd grown an extra nose.

'The first time they laid eyes on each other,' he said. 'You didn't notice?'

Noah scowled.

Emir said, 'I guess I should also point out that they don't know that we all know. They think they're keeping it a really big secret. So don't spoil it for them, okay?'

'Right,' Noah said, frowning.

'Problem?' Emir said.

'No,' Noah said. 'It's just that it's a bit gross, isn't it?'

'What do you mean "gross"?'

'Well, he's old and … and … he tried to kill me!'

'For goodness sake, Noah – he only tried to kill you once. Get over it. And anyway, he's not that old – early twenties – same as Jemima. It's just the goatee makes him look so sophisticated.'

'Well, he could do with a haircut,' Noah said.

'A warrior of the Order of Elani is a great catch. There are very exacting standards one has to meet to be accepted as one of Elani's knights. Montana upholds them; she accepts only the best. And young Ardis, he has the High Priestess's blessing.'

'It's still gross,' Noah said.

'That'll be you one day,' Emir said, 'swooning over some guy.'

Noah grimaced. 'God, I hope not,' she said.

'Or maybe,' he said, 'you'll have some guy swooning over you.'

'I don't think so.'

'You're right,' Emir said, 'that is hard to imagine.'

Her reflexive retort about it being equally hard to imagine anyone swooning over him, was interrupted by Sachin's return.

'Right,' Sachin said. 'Plan for the rest of today is this. Alan and I are going out to run a couple of errands. Noah is going to stay in this room and get to work on her collection for the fashion show.'

'Which one?' Noah asked, wanting to make sure she was doing exactly what Sachin had in mind and not risk his displeasure once again.

He frowned. 'What do you mean, "which one"?'

'Which fashion show? The one at home, or the one at the Summer Solstice Festival?'

'Stick to your one at home for now. You might be back there sooner rather than later at the rate you're going.'

'Roger that,' she said.

A quizzical scowl marred Sachin's boyish face momentarily but he moved on quickly.

'In the morning, Noah and I will be going to Scratch & Denton – a second hand shop of musical instruments,' Sachin said.

'And we'd be going there because …?' Noah prompted.

'Because you're going to try playing some musical instruments. See if you can follow this logic. We'll try you out on a variety of instruments; if there are any that you are particularly good at – maybe we'll have some idea of the key we are looking for.'

'Okay, I get it,' Noah said.

'Good,' Sachin said, raising his eyes dramatically to the heavens. 'Maybe there is some hope after all.'

He headed for the door, pausing only to speak to Emir. 'Make sure she stays here,' Sachin said.

'I will, Major,' Emir said.

While Emir stood guard, Chase pried herself away from Ardis to draw up the pattern pieces for each of the designs in Noah's collection. Noah immersed herself in the fabrics. She took each one in turn, testing the music of each piece. Surprisingly, she found that by sensing the fabric in this way she got new ideas about what outfit to make and how to best use the fabric. There was more to the fabric than just the look of it. It had deeper qualities that she hadn't been aware of before.

Three hours later she was swimming in a sea of swatches and sketches. It finally occurred to her to look up. Ardis was gone but Chase and Emir were still with her.

'What are you doing?' she asked Chase.

'Just writing down an idea,' Chase said. She shrugged apologetically, adding, 'Inspiration struck.'

'Understand,' Noah said, nodding.

Emir picked up one of Noah's sketches.

'This is a great sketch, Noah,' he said.

'Don't sound so surprised,' Noah replied curtly.

He frowned and Noah instantly regretted her tone. He put the sketch back down on the pile and went back to his chair.

'I'm sorry,' she said. 'I didn't mean to be snippy.'

He shrugged while Chase picked up the sketch, studied it, looked at Noah and then back at the sketch.

'It'll look great on you,' Noah cooed.

Chase glared at her. 'I will *not* be wearing *that*,' she declared.

'Oh, come on,' Noah said. 'You'll like it once you try it. You'll see.'

'I would not be seen dead in that,' she replied. 'And besides, are you sure that bit goes at the front?'

'Of course I'm sure,' Noah said. 'I will say though, as far as models go … I wish you were about a foot taller. That would have been really convenient.'

'Well, really! I suppose you're going to say that you wish my bum was—'

'Alright ladies, break it up,' Emir said. 'Jemima, go and make some tea.'

Chase said, 'Why do I have to make the tea? Just because I'm a girl …'

'It's not because you're a girl. It's because Noah is to stay in this room and I am to stay in here with her. Need I remind you what happened earlier when you two were left to your own devices?'

'No,' Chase replied. 'But need I remind you that *I* wasn't the one who climbed out of the window?'

'So then I can trust you to make tea,' Emir replied. 'Off you go.'

Muttering under her breath, the girl stalked out of the room on her tiptoes, looking back over her shoulder trying to assess the size of her rear-end as she went.

Chapter 14

'It's just around this corner,' Sachin said.

'Thank goodness,' Noah said. 'I was starting to wish we'd ridden the horses.'

'It's not that far,' Sachin replied shortly.

It wasn't the distance they'd walked through Leninstar's bustling streets that bothered Noah, but she didn't dare say so to Sachin. Though the people they passed appeared to pay them no notice, Noah was vigilant. She walked the streets of the royal city with a fugitive. The sooner they were indoors, the better she'd like it.

'Here,' Sachin said.

A large wooden sign hung above the entranceway. *Scratch & Denton*.

'Welcome to Scratch & Denton, Major Sachin!' cried a voice as they entered.

Locating its source, Noah was confronted by a lanky young fellow in a black T-shirt and an emerald, blue and black kilt. No shoes were in evidence but a colourful, embroidered band encircled his left ankle. Curiously, all his fingernails were painted different colours, and Noah would like to have introduced his black locks to a comb. His hair looked clean though, which made her think that he purposely cultivated the tousled arrangement.

'I'm Scratch,' he said extending his hand to Noah.

'Noah Chord,' she said, shaking the offered hand. 'Nice place you've got here.'

'Thank you,' he said, smiling.

Nice ... and very cluttered, Noah thought. She didn't have much experience with musical instruments but she was sure that every conceivable type of instrument that existed, was here. It was difficult to estimate how many instruments there might be. There was no spare space. Benches and shelves lined the walls and glass cabinets huddled on the floor like pigs in a pen. All were overflowing. In between instruments there were pieces of instruments.

Scratch reached behind a cabinet.

'Shall we get started?' he asked, brandishing a guitar.

'Sure,' Noah said, taking the instrument from him. 'Where do I blow into it?'

Sachin rolled his eyes as Scratch swooped to rescue the guitar from her grasp.

'What—' Noah started to say.

'Try this,' Scratch said, thrusting a harmonica into her hands.

Noah inspected it and put it to her lips and blew.

Nothing.

Scratch said, 'Other side.'

'She had a fifty-fifty chance,' Sachin said, 'and still she got it wrong. Give her a tambourine.'

Scratch obliged. He and Sachin watched for a minute while Noah shook, hit, tinkled and scraped at the tambourine.

'Creative, but no sense of rhythm,' Scratch noted.

Noah frowned. 'Give me a break. Ten days ago I was deaf.'

'What about a xylophone?' Scratch suggested.

Sachin grimaced. 'Let's come back to percussion at the end. Seriously, if the 13th key is a percussion instrument, we're in deep trouble. Clarinet.'

Scratch handed Noah a wooden clarinet.

'That's a good start,' Scratch said. 'She knows which end to put in her face at least.'

'I've seen Major Maggie play one of these,' Noah said.

'What strength reed have you got on there, Scratch?' Sachin asked.

'One,' Scratch replied.

The Major nodded as Noah blew tentatively into the mouthpiece.
Honk.

'Is it supposed to sound like that?' she asked.

Scratch and Sachin shook their heads in unison.

'Try curling your bottom lip under and resting your top teeth on the mouthpiece,' Scratch suggested.

Noah took a deep breath this time and shot a solid breath through the instrument and instantly wished she hadn't. Scratch disappeared behind the counter and Sachin danced around with his hands over his ears screaming, 'Make it stop! Make it stop!'

'No, not keen on that one,' Noah said. 'Got something else?'

'Follow me,' Scratch said.

Noah did her best to keep up with the shop owner as he wound his way between the cabinets.

'Try this,' he said.

Noah looked at the big brown thing with legs. 'There's a stool,' she said.

'You sit on that part, Noah,' Scratch said. To Sachin he said, 'Still think she's the one?'

'I don't blow into this one, do I?' Noah said.

'No, Noah. But try opening the lid …' Scratch replied.

'She has to be the one,' Sachin said.

'Are you trying to convince yourself or me?' Scratch said.

Noah looked at the pair. 'You know I can hear you, right?'

Sachin pointed to the keyboard.

Obediently, Noah put her hands to the keys and plinked and plonked away on the old harpsichord, testing out single notes and combinations of notes – some of which worked, and some that didn't.

'Chord by name, but not by nature it would seem,' Scratch said, wincing at the excruciating recipe of notes she'd just concocted. 'You're going to have to find the Descera.'

'I know,' Sachin said, nodding. 'I don't suppose you've seen any around lately?'

'If there are really any of them left,' Scratch said, 'I'd bet that they're hiding deep underground – tucked up safe in their ancient cities – well away from human hustle and bustle. And hopefully, protecting the 13th key.'

'They'll know Noah is here,' Sachin said. 'I'm hoping that they'll find us.'

'Even if you find them—'

'*When* we find them,' Sachin corrected.

'Right. *When* you find them, do you think they'll tell you where or what the 13th key is? I've heard talk that the Descera didn't even make the 13th key. People are saying the 13th key was brought here from another planet tens of thousands of years ago by a race of beings who wished it never to be found. It is a talisman of such great power, they say, that it is not safe to use. That being the case, it was buried deep, deep underground so that none could find it.'

'Sounds like a story spread around by Orville to scare people,' Sachin said. 'Look, the Descera made the original twelve keys. If I were old enough to bet legally, then I'd wager that they made the 13th key too.'

'That's logical I guess.' Scratch cringed at yet another odd assortment of notes from the harpsichord. 'How long should we let her keep doing that?'

'Leave her a bit longer,' Sachin said.

'Okay,' Scratch replied. 'But if I get another customer, she stops.'

Sachin grinned. 'Absolutely.'

'You know, if Orville finds the 13th key first, he will destroy it,' Scratch said.

'Yes, I know.'

'Word has it that he wants to destroy *all* the keys.'

'Yes,' Sachin said.

'He got your flute when he arrested you?'

'No,' Sachin said with a wink. 'He got a wonderful replica.'

'So everyone is happy then.' Scratch nodded approvingly.

'Until Orville finds out, yes – everyone is happy.'

'Well, I'll be happier when Noah stops plonking around on my harpsichord,' Scratch said.

'Maybe you could show her how it's meant to be played,' Sachin said.

'Right you are, little master.'

'I like this,' Noah declared. 'Just imagine if my parents had named me Harpsi, instead of Noah. Then I'd be Harpsi Chord. Harpsichord. Get it?'

'Yes, Noah,' Scratch said. 'We get it. But now, we want you to get *off*.'

'Wait a minute,' she said. 'I've been working on something here. Just listen to this. If I press this key, this key and this key – they all sound the same, but different. How cool is that?'

'She's discovered octaves,' Scratch noted.

'But there's more,' she said.

'If I press this one and this one together – it sounds nice …'

'That's a major third, Noah,' Sachin said.

'And this one and this one still sound nice but somehow sad.'

'A minor third.'

'This one sounds kind of weird …'

Scratch patted her on the head, 'A minor with an augmented fifth. A chord for Miss Chord, I do declare!'

'But watch what happens when I put four notes together. This one—'

Sachin and Scratch watched as she struck a D.

'Then this one.'

An F#.

'This one.'

A.

'And then this one.'

What was meant to sound like middle C actually sounded more like a rat squeaking an E in the octave above middle C.

'What the—'

Noah hit the note again.

Squeak.

Noah looked at Scratch.

'It wasn't doing that before,' she said.

'It shouldn't do that,' Scratch said. 'Let me try.'

Scratch pressed the key twice, just for good measure.

Squeak. Squeak.

When Sachin had his turn, he got –

'Stop that!'

Noah pushed herself back from the keyboard so fast that she toppled off the stool, which also fell over. Scratch narrowly avoided having his toes crushed by leaping out of the way of the falling stool but in doing so, revealed to Noah exactly what men wear under their kilts, which she would rather have read about than witnessed firsthand.

Reefing up the main lid of the harpsichord revealed a pair of rats. One of them was shaking an angry fist at the trio above them.

'Rats!' Sachin exclaimed.

'Talking rats!' Scratch added.

'Where?' squeaked the rats as they ran around in a mad panic. 'Rats! Rats! Look out for the rats!'

'What the hell are they doing?' Noah breathed.

Slap.

'Ouch! What was that for?' Noah asked Scratch, rubbing her stinging arm.

'Watch your language, young lady,' Scratch said. 'You sound cheap.'

'What did I say?'

'I'm not repeating it,' Scratch replied loftily.

'You said "hell",' said one of the rats.

'You stop it too,' Scratch admonished. 'If I catch you, you'll be sorry.'

'Right, enough!' Noah demanded. 'Everybody stop and be quiet! This is ridiculous. Whoever heard of talking rats?'

At the mention of rats, the rats raced around each other again.

'STOP IT!' Scratch roared.

Everyone, human and rodent, stopped.

'Now,' he continued in a calm voice, 'no one is going to move a muscle even if, and let me make this perfectly clear, even if someone does say "rats".'

He paused to make sure his directive was followed. The rats flinched but they didn't move from the spot.

'Right,' he said to the rat who had spoken first. 'Who are you and what are you doing in my harpsichord?'

'I am Archie,' the rodent said. 'My wife and I live here.'

'How can that be?' Scratch said. 'I have this shop fumigated every year to kill rats and cockroaches.'

'For which we are very grateful,' Archie replied. 'Rats are disgusting creatures.'

'But you are rats,' Scratch pointed out.

'I should say not!' he declared emphatically.

'You look like rats,' Sachin put in.

'To the untrained eye perhaps,' Archie replied haughtily. 'And might I ask, who *you* are and what you are doing here?'

'I am Scratch. This is *my* shop,' he said. 'This is Major Sachin and this is Noah Chord.'

At the mention of Noah's name, the rats – or whatever they were – started whispering animatedly.

'Why is she so interesting, I wonder,' Scratch said.

'It is my natural charm,' Noah declared. 'People find me fascinating.'

'Settle down, Noah. They're not people. They're rats. Rats find you fascinating.'

'Stop saying that,' Archie demanded. 'We are NOT rats.'

'Well, what are you then?'

'Not telling.'

'Why not?'

'Because.'

'Because why?'

'Because we don't like you!'

'Why not?'

'Because you called us rats.'

Scratch threw his hands in the air and walked off.

'Where are you going?' Sachin asked.

'To find something that will eradicate *pseudo*-rats,' he called back over his shoulder.

When Scratch had disappeared into the back of his shop, Noah studied the creatures. They weren't rats. Their ears were too long and they had no tails.

'Hey!'

Noah and Sachin looked at Archie.

'We know who you seek, Major Sachin.'

'Did you just wink at me?' Sachin said.

Archie nodded. 'We know you seek the Descera.'

'Oooohhhh,' Sachin said. 'And what do you know of the Descera?'

'Hold that thought,' Archie said before scampering out over the edge of the harpsichord, closely followed by his wife.

Noah and Sachin craned their necks to see where the pair had gone.

'No peeking,' Archie said from somewhere underneath the instrument.

Noah frowned and looked at Sachin who shrugged. When Noah turned back, two people stood on the other side of the harpsichord.

'Where did *you* come from?' Noah said.

The man said, 'I am Archie and this is my wife, Edwina.'

Noah walked over to the woman.

'I've seen you before,' Noah said. 'My first night here, when I was holding Sachin's flute – I saw you.'

'Yes, Noah,' Edwina replied. 'I made that key – that's why I was able to communicate with you through it. I wanted you to know we were waiting for you.'

'You're the Descera,' Noah said, now noticing the woman's unusual eyes – round and dark.

'Edwina?' Sachin whispered, drawing his flute from a pocket.

Edwina smiled at him and pointed to the flute. 'May I?'

The boy laid the flute across her outstretched hands and watched as she inspected the instrument.

'It has been an age since I held her,' she said, 'and while she bears the scars of those long years, she is as vital now as she ever was.'

Without warning, Sachin threw his arms around the Desceran lady. After a few moments he pulled back, and at a time when the appropriate words seemed impossible to find, Sachin went with the easy option of choosing inappropriate words instead.

'So how *old* are you?' he asked.

Noah imagined what Emir's reaction might have been but Edwina laughed.

'To be truthful, I do not remember,' she said. 'But even if I did, it would mean little to you. We do not measure time the same way you do. But I think we could safely say a good many thousands of your years have passed since I was born.'

'Did you make a key too, Archie?' Noah asked.

Archie shook his head. 'I am not skilled in the making of keys,' he said.

'I don't imagine there's a lot of work around for that skillset,' Noah noted. 'It's quite specific, isn't it?'

'Can you tell us about the 13th key?' Sachin said.

Archie and Edwina looked at each other. A tear ran down the Desceran lady's cheek.

'Our task is almost done, our time almost up,' she said to her husband.

Archie nodded.

'What task?' Sachin asked.

'Our task,' Archie said, with a loving look at his wife, 'is to give Noah a message. When we have fulfilled this task, we can go.'

'Go where?' Noah said.

Sachin nudged Noah with his elbow. In a quiet voice he said, 'He means they are going to die, Noah.'

'Yes,' Edwina said. 'At long last, we will rest. The time of the Descera is at its end.'

Though Noah had only just met them, her heart swelled with sorrow. 'That's terrible,' she whispered.

'Not terrible, Noah,' Edwina said. 'It is long overdue.'

'Are there others?' Sachin asked.

'A few,' Archie said. 'Mostly we live in the deep – haunting the ancient underground cities below Mellifont, Leninstar, Seychelles, Jagar ...'

'Why are there so few of you?' Noah asked.

'Basically because we didn't use the keys properly,' he said. 'The Descera are children of fire, children of lava, born to live underground where the blood of Xan courses through Talisker's veins. The Pyranhi – a race that makes us look young – gifted us firestone with the plans for the twelve keys. We made the keys and with them fashioned our great cities – like Mellifont – where we lived for millennia. But we were so busy building our cities and living our lives that we forgot about Xan and our responsibilities to her. Eventually we realised that the lava was drying up and that if we didn't do something, we would be lost. Despite our efforts, our race declined over many years and when the children of the sun appeared – humans – we gifted the keys to them in the hope that they would make better use of them than we did.'

'Now,' Edwina said to Noah, 'you have returned to Talisker and you have a job to do. You must use the 13th key to rid this world of the evil that threatens it.'

'I don't suppose you have it on you?' Noah asked.

Both Descera shook their heads. 'We don't have it,' Archie said, 'but our message will set you on the path to find it.'

Noah held up her hand and took a deep breath. She pictured her parents' faces. What would they want her to do with the 13th key? If it was so dangerous, maybe it would be a good thing if Orville destroyed it. And if Orville knew her mother, perhaps she'd want Noah to give it to him. It was confusing but not this day's crisis. Since Archie and Edwina didn't have the key, she didn't have to decide what to do with it yet.

'Before we get to the message,' Noah said, 'can I ask a question?'

Edwina smiled. 'Certainly.'

Noah lifted the hem of her top. 'Did either of you give me this?'

'We did not brand you with the mark of the Dragonsbane,' Archie said, 'but our message is from the one who did. You must go to Ironside and seek him out.'

'Him?' Noah said.

'The Descera, Seth,' Archie clarified. 'He awaits you at Dragonhall.'

'Where the Dragonsbane lives?' Noah asked.

'Yes,' Archie said.

'We will go there,' Sachin said.

'Stopping at Seychelles on the way,' Edwina put in.

Sachin's face contorted. 'Seychelles is not "on the way". It's three hundred kilometres north of here and we need to go west to get to Ironside.'

'And yet you must go there,' Archie said. 'You must witness and understand the evil that is happening there.'

'And then to Ironside?' Sachin said.

'And then to Ironside,' Archie confirmed.

Chapter 15

'They should be back by now,' Sachin said as he paced around the living room of their quarters in Mrs Sloane's boarding house.

'You're going to wear a track in the floorboards if you don't stop that,' Noah said, sharing his concern that Emir, Montana and Ardis were late, but not willing to show it.

'And you're making me dizzy,' Chase added, tapping her pen on her notebook.

Noah stroked Raven's head. It wasn't often that he would sit quietly for an extended period with his head resting on her lap. He was anxious too and that bothered Noah.

Patting the seat beside him at the table, Alan said, 'Come and sit with us, Major. Tell us about your trip to Scratch & Denton. I think I really will explode if I have to wait any longer. And anyway, if you start the story, they're bound to turn up.'

'I hope you're right,' Sachin said. He frowned. 'We found the Descera,' he said as he took a seat between Alan and Chase.

'Just like that?' Chase said, shaking her head as she put pen to paper. 'You just walked into the shop and there they were?'

'No,' Sachin admitted. 'They were disguised as rats and hiding in a harpsichord.'

'A harpsichord?' Alan said. 'That would certainly be roomy.'

'I brought it back with me,' Noah said. 'Look.'

Noah opened a pocket for Chase.

'Is that it? The 13th key?' Chase asked dubiously as she peered into Noah's pocket, inspecting the miniaturised harpsichord inside.

'No,' Noah said.

'Thank goodness for that,' she said.

'Why do you say that?' Noah asked.

'Well, you can't find it yet,' Chase replied.

'Why not?'

'No suspense,' Chase said. 'It's a necessary literary plot device. It's going to be a crap story if you find the key so – ouch!' She turned to Sachin. 'What did you do that for?'

Noah smirked as the budding author rubbed her stinging arm.

'Girls of today,' Sachin said, shaking his head. 'Such potty mouths. It's shocking.'

Chase looked imploringly at Noah. 'What did I say?'

'I'm not repeating it,' Noah said. 'I've been slapped once today already.'

'Right,' Chase said at length. 'Well, if it's not the key, why did you take it?'

'I just liked it,' Noah said, 'and besides, we have the same last name.'

'Are they still in there?' Alan said.

At a quizzical look from Noah, he said, 'The Descera. Sachin said they were disguised as rats and hiding in the harpsichord.'

Sachin shook his head. 'No. They're … gone.'

'Gone where?' Alan asked as Chase put pen to paper.

'They've … passed on,' Sachin said. 'They've been waiting for Noah to come so they could give her a message. And now that they've done that …'

Alan's eyes shone. 'What message?'

'We need to go to Ironside,' Noah said, 'to see the Descera, Seth. He will be able to tell us about the 13th key.'

'Ironside,' Alan said, rubbing his hands together. 'That is going to be awesome! I wonder what the Dragonsbane would think about my theory that numbers underpin the music of our world. Her knowledge would be—'

The door swung open and a hooded figure slipped through the doorway. Noah and her companions at the table stood up as Emir closed and locked the door behind him. He turned and pushed back his hood.

'We need to leave now,' he said.

'What happened to your face?' Sachin said.

'The king's guards found us.'

Emir's face looked like a well-used painter's palette. Smudges of purple and blue and grey and yellow intermingled as the bruising developed, streaked with gashes of red.

'Montana?' Sachin said. 'Where's Montana?'

'Leaving the city already,' Emir said without emotion. 'Ardis is escorting her. But we need to leave too. It's not safe here.'

♫♫

Their new hideout was a small hut a day's ride out of Leninstar. They'd ridden hard during the night to put some distance between themselves and the royal city. Sachin was keen to keep moving but Emir had advised a twenty-four-hour rest stop to throw any pursuit. He'd suggested that the guards would not expect them to stop so soon. With luck, anyone following would overtake them.

Noah sat amongst the fabrics and sewing paraphernalia that Chase had unpacked for her.

'Are you going to do something other than toy with those fine fabrics?' Chase asked.

Noah frowned. 'Give me a break. I'm thinking.'

'About what?'

'About what to cut out next,' she replied absently.

'Liar,' Chase said.

'Pardon?'

'Liar,' Chase repeated. 'You've got a pile of great sketches there,' she pointed, indicating a pile of papers behind Noah, 'but you need to pick one up and *get started*.'

'Yeah, yeah.'

Noah continued to sit and finger an elaborate piece of rust-coloured brocade. This was partly what she'd come to Talisker for – the chance to source unique fabrics for her collection – but her journey so far wasn't as she'd imagined it. Things had become complicated and confusing. There were so many questions she wanted to ask her parents. Noah looked at her hand where her mother's ring had been. She missed wearing it but she understood why Sachin had told her to remove it. Wearing an Academy ring drew unwanted attention.

Chase went to Noah's pile of sketches and rifled through them.

'The boys will be gone for hours,' Chase said. 'Without distractions, if we knuckle down, we could have all the pattern templates done by the end of the day.'

The only male still inside the hut was Raven who dozed fitfully in the corner. Emir, Sachin and Alan were tending to the horses and patrolling the area.

Noah picked up the sketch on top of the pile; a suit for the men's formal-wear category. It wasn't one of her preferred categories. Suits were so mundane – usually. While her design differed little from what she might have done back home, the fabrics here opened up exciting possibilities for her. She'd never dreamt of using silk and corduroy in combination but the weaves here brought themselves to life in her mind. Pushing aside thoughts of having to bully Emir into being her model, she started drawing her pattern templates.

Once she'd started she worked for a solid eight hours, barely lifting her eyes from her work. At some point Chase had delivered her dinner. Later she noticed the plate had disappeared although she couldn't remember what she'd had. Sachin, Emir and Alan had returned at dusk but Noah had ignored them and kept working. Chase seemed more than happy to play hostess for which Noah was grateful. Sachin had set up a light for her so she could keep working into the night.

'Noah,' Sachin said.

She looked up from her work as Sachin placed a cup of water in front of her.

'Thanks,' she said, surprised by the fact that the Major was waiting on her. Suddenly realising how hungry she was, she said, 'I don't suppose there's anything to eat?'

'Still hungry?'

'Famished actually,' she said.

'Hmmm,' Sachin said. 'I suspected as much. I don't think *you* had your dinner. I suspect Raven enjoyed the dried beef though.'

Noah smiled, unsurprised. 'He does like dried beef.'

'I'll get you some while Emir gives you your present,' he said.

'Present?'

Grimacing in pain, Emir reached into one of the pockets on his trousers. He still carried his wounds from yesterday's encounter with the king's guards and Sachin was unwilling to risk using raiki to heal them. The king's guards would be out looking for them. If anyone heard the music, they'd be captured for sure. It was also why there was only dried beef for dinner. Sachin wouldn't risk a fire.

With difficulty, Emir pulled a sewing machine out of his pocket and placed it in front of Noah on the small table.

'That is so cool,' Chase said, hovering at Noah's elbow as Emir found the treadle to attach to it. 'It looks like one my grandmother had. The one I learned to sew on.' Chase sighed. 'I spent hours pushing that pedal for Nana while she sewed the most beautiful clothes. Truth be known she'd rather have worked the treadle herself but I just loved to be part of her sewing.'

Noah looked at Emir. 'Thank you,' she said. 'That's very thoughtful.'

'I believe it is a necessary tool,' he said.

'Do you like it?' Sachin said from the other end of the hut where he rummaged through a bag for the dinner supplies.

'Yes, thank you,' Noah called back.

'Are you going to start sewing tonight?' Emir asked.

'Yes,' Noah said, keen to give the machine a run, 'but I'll stop when you all want to go to sleep.'

'Sew for as long as you like,' Emir said. 'Apparently it's very quiet. We won't hear a thing.'

Sachin brought Noah dinner which she accepted enthusiastically. She really was ravenous. Raven crawled over to lie at her feet.

'No,' she said. 'You've had yours. This is mine.'

He whined in protest but it got him nowhere.

'Alan, Raven,' Sachin said, 'bedtime. The girls have got work to do. Emir, first guard shift.'

As the boys dossed down on their swags around the inner walls of the single-room hut, Noah selected the first pieces that needed sewing.

Chase was almost beside herself. 'Can I thread it for you?' she asked.

'Go for your life,' Noah said. 'Navy blue if you don't mind.'

'Suit first?'

Noah nodded as she started pinning the first pieces together. Chase hummed to herself as she worked. Noah wondered if she'd always hummed. It was something she'd never have known about her friend if they hadn't come to Talisker. Noah listened contently for the next hour until Chase fell asleep at the table.

Noah nudged her gently. 'Chase,' she said, 'go and grab a couple of hours' sleep.'

'I think I will,' Chase replied. 'I'll be back.'

As Chase settled herself on her swag, Noah kept sewing. No one stirred. The machine was so quiet it was eerie. Sometime in the wee hours of the morning she was ready for a model. To her surprise she found Emir sitting quietly in the corner.

'Have you slept?' Noah asked.

'No,' he said as he stood up, wincing as he did so. 'Chase said you'd need a model. I wasn't sure when you'd be ready. I decided just to wait,' he said.

'Oh,' Noah said. 'Thanks.'

He walked over to where Noah was working.

'I imagine riding with those injuries was pretty painful,' she said.

'Yeah, I've had more fun,' Emir admitted. 'What do you need tried on?'

'Shirt.'

Noah handed him the garment.

'I'm going to need some help. I've got a couple of cracked ribs,' he said. 'I can't get this off …'

She helped him out of his shirt, having to stand on a block of timber to do so. Unlike his heavily tattooed arms, his torso was devoid of artwork. However, there was presently an impressive array of welts, bruises and cuts.

'I'm sorry about this,' Noah said as she pulled the shirt over his head.

He shrugged. 'Needs to be done.'

It did, Noah knew. She got right to work, pinning here and there.

'I'm glad you started with the top rather than trousers, though,' Emir said.

She looked up at him. He smirked lamely at her. She returned a weak smile.

'Me too,' she said honestly.

What a time for him to start joking around, she thought as she pinned the side seams. He'd been the ice man from day one. Why he'd decided to lighten up now was beyond Noah.

'Do you need me to lift my arms?' he asked.

'I can work around it,' she mumbled through a mouthful of pins.

'I can manage,' he said, raising his left arm without warning.

As Noah had chosen that moment to change position, he collected her in the eye with his hand.

'Ouch,' she exclaimed, more in shock than in pain.

'Oh, I'm sorry,' he said. 'Are you okay?'

As he bent down to see if she was alright, Noah stood up – head-butting him in the process.

Emir grunted.

'What is going *on*?'

It was Alan. The kerfuffle had woken him.

'Nothing,' Emir said, dabbing blood from his lip.

Alan looked from him to Noah, who was still clutching her eye.

'Doesn't look like nothing,' he said. 'Perhaps I can help? I could be your model?'

Even with the 13th key Noah didn't think Alan could be turned into model material but she knew it would be rude to say so.

'If you could help Emir,' she said, 'that'd be great.'

'I've actually had modelling experience,' Alan said.

'Oh yes?' Noah said.

'You might recall that I like to knit,' Alan said. 'I had a request one year to present a range of knitted garments to the House of Wind. It was a roaring success and I must say, I really enjoyed the modelling gig.'

'You modelled a beanie and scarf,' Emir said.

Alan beamed with pride.

'Which I'm sure were lovely,' Noah said, 'but if we could get this shirt pinned? I'm really tired …'

'Of course, of course,' Alan said.

With Noah giving instructions and Alan coordinating Emir's arm movements, the necessary pinning was achieved quickly and without further incident. To Noah's relief, Alan attended to Emir's undressing and redressing while she tidied up her chattels.

'Now get some sleep you two,' Alan said. 'There are only a few hours until dawn and we have a long and dangerous ride ahead of us.'

♪♫

'Horses everyone,' Emir said.

The cabin emptied in seconds. Noah had all her possessions packed safely in the pockets of her trousers. When Alan had issued her the pants, they'd had only one pocket. Now there were dozens. Her harpsichord was in one, her sewing machine in another. All her sketches were safely stored, as were her pattern templates and fabrics. Even her school bag was tucked away.

'Do you hear something?' Chase said as Noah settled herself in the saddle.

'Sounds like horses,' Noah said.

'It is horses,' Sachin said quietly as the mounted group drew together.

A bird whistle broke the dawn quiet and Sachin relaxed visibly. Within moments, Montana arrived with four riders.

'High Priestess!' Sachin said. 'What news?'

Montana's four soldiers took their places around her. Noah looked at Chase who beamed when she saw Ardis among them.

'Orville has left Leninstar for Seychelles,' Montana said. 'That is where they are generating the electricity. He must have concerns about the project if he's going there personally.'

'How far is it from Seychelles to Leninstar City?' Noah asked.

'About three hundred kilometres,' Emir replied.

'Why generate the electricity so far away?' Chase said.

'It's a strategic point,' Emir explained. 'There are many underground cities across Talisker, thanks to the Descera, and they are linked by a comprehensive tunnel system. Seychelles is the point where tunnels from all seven royal cities converge. King Tambian wants to show his fellow kings that he can generate electricity in Seychelles and then run it through wires in the existing tunnel system to Leninstar City. If he can do this, then the wiring could be run to the other cities as well. He wants them to support his initiative and get involved in it.'

'And contribute to the cost,' Montana added.

'Yes,' Emir said.

Alan frowned. 'There are hundreds of kilometres to cover,' he said. 'Aside from the cost of the wiring and the logistics of installing it all, they'd need a lot of booster stations.' His eyes widened, like a child standing in front of a wall of games and sweets.

'You can do all the calculations as we ride,' Emir said. 'We need to get going.'

'Where are we going?' Montana asked.

'To Seychelles,' Sachin said.

The High Priestess shook her head as though she'd misheard him. 'Seychelles? Did you not hear what I just said? Orville is on his way there now.'

'Yes,' Sachin said, 'but it is where the Descera said Noah must go.'

'You've seen the Descera?' Montana said.

Noah and Sachin nodded.

'Well,' Montana said. 'That *is* interesting. Where did you see them?'

Nudging his horse into motion with his heels, Sachin said, 'We'll fill you in on the way.'

Chapter 16

Noah peered through the sparse canopy at the mountain range that loomed above her. 'I can see why the Descera went underground,' she said. 'That'd be a bugger to climb.'

'Indeed,' Emir said as he dismounted.

'There will be goblins,' Sachin said. 'We must be careful.'

Butterflies stirred in Noah's stomach. She wished Raven and Chase were here. She knew they were safer where they were and that was some consolation, but she could have done with the moral support.

Turning to Sachin, Noah said, 'I don't suppose there's any chance that you'd half kill me again now, is there?'

'No,' Sachin said flatly.

'I thought not,' Noah said, 'but it was worth a try.'

'The Descera are right,' Sachin said. 'If we're going to bring down this network, we need to know how it works. The only way to do that is to get inside and see it.'

'It's a great theory,' Noah conceded. 'My only problem is that if we don't make it out alive …' She left her sentence unfinished.

'Well, let's just make sure we do,' Sachin said. 'Now shush, there'll be goblins at the entrance and we need to surprise them to neutralise them.'

Neutralise, Noah thought, failing to suppress a shudder. After their encounter with goblins in the forest, she didn't like them, yet the thought of killing things made her squeamish.

Emir drew his sword and took the lead. Sachin fell in behind and motioned for Noah to follow him. She took great care with each step on the rocky path, not wanting to draw attention with the sound of rocks grinding underfoot. Though it took only a few minutes to reach the entranceway it felt a lot longer than that to Noah.

When they reached the iron gate that marked the entrance to the ancient underground city, they found two goblins lying on the ground, blood still seeping from gashes across their throats.

From behind them a voice said, 'Lower your sword, soldier. You are safe for now.'

Before Noah could spin around, Emir shoved her aside.

'Who are you?' he demanded.

'Emir,' Sachin said urgently, 'they are Descera. Lower your sword.'

Emir hesitated only a moment before putting his sword in its sheath. He nodded to the two male Descera before him. 'I meant no offence,' he said.

'None taken,' said the Descera on the left. 'I am Benji and this is Saul. We are the last guardians of Seychelles.'

Noah nodded. 'Archie and Edwina said there were still Descera who guarded the ancient cities.'

Saul smiled. 'Archie and Edwina advised us that you were coming, Noah. We will ensure you see what you need to see here before you go to Ironside to meet Seth.'

'And this is your last task?' Noah asked.

It was Benji's turn to smile. 'Yes, Noah. This is our last task. Now let's move'—he pointed to the corpses—'before reinforcements arrive.'

Benji pushed open the gate and Saul strode through. Benji motioned for them to follow. As the darkness of the underground swallowed them up, Noah held her breath.

'We will give you light,' Saul assured her.

Noah noticed the faint light around the Descera and felt a little better.

'This city is old, very old,' Benji said as they entered the tunnel. 'There is still an active lava vein under the city. Can you feel it, Noah?'

'I feel something,' she said softly.

'The lava is the blood of the dragon,' Benji said. 'That is the dragon-song you can feel.'

In the lava's music Noah heard an ancient song – a lullaby of primordial times. The sonorous melody was of a more vital time, long in the past, when Xan first slept. She could tell the song wasn't what it once was. She could pick where the music was fraying. Though the lava was waning – its pulse weaker now – the music still compelled her. As the song swam around her, Noah marvelled at how her own music blended with that of the lava. She drifted along with the melody as she walked, excited at what she could sense.

'Orville and his wizards are using the dragonsong in the lava to make the electricity,' Saul said. 'We will show you where this happens.'

'I thought they used blood magic,' Noah said.

'They do,' Saul replied. 'They use musical instruments like the adepts do, but they use blood rather than firestone to *enhance* the music – to give it its power.'

'There is a staircase coming up,' Benji said. 'It will take us deep into the city. It is narrow, steep and long. You must take care.'

'Right,' Noah said. 'Take care on the stairs. Got it.'

By the time they reached the bottom of the staircase, Noah was almost too dizzy and exhausted to chastise Benji but she dug deep.

'You need to work on your safety briefing,' Noah said, breathlessly. 'That was *torture.*'

'It is on this level of the city that the wizards perform their magic,' Saul said. 'That staircase is one they don't use. *We* use it so we don't run into any of them.'

Noah nodded as she massaged her aching quadriceps. 'Where to now?'

'Follow me,' Saul said.

With Sachin and Emir, Noah followed the Descera along another tunnel.

'The dragonsong is getting stronger,' Noah said.

'We are close,' Saul replied.

They walked for several minutes in silence before Sachin said, 'I hear the music of the wizards.'

'And it's getting really hot in here,' Noah added.

Benji turned and nodded, putting his finger over his lips. He walked only another few dozen steps before putting up his hand again, this time to signal a halt. Beyond the next turn, light was visible. Noah stopped, crouching behind a rocky outcrop. Emir and Sachin took a position on either side of her. They all looked up.

Even the grandeur of Mellifont had not prepared Noah for this. The cavernous interior of the mountain seemed to spiral away into the heavens. The ceiling – if indeed there was one – was so high overhead that Noah couldn't see it. A metal pylon, like a compass needle, protruded from ground level and disappeared into the darkness high above. Tier upon tier encircled the cavern and stretched away above them. And on each one, were statues. Hundreds of them. Statues of the Descera, looking down, bearing witness to the work of Orville and his wizards. Noah followed their frozen stares.

A huge, circular pit in the floor was surrounded by a brick wall – about three metres high – with open vents that gave a glimpse of the fiery lava inside. A metal dome sat atop the brick balustrade and the metal spire protruded from its top. Flashes of blue light, like lightning, crackled around the dome, dancing to the tune of the thirteen wizards that sat around the circumference of the wall, each with a musical instrument in hand. The music they played was clearly audible even over the roar of the lava and the crackling of the electricity.

Saul tapped Noah on the shoulder and pointed across to the right of the cavern. She looked to where he pointed. A wooden trough protruded from the wall on the second tier and sloped down to almost meet with one of the vents on top of the brick wall. A trickle of blood flowed from the lip of the trough into the lava.

'The blood is what powers the wizards' spell,' Saul whispered into her ear. 'Can you see the conduits further up?'

Thankful to look away from the blood trough, Noah looked up. She saw a pipe leading from the central column away to the left of the cavern.

'I see it,' Noah said.

'That is the wiring that will go to Leninstar City,' Saul said. 'There are tunnels from here to all the capital cities in Talisker. Only one pipeline has been built so far – the one to Leninstar.'

'So we need to destroy all this,' Noah said.

'Not today,' Saul said.

Noah stared at him. 'Why not? We're here! We might as well.'

Saul shook his head. 'We are not enough,' he said. 'And besides, if the adepts can find a supply of firestone, this facility will be very useful. We want to undermine the *way* the electricity is being generated – not electricity itself.'

Before Noah could reply, a sword tip protruded from Saul's chest. The Descera's eyes widened as blood spurted from him. As Noah fell backwards in shock, two arms slipped under her armpits and wrenched her to her feet.

'Let me go!' she cried, struggling against her unseen captor.

'Noah, how lovely of you to join us.'

Noah turned her head. Orville smiled at her.

'I have been trying to catch those Descera for months now,' he said. 'It's nice to finally be rid of them.'

Benji and Saul lay motionless at her feet. To her horror she could also sense their blood as it oozed across the dirt floor. She looked left and then right. Sachin and Emir struggled in vain against the goblins that held them. Her stomach clenched in revulsion as she struggled to block an image of what held her.

'Major Sachin,' Orville said. 'I hope, when I return you to the king's jail, that you will do me the honour of staying there this time.'

'Don't count on it,' Sachin said.

'Well, I think you'll have more difficulty breaking out of the king's dungeon in Leninstar,' Orville said. 'I expect you to be a good boy and sit in a cell for three weeks and stay out of my way until the Solstice Festival.'

'We're here to kill you,' Emir said bluntly.

As Orville smiled, Noah wondered how a man of such ill-repute could be so handsome.

'You should have made an appointment, Emir,' he said. 'Today is not really good for me. I still have a lot of work to do. And anyway, I need *you* to look after Noah.'

'I don't need looking after,' Noah said.

'You've got a hectic schedule,' Orville said. 'What with finding the 13th key for me and putting together your Solstice collection ...'

'Even *if* she finds the 13th key, she's not giving it to you,' Emir said.

Orville smiled at Noah. 'We'll see,' he said.

Noah's heart beat faster. It probably wasn't a good idea to give it to him, but could she use it as leverage to find out more about her parents?

'Noah,' Orville said, 'did you make that top you're wearing?'

Caught off guard by the change in topic, Noah reflexively said, 'Yes.'

'I like it,' he said. 'While you are working on your Solstice collection, you will design something fabulous for me to wear to the gala event.'

'*What!*'

'I need something absolutely magnificent to wear to the Festival – something completely out-of-this-world. I'm sure you can come up with something fitting.'

'As far as I'm aware, she doesn't make coffins,' Emir said.

Orville gave Emir the same long-suffering look Noah's English teacher, Mr Brennan, had inflicted on her many times. '*I* make the jokes around here,' Orville said.

'Where is that blood coming from?' Noah said, looking towards the chute.

'A storage tank,' Orville said.

'And how does it get into the storage tank?'

'Donations,' he said, running a hand through his wilful hair. 'Look. This is all completely legal. The king has passed a law validating the use of blood magic and a law requiring that convicted criminals compulsorily donate all their blood for the good of humanity. This facility here is legitimate.'

'Donate all their blood?' Sachin echoed. 'So you're slaughtering them here too?'

'It is easier to transport the blood here in bodies rather than barrels,' Orville said.

'It's a slaughterhouse,' Noah said in disgust.

'Blood collection facility,' Orville corrected her. 'The blood we collect here will power the new technology for the kingdom. Thanks to me the people of Talisker will have electricity, factories and cars – the things on Earth that people here crave. And all powered by blood. Power from the people, for the people.'

'How do these people even know about Earth technology?' Noah said.

'I told them,' he said smugly. 'Create a demand and then fill the supply.'

'How do *you* know about Earth technology?' Noah asked.

'You'd be surprised at what I know, Noah,' he said with a wink. 'Anyway, they have very little here in the way of natural resources so blood is the obvious choice.'

When no one responded, Orville continued.

'But that's not the whole story. This isn't really about electricity at all. It's about world domination. With this blood stock I intend to destroy this world.'

He paused, presumably for effect.

'Well, if you destroy the world, you're not going to be dominating it for very long, are you?' Emir said.

'True,' he said, 'but I don't need to. I just want the dragon.'

'You *just* want the dragon?' Sachin said.

'Why are you telling us all this?' Noah asked.

'Why?' Orville said. 'Because I think genius should not go unappreciated.'

'And?' Noah prompted.

Orville smiled as he stroked his chin. 'And ... if you deliver the 13th key to me and help me achieve my goal, Noah – I will let you live.'

'You will get the 13th key over my dead body,' Sachin said.

Orville looked down at the diminutive Major. 'Probably,' he replied. 'But for now, we all have a job to do. Sachin, I'm sending you back to Leninstar City where you will stay in the dungeon until the Solstice. Emir, you are now Noah's chaperone. You will protect her while she hunts for the 13th key. Noah, when you *find* the 13th key, you will bring it to me. In the meantime, I will get this electricity network operating to keep King Tambian happy. Any questions?'

No one spoke.

'Good,' Orville said. To the goblins, he said, 'Get them out of here.'

♪♪

The evening campfire was a sombre affair. Dinner was done and Noah, Chase, Emir, Ardis and Alan sat around the crackling fire. The goblins had attacked the safe-house while Noah, Sachin and Emir had been in Seychelles. Two of Montana's guards were dead and after hearing about the slaughter of prisoners in Seychelles, the High Priestess had taken one of her remaining warriors back to the facility to try to save some of the condemned. She'd left Ardis to help Emir escort the rest of the group to Ironside. But Noah's biggest problem was Raven. He'd gone missing in the melee.

'May I say something about Raven?' Ardis said.

Instantly wary, Noah eyeballed him across the campfire. Given the injuries Raven had inflicted on him, Noah had good reason to suspect that Ardis might not paint her beloved canine in the most favourable light.

'That would depend on what you wanted to say,' she said.

'Let him speak, Noah,' Chase said. 'It'll be fine.'

'As long as you're not going to try to make a joke about him being a pain in the behind, go ahead,' Noah said.

Ardis shook his head. 'I think this is not a time for joking,' he said. 'Raven is a loyal companion. He is a brave and fierce fighter and he is clever. Aside from his inability to wield a sword, he is a fine warrior. I hope I get to fight alongside him someday.'

'Is?' Alan said. 'Don't you mean was?'

Tears blurred Noah's vision, but not before she caught Emir's withering look at Alan.

Possibly to stop Alan talking again, Ardis said, 'How did he come to be your companion?'

Noah shook her head as a hot lump lodged in her throat. 'I can't,' she whispered.

'You can,' Chase said softly. 'Please.'

Noah took a steadying breath. Her parents had told her the story many times because Noah had asked to hear it so many times. But she'd never actually told the story herself before.

'According to my parents,' she began, 'I was a fussy baby. I didn't sleep well. One particular night when I was only a few months old, my mother was lying in bed listening to the baby monitor. She heard scratching noises in my room. Thinking there were rats, she jumped out of bed to investigate. Unfortunately, she got her foot tangled in the bed sheet and tripped over. She'd actually broken her wrist but she didn't find that out until later.

'She went to my room and turned on the light, expecting to see rodents scurrying around but there was nothing. The scratching had stopped. She looked everywhere but couldn't find anything. No rats, no nothing. Mum decided that her wrist needed attention so I was bundled up for a trip to the hospital. But when Mum and Dad opened the front door they got the fright of their lives. There was this *thing* sitting on the veranda. At first they thought it was a giant rat – they had rats on the brain obviously – but they realised pretty quickly that it was actually a puppy. But Mum was cranky by then. Her wrist was really sore.

'She yelled at the puppy to shoo him away, and then went on to the hospital to get her wrist set. It was nearly sunrise by the time we got back home again and there was no sign of the puppy. By then they'd figured that he was the one they'd heard scratching – trying to get into my room from the veranda.

'So they put me back in my cot and went back to bed. When Mum woke up later and went to my room to check on me she found the puppy asleep in the cot with me, curled up at my feet. Once she'd checked to see that I was alive she went to fetch my father. When he picked up the dog, it whimpered and I started to cry. Dad put the dog back in the cot, the dog went back to sleep and so did I.

'They put ads in the paper and pinned up notices in the local stores to see if anyone had lost a puppy but they got no response. They tried keeping him outside – Mum didn't like the idea of a dog inside the house, let alone sleeping in my cot – but he scratched at the doors until they let him in. We've been together ever since.'

Noah wished she could have said the same thing about her parents. She dragged her mind back to the present. Chase was scribbling in her journal.

'Chase you can't be serious! Tell me you're not writing this down,' Noah said.

'Are you kidding? It's great backstory. Fate brought you two together. This kind of detail is important in a novel, Noah.'

Noah closed her eyes for a moment and then looked at her friend. 'I hope *your* story turns out better than this one.'

'What do you mean?' Chase asked.

'Well, this one is going to hell in a handbasket at the moment, isn't it? It's hard to imagine things could get any worse. Raven's gone. Sachin's gone. How are we supposed to find the 13th key without Sachin?'

'We go to Ironside,' Emir said, 'just like the Descera said … and we go from there.'

'We've only got three weeks,' Noah said.

Emir's face was grim. 'Jagar is two days' ride from here. We will charter a boat to Ironside. While we're in Jagar, you girls can do whatever shopping you need to do to finish your collection. Once we've been to Ironside, we'll reassess and plot our next move.'

'What about the Dragonsbane?' Noah said. 'We know we're looking for the Descera, Seth, but what am I supposed to do about the Dragonsbane?'

Emir looked at her. 'Do about her?'

'I'm supposed to take her job. That could be awkward,' Noah said. 'And what is her name again?'

'Ursula,' Emir said. 'The Dragonsbane's name is Ursula.'

Noah thought about the flaming rocks and the message the Dragonsbane had sent her on her first night in Talisker. *Noah Chord beware.* Beware. Anger surged through Noah. Her beloved Alsatian was gone. She feared nothing now.

'I think Ursula had best beware,' Noah said. In the silence that followed, she added, 'If you'll excuse me, I'm going to turn in.'

Chase put her arm around her. 'It's going to be okay, Noah,' she said. 'Not for me,' she said. 'Not unless Raven comes back.'

Noah left her companions at the fire and crawled into her swag. She lay on her back, studying the stars. The day after tomorrow they'd be in Jagar. She'd be able to shop and hopefully make progress on her collection. The Solstice Festival, featuring Orville's farcical fashion extravaganza to select a successor for the king's late tailor, was now only twenty days away. She had a lot of work to do. Reviewing her collection in her mind for the umpteenth time, Noah made a mental list of things she needed to purchase in Jagar.

When she could think of nothing else to add to her list, Noah closed her eyes. She focused on her breathing – the feel of it, the sound of it. Gradually she relaxed. She let her mind drift through her inner catalogue of all the things she'd seen since arriving on Talisker – some things beautiful, some not. The majesty of Mellifont shone against a backdrop of darkness – the evil forest, the grom, goblins and the firestorm. But it was the people Noah found more problematic. With Montana as the exception, the supposed "good guys" were difficult to get along with – Sachin was precocious, Emir was aloof and humourless, Alan was nauseating and Brinn was haughty. Ardis had a category all his own. Though he tried to be pleasant, Noah just couldn't warm to someone who'd tried to skewer her on a sword. And why was the ultimate "bad guy" – who clearly *was* bad, as evidenced by the atrocities at Seychelles – so charismatic?

She moved on, not allowing her mind to dwell on any one thing too long. She thought of the harpsichord she'd procured from Scratch & Denton. That had been quite the experience. Archie and Edwina had seemed a lovely couple but now they were gone, as were Saul and Benji. The Descera – children of fire, who'd made the twelve keys that the Majors used to keep the world in order – were almost all gone.

Emptying her head of all thoughts, Noah tuned in to the music around her. As she listened, testing her perceptions here and there, she found Emir nearby. She couldn't see him but she could sense his musical signature.

'You don't have to spy on me,' she said.

'I'm guarding you,' he said without moving.

'I don't need guarding,' she replied.

Without being able to see him, Noah knew he had shrugged in response.

'And don't shrug at me,' she snapped.

'Fine,' he said, standing up. 'Yell if you need anything.'

Once she was sure he was back at the campfire, Noah let her senses collapse into the ground beneath her. Someone had seen fit to protect her hearing so Noah tried to put it to good use. To her surprise it was easier than she thought. Tunnels of various sizes snaked and twisted throughout the ground under her. This world was far from solid. Some tunnels connected the subterranean cities of Talisker, others carried lava – the blood of the dragon. As the stars made their way across the sky, Noah marvelled at the underground network carved out by the ancient race and it galled her that Orville had defiled Seychelles with his macabre facility. He was clever. The Solstice Festival celebrations provided the perfect smokescreen for his ultimate plan. It was difficult to see how to stop him.

Chapter 17

Noah and Chase had scoured the Jagar markets all day.

'We should get going,' Chase said. 'If we're gone too long the others will worry.'

'Yep, almost done,' Noah replied as she handed over two dinah for some translucent beads.

She thanked the stallholder and stashed her latest acquisition in one of the five bags she now had. 'Right,' she said to Chase, 'that's the end of our pocket money. Let's go.'

The two girls made their way out of the crowded bazaar and onto the main street. Horse-drawn carriages whizzed up and down the street. At least Noah was able to walk alongside the goat lane now without staring. Horses and carriages had the run of the centre section of the road with the goat lane being closest to the footpath. Although it was called the goat lane, it was in fact dedicated to any small, four-legged beast that needed to travel through the city. There were no refrigerated trucks on Talisker so meat had to bring itself into town.

A young girl with golden ringlets streaming from a high ponytail skipped up to Noah.

'Are you Noah Chord?' she blurted.

Without breaking stride Noah said, 'No.'

'Are you sure?' the girl said.

'Very sure,' Noah said firmly.

'Well, I reckon you are,' she said, 'so I'm going to give you this note. It's from my aunty.'

The girl – who could not have been more than nine or ten – stuffed something into one of Noah's parcels. Her mission accomplished she said, 'Okay, bye,' and skipped off up the street.

Chase frowned. 'We need to get back to the others.'

Noah nodded but said nothing.

Noah's stomach churned. If a young girl could pick her in a crowded place it wasn't going to take much for Orville's minions to find her. She forced herself to walk more slowly and then she laughed out loud. At her side, Chase nearly jumped out of her skin.

'What are you—?'

'Work with me here,' Noah whispered. And then in a louder voice, she said, 'And you wouldn't *believe* what he did next, Ellie. It was *unbelievable!*'

Ever the fictioneer, Chase, fell into character.

'Well, don't hold out on me,' she said effusively. 'Tell me, what did he do next?'

'He emptied the ice-bucket over her head!'

Chase's eyes widened but not in a good way.

'What's an ice-bucket?' she said.

Noah winced. They didn't have ice-buckets here. They didn't have ice. They didn't have freezers. So much for being inconspicuous.

'*Rice* bucket,' Noah gushed. 'I said *rice bucket*. Who ever heard of an ice-bucket?'

'Oh, of course. A rice bucket. Silly me. Need my ears cleaned out,' Chase said.

'I should say so,' Noah said.

They walked the rest of the way back to the boarding house in silence.

'I've not heard of a rice bucket either,' Ardis said dubiously when Chase related the story to him.

'Well, that was the best I could do on such short notice,' Noah said defensively. 'Now be quiet, I'm trying to listen.'

In her hand she held the swatch of fabric that the girl in the street had stuffed into her bag. Many of the Taliskeran fabrics she'd explored sang to her but this one was different. Very different. And Noah was having difficulty nailing down what set this particular fabric apart from the others. It was white – it had little going for it in the visual appeal department – but there was much more to it than that. With so much background noise though, it was hard for her to focus. The situation was not improved by Emir and Alan's return.

'Successful trip?' Chase asked.

'Yes,' Alan said. 'The boat is booked. We leave at dawn.'

'Tomorrow?' Noah asked.

'Yes, tomorrow,' Emir said shortly. 'Is that a problem?'

She handed him the swatch. 'I need to get some more of this.'

'Why didn't you get it while you were out?'

Noah quickly explained how she'd come by the sample.

'I don't like it,' Emir said. 'It sounds like a trap.'

'I know how it sounds and I agree with you but … this fabric is special. Really special. There are easier ways to lure people into a trap than to create a fabric like this.'

Emir held her gaze for a moment. 'We will go now then.'

Chase jumped up.

'Not you,' Emir said to her. 'You stay here with Ardis and Alan.'

She sat down obediently.

'Would you mind doing some sewing while I'm gone?' Noah said.

'My pleasure,' Chase said, beaming.

Noah and Emir walked several blocks before locating the address on the business card that had been attached to the swatch.

'You're sure this is the place?' Emir asked doubtfully.

Noah held up the business card. 'According to this, it is,' Noah said as they walked up to the door. 'The Purring Pussy. It's a shame Brinn isn't here, she'd probably like this place. I wonder where she is …'

'I couldn't say,' Emir replied. 'But I'd venture, wherever she is, she's probably very pleased she's not here.'

'You're probably right,' Noah said. 'I don't think cats are capable of having a good time.'

Emir gave her a sideways look.

'What?' Noah said.

'Never mind,' he replied. 'Let's just get this over with.'

'What is your problem? You look like a man who's about to get a prostate check. Relax. It's just shopping.'

'Right,' he said. 'Just stay close, okay?'

'Okay,' she said, opening the door.

The young girl from the market appeared. 'Hi, Noah,' she said cheerily. 'My aunty is expecting you. Come on through.'

She skipped off. As Noah and Emir followed her, Noah wished that she could stop and inspect the lavish furnishings of the reception area more closely. It was unlike any fabric shop she had ever been in. Past the reception area snaked a winding staircase. Noah mounted the stairs, admiring the ornately carved, dark mahogany handrails. The staircase ended at a T intersection where the youngster took a left turn.

Gold doors lined the blue carpeted hallway they walked down. It reminded Noah of a hotel. The layout was even more unusual than that of Bibs & Bobs. When they reached the end of the hallway, the girl knocked on the last door on the right.

A woman's voice said, 'Enter.'

They did so and found a woman with so many wrinkles that she could have pulled up her socks by raising her eyebrows. Thin as a whip she stood as tall as Noah but her extravagant beehive hairstyle added an extra foot.

'Thank you, Melody. You may run along and play now.'

'Thank you, Aunty Scilly,' she said and scampered back out the door.

'Welcome, my dear Noah,' she gushed once the youngster was gone. She extended a hand heavily laden with rings. 'So glad you could make it. I'm Madame Priscilla.'

Noah accepted the proffered hand and bowed. She hadn't realised she'd be dealing with someone of rank.

'Thank you for the invitation, Madame,' she said politely. 'This is my friend, Emir.'

Given their tumultuous history, it felt strange to introduce Emir as her friend but one had to be polite.

'Your friend, indeed,' Madame Priscilla said, eyeing him up and down. 'If you ever need work I could squeeze you in here,' she said, winking at him.

'Not a chance,' he replied stiffly.

Emir could be so rude. Considering how often he'd lectured Major Sachin on appropriate behaviour, Noah thought Emir was a bit of a hypocrite. Thankfully Madame Priscilla just smiled.

'So you've come about the fabric?' she said.

'Yes, Madame,' Noah said.

'What did you think of it?'

Aware that the negotiations had now begun Noah chose her words carefully.

'It has a nice feel to it but it's rather plain to look at,' she said.

Settling herself gingerly into the armchair behind her desk, Madame Priscilla said, 'Plain to look at? Yes. It is at present a blank canvas, so to speak. I know you are entering a collection at the Solstice Festival, Noah, but I don't know what colours you need. I can arrange for any colour you desire. The most important thing for me was to have you feel it. I'm sure you can appreciate its unique quality.'

The hairs on the back of Noah's neck prickled. Perhaps she'd made a mistake. Perhaps this woman was going to be competing with her at the Solstice Festival and this was her way of gaining information about Noah's collection. Or worse, maybe she was aiming to sabotage Noah's collection. With what Noah had gleaned of the fabric's capabilities, it was very possible that instead of Noah winning the competition with it, the fabric could in fact be used against her.

'Yes, Madame. I can appreciate its unique quality. May I ask who made it?'

'You may certainly ask,' Madame Priscilla said, 'but I shan't tell you. Weavers are a secretive lot and they do not divulge the secrets of their craft. That's even easier to do if people don't know who they are. You understand, I'm sure.'

It was a plausible story Noah had to admit but alarm bells were ringing. This was an extraordinary piece of material. Noah didn't understand it fully but she knew enough to know that this was not an accidental creation. It had a mysterious, sophisticated and danger-ous music to it. This would have taken some serious expertise to make. Expensive expertise.

'So you make colours to order?' Noah said.

'Yes, dear,' she replied.

Noah appeared to think hard, which was not too much of a stretch considering she was thinking hard, but just not about what Madame Priscilla thought she was thinking about.

'So what colours have you sold so far? Do you have some other samples?'

Madame Priscilla had been around too long to show she was sur-prised by anything. Instead, she gave Noah what was supposed to be a grandmotherly smile – and it would have been if Noah's grandmother had been a crocodile.

'My dear there have been no other colours, no other customers,' she said smoothly. 'I have only one roll of this material. I'm sure you can understand why. It's tricky to make.'

That was most likely true. And it was going to make it very expen-sive unless Noah could find some kind of leverage.

'So why me then?' Noah asked. 'Why are you offering it to me? I'm not the only designer entering the Solstice Festival competition.'

'That's true,' she replied. 'You are not the only entrant. But I think you can actually win it.'

'Why do you care if I win or not?'

'Well, because it's good for business. If my name is associated with the winning designer that will bring more customers through my doors.'

'And won't the king love that,' Emir said.

When both Madame Priscilla and Noah frowned at him, he went quiet again.

'And secondly,' she continued, 'Orville Kurz needs to be put in his place. You need to win this competition to get access to the king. You need to convince him how dangerous Orville is and that he needs to be fed to the grom.'

'So you don't like Orville either?'

'Absolutely not,' Madame Priscilla snorted. 'Frightful little twerp he is.'

'At least we agree on one thing,' Emir muttered.

'Don't mutter under your breath, young man,' she said. 'It's unseemly.'

Emir's jaw dropped and Noah thought his eyes might bulge out of their sockets.

'Muttering under one's breath is unseemly?' he sputtered. 'What do you call what goes on here then?'

'Enough, Emir,' Noah said. 'This is the reality of negotiating. If you don't have the stomach for it, perhaps you should wait outside.'

Madame Priscilla smiled sweetly while Emir continued to glower at her.

Aware that time was of the essence, Noah cut to the chase.

'So what's your price?'

'Ten thousand dinah,' she said.

Noah gasped. 'Ten thousand? Even if I had that much I wouldn't pay it.'

'Ah, but you would,' Madame Priscilla crooned. 'It's a small investment for a lifetime career as the king's Tailor.'

'Well, it's a moot point, because we don't have that much,' Emir said flatly.

'Okay,' Madame Priscilla said, 'here's my offer. Two thousand dinah but with three conditions.'

'Which are?' Emir asked, drawing his sword.

To Noah's surprise Madame Priscilla laughed.

'I wondered if you had a sword in your pocket,' she wheezed as she spoke. 'Now put that away, young man. You won't be needing that in here.'

Noah glared at Emir.

'Anyway,' the old lady said, 'my conditions are these. One, you get rid of that Orville Kurz. And by get rid of, I mean he has to be dead. Two, if you win you name me as your principal sponsor. Three, you promise not to take over my business while I am alive.'

'What makes you think I want to take over your business?' Noah asked.

'Yeah, what makes you think she wants to take over your business?' Emir repeated.

Noah couldn't figure out for the life of her what had gotten into Emir. At this rate they weren't going to make it out of Jagar alive and it would have nothing to do with Orville's minions.

'So do we have a deal?' Madame Priscilla asked.

Extending her hand, Noah said, 'Deal.'

Madame Priscilla's face just about split in two.

'Well now, let's get the paperwork in order,' she said, pushing a pile of parchment and a pen across the desk to Noah.

Noah flicked through the parchments, noting that the deal she'd just struck had been written in advance. 'You knew I'd agree,' she said.

'Yes,' the old lady said.

When Noah was finished signing the documents, she pushed them back across the table.

Madame Priscilla swept them up and tied them in a roll with a gold ribbon. 'And now the only thing I need to know,' she said, 'is what colour you'd like that fabric in.'

♪♫

'You should get some sleep, Noah,' Emir said.

She looked up from her sewing machine. 'I'm not tired.'

'You have a big day ahead of you.'

'I'm trying not to think about it.'

'You're going to have a battle on your hands. You—'

'How about you do your job and let me worry about mine,' Noah said. 'Deal?'

'Fine,' he said, folding his arms across his chest.

She judged it was only a little after midnight. Chase, Alan and Ardis were asleep in the next room. The prospect of the journey to Ironside and a possible meeting with the Dragonsbane had all but guaranteed her insomnia though.

'What did you find out today about Orville's plans?' Noah asked, needing more of a distraction than her sewing could provide.

'News has it that the king's army is currently on its way to Mellifont,' he said.

'His whole army?'

'More or less.'

'Why?'

'To destroy it.'

Noah jumped to her feet. 'What do you mean destroy it? Why?'

'A Major of the Academy broke into the facility at Seychelles,' he said, 'and several hundred prisoners were released.'

'Montana succeeded,' Noah mused.

'Maybe,' Emir said.

Noah looked at him.

Emir said, 'Orville could be exaggerating to justify his response. Anyway, it amounts to treason and someone needs to be accountable. It was just the excuse Orville needed to invade Mellifont.'

'Surely they can't do that,' Noah insisted. 'It's not right. Does the king know Orville was slaughtering all those people?'

'I do not know what the king knows,' Emir said.

'Is this bothering you at all?' Noah asked.

'Of course it is.'

'You'd never know it.'

He held her gaze. 'What would you like me to do?' he asked.

Noah threw her arms in the air. 'Oh, I don't know. Show some emotion perhaps? Maybe try a frown? I know you can do those. I've had quite a few of them directed at me.'

'Getting emotional serves no purpose, Noah,' he said. 'In fact, it clouds one's ability to think and act clearly. I have a job to do and I intend doing it – without any theatrics.'

'You're unbelievable,' Noah said, shaking her head.

Before Emir could respond, Chase stuck her head through the doorway.

'Do you two want to keep it down?' she said. 'People are trying to sleep in here.'

'The king's army is marching on Mellifont,' Noah said.

'What!' Chase said, instantly awake.

'Retribution for what Montana has done at Seychelles, apparently,' Noah explained.

Chase looked at Emir. 'The king has sent his army on Orville's advice?' she said.

'I'd expect so.'

'So by the time the Solstice Festival kicks off, there won't be many troops on the ground in the king's city,' she observed.

'Correct.'

'Don't you think as king, you'd be suspicious about someone wanting to clear out your army?'

'I would be,' Emir said, 'but then, I'm not the king.'

'Pity,' Chase said. 'You'd make a good king.'

Chapter 18

The boat ride from Jagar to the island of Ironside was uneventful. Aside from the mountain peaks at the northern and southern ends of the island, the land was remarkably flat. The Dragonsbane's abode looked like an enormous dragon curled up, sleeping under the watchful gaze of the mountains.

'Who built that?' Noah asked.

'The Descera,' Alan said.

'I thought they were more underground types,' Noah said.

'They mostly were,' Alan replied.

It was the most incredible building Noah had ever seen – a copper coloured monolith, scales gleaming in the morning sun. From where Noah stood she could see the overlapping scales had been strategically placed to create the shingled exterior of the structure. The shingles were not shut tight though. Like a bird ruffling its feathers, the scales had gaps between them.

Leaving their boat captain waiting in a sheltered cove, the party made their way towards Dragonhall.

'Are we going in there?' Alan asked when they reached the edge of the moat that encircled the structure.

'I guess so,' Noah said. 'I don't suppose the Dragonsbane is going to come out here to give me her job and her blessing.'

'No sign of Seth,' Emir noted.

'Maybe he's waiting inside,' Ardis said.

'That bridge doesn't look very sturdy,' Chase said.

'No,' Ardis agreed. 'And that lava down there looks pretty hot.'

'We'll just have to go one at a time,' Noah said.

They walked towards the rickety wooden bridge that hung in a slovenly fashion across the lava-filled moat.

'I'll go first,' Emir said.

As he went to step onto the bridge a large, flaming bird whooshed up in front of him. It flapped its wings dramatically and let out a long, eardrum-rending screech. Everyone clamped their hands over their ears. After a few long moments, Noah risked a glimpse at the bird. The flames subsided as the phoenix landed. He stood a head taller than Noah, almost as tall as Emir, and his plumage was a shimmering royal blue. When he moved though, it changed colour, became a deep maroon.

'I am Cecil,' it squawked. 'Who are you?'

Trying not to show her surprise that the bird could talk, Noah said, 'I am Noah Chord.'

'Noah?' the phoenix said. 'Funny name for a girl isn't it?'

'Apparently,' Noah said. 'I have come to see the Dragonsbane.'

'What is your business with the Dragonsbane?' the phoenix said.

'I've come to replace her,' Noah said, twirling her mother's ring on her finger. Emir had suggested she wear it for her meeting with the Dragonsbane. Noah didn't know if the Academy ring would give her any extra credibility but she was glad to have it on again.

'You bear the mark?'

'I do,' Noah said.

'Does anyone else bear the mark of the Dragonsbane?' the bird asked.

The others shook their heads.

The phoenix nodded, his plumage shimmering as he did so. 'So Noah is the only one who may enter. The rest of you will have to wait here.'

'Could just one of us go with her? For moral support?' Chase asked. 'I'm her best friend. I have no sword – I won't be any trouble.'

'No,' Cecil said. 'Only those that bear the mark may enter Dragonhall.'

Noah wondered if Raven would have been allowed to accompany her. A hot lump lodged in her throat again at the thought of her companion but she refused to cry. *I'm going to find you, Raven,* she thought. *Once I find the 13th key, I will use it to find you.*

'Okay Noah, you need to follow me,' the phoenix said. 'We will be crossing via the footbridge today – I'll just run through the safety demonstration with you first.'

Noah looked at the bridge and then back at the phoenix.

'Your feet should stay on the wooden boards,' he advised, 'and you should maintain a steady walking pace. There is no running and definitely no swinging. Do I make myself clear?'

'Inescapably clear,' Noah said.

'Good. Your emergency exit is located here,' he said, pointing down into the moat.

She prayed she wouldn't need to use the emergency exit but the look of the bridge didn't fill her with confidence.

'Ready to go?' he asked.

'Almost,' Noah said.

She turned to Chase. 'Do you want me to take your voice recorder?'

'That's very sweet of you to offer,' she said, 'but … how about you just come back safely and tell me all about it.'

'You sure?'

Chase threw her arms around her friend. 'I'm sure.'

'Okay,' Noah said. 'You got it.'

'Good luck, Noah,' Ardis said. 'May Elani see you safely through this trial.'

'Thanks, Ardis,' she said.

Alan hugged her. 'You'll be great,' he said. 'Just stay strong and don't let her bully you. Don't let her fifty years' experience bother you. This is your destiny. You need to—'

Emir interrupted. 'That's quite enough, Alan,' he said.

Noah looked at Emir.

'We'll be here when you get back,' he said.

'Right,' Noah said. She turned to the phoenix. 'Ready.'

'Follow me,' he said.

Noah followed him across the bridge. It felt surprisingly solid underfoot but she was not tempted to run or swing on it. Nor did she look down. The heat radiating from the molten rock below made breathing difficult and the smell was putrid. Through the shimmering heat haze, she focused on the end of the bridge.

When she stepped off the bridge, she breathed a sigh of relief.

'I leave you here,' Cecil said. 'It was a pleasure escorting you. Maybe I'll see you for the return trip.'

'I hope so,' Noah said. 'Thanks.'

As the phoenix flew off, Noah contemplated the corridor before her. The sleeping dragon's long tail wrapped protectively around the body but left a small gap, making a curved passage. Noah walked along the corridor to the entranceway – there was no door. Buildings generally only had doors to keep things out – people, animals. This fortress had its own defences though. Only those with the mark of the Dragonsbane could enter.

'What took you so long?' Brinn asked.

Noah flinched at the cat's sudden appearance. 'I had to sweet-talk the phoenix,' she said.

Brinn licked her paw. 'Sweet-talk you say? Well, in that case, I understand why you took so long.'

'Very funny,' Noah said. 'What are you doing here? How did you get in here? I thought only those with the mark of the Dragonsbane could come in here.'

'So many words!' Brinn said. 'Just for a change, try thinking. Why do you think I was able to enter this place?'

'Because you're the Dragonsbane?'

'Good thinking, but no.'

Noah thought hard. Something niggled at the edge of her memory. When she'd first arrived on Talisker, the only voice she'd been able to hear initially had been Brinn's. She'd asked Emir how that was possible. Dragging the conversation from the recesses of her memory she heard his voice in her mind.

'Well you know that you can train dogs, but you can't train cats. That's because cats refuse to follow rules. Well this cat,' Emir had nodded his head towards Brinn, *'refuses to follow any rules. She defies all rules, even rules of nature it seems. I have no idea how she does it.'*

'You're here because you refuse to follow rules,' Noah said.

'I don't like rules, that is true,' Brinn said slowly, 'but I didn't need to break any rules on this occasion.'

Noah was short on time and patience. 'Look only someone who *bears the mark of the Dragonsbane* can come in here,' she said. Realisation washed over her like warm honey. 'You have the brand?'

Brinn sighed. 'Finally!'

'Who branded you?'

'That's not important right now—'

'You branded yourself, didn't you!' Noah said. 'You stole the brand and put it on yourself.'

'Purr-loined,' she said. 'Cats don't steal things. They purr-loin them.'

'Whatever you say. Where is it?'

'On my stomach.'

'Can I see it?'

'No.'

'Why not?'

'Because it's private,' she said haughtily.

'I showed you mine,' Noah replied, thinking back to their first meeting in the forest behind her Aunt Polly's house.

'So?'

Vexed, Noah stared at the feline. 'You've got more than one brand, haven't you,' she said.

'Look, can we get on with this?' Brinn suggested.

Noah knew she wasn't going to get a straight answer. 'Sure,' she replied. 'Lead on.'

They continued down the corridor until they reached another hairpin bend. Rounding the bend brought them into what could best be described as a cathedral.

'Whoa,' Noah breathed.

Brinn stared at her. 'Is that all you've got to say? This is arguably the most magnificent hall in all of Talisker and all you've got to say is "whoa"?'

Noah wished that Chase were here. She'd have done it justice. But Chase wasn't here so Noah had to appreciate the splendour around her without being able to articulate it to the cat's satisfaction. None of the shingled scales that Noah had seen on the exterior of the structure was visible from the inside. Intricately carved sandstone columns stretched up to the vaulted ceiling, itself an enormous fresco. Had Noah had the time, she might have spent hours following the story of Talisker's creation as depicted on the ceiling, but today there was no time. The most breath-taking feature of the hall, however, was the stained-glass window at the far end. Not so much a window, as a wall, it showed Xan kneeling at the foot of a cloaked figure.

'Who is that?' Noah asked, pointing to the robed figure.

'That is Trixit, the first Dragonsbane.'

'Xan is magnificent,' Noah murmured. 'I thought dragons were one colour but she has many shades. Her scales remind me of opals.'

Brinn nodded. 'Opals are found on many worlds,' she said. 'As Xan travelled with Jong she shed old scales as new ones grew. These old scales floated around in the ether for eons and when worlds were made, they were part of the matter that was used to make them. That is why you have opals on Earth.'

Noah thought for a moment.

'Talisker must have heaps then,' she reasoned.

'Not as many as on Earth actually,' Brinn said. 'But we have firestone – the living scales of Xan. They are buried deep underground so we are safe.'

'Safe?' Noah said.

'Like I said, scales have powerful magical properties. In the wrong hands the results would be devastating.'

'The Descera had one to make the twelve keys, didn't they?' Noah asked as she watched rays of sunlight dancing through the myriad colours of the stained-glass pane.

'Small pieces of one,' Brinn corrected. 'One whole scale would be bigger than several people.'

'*One scale?* That would make the dragon ...'

'Pretty big,' Brinn finished. 'Anyway, back to the firestone. Just a small portion – about the size of your index finger – was enough to make the twelve keys. Well, we could stand around all day discussing such things but we are pressed for time. We need to find the Dragonsbane. Come on, follow me.'

Without waiting for a reply, the feline sauntered off towards the immense stained-glass artwork. Reaching a seemingly random spot in front of the window, she sat.

'You'll have to open it,' Brinn said. 'I have no opposable thumb.'

'Open what?' Noah asked. 'The window?'

'Are you daft? Of course not the window! Look at the size of it. How would you open it?'

'I don't know!' Noah snapped. 'But what else is there to open?'

'How about the trap door?' Brinn said, inclining her head towards the floor.

On closer inspection, Noah could see a small handle on the floor although there were no cracks or joins to indicate that there was a door in the vicinity. Deciding that arguing this point would be futile, Noah gripped the handle and pulled. The handle disappeared as did the floor around it to reveal a set of stairs.

'Off to the crypts we go,' Brinn purred.

Noah shuddered.

'Crypts?'

'Crypts,' Brinn said. 'Don't worry, they're quite lovely. Much better than the dungeon. Just be thankful we're not going there.'

'I'm a little tired of being underground. Isn't there anywhere we can go that isn't underground?'

'Well, of course there are places we can go that aren't beneath the surface,' Brinn said as she trotted off down the stairs. 'The main chamber contains a labyrinth of exciting nooks and crannies.'

'Well, why can't we explore some of those?'

'Because, that's not where the Dragonsbane is!'

'Fine.'

'And anyway,' Brinn added, 'some of those quarters are extremely dangerous. They lead to dark places – places outside our time.'

'Really?'

'Don't worry about that today, Noah,' Brinn said. 'Let's just focus on the job at hand. You need to be Dragonsbane. I hope you've got your wits about you.'

'Sure,' she replied.

Noah followed Brinn in silence, content to admire the artwork on the walls as they descended the staircase to the crypts. Like in Mellifont, the walls here glowed with soft light. When they reached the junction at the bottom, the feline took a left turn without hesitation. They proceeded to wind through passageway after passageway, taking a left here, a right there ... up a set of stairs on the left, along another corridor and then up another set of stairs on the right ... passing scores of identical doors until Noah was completely disoriented.

'I hope you know where you're going,' Noah said.

Brinn didn't answer, taking half a dozen more steps before stopping before a door that looked exactly like every other one they'd passed on the way.

'This one,' the cat said.

Noah opened the door. Despite the fact that the room was small and underground, it was well lit and homely. The desk was strewn with papers, pencils, teacups and plates while the aroma of freshly baked cake leaked from the potbelly stove that lurked in the corner. The kettle on the stove top rattled gently as its contents bubbled away. Noah was surprised to see a familiar face sitting behind the cluttered desk.

'Just in time,' the old woman smiled. 'Would you care for some tea?'

'I would love some tea,' Noah said, 'but Madame Priscilla, what are *you* doing here?'

Brinn snorted derisively. 'You are a bottomless pit of stupid questions, aren't you,' the cat said. 'What do you think she's doing here?'

'Besides making tea, you mean?' Noah asked sarcastically.

In response, the cat narrowed her eyes.

'Besides making tea and doing crossword puzzles, you mean?' Madame Priscilla said.

Brinn sighed. 'Yes. Besides all that.'

'You're the Dragonsbane?' Noah asked.

Madame Priscilla winked at her. 'Right you are, my girl. Right you are,' she said as she got up from the desk to fetch some fresh teacups from the small sideboard next to the stove.

'But how can you be the Dragonsbane?' Noah said. 'I thought the Dragonsbane's name was Ursula. And what about your fabric shop in Jagar?'

'What fabric shop?' Brinn cut in.

'The Purring Pussy,' Noah replied on Madame Priscilla's behalf.

Brinn's little tiger face contorted in confusion. 'That's not a fabric shop, it's a den of iniquity.'

Madame Priscilla laughed, with every wrinkle on her face joining in. 'That is why cats should not talk,' she said. 'They mix up their words. Although I must say it is very entertaining. What Brinn means, dear, is a den of *ingenuity*.'

Brinn scowled and moved over to sit in protest in front of an empty bowl.

While retrieving a bag of cat treats from the sideboard and emptying its entire contents into Brinn's bowl, Madame Priscilla took the opportunity to clarify.

'I own a number of businesses with my sister, Gwen,' she said, 'so when I retire from this position, I will be financially secure. Gwen runs the businesses on a day-to-day basis because, as you can imagine, my responsibilities here take a lot of my time. Now The Purring Pussy is primarily an *accommodation* service—'

At that point Brinn appeared to choke on her biscuits but recovered – remarkably quickly.

'But there are a number of related activities that we also run,' she continued as she cleared a skerrick of space on the desk on which to set down Noah's teacup. 'We run a recreational facility – people like to engage in a wide variety of activities while they are staying with us at The Purring Pussy.'

Brinn coughed again and Madame Priscilla glared at her.

'So we employ about twenty people making and maintaining the equipment in that division. There is the fabric division – which you know about – that produces all the materials for the sheets, towels and furnishings. We also run a laundry service – the sheets and towels don't just wash themselves, you know. And of course there is our catering company.'

'So who is Ursula?' Noah asked.

'I am Ursula,' Madame Priscilla replied. 'Madame Priscilla is just my business name.'

'So if your sister runs the business, why were you in Jagar yesterday?' Noah asked.

'I wanted to meet you. And to make sure you got my special fabric,' Madame Priscilla said.

'How did you know I would be there?'

'Noah,' she said, 'I *always* know where you are.'

Noah thought of the burning rocks. *Noah Chord beware.*

'Right,' Noah said. 'So what do we do now?'

'Now,' the Dragonsbane said, 'we have tea and cake.'

'And what about me being Dragonsbane?' Noah asked.

'Well, unfortunately that's out of the question,' Madame Priscilla said.

'Why is that?' Noah asked. 'I have the mark.'

'Yes, yes,' Madame Priscilla said. 'I know all about that, but do you remember when you visited me in Jagar, that you made a promise?'

'Promise?' Noah asked.

'Promise?' Brinn echoed.

'Yes, a promise,' Madame Priscilla said. 'Well, more like a signed contract actually.'

Noah picked up her teacup from the table as Madame Priscilla, spritely beyond her advanced years, leapt to retrieve the cake from the oven.

'A signed contract?' Brinn said as she landed nimbly on the spot recently vacated by Noah's teacup. 'What have you done?'

Noah jumped, startled by the sudden appearance of the miniature tiger on the table before her. The saucer was the only thing that saved her from a nasty burn.

'Don't *do* that,' she snapped. 'You'll give me a heart attack.'

'What did you sign?' Brinn insisted.

As the fragrant teacake was served up, Noah quickly explained the terms of the deal she'd struck to purchase the special fabric from Madame Priscilla.

'May I see these *alleged* documents?' Brinn said icily.

'But of course,' the Dragonsbane replied, selecting a wad of parchments from the clutter on the table.

'Great filing system,' Brinn muttered as she started perusing the documents.

'As long as I know where they are, that's all that matters,' Madame Priscilla said, popping a morsel of cake into her mouth.

Brinn looked at Noah. 'Read,' she demanded.

Noah read from the contract as the cat listened intently.

'I have no problem with condition one – eliminating Orville Kurz,' Brinn said, 'and I can live with you naming Madame Priscilla as your sponsor should you win at the fashion gala, but the third condition is a problem.'

Noah frowned. 'When I agreed that I wouldn't take over her business, I didn't know she meant this one here in Dragonhall.'

'I don't suppose this is the only copy,' Brinn said to Madame Priscilla.

'No,' the Dragonsbane replied. 'That wouldn't be good business now, would it?'

'How many copies?'

'Three.'

Brinn's face betrayed nothing of her thoughts, but her raised hackles screamed her displeasure. If Noah had had hackles, hers too would have been raised. The Dragonsbane had tricked her. She'd known all along about Noah's mark and had manipulated the situation to prevent her taking the role.

'So you see,' Madame Priscilla crooned, 'destroying the contract is not an option.'

Brinn didn't answer. Noah cursed. Madame Priscilla looked relieved.

'Doesn't the contract say that I can't take the position while she's alive?' Noah asked.

Both Brinn and the Dragonsbane looked at her in surprise.

'Yes,' Brinn said slowly. 'But killing her doesn't help us either.'

Again, Madame Priscilla looked relieved.

'Why not?' Noah asked, annoyed.

'It is preferable that the office of the Dragonsbane pass from one living person to another.'

'Why?'

'The short answer to that question is paperwork. Between two living people, the incumbent simply submits a completed Form 23PS (Change of Tenancy) for Dragonhall and all's good.'

'But if the incumbent dies, the process is so much more cumbersome,' Madame Priscilla said. 'Did you know there are eleven forms that need to be completed and filed before the selection process even begins? And the selection process is a nightmare,' the Dragonsbane said dramatically. 'Everyone with a birthbrand has to be summonsed and put before a panel. You can imagine how difficult it is tracking down everyone who has a brand. They keep a register, of course, but it is notoriously difficult to keep track of everyone.'

'I wouldn't have thought they branded too many people with this particular brand,' Noah commented.

'You'd be surprised,' Madame Priscilla said.

'*Anyway,*' Brinn cut in, 'the continued existence of this world relies on Noah being Dragonsbane so we need to get this mess sorted out.'

'That's a bit dramatic, don't you think?'

'Dramatic it may be but it also happens to be true,' Brinn growled.

'Sorry, can't help you,' Madame Priscilla said. 'We have a contract that is like a fish's bottom.'

Noah raised an eyebrow.

'Watertight,' she said, laughing uproariously as she did so.

'Then we need a new contract,' Brinn said.

Madame Priscilla gave a semi-apologetic shrug. 'I'm happy with the current one.'

'You do realise,' Brinn said, 'that if Orville's plan succeeds, you won't be Dragonsbane because Talisker will no longer exist?'

Madame Priscilla picked up the contract. 'According to clause 1 in this contract, Noah is responsible for ridding the world of Orville Kurz. If she fails to do this, I'll have grounds to sue her for breach of contract,' she declared.

'Again Madame Priscilla,' Brinn said wearily, 'if Noah doesn't rid the world of Orville Kurz, you won't be suing her because *you'll be dead*, along with everyone else.'

'Well, as long as she holds up her end of the contract, we'll all be fine.'

'Which brings me to my other point,' Brinn said. 'Noah needs to be Dragonsbane to hold up her end of the contract.'

'Well, that can't happen because according to the contract—'

'*Be QUIET!*' Brinn roared.

Both Noah and Madame Priscilla jumped.

'This is getting us nowhere,' Brinn growled. 'Stop yabbering so I can think.'

Taking her life in her hands, Noah whispered in Brinn's ear. The cat stared at her like she'd never seen her before and continued to do so for a full minute. Noah held her breath.

'My girl, you're worth your weight in cat biscuits! That might just work.'

Chapter 19

'What might just work?' Madame Priscilla asked.

'Well, as per the contract you can't make Noah Dragonsbane.'

'Agreed.'

'But you could make *me* Dragonsbane,' Brinn said.

'But you're a cat,' she replied.

'To the untrained eye perhaps, but that is not important right now. I bear the mark. *Technically,* you could bestow the office of Dragonsbane on me.'

Madame Priscilla reached across the table, broke herself off another morsel of cake and popped it in her mouth.

'Technically I guess I could. And then what? You'll bestow it on Noah?'

'That is her plan, yes,' Brinn nodded. 'Quite simple, yet brilliant.'

'And why would I want to do that?' she said as she chewed.

'Because you have the good of Talisker at heart and you want to ensure Noah is in the perfect position to put Orville Kurz in his place,' Brinn said. 'Have you forgotten the prophecy? *The thirteenth key the world shall need, for evil to be brought to heel – One of two, the Dragon's bane must rise; and the music wield.*'

Madame Priscilla said, 'Have you found the 13th key, Noah?'

'No,' Noah admitted.

'Has anyone?'

'Not that I know of,' Noah said.

'Well, until such time as the 13th key comes to light, I don't feel inclined to hand over the title of Dragonsbane,' Madame Priscilla said, 'especially to someone with such limited experience. I think Dr Grainger is eminently more qualified.'

'Then why did you give me the fabric?' Noah asked.

'I didn't *give* it to you,' Madame Priscilla said. 'I *sold* it to you. And I did so because I think you have the talent to use it against Orville. As far as being Dragonsbane and using the 13th key to save the world, my money's on Dr Grainger.'

'But he's not here,' Noah said.

'He's on his way,' Madame Priscilla said.

Goosebumps prickled over Noah's skin. 'How close?'

'He'll be here today.'

Noah's eyes narrowed. 'This is a test?' she asked.

'Not really,' the Dragonsbane replied. 'I have no intention of making you Dragonsbane because I don't think you can discharge the duties of the office.'

With her hands in her lap, Noah twirled her mother's ring on her finger. She thought of her parents and of Raven. She pictured them all standing behind her. *I have to do this,* she thought. *I will not fail. I need a plan. I need time.*

'Fair enough,' Noah said. 'Well, if we don't need to worry about that anymore, let's enjoy our tea and cake.'

'Excellent,' Madame Priscilla said, raising her teacup. 'Perhaps you'd like to help me with my crossword. It's a cryptic puzzle and I've just got one last clue to complete before I can send it away to claim my prize.'

'Um, I haven't really done many crosswords,' Noah said. 'Particularly cryptic ones. They're harder; aren't they?'

'They can be a downright pest,' Madame Priscilla agreed, handing the puzzle to Noah. 'I've been stuck on this particular clue for days now. It's starting to drive me up the wall!'

Noah read the clue aloud. 'Triad in I# major,' she said. 'What does that mean?'

Brinn purred. 'Tell me about this crossword puzzle,' she said. 'The prize, what would it be?'

'The prize is but a mere trifle,' Madame Priscilla said casually. 'The real reward is actually completing the puzzle.'

Stepping daintily through the chaos on the table, Brinn said, 'If that were true, surely you'd want the gratification of solving the final clue yourself.'

Noah had time only to glimpse the Dragonsbane's tight smile before her view was obscured by the cat plonking herself down in front of the wily businesswoman.

'I've solved all the other clues,' she countered.

'How many?'

'A lot.'

Despite her limited experience with completing crosswords, Noah had seen many of them. Aunt Polly was an avid crossword fan. Noah at least knew something of their structure.

'Where are the other clues?' Noah asked. 'Why are there no other boxes?'

'This is not your regular crossword,' Madame Priscilla said. 'The words disappear when you put them in correctly.'

Brinn and the Dragonsbane continued their banter while Noah studied the crossword puzzle more closely. She'd had one good idea – gaining the office of Dragonsbane via Brinn and thus circumventing the problem of the contract was, as Brinn had said, brilliant. But it was not enough. Buoyed by her recent success, she set her mind to deciphering the crossword puzzle. An idea occurred to her. On impulse she placed her hands over the crossword puzzle and then closed her eyes. She tried listening to it rather than seeing it.

Her task was made more difficult by Brinn and Madame Priscilla's squabbling, but Noah concentrated intently. And it paid off.

'It's a test!' she cried.

'Of course it's a test,' Madame Priscilla said. 'It is a test of word knowledge and problem-solving skills.'

'It's more than that,' Noah argued. 'This is a test of the *Dragonsbane's* word knowledge and problem-solving skills.'

'Is that so?' Brinn mused. 'Keep this up, Chord and I might even be tempted to rub up against you. I believe we finally have something to bargain with.'

'You have nothing to bargain with,' the Dragonsbane said.

'On the contrary,' Brinn said, 'if you can't submit your test you'll be de-registered. You won't be able to be Dragonsbane anyway,' Brinn said. 'You might as well give it up now. Make me Dragonsbane.'

From her seat across the table from the Dragonsbane Noah reached out her perceptions to listen to the old woman's music. Noah was instantly aware of her strength. This woman was a seasoned campaigner. She'd been around for a long time and negotiated her way in and out of countless hairy situations. Showing weakness was not an option. Noah dug a little deeper. The Dragonsbane did not believe she was beaten. She was still formulating plans and revising options.

'I think not,' Madame Priscilla said haughtily. 'I'd rather wait and be de-registered.'

They were at an impasse.

'Say I solve the final clue,' Noah said. 'Your registration will be renewed and then you can make Brinn Dragonsbane.'

'Are you listening to yourself?' Madame Priscilla said. 'If my registration is renewed I'm just going to continue to be Dragonsbane. I'm not going to hand it over to *her*.'

'That is kind of a daft idea,' Brinn agreed.

Noah shook her head impatiently. 'If I can solve this, surely you should consider me to be Dragonsbane.'

Madame Priscilla shook her head. 'It's not enough to push Dr Grainger out of the running,' she said.

'What if I solve this *and* find the 13th key,' Noah said. 'Is that enough?'

'You're ambitious, I'll give you that,' the Dragonsbane said.

'Crossword puzzle now,' Noah said, '13th key by the end of the week.'

The only sound in the room was the kettle rattling on the stove.

'Crossword now,' Madame Priscilla agreed, 'and you have three days to find the 13th key. If you do those things, I will then test Brinn and Dr Grainger for the position of Dragonsbane.'

'Done!' Noah said.

'So come on, Noah,' Brinn purred, 'put us out of our misery. Write the answer on that crossword puzzle and let's get on with this.'

'Ah y-yes, about that …' Noah stammered.

'Tell me you know the answer,' Brinn said.

'Well—'

'You've got to be kidding – the way you were negotiating I thought you knew the answer!'

'Just give me a couple of minutes,' she said.

'*A couple of minutes?*' Madame Priscilla said. 'I've been Dragonsbane for fif- … a long time and I've worked on that clue for months without success. What makes you think you can get it in a couple of minutes?'

'Months?' Brinn said. 'A minute ago you said you'd been working on it for a couple of days.'

Noah had no idea how she was going to come up with the answer but she had to do it quickly. She cursed her own stupidity. Not being able to solve a crossword puzzle clue was one kind of stupid – and not a kind of stupid that particularly bothered her per se. But brokering a deal that relied on her being able to solve a crossword puzzle clue – that was a whole other kind of stupid.

As the seconds ticked by, the pressure mounted. Madame Priscilla continued glaring at her across the table. Brinn appeared to be focused on her grooming routine but Noah knew better.

'I need to get out of here,' she whispered. 'I need space.'

Snatching up the crossword puzzle, she bolted out the door.

'Noah! Stop!' the Dragonsbane called. '*You'll get lost.*'

Noah had been disoriented when Brinn led her into the crypts but everything was clear to her now. Not only had she absorbed the flow of music that she'd heard on the way through but she could follow it in reverse to find her way out. That lifted her spirits a little but she still had a lot more things to get off her mind before she could even begin to focus on solving the crossword clue.

Something brushed against her leg and she squealed in surprise.

'Brinn!' Noah said. 'Leave me alone. I need to think. I need space.'

'Yes,' she replied. 'And I'm right here to make sure you get it.'

Noah ran faster. 'You don't get it. When I say I need space, I mean I don't want anyone around. That includes you!'

Brinn hissed. 'Just follow me. You'll have all the space you need.'

With that she took off ahead, taking a left at the next T intersection where Noah would have gone right. At heart she was still a dog person; trusting a cat didn't come easily. Noah hesitated for only a moment. The lure of space was strong and so far Brinn hadn't done anything that showed her to be untrustworthy.

Less than a dozen steps down the corridor the cat stopped in front of a door. All the doors looked the same to Noah but Brinn was insistent.

'I will guard this door for as long as it takes,' she said. 'Go.'

Noah nodded and did as she was told. She stepped through the doorway and let out a long, slow breath.

'Wow!' she said.

She had space all right. She'd stepped through a doorway expecting to have a small room where she could think without distraction, but sensationally she'd ended up outside in the shade of a magnificent, lone sequoia, the only vertical object that rose higher than her shins.

Noah spun round. There was no sign of the doorway she'd come through or of Brinn. Lush, spongy grass sprawled to the horizon in all directions, interrupted only by tufts of wildflowers that sprouted here and there like errant hairs on an old man's ears. She didn't know where she was outside of, but she certainly wasn't outside Dragonhall. With no time to try to fathom what was going on, Noah plonked herself down in the dappled shade of the sequoia.

Smoothing the crossword puzzle out on the ground in front of her she considered the clue. *Triad in I# major.* Nothing. No idea. A wave of panic washed over her. She really needed to solve this clue. *Maybe it's like being caught in a rip at the beach,* she thought. *Don't fight the rip, just go with it.* Taking a deep breath, she waited until the panic passed. *Triad in I# major.*

Sachin had said something about triads. Obviously it had something to do with three. Three something. Three notes. Three notes made a chord. Chord. Maybe it had something to do with her name. It wasn't much, and nowhere near definitive, but it was progress … she hoped.

I#? That was confusing. As far as she knew there was no key of "I". All the ones from A to G she'd heard of but not "I". As she mulled it over she became increasingly sure that there was some connection between the "I", chord and key. It was too much of a coincidence that there was chord and key together. Wasn't she supposed to find the 13th key? And possibly the "I" wasn't really key signature but a personal pronoun. She let her mind wander. *I, Noah Chord, have the 13th key …*

She leapt to her feet.

Did she? Did she already have it?

In a frenzy she emptied her pockets. If she really did have the key, it must be in a pocket somewhere. It took her several minutes to empty them all – it was amazing how much stuff she'd managed to accumulate in only a few weeks. Surveying the array of stuff strewn on the lawn, she let the pictures sink into her mind. Most of the items before her related to her collection but there were still a lot of things that didn't. There were a couple of things she didn't even recognise.

'Okay,' she said aloud, 'now it's time to listen to everything.'

Deciding to leave her sewing chattels until last she started on one of the souvenirs she'd picked up in the markets in Leninstar. Suddenly, she leapt to her feet.

'Brinn!' she cried, as she stuffed things back into her pockets. 'Brinn! Open the door.'

No door appeared but Brinn's head popped out of the tree trunk.

'Got the answer?' she asked.

'Yes! *Yes!*'

'Good. Follow me.'

Noah didn't hesitate before launching herself at the sequoia's trunk. She followed the little tiger as she scampered through the corridors under Dragonhall. The Dragonsbane stood as Noah and Brinn entered the room.

'Do you have the answer?' Madame Priscilla demanded.

'I believe so,' Noah replied, unable to keep a little smugness out of her voice. 'How many letters was it?'

'Eleven.'

Noah made a show of counting on her fingers as she reviewed her answer in her head. She smiled. 'Yep, I believe I've got it.'

Madame Priscilla returned something of a smile. 'And it would be,' she prompted.

'Well, when you think about it, it's really quite—'

'The answer,' Brinn interrupted. 'We don't have time to mess around.'

'Oh right,' Noah said, deflating slightly.

She was proud of herself for solving the clue and wanted to fully enjoy the moment. 'For the record,' Noah said, 'Chase would have preferred for me to build the suspense.'

'Answer,' Brinn demanded.

Noah nodded. 'Harpsichord,' she said.

'*Harpsichord?*' Madame Priscilla repeated. 'Are you sure?'

'It fits,' Brinn said.

'I know it fits,' the Dragonsbane snapped, 'but is it right?'

'Only one way to find out,' Noah said, reaching for a pen.

Madame Priscilla snatched the pen up from the table before Noah could retrieve it.

'We only have one chance at this,' she said, 'I need to be convinced that it is right.'

Brinn flicked an ear in irritation but agreed. 'A quick explanation, if you will, Miss Chord.'

'Gee, make up your minds,' Noah said, rolling her eyes. 'I was going to explain it before and you didn't want an explanation. You just wanted the answer. "We don't have time to mess around," you said. And now that I've given you just the answer, you want the explanation.'

'Just do it,' Brinn growled.

'Okay,' Noah said. 'Triad in I# major is the clue. A triad is a chord, right?'

Both Brinn and Madame Priscilla nodded.

'I#, if you spell it out, is "I sharp". So put all that together 'I sharp' and 'chord' and you get "I sharp chord". Unscramble the letters and you get "harpsichord".'

'Sounds plausible,' the Dragonsbane admitted.

'It's right,' Noah said. 'I heard it.'

'You heard it?'

Noah nodded.

'I listened to the clue – like you, I can tune into things – and I listened to a harpsichord. They match.'

Madame Priscilla was a mask of scepticism. 'So you "listened" to the crossword clue,' she said.

'Yep.'

'As you say, I can tune into things and I can't hear anything.'

'I can,' Noah insisted.

For a moment the Dragonsbane considered her predicament. 'Okay, let's do it.'

Noah took the reluctantly proffered pen. She looked at the eleven small boxes down the bottom of the page. Inanimate though they were, they seemed to glare balefully at her. It was a password. It didn't bear thinking about what might happen if she was wrong. She steadied her hand, inhaled deeply.

Noah wrote in the solution.

Nothing happened. She didn't know what she expected to happen but it wasn't nothing. Surely there'd be something.

'What now?' she asked.

'Patience,' Brinn purred. 'Patience.'

It took a few moments but all of a sudden, the ink on the page started to move. Like black raindrops on a windowpane, the ink beaded and slid down the page, pooling at the bottom. Then it started to swirl around the page, counter-clockwise. A blinding flash of light erupted from the page.

Noah instinctively turned away.

'Look.'

Noah dared a peek. There was a message on the page. In pulsating hues of all shades of blue, the message read:

Congratulations Madame Priscilla, on passing your decennial exam. Your re-registration is now complete. Please file this certificate in a safe place.

Kind regards,

Callinan (Chief Seer)

'So, Dragonsbane,' Brinn said, 'our deal?'

Madame Priscilla nodded slowly. 'I will wait three days,' she said. 'If you do not return with the 13th key in that time, I will make Dr Grainger the new Dragonsbane.'

Chapter 20

Noah closed the door behind her, leaving Madame Priscilla to her work. She looked left and right along the corridor.

'If I were a Descera, where would I wait?' Noah said aloud.

'How about right here?' a voice answered her.

Noah spun to her left. 'You really shouldn't do that,' she said to the tall Descera. 'You're as bad as Brinn.'

'I'm Seth,' he said, smiling.

'I figured that,' Noah replied, extending her hand.

As the Descera shook her hand, he said, 'And where is Brinn anyway?'

'No idea,' Noah said. 'Gone again.'

'I am glad you're here,' Seth said, his face turning serious. 'There is someone else I'd like you to meet. Follow me.'

Noah fell in behind the Descera but he stopped at the second doorway on their right.

'In here,' he said.

As Noah entered the domed room, she shielded her eyes from the light. A large pool of lava bubbled away in a deep pit in the floor. A brick wall about half a metre high surrounded it. Noah walked forward over the slate tiles to peer over the edge. The heat assaulted her face and made her squeeze her eyes shut. When she dared open them again she saw the phoenix emerge from the pit and land on the wall.

'Hello, Noah,' the fiery bird said.

'Hello, Cecil,' she said. Turning to Seth, she added, 'We've already met.'

'Yes, I know,' Seth replied. Pointing across the room, he said, 'This is who I wanted you to meet.'

Through the heat haze, Noah peered at the young man walking towards her. He was tall and lean and wore a grey robe like Seth's. His jet-black hair was pulled back from his face in a low ponytail, revealing the impossibly pale skin of his face. *Has he never seen the sun?* Noah wondered. She saw his unsteady gait as he walked and noticed that he kept his eyes down, as if concentrating on every step. When he stopped in front of her, he looked up. Noah's heart froze.

'No,' she whispered. 'No, no, no. It can't be …'

'It is, Noah,' Seth said gently. 'This is Raven, in his proper form.'

'Proper form?' she said, unable to look away from the eyes she knew so well.

'Hello, Noah,' Raven croaked. 'It's good to see you again.'

'He still needs to exercise his vocal cords,' Seth explained, 'but he'll be fine.'

'Fine?' Noah repeated. 'How it this *fine?*'

'Raven is your brother, Noah,' Seth said. 'Your *twin* brother.'

Raven stepped forward and put his arms around her. Heart thumping, Noah returned the gentle hug.

'Hey, Sis,' Raven said.

'How can this be?' she whispered.

Seth said, 'You two need to get re-acquainted but there are things I must tell you – show you – so you understand what's at stake here. Come.'

As the phoenix settled on the brick wall behind them, Seth led Noah and Raven to a section of pale grey wall.

'Sit,' Seth said. 'I will tell you and show you how this came to be.'

Noah and Raven sat on the floor. As Noah settled herself, she looked sideways at her brother, trying to think of something to say to him. Nothing presented itself. After everything she learnt about her family since arriving on Talisker, she probably shouldn't have been surprised that her Alsatian was actually her brother.

Raven caught her eye. 'It's great to be taller than you at last, Noah,' he said with a wink.

She smiled at him and shook her head. 'You're funny,' she said.

'Surprised?'

'Yes.'

Cocking his head to one side, Raven said, 'In a good way?'

Noah put her hand on his knee. 'Yes, Raven,' she said softly. 'It's nice to have real family again – and having a twin is pretty cool.'

She would miss her dog but she couldn't tell him that. *I'll just look at his eyes,* she thought. His puppy eyes would be a lasting reminder.

'Are you comfortable?' Seth asked.

The twins nodded. Noah said, 'Yes, please begin.'

The Descera nodded. 'Your mother grew up on a farm about fifty kilometres south-east of Seychelles,' Seth began. '*Her* mother died during childbirth so Isla was raised by her father. She didn't have an easy time of it – her father didn't cope well after his wife's death. He became an alcoholic. Isla had dreams of going to Mellifont but found herself working the farm so that she and her father could at least eat.'

Noah seized on the mention of Mellifont. 'My mother played an instrument?'

Seth nodded. 'She played the viola and she did go to Mellifont for one of their quarterly immersion programs.'

'What's an immersion program?' Noah asked.

'Once a quarter, the Academy hosts a group of students who aspire to be Notaries. All prospective adepts begin their lives in Mellifont as Notaries. They are entry level positions and they can choose to remain Notaries or they might train for more advanced positions.'

'How long did my mother—' Noah started to say but was distracted when Raven nudged her. She looked at him.

'Our mother,' Raven corrected her. 'How long did *our* mother stay in Mellifont?'

'A fortnight,' Seth replied. 'Isla was paired up with a resident Notary called Jimmy, who was smitten with her. In a valiant effort to impress her, he took her on a date – to Earth. And Isla *was* impressed but alas for poor Jimmy, it wasn't with him that she was impressed. Isla thought

Earth was just the most wonderful place. She was greatly attracted to it *and* to a particular person that she met there.

'Dad?' Noah guessed.

Seth nodded. 'Striker Chord was as besotted with Isla as she was with him, so when she returned home, he came with her.'

'Did he go to Mellifont?' Noah asked.

'No,' Seth said. 'Isla decided to defer her studies at the Academy and went back to the family farm. Her father, Tulson, was in poor health. He wanted to shut himself off from the world. The house was in two sections so Isla lived in one section, Tulson in the other. With Tulson confined to his quarters, Isla and Striker could come and go without anyone noticing.'

Noah found it difficult to picture her parents as teenagers sneaking into each other's rooms at night, particularly when their rooms were on completely separate worlds. This was certainly a side of her parents that she'd never seen.

'How long did this go on for?' Noah said.

'About five years,' Seth said. 'That's when Isla discovered she was pregnant. Her father had passed away the year before so Isla and Striker had been spending a lot of time at the farm.'

Noah was stunned that such an arrangement could continue for so long without arousing suspicion. 'Did Dad's family know?'

Seth shrugged. 'I don't know.'

'I can't imagine Aunt Polly approving of that.'

The Descera continued his narration. 'Isla decided she wanted to have her baby on Talisker. The farm was hers now and it was home. She didn't know though, until you were both born, that she was having twins.'

'Yikes,' Noah said.

Seth smiled. 'That was your father's reaction too.'

'He was here for our births?' Raven asked.

'Absolutely. They were married by then and Striker was happy to be wherever his wife wanted to be. He loved the farm almost as much as she did and when the two of you arrived, they were both over the moon.'

'So what happened?'

Seth's face turned grim. 'Then I came along.' He paused and took a deep breath. 'I want to show you both something,' he said. Pointing to the wall, he said, 'Watch.'

Noah and Raven looked at the grey rock.

Seth said, 'From my mind, I'm going to project what I saw the night I came to the farm to brand you, Noah.'

Turning his attention to the wall before them, he closed his eyes. After a moment or two a large, pale blue weatherboard barn wriggled into focus on the grey stone. In fact, it looked like two barns joined by an elevated walkway. The walkway was enclosed and Noah could now see how her mother and grandfather could have lived separate lives while in the same dwelling.

To one side of the barn was a fenced expanse of grass where a few long-haired cows grazed in the fading daylight. On the other side was a stand of olive trees. But Noah barely noticed these details. Her eyes were on the man digging in the dirt in front of the barn. Her father. Tears filled her eyes at the sight of him.

She flinched when Raven put his hand on her knee. She could feel him looking at her. Without taking her eyes from the wall, she squeezed his hand and whispered, 'Keep watching, Raven.'

The movie from Seth's memory showed Striker digging two shallow holes, a couple of feet apart. *Like little graves,* Noah thought. Once satisfied with the holes, her father moved a short distance away to set a flame to some carefully arranged kindling. He did this at three more piles that served to form a diamond shape around the holes.

'One pyre at each of the compass points,' Seth explained.

Butterflies stirred in Noah's stomach as she watched her mother walk out of the barn. Her long, dark hair was loose and hung in shiny waves over the embroidered bodice of her cream and scarlet gown. Noah's gaze was torn between the beautiful garment, the black case under her arm and the dazzling smile her mother wore. Isla kissed her husband tenderly as he stood back to admire his handiwork.

Striker spoke. 'Almost ready?' he asked.

Both Noah and Raven flinched at the sound of their father's voice.

'The children and I are ready and this looks perfect out here,' Isla replied, surveying the fires and the freshly dug earth. 'You should go and get cleaned up before the sun sets.'

'Aye, aye,' he said.

He disappeared inside the barn as Isla laid the black case on the ground between the two holes. She opened the case but left the viola and bow inside. While she waited she found a stick and drew lines in the dirt to connect each of the fires. When she was done she went back inside.

Seth said, 'What you are about to see is a sacred ceremony. It is customary here on Talisker. Do not be alarmed. You both survive it.'

'Does Raven become a dog?' Noah asked.

'No,' Seth said. 'That is not customary. You will not see that.'

Noah twirled her ring on her finger as her parents emerged from the barn, each cradling a sleeping baby wrapped in a purple rug. Without speaking they made their way into the diamond and laid the babies in the holes.

'No prizes for guessing which one is you,' Noah said to her brother. 'Check out your hair.'

As the flames from the four fires licked hungrily at the new night's air, Isla took her viola from its case. Striker sat on the ground at the babies' feet, head bowed.

Standing inside the diamond opposite her husband, Isla took a deep breath. 'Elani, here is our daughter, Noah, and our son, Alex,' she said.

'Alex?' Raven said. 'My name was Alex?'

Seth nodded. 'Yes.'

'Alex is a fine name,' Noah said.

Raven nodded. 'Yes. I think I'll stick with Raven though.'

The twins watched as Isla tucked the viola under her chin and started to play. It was an hypnotic melody, the flames dancing higher in response. At her nod, Striker got to his feet and drew a small paper sachet from his breast pocket. He went to the fire at the northern point of the diamond, emptying a portion of the contents of the sachet into his open palm as he walked.

'That's cinnamon and cloves,' Seth said.

Striker threw the spice mix onto the fire before moving to the other three points to do the same thing. Isla's tune took on a more syncopated rhythm. She chanted softly in a language that Noah didn't understand. As she did so, a figure started to form in the fire on the eastern side. A dragon took shape, stretched its wings and began darting in and out of the flames. Across the diamond another figure emerged. This one had a human form.

'Xan and Elani,' Seth said.

The fiery human figure strode to stand between the two children. The dragon flew menacingly around the diamond, showering the ground with cinders. As the music from Isla's viola picked up tempo, the dragon's circles grew faster and tighter. When Isla dragged her bow across three strings simultaneously, Elani whipped his flaming arms skywards and Xan spiralled towards the heavens.

Isla's song got softer and softer as the dragon climbed higher and higher. When Xan was little more than a flaming dot in the night sky, Isla plucked a solitary note. Elani dropped his arms and the dragon started her descent. Like a meteor, she hurtled towards the oblivious infants.

Despite knowing that she must have survived this episode, Noah held her breath as the dragon sped towards her.

Xan was barely a metre from the babies when Elani launched himself at the dragon – spearing her through the heart. Sparks rained down like a New Year's Eve fireworks show.

'Ouroboros!' Isla cried.

On her command the sparks fell in a perfect circle around where Noah and Raven lay. Flames sprang from the bare ground. The fort of fire burned high, concealing the babies from view.

Isla switched to a lilting melody which appeared to have a calming effect on the wall of flames. The flames eventually died down leaving a glowing orange ring around the holes containing the babies.

Isla stopped playing and put her viola on the ground between the twins. She knelt at Noah's feet as Striker knelt at the feet of his son.

'Feel the music and warmth of the earth, little ones,' she said. 'It is a part of you – as you are of it.'

The proud parents pushed warm soil into the holes and packed it around the infants. Noah opened her eyes and smiled at her mother. She reached up her arms brandishing two fistfuls of dirt. Isla lay down next to her, emptying one hand and then the other. She let her daughter explore her face with her grubby little hands.

'I've never heard of that happening on Earth,' Noah said. 'In fact, it would probably be considered child abuse.'

Seth scowled. 'It is a beautiful and sacred ceremony,' he said. 'It doesn't happen on Earth because they don't have the same connection with their world that Taliskerans do.'

'I get it,' Noah said, slapping her palm against her forehead. 'I get it! I *finally* get it. I know what they mean now! *That's* what it means.'

'Slow down, Noah,' Raven said. 'What are you talking about?'

'In the prophecy,' Noah said, 'when it says "one of two". It's not one of two with the Dragonsbane's mark – it's one of two *twins*.'

'Yes,' Seth said. 'That's why I changed Raven into a dog. To hide the fact that you were a twin.'

'Seems extreme,' Noah said.

'I had limited options,' Seth said. 'It was either kill him, separate the two of you or turn him into a dog. Can we continue?'

'Please do,' Noah said.

'I'm going to skip forward a bit to where your parents discover Raven's disappearance,' Seth said.

Isla entered the babies' room to discover one of them missing. For a moment she stood in shocked disbelief before calling for her husband.

Striker arrived within moments, out of breath. 'What's wrong?' he asked.

Isla pointed to the empty crib. When Striker picked up the purple blanket, a folded piece of parchment fell onto the mattress. He snatched up the piece of paper, unfolding it hastily.

'What does it say?' Isla asked.

Dutifully Striker read the note.

'Your baby boy is safe,' he read. 'You must not try to find him. That will put his life – and yours – in danger. Your daughter bears a mark that puts you all at risk. It is for your whole family's safety that I have taken

Alex with me. He will be returned to you – but it is likely that it will not be for some time. I can't stress strongly enough that you must not try to find him. This is important. Mention Alex to no one. No one.'

The last word was barely out of his mouth when the paper spontaneously burst into flame. Striker dropped the burning note. Harmless ash settled on the floor.

'What is going on here?' Striker asked. 'What mark has Noah got? Who's taken Alex?'

Isla peeled off the blanket that covered her daughter and inspected the brand that Seth had left on her.

'It is the mark of the Dragonsbane,' Isla said. 'It means one day Noah will have a very important job to do.'

'And what about Alex?' Striker said. 'Who took him?'

'Presumably the seer who branded Noah,' Isla said softly. 'This is strange. Usually birthbrands are applied at a formal ceremony. Families get notice, time to arrange things. We didn't get that. There is something very strange going on here.'

Isla cradled her daughter close.

'What do we do?' Striker said.

'We must leave here … leave Talisker. We must take Noah to safety.'

'And Alex?' Striker said.

'We'll search for him. Discreetly. We need time and space to get a plan together.'

Noah felt numb. It was astounding to think that a little stamp could turn four lives upside-down. Her parents had lost their son and left their beloved farm, and ultimately lost their lives. Raven had been turned into a dog and Noah had spent her life as a deaf-mute.

Noah turned to look at the Descera. 'Why us?' she said.

'It is destiny, Noah,' Seth said. 'We Descera identified your family hundreds of years ago as being instrumental in saving Talisker from a great evil. That great evil is now upon us. It has arrived in your time – it is up to you to stop it.'

Noah felt a hand on her shoulder. She turned to Raven.

'It's *our* time,' he croaked. 'We'll do this together. Two heads are better than one.'

A hot lump burned in Noah's throat. She nodded.

Seth said, 'Well, you can't do it without the 13th key.'

Noah stood up. 'You know where it is?' she asked.

He nodded. 'May I have your ring?'

Noah was taken aback. 'My ring? What for?'

'Please trust me,' the Descera said as the phoenix appeared at his side.

Noah frowned as she slipped her mother's Academy ring from her finger. Reluctantly she went to place it on Seth's outstretched palm but without warning, the phoenix nipped it out of her fingers.

'Hey!' Noah cried.

Before she could make a grab at the bird, the phoenix disappeared over the edge of the brick wall. Noah raced after him with Raven at her side. She looked over the wall. The heat assaulted her face. Blinking away tears, Noah looked for Cecil, but there was no sign of him. *No,* Noah thought. *No, no, no.*

Noah spun around to face Seth. 'Where's he gone with my ring?'

'Patience, Noah,' Seth said calmly. 'He will return.'

Cecil re-emerged within seconds, alighting gracefully on the slate tiles. The phoenix bobbed down and placed her ring on the rocky ground. 'Give it a minute before you pick it up,' he warned. 'It'll be very hot.'

'No kidding?' she said, surprised the ring had survived a dip in the lava.

Unable to wait until it cooled, Noah dropped down on her hands and knees to inspect her mother's ring. 'Wow!' she said, staring at the multi-coloured stone, 'What's happened to my sapphire?'

'It is not a sapphire,' Seth said. 'It never was. That is a piece of fire-stone – dragonscale. I put a charm on it before I entrusted it to your family, Noah. I had to disguise it. No one could know what it really was. But now, by immersing the stone in lava, its bindings have been burned away. It has been returned to its original state.'

'So this piece of firestone has been in my family for six hundred years?' Noah said.

'Our family,' Raven said.

'Our family,' Noah echoed.

'Yes,' Seth said, picking up the ring from the floor and handing it to Noah. 'It has been in your family, ready for the time when it would be needed.'

Noah put the ring on her finger. 'That time being now,' she said.

'That time is now,' Seth confirmed. 'And now we make the 13th key.'

'Make it?' Noah said. 'Did you say *make* the 13th key?'

'Yes,' Seth said. 'We need to make the 13th key.'

Noah stared at him. 'We?'

'Think you can do it yourself?' Seth said.

'Of course not,' Noah said. 'I've got no idea how to make it.'

'Then you'll be needing my help,' the Descera said.

'And mine,' Cecil said.

'Okay,' Raven said. 'Let's make this thing.'

Chapter 21

'What are we going to make the key out of?' Noah asked, looking around the room.

'What are we going to make it *with*?' Raven added. 'There are no tools.'

'So many questions,' Seth chided gently.

Cecil shook himself from beak to tail tip, fluffing his two-tone plumage before composing himself to begin work.

'Please kneel down before the wall,' Seth said. 'Noah on my left, Raven on my right.'

The twins did as instructed.

'This is a significant day in the history of our world,' the Descera said once they were in position. 'Today the 13th key will be made. While the making of the key signifies great hope for Talisker, you must also recognise the danger such a power represents. In the wrong hands, the 13th key will condemn our world rather than save it.'

'So we can't let Orville get his hands on it,' Noah said.

'That is correct,' Cecil said. 'He needs it to accomplish his goal. If he acquires it, Talisker will be destroyed.'

'Okay,' Noah said, 'we will keep it safe.'

Raven nodded his agreement.

'Good. Now, the first thing you need to know is that the 13th key is not an "it",' Seth said looking at Noah, 'but a "she".'

A shudder raked through her body. 'You can't be serious.'

Seth nodded his head. 'Yes, Noah. *You* are the 13th key, or you will be once we are finished here.'

'That's ridiculous,' Noah said. 'How can the 13th key be a person?' Her blood went cold. In a whisper, she said, 'You're going to turn me into an instrument? You're going to kill me?'

Raven growled.

The phoenix burst into flame. 'At ease, Raven,' Cecil said. 'You have passed your first test.'

Raven stopped growling. He cocked his head. 'Test?'

'You are to protect your sister. You are the guardian of the 13th key,' he said. 'At the first sign of danger you reacted instinctively. That is good.'

'What are you going to do to me then?' Noah asked.

'Basically, you will be fused with the firestone,' Seth said. 'It will be part of you and you part of it. Each of the twelve existing keys has a piece of firestone in it; you will be no different in that regard. The big difference will be that you are a living, breathing instrument – not one made of metal or wood.'

Chase is going to love this, Noah thought, but she wasn't so keen on the idea herself. She looked at her ring.

'Ready to get started then?' Seth said.

Noah looked at her brother who, to her surprise, winked at her. She smiled. 'Ready.'

Seth nodded to Cecil.

The phoenix said, 'Okay. I'm going to take you for a dip in the lava—'

'What!' Noah said. 'Are you crazy? I thought you said you weren't going to hurt me.'

'Oh, for goodness sake!' Cecil said. 'Can you just listen without interrupting? I said I wasn't going to harm you and I won't. Okay?'

'Okay,' Noah mumbled.

'Promise that you won't interrupt again?'

'I promise.'

'Good. Now I need to immerse you in the lava because only when the firestone is surrounded by the dragon's blood can you weave its music with your own. And that's what you need to do. I said before that you need to be "fused" with the firestone, but what we're actually doing is intertwining your music with the music of the firestone. Now, what I need to do to protect you from the heat of the lava is to tuck you in my pouch.'

The phoenix stopped, checking to see if she would interrupt. Once satisfied that she wouldn't, he continued, 'All phoenixes have a pouch – males and females – and that will protect you from the heat. It's not the heat that is important in this process, it's the music. You need to be surrounded by the music of the lava. Now before you tell me that you won't fit in my pouch, I've already thought of a plan for that.'

'And that would be?'

'You're going to climb into one of the pockets in your trousers. Raven here, will then roll them up and pop them in my pouch and then I'll dive into the lava.'

Seth took off his robe and handed it to Noah. Thankful the Descera had trousers on, she put on the robe and slipped her own trousers off.

'I'm ready,' she said, handing her trousers to her brother.

Raven opened a pocket for her. Noah looked into the small space and wondered if they were really designed to have people in them.

'Wish me luck,' she said as she stepped into the pocket.

'Good luck,' he said.

Instinctively, she closed her eyes. She felt a brief tingling sensation, like being zapped all over with static electricity. When she opened her eyes, she didn't feel any different. She looked around her and the black fabric walls told her she was inside the pocket. Noah inspected her hands, arms and legs. They didn't look any different, just as they didn't feel any different. But when she looked up and saw Raven looking down at her, she knew she'd shrunk. Her brother's head seemed impossibly big.

She gave him the thumbs up. 'Be careful when you roll up the trousers,' she called.

He nodded and returned her gesture before buttoning the pocket closed. Darkness descended instantly. Noah held her breath and reached for something to hold onto. She felt like she was in a dark elevator ready to plummet to the ground at any moment. Finding nothing to hold onto, she decided to lie down.

The falling sensation never came and Noah wondered what was going on. Had the trousers been designed so that the movement of the wearer could not be felt inside the pockets? If so, that would imply that they'd been designed to carry live cargo. Inanimate objects wouldn't get motion sickness. She couldn't remember the name of the Major who'd invented the trousers, but if she survived this she would find out who it was and thank him personally.

Alone in the dark, Noah realised she knew what to do but not how to do it. Neither Seth nor Cecil had told her how to weave her own music with that of the firestone. As she contemplated her plight she felt the ring on her finger heating up. *I must be in the lava*, she thought. She sat up and looked at the ring. In defiance of the darkness, the iridescent colours shone out. She brought the ring closer to her eyes and peered intently into the stone.

At first the bright colours hurt her eyes but as they adjusted she realised she could see into the stone. Even though it appeared to be only half a centimetre thick, she felt like she was looking into the depths of space. The swirls and spots were more layered than she'd thought. She felt like she was looking into another universe – galaxy after galaxy greeted her the deeper she looked. Planets and moons clustered reverently around bright stars while quasars lurked on the galactic outskirts. Comets and meteors shot across space in a futile attempt to draw attention away from mesmerising multi-coloured nebula.

Seth's voice came to her. *You are looking back through time, Noah. You are seeing what Elani created.*

If I keep looking further and further, will I see the beginning of time?

Eventually, yes.

Cool.

But it will take you until the end of time to do it.

Not cool. Noah thought for a moment. *Does that mean we're halfway then?*

Halfway?

Halfway through time. If it takes me until the end of time to look back to the beginning, surely that means we're halfway.

It doesn't work like that, Noah. Time isn't linear.

Oh.

You need to close your eyes, Noah.

But it's so beautiful.

Yes, but you need to listen to the stone, not look at it. Looking at it will distract you. You must listen to the stone and listen to yourself and weave the music together.

How?

Noah, that is for you to figure out. I am here as your guide only. I cannot make the key, nor can anyone else. It is up to you to become the 13th key, without anyone else's interference. Be who you want to be.

Thanks. You're a big help.

You're welcome. Just let me know when you're done.

Right.

Noah lay down again and closed her eyes. She took several slow, deep breaths and listened to the music of the firestone. Being a piece of dragonscale, she had expected its music to be violent and discordant but it was quite the opposite. It was as beautiful as it was complex. In comparison she found her own music to be of variable quality. How was she supposed to weave them together? It would be like trying to weave course hessian with fine organza. Her heart sank. Sachin had told her that everyone had their own unique musical signature but until now she hadn't considered that there would be a difference in the quality of the music.

Do not despair, Seth said. *You are human. You are not supposed to be perfect. If you were perfect, you would not be human.*

But doesn't the 13th key have to be perfect?

No. Nothing perfect can endure in an imperfect world. As the 13th key, you have a job to do but it is still only a part of who you are. You are human; an imperfect being with many faults. Your music will change over your lifetime as you grow and learn but you can't change everything now. Remember, being the 13th key is only a part of who you are. Take of the firestone only what you need now, what fits. If you change too much you will no longer be you.

Noah could think of a few people who would consider that a good idea – her Aunt Polly, Mr Brennan and Emir topped that list. She took a deep breath, pushed such thoughts aside. Nothing would be gained by lying around worrying about her faults. If she wanted to live long enough to fix some of them, she had a job to do.

Patterns. It was all about patterns. And contrasts. Noah thought about hessian and organza again. She remembered a handbag she'd seen once in a second-hand shop in Sayle. It was cheap, white vinyl covered in hessian. White vinyl flowers with button centres had been sewn onto the hessian to decorate the front of the bag and the effect – while rustic – had been striking. Maybe, just maybe this could work. With an image of the handbag in her mind, she listened to her own music and pictured it as a piece of hessian. Against that backdrop she decorated it with rosettes of organza – music from the firestone.

When she was happy with her work she called in her mind to Seth.

Done? he asked.

Yes, she said. *I'm done.*

♪♫

Madame Priscilla looked up. 'Back so soon, Noah?' she said. 'Did you get lost?'

'No,' Noah said.

'I see you've found a friend,' she said, eyeing Raven.

'He's my brother,' Noah said.

Madame Priscilla frowned. 'What's he doing here?' she asked. 'Only those with the mark of the Dragonsbane may enter Dragonhall.'

'Unless they're escorted by a Descera,' Noah said. 'I found him in one of your rooms.'

'Descera?' Madame Priscilla said. 'You found a Descera here?'

Noah nodded. 'I did.'

The Dragonsbane sat back in her chair and laced her fingers over her abdomen. 'Then can I assume you found the 13th key?'

Again, Noah nodded. 'I did.'

Brinn slinked out from under the sideboard. 'About time,' the cat said. 'Dr Grainger is on his way over the bridge as we speak. We need to get this sorted out.'

'May I see the 13th key?' Madame Priscilla asked.

'You're looking at her,' Noah said.

The Dragonsbane's eyes narrowed. 'Her?'

'Me,' Noah clarified.

'Do you really expect me to believe that the 13th key is a person?' she said.

'Yep,' Noah said calmly. 'If you listen, you should be able to tell.'

Madame Priscilla closed her eyes for several moments. When she opened them she said, 'Well, that was unexpected. The Descera are cunning – a good play.'

'Our bargain?' Brinn prompted.

The Dragonsbane rose from her chair. 'Yes,' she said, looking at Noah's ring. 'We do not have much time.'

Raven moved closer to Noah. 'Priscilla, what do you think you're doing?' he asked.

Madame Priscilla strode across the room and reached behind a bookshelf on the far side. 'Trying to protect your sister,' she said, withdrawing her hand to reveal a long wooden staff. The old woman looked at Noah, 'No one can know that you are the 13th key. This'—she tapped the staff on the floor—'is my staff. It is made of petrified olluka wood and I use it to tune into the dragonsong. We will attach the stone from your ring to this staff and you will present it to the Academy as the 13th key.'

'What's olluka wood?' Noah asked.

'Olluka means flame,' Madame Priscilla said. 'So olluka trees are flame trees. They grow underground, rooted in lava – Xan's blood. They are massive, majestic trees.'

Mesmerised by the dark wood, Noah said, 'It's beautiful.'

The Dragonsbane nodded. 'And powerful. You wouldn't be here if it weren't for the olluka trees.'

'How's that?'

'Olluka trees connect our worlds. They act as portals. That's how you came here.'

Thinking of the weedy sapling she'd encountered in the woods behind Aunt Polly's house, Noah frowned. 'They must look better here.'

'What you saw was the very tip of a branch that has reached out from here – crossing space and time – to connect to Earth.'

Trees that grew through space? *I shouldn't be surprised,* Noah thought.

Brinn jumped up on the table. 'Dr Grainger is inside Dragonhall.'

'Noah, give me your ring,' Madame Priscilla said. 'Brinn, you and Raven organise the paperwork to make Noah Dragonsbane. It's on the table over there.'

'You're not going to make me Dragonsbane?' Brinn asked.

'Things have changed,' Madame Priscilla said as she accepted Noah's ring. 'There is no time to mess about. The Descera have demonstrated their faith in this girl so I must follow their lead. She will be Dragonsbane and have a staff that looks like the 13th key before Dr Grainger walks through that door.'

Raven, still exercising his vocal cords, said, 'Should I stop him?'

'No,' Noah said. 'He is still part of this. I know what he needs to do.'

The Dragonsbane gave a curt nod as she prised the piece of firestone from Noah's ring with a knife from the table.

'How will we stick it to the wood?' Noah asked.

Madame Priscilla handed the stone and the staff to her. 'You're the 13th key, Noah. You and the stone are one. Tell it what to do.'

The staff was cool and not as heavy as she expected. It fit comfortably in her hand and while generally straight, it retained the character of the tree branch it had been. Noah marvelled at the small knots and bumps that covered its dark surface. Dark lines also scored its surface, like etchings of an artist. Noah held the firestone over one of the knots and closed her eyes. She listened to the music of the ancient wood. In her mind she bound the music of the stone and wood together. Noah opened her eyes.

'Good,' Madame Priscilla said. 'Now Noah, sit in that chair.'

The Dragonsbane pointed. Noah sat.

Madame Priscilla turned her attention to Raven and Brinn. 'Paperwork?'

'Awaiting your signature,' Brinn said.

The Dragonsbane took her seat and snatched a pen from the table as someone knocked on the door.

'Come in,' Madame Priscilla said as she scrawled her name across the paperwork Raven put in front of her.

Raven moved to stand behind his sister's chair as the door opened. A wiry man in Academy garb strode into the room, his surprise at the other guests obvious.

'Dragonsbane,' Dr Grainger said with a bow to Madame Priscilla. 'What is happening here?'

Madame Priscilla rose to shake the doctor's hand. 'It is good to see you Dr Grainger, but I am no longer Dragonsbane. That is now Noah's job.'

The man's eyes widened, his eyebrows arcing in perfect symmetry. 'Why did you do that?' he asked.

'She has the 13th key,' Madame Priscilla said.

His grey eyes bored into Noah. 'The staff?' he said. 'That's the 13th key?'

Noah nodded, turning the staff slightly so he could see the firestone embedded into its surface.

'What sorcery is this?' he demanded. 'That is the staff of the Dragonsbane – always has been. How is it that it now bears a piece of firestone? Where did it come from?'

'From here,' Noah said, showing him the empty setting on her Academy ring.

'We have much to discuss, Dr Grainger,' Brinn said. 'Please sit down.'

The doctor perched on a seat but looked far from comfortable. Noah had some sympathy for him. She felt very uneasy.

'Dr Grainger,' Noah said. 'I understand that you're unhappy with what's been done here but we all have a job to do and we need to get started quickly.'

Dr Grainger glared at her. 'You're not going to be giving me orders, Miss Chord,' he said coldly.

'Of course not,' Noah said, 'but I will tell you what I know. I've been to Seychelles and seen the generator that Orville will use in his electricity network. Sachin was captured and is on his way to Leninstar which is where I am going from here. The other problem is that King Tambian's army is marching on Mellifont now.'

'Yes, I know,' he said. 'I heard that in Jagar last night.'

Noah nodded. 'As I did. So someone has to get back to Mellifont and evacuate the city.'

'And you think that "someone" is me?' he said.

'Yes,' Noah said.

'Even if I get back before the army—'

'Which you should,' Brinn interrupted.

Dr Grainger turned his withering gaze on the feline. 'Even if I get back before the army, there won't be time to clear the city.'

'There is a quicker way back that will buy us time,' Noah said.

'Oh yes? And what's that?'

'Through the lava tunnels,' Noah said.

Dr Grainger snorted. 'Lava tunnels have lava in them, don't they?'

'Yes,' she said.

'I've heard that lava is pretty hot,' the doctor replied.

Noah explained about the phoenix's pouch and how she had been immersed in lava while inside one of the pockets in her trousers.

'I have spoken to the phoenix,' Noah said. 'He will take you to Mellifont through the lava tunnels. Then you'll have time to evacuate everyone to the underground.'

'The army won't have a target,' Dr Grainger said, rubbing his chin.

'Correct,' Noah said.

A reluctant smile creased the doctor's face. 'I'm picturing the king's army storming an empty city …'

'Entertaining?' Madame Priscilla asked.

'Somewhat entertaining,' Dr Grainger admitted.

Brinn purred. 'Then what are we waiting for?'

♪♫

Noah decided to chance the rickety bridge over the moat on her own. Being Dragonsbane and the 13th key had to count for something. Although she wanted to run to get off the bridge sooner, she forced herself to walk calmly. When she reached the other side where her friends waited, she almost collapsed with relief.

Chase grabbed her in a suffocating hug. 'So glad you're back,' she said.

'Successful meeting?' Emir asked as he physically restrained Alan from joining in the hug.

Unable to suck in enough air to answer his question in words, Noah nodded.

'Jemima, unhand her,' Emir said.

Reluctantly, Chase did as she was told. 'You're Dragonsbane?' she said to Noah as she released her.

'Yes, I am.'

Alan applauded enthusiastically. 'Congratulations, Noah!' he said as Chase launched herself at Noah again.

This time both girls ended up on the ground. Emir and Ardis looked at each other. Emir shrugged while Ardis shook his head.

As Ardis pulled Chase off Noah, Emir said, 'You need to control yourself, Jemima. You almost knocked her into the moat. What an inglorious end that would be for Talisker's new Dragonsbane – to be killed in a freak hugging accident.'

Emir offered Noah his hand. Surprised but not wanting to seem ungrateful, she let him help her to her feet.

'Thanks,' she said.

He nodded then looked at the staff on the ground. '13th key?' he asked.

'Yes,' Noah said. 'I made it.'

'Made it?' Emir said.

'With help from Seth and Cecil,' Noah replied.

Chase squealed. 'That is priceless. I so didn't see that coming. What a great twist,' she said.

'That's amazing,' Alan said, staring in wonder at the staff. 'You've really outdone yourself.'

Noah gazed at the firestone in the staff. 'That's the stone from my mother's ring. It was a piece of firestone the whole time. The Descera had put a charm on it so no one would detect it.'

'Fabulous,' Chase breathed.

'But the best part,' Noah continued with a smile, 'is that now, I have my very own wand.'

Chase's eyes widened in horror.

Alan placed himself between the girls but Ardis was quicker. The Elani warrior took Chase's wrists and held them behind her back.

'Noah,' Emir said, 'you've had your fun. I trust that's the last time we're going to hear that?'

'I make no promises,' Noah said, 'but yes, I've had my fun … for now. I have another surprise for you though,' she continued. 'There is someone I need you to meet.'

A look of panic swept across Chase's face. Breaking free of Ardis's grip, she clamped her hands over her ears and bolted as if a swarm of goblins was after her.

'Suspense junkie,' Emir muttered as Ardis strolled off after her.

As Noah looked at Emir, a thought occurred to her. 'You like her, don't you?' she said.

'Jemima?' Emir replied. 'She's hard not to like.'

Chase was intense and undoubtedly crazy but that made her a lot of fun to be around.

'Does Ardis know about this?' Noah said.

To her surprise, Emir smiled. 'I don't like her that much,' he said. 'She's better with a bit of distance – like a tornado. From a distance, a tornado is quite spectacular to watch but, if you get too close, you get sucked into the chaos and it's mostly just painful.'

'You know, I think she'd actually like that analogy,' Noah said as her friend returned under escort.

'Okay,' Chase said reluctantly. 'I'm ready.'

Noah gave her friend a sympathetic smile and then opened her pocket. Raven sprang from inside, landing nimbly beside his sister.

'Whoa!' Chase said. 'You can carry people in there?'

'Yep,' Noah said. 'This is my twin brother, Alex.' Looking at her brother, she added, 'But unless you want to get bitten, you should probably call him Raven.'

Chase gasped. 'Raven! Oh my goodness! One of two! That's cool.'

Noah smiled and nodded.

Ardis stepped forward first, hand extended. 'Nice to see you again, *Raven*,' he said. 'Having experienced your biting before, I am happy to call you Raven to avoid a repeat of that.'

Raven blushed. 'Yeah,' he said, his speech still strained. 'Sorry about that.'

Alan and Emir re-introduced themselves to Raven in turn and Chase hugged him.

'You must be relieved to have found him,' Chase said to Noah.

'Absolutely,' Noah said. 'One of the Descera at Seychelles found him and brought him here to Ironside using the underground tunnels. Seth returned him to human form and they've been waiting for us to arrive.'

Chase beamed. 'You can fill me in on all the details later.'

'We'll have time on the way to Leninstar,' Noah said.

'And speaking of Leninstar,' Emir said. 'We need to get going.'

Chapter 22

'Well, we have loads to do,' Chase said, surveying the table that was currently blanketed in sketches, pattern pieces and fabrics.

'You got that right,' Noah agreed.

They had one more night before they reached Leninstar and Noah needed to put some work into her collection. It was the same cabin they'd stayed in on their way out of the royal city to Seychelles and, for now, the girls had it to themselves. But Noah was finding motivation difficult to come by.

'Look, how long are you going to mope about like this?' Chase said.

Noah frowned. 'I am *not* moping,' she said, 'but if I *were*, I think I have good reason.'

'Piffle,' Chase replied. 'You lost a dog but you gained a brother.'

'Bugger off, Chase. I'm allowed to grieve for my dog.'

'Undoubtedly. Grieving is one thing, but moping is quite different. We need to get this collection sorted – moping about will get us nowhere. There's a limit to how long you can do this.'

Noah glared at her friend. Chase's complexion was at present far from flawless – her flushed cheeks revealing her consternation at Noah's behaviour.

'So in your *vast* experience of the world, how long would be acceptable for me to "mope about"?' Noah asked.

Ignoring the sarcasm, Chase considered her question. 'I'd say about two pages.'

'I'm sorry?' Noah said.

'Two pages … three – tops,' she declared.

Noah shook her head. 'Bloody fantasy writers,' she muttered under her breath.

'Fictioneer,' Chase said as she pushed to her feet. 'Raven's the one I feel sorry for. *He* was stuck in a dog's body for sixteen years.'

'Yeah, I know that,' Noah said. 'Thanks for the guilt trip.' Noah chewed her bottom lip. 'He was such a fabulous dog.'

'With a particularly casual attitude to obedience, as I recall,' Chase said with a smile.

'Sometimes,' Noah conceded.

Chase changed the subject. 'Did you ever think you'd be vying for the position of royal tailor?'

Noah shook her head. 'If you'd said that to me, even a month ago, I'd have thought you were crazy. A month ago I had the Junior Design State Titles in my sights but now …'

'But now what?' Chase asked.

Noah hesitated, not sure how to put her thoughts into words.

'But now it's the furthest thing from my mind,' she said finally.

Chase looked at her. 'Okay, so where do we start?'

'First, let's make sure we've got all the designs we need for each category,' Noah said. 'I've been distracted for the past few days. I need to get my head back in the right space.'

'Okay,' Chase said. 'We have four categories – Ceremonial, Formal wear, Loungewear and Casual. In each of those categories you need to consider the king, the queen, Princess Catriona and Baby Vernon – sixteen outfits in all – less the four that you've finished already. That leaves twelve to go.'

'Thirteen,' Noah corrected her.

Chase raised an eyebrow.

'Orville,' she said.

'Then make that fourteen,' Chase said.

It was Noah's turn to raise an eyebrow.

'If he's getting one then I, as your best friend, want one too.'

Noah smiled. 'Goes without saying—'

'And Raven will need something too.'

'Settle down – the Festival is in a fortnight's time and we're going to be pushing it to get the thirteen done that we need.'

'Fourteen, you mean,' Chase said.

'Okay, fourteen,' Noah said. 'If we've got fourteen then we really do need to get started.'

Chase saluted. 'I'm at your service,' she said. 'I can finish the queen's lounging outfit tonight.'

'Great,' Noah said, 'I'll finish Princess Catriona's formal dress and we'll have six completed outfits.'

The girls worked for two hours before Alan and Raven returned. Noah looked up when the door opened. Her brother's arm was draped around Alan's neck and the Academy auditor practically dragged his taller companion through the doorway.

'Raven,' Noah said, 'are you okay?'

'Fine,' Raven said, wheezing. 'Ardis … is … a … tough … teacher.'

Alan eased Raven onto his swag – a feat made more difficult by the sword hanging in its sheath at Raven's side.

'We could take the sword off?' Alan suggested.

'It's fine … where it … is,' Raven said, pushing sweaty hair back from his brow. 'Just fine.'

'If you want to be a warrior, you'll have to work hard,' Chase said.

'Yeah,' Raven said. 'That's what Ardis said.'

Noah returned to her duties. She was never happier than when in the midst of a sea of haberdashery. Sitting at her sewing machine was cathartic. She whizzed through the pieces she'd had pinned for the princess's formal dress, enjoying the steady rhythm of the stitching.

'I need a model,' Noah declared when she was done. 'Is there a would-be princess in here anywhere?'

To Noah's surprise, Alan struck a pose.

Noah grimaced. 'Exactly what look are you going for there?' she asked.

'Regal yet demure,' Alan said. 'How'd I do?'

Noah burst out laughing as she passed the dress to Chase. 'I think Chase is more Princess Catriona's size,' she said.

'It couldn't have been that bad,' Alan said affecting an extravagant pout.

'You're right – it wasn't that bad,' Noah admitted.

Alan looked relieved, which was in stark contrast to Chase who eyed the dress like it might bite her.

'Thank you,' Alan said. 'As I think I mentioned to you before, I have done some modelling.'

'It wasn't that *bad*,' Noah repeated, 'it was *worse*.'

'You'd want to be careful, Noah,' Alan warned, wagging a pudgy finger at her. 'The day will come when you need my modelling expertise …'

'Okay, yes. I'm sorry, Alan,' Noah replied, trying her best to look repentant, 'but in the meantime, could you look after Raven?'

Happy to be of service, Alan went to work.

'He's developed quite the sense of humour, hasn't he?' Chase said as she watched Alan attend to his assigned task.

Noah looked at her friend. 'What?'

'Alan? Modelling? That's pretty funny.'

'I don't think he's joking, Chase.'

Chase shook her head. 'It's got to be auditor humour. Surely.'

'I wouldn't count on it. Now come on. Let's get this dress sorted.'

Once Noah had helped her friend into the dress, she began the momentous task of cinching, tucking and pinning the multi-layered gown.

'Will you be ready for me to start the beading on the bodice tonight?' Chase asked.

Stabbing a pin into her pincushion, Noah said, 'I hope so but it'll take me a while to hand stitch all the scalloping into this skirt.'

'Have you started my suit yet?' Raven asked, once he'd regained his breath.

His speech was improving – probably a result of all the practice he was getting. Noah thought he was trying to make up for the sixteen years he hadn't been able to talk.

'Not yet,' she said, 'but don't worry, it's under control.'

'Really?'

'Yes,' Noah lied.

Brinn's sudden appearance cut off any reply Raven might have made.

'Where are the boys?' Brinn asked.

'Emir and Ardis?' Noah said.

'Yes, that is who I'm referring to,' Brinn said. 'Have you picked up others?'

Noah frowned. 'Of course not. What do you take us for?'

Before Brinn could respond, Chase jumped in. 'That was a rhetorical question, Brinn. It does not require an answer.'

'Pity,' Brinn said. 'So where are they?'

'They're guarding the camp,' Chase said.

'Obviously they are not guarding against cats. Lucky for me. Anyway,' she said, with a glance towards the corner, 'I'm glad to see the staff is safe.'

Unable to help herself, Noah said, 'My wand, you mean?'

'No,' Brinn said, her tone echoing the look of disgust on Chase's face, 'I meant the staff.'

'The 13th key,' Alan said, not wanting to be left out of the conversation.

'Yes,' said Chase, 'the 13th key. Show some respect, Noah.'

Noah did her best not to wince. She felt guilty about lying to Chase about the true nature of the 13th key. There'd be a ruckus if Chase ever learned the truth and not just because Noah had lied to her. Chase was thrilled with the "elegant convergence of plot elements", as she called it. She thought that combining the Dragonsbane's staff with the firestone concealed in the Academy ring that had passed through Noah's family for hundreds of years, was masterful. Madame Priscilla's impromptu solution to hiding Noah's secret had blindsided Chase – something that only enhanced Noah's respect for the former Dragonsbane.

Noah looked at the empty setting on her ring. 'I have respect,' she said quietly. 'If it wasn't for that stone … we'd be living a quiet life on a farm with our parents.'

'The farm is yours now, you know,' Brinn said.

'What? Really?' Noah said.

Raven sat up. '*Ours*, you mean? The farm belongs to *us*.'

'No,' Brinn said. 'I mean the farm belongs to Noah.'

Noah's eyes narrowed. 'How do you know that?'

'I know a great many things,' the cat bragged, 'but how I know them is none of your business.'

'Fine,' Noah said. 'Just tell us what you know. Please.'

'Okay,' Brinn said. 'Before your parents left Talisker, they made sure you were registered – the farm would never pass to you if your birth wasn't recorded here. Your mother then organised for a friend of hers to manage the farm in their absence. Now that they've passed, Leila holds the farm in trust for you until you return and claim it. As Seth advised, Raven's birth was never registered so technically, he doesn't have a share in the farm.'

Noah looked at her brother. 'It is *ours*,' she assured him.

Brinn said, 'Your parents returned to the farm on many occasions after you were given the birthbrand. It was partly to check on the farm but mostly to maintain a connection with their son since that was the last place they saw him. There is a cairn where he lay during the ceremony that Seth showed you. On every visit they laid a stone in his memory.'

'I'd like to see it someday,' Noah said wistfully.

'Save the world,' Brinn said, 'and I'll take you there myself.'

'You're on,' Noah said.

Brinn jumped up onto the table and stretched. 'Have you thought about how to use the fabric you got from Madame Priscilla?' she asked.

'I've thought about it,' Noah said, 'but I haven't come up with anything yet.'

Of all the exotic fabrics Noah had purchased on Talisker, the material she'd procured from Madame Priscilla was unique. Strange. Powerful. Dangerous. It could be a weapon – she knew that much – but she didn't know how to make it work.

'Give it to Alan,' Brinn said.

Noah looked at the cat and then at Alan. Alan looked like he'd won a lottery. A big lottery.

'Really?' Noah said.

Brinn licked her paw and then said, 'Yes. Really.'

Shaking her head but secretly grateful for something to keep Alan out of her hair, Noah retrieved the swatch of fabric from her pocket. Alan accepted it reverently – and to Noah's astonishment, silently – and went to sit in the corner. He settled himself and focused on his task. Even when the cabin door opened, Alan didn't look around.

Emir entered. He looked at Brinn and nodded. 'Here to escort us to Leninstar?' he asked.

'Not to escort you exactly,' the cat said, 'but I have a suggestion.'

Emir raised an eyebrow. 'Jemima, could you go and find Ardis, please? He'll need to hear this plan.'

'I'll go,' Raven offered, struggling to his feet.

'No, no,' Chase said. 'I'll go – be back in a minute.'

Noah watched her friend make a concerted effort to walk rather than skip out of the room.

'Do you have to encourage her?' Noah said to Emir once Chase was out the door.

'I don't know what you're talking about,' he said.

'You do know what I'm talking about,' Noah replied, 'and you also know that I think it's gross.'

Emir gave her a cool stare. 'What you think is irrelevant,' he said. 'I would have thought you'd be happy for your friend.'

'And you're still not to let on that we all know that they like each other,' Raven added. 'They still think we don't know what's going on.'

In truth Noah didn't want to know exactly what was going on between Chase and Ardis, so confronting her friend about it was the last thing on her mind. 'Perhaps we could all just focus on the job at hand?' she suggested.

Chapter 23

Leninstar was buzzing. The Solstice Festival was less than a fortnight away and preparations were in full swing. There would be celebrations across Talisker, but those in the king's city would be the most extravagant and audacious. According to Alan, the Solstice Festival on Talisker was always a spectacular affair but this one was different. Very different. Not only would the king be hosting a fashion gala to choose his new tailor, but Orville would deliver his promised new technology – electricity.

With electricity, the residents of Talisker would have reliable lighting and heating. Factories would be constructed to manufacture everything their hearts desired. Taliskerans coveted the Earth technologies Orville had shown them – cars, phones, kitchen appliances, televisions – and with blood magic, they had the means to produce the electricity required to deliver them. Orville's plan had captured the popular imagination but Taliskerans would see none of it if his plan succeeded.

As Noah and Emir walked along the main street, Noah watched the workmen erecting electric street lights and, although the day was warm, she shuddered. They walked in silence until they reached the palace gates.

'In we go,' Emir said.

'Looks busy,' Noah replied as she surveyed the crowds in the palace grounds.

'Lots of things for people to see,' Emir said.

'We'll never convince them that Orville's the bad guy,' she said.

'No, we won't,' Emir agreed. 'Have you noticed that he's not taking the credit for himself? He's actually making the king the focal point.'

'Why would he do that?' Noah asked.

'He's smart,' Emir said. 'If he had the adulation of the people, the king would see him as a threat. Kings generally don't like threats – they tend to eliminate them.'

'But if the people are happy and the king's happy, Orville is free to call the shots,' Noah said.

'Correct.'

They continued walking towards the palace and Noah's stomach churned. 'There are still a lot of the king's soldiers about,' she said. 'They're obviously not all in Mellifont.'

Emir nodded. 'You can bet that there are only enough here to maintain public order. Of course, there'll be increased crowds for such a huge event and Orville needs to keep order to ensure things go to plan.'

'He really is dangerously clever, isn't he,' she said.

'Yes. Now buy yourself some roasted corn and wait for me here.'

Without waiting for her reply, Emir strode away. Blood pounded in Noah's ears as she ordered the snack she didn't feel like eating. Her stomach churned painfully but she forced herself to munch on the corn while she awaited Emir's return. She watched Leninstar's residents to distract herself. Brinn's plan was good in theory but it was no picnic. Noah wished Emir would hurry up. She was only halfway through the snack when someone grabbed her elbow.

'You need to come with me, Miss,' said Emir, dressed in a soldier's uniform, 'and you won't make any trouble.'

Noah looked at him. 'Why? Where are we going?' she asked.

'To security,' he said. 'Now move.'

'I haven't done anything,' she said indignantly.

'You'll come quietly or I can call more guards,' he said. 'Up to you.'

Noah mumbled under her breath and hoped the show was convincing for those around them. Emir yanked her arm to get her moving.

'Ouch!' she exclaimed.

'If you cooperate, it won't hurt,' he said.

Noah frowned. It needed to look authentic but she suspected Emir was actually enjoying his role. She continued her show of resistance until they reached the palace doors. *This isn't going to work,* she thought as they approached the main doors. Four soldiers, two on either side of the doors, stood guard.

One of them nodded at Emir. 'Where're you taking her?' he asked.

'Security station,' Emir said flatly. 'She claims to be a designer competing in the king's Fashion Gala. Wants a copy of the conditions.'

'Process her,' the guard replied.

Emir put his closed fist over his breastplate. The soldier returned the gesture and then waved them through.

'You know where the office is?' Emir said quietly.

Noah nodded. 'Not far.'

She led Emir to the room where she'd got her application form on her last visit.

'Are you going to kick the door down?' she asked.

Emir gave her a cool stare. 'Perhaps I'll try the handle first,' he said. He turned the handle and the door gave way easily.

'Just for the record, Chase would have preferred you to kick it down,' Noah said.

The study was relatively small but opulently furnished. Orville sat behind a mahogany desk. He looked up as they entered the room and smiled.

'Ah,' he said. 'You made it. I'm so pleased.'

'We need a room,' Emir said. 'Things are kind of busy in town at the moment and we're having trouble securing accommodation.'

'Indeed,' Orville said. 'I'm sure I can arrange something. *Guards!*'

The outer door to the study opened and two soldiers appeared.

'What is your bidding, Lord Orville?' one asked.

'Take this soldier,' he said, waving in Emir's direction, 'to find suitable accommodation for Miss Chord here. She'll need secure premises for her and her entourage so she can finish her collection for the fashion gala at the Solstice Festival.'

'As you wish, my Lord,' the soldier said.

Without a backward glance, Emir left with the two guards.

Before the door had closed, Orville said, 'Have you started my suit for the Gala?'

'It's still in the design phase,' Noah said.

Orville stood and walked out from behind his desk to stand in front of her. She felt her chest tighten. Once again she cursed his good looks.

'Have you found the 13th key?' he asked.

'No.'

'Tut-tut, Noah,' he said, wagging his finger. 'You're a terrible liar. Let's try that again. Have you found the 13th key?'

'Yes,' she said.

'May I see it?'

'No.'

'No?'

'I don't have it here,' she said.

Orville looked at her trousers. 'Are you *sure* it's not in one of those pockets?'

Noah smiled. 'I left it with my friends,' she said.

An almost imperceptible frown swept across his face. 'You're too trusting, Noah,' he said. 'Anyway, I'll see it when you all get here.'

To her surprise, he took her hands in his. His hands were soft but his grip was strong. He pulled her closer to him.

Orville smiled. 'I'm going to kiss you, Noah,' he said.

He pressed his lips gently onto hers. She didn't know if he was a good kisser or not – never having kissed a boy before – but she decided that she was enjoying it. It was wrong on so many levels she knew, him being the evil egomaniac that was just about to destroy the world and all, but it couldn't be totally bad … surely … not if it felt this good … could it?

Noah hadn't expected her first kiss to be like this. In fact, she hadn't given much thought to what her first kiss – or any kiss for that matter – would be like. Her passion was fashion, not boys.

Without warning Chase's face flashed in her mind. Even though it was an apparition, it was clear that the apparition was not happy.

What are you doing? it asked.

None of your business, Noah told it.

You can't be doing that, it insisted.

It's research, Noah said.

What?

Research, she repeated. *I can find out a lot about him this way …*

And it was true, Noah had found out something. She didn't know how or if it would help her – but she knew one thing. Orville was not from Talisker – not totally. He was like her – part Taliskeran and part Earthling.

♪♫

'Noah, what are you doing?' Emir asked.

'I'm getting my things together,' she said.

'No, you're not. You're just moving things around. Get that stuff packed and hurry up. I don't know why you had to take all that stuff out in the first place. You knew we were going to set up at the palace,' he said.

Six soldiers waited outside the room Mrs Sloane had given them for the day. The house mistress was fully booked for the Solstice Festival and she'd only been able to put them up for one night. Once the soldiers escorted them to the palace, they would be under house arrest. Brinn's master plan.

'Noah, what is wrong with you?' Chase asked, shaking her head.

'Nothing,' Noah said. 'Would you all just lay off me? How do you expect me to get organised when you're badgering me constantly?'

Chase grabbed Noah's wrists. Startled, Noah looked up.

'What—'

'Shush,' Chase said, 'just look at me.'

Noah squirmed as her friend peered at her for several moments.

'Right, my girl, you're coming with me,' Chase declared.

'Where are you going?' Emir said.

'I'm just going to have a quick word with Noah in the next room. We'll be right back. You all just wait here.'

Chase dragged her though the doorway into the adjoining room where they found Brinn lying on the table.

234

'Afternoon, girls,' she purred, 'almost ready to go and camp at the palace?'

Past being surprised by the cat's unheralded appearances, Chase said, 'Busy here, Brinn. Give us a moment would you?'

'Go for it,' Brinn replied, stretching extravagantly.

Chase turned her attention back to Noah. 'Spill,' she demanded.

'Spill what?' Noah said.

'What happened at the palace? What did Orville do to you?'

Noah felt the heat rising in her cheeks and look down. 'Nothing, nothing,' she said.

'Look at me,' Chase said.

Reluctantly, Noah did.

Chase's eyes narrowed. 'Why are you blushing?' she asked. 'He kissed you, didn't he!'

For someone who so loved suspense, she could be very blunt at times.

'The plot thickens,' Brinn said as she jumped down from the table to rub against Noah's leg.

That unsettled Noah more than Chase's interrogation. Brinn had never showed Noah even the slightest hint of affection and she sincerely hoped she refrained from any future demonstrations.

Chase put a hand on each of her shoulders. Noah winced as Chase's fingers dug into her flesh.

'That hurts,' Noah said.

'Good,' Chase said. 'If you're feeling pain it means you are focused. That's what I need from you at the moment. Now, tell me everything that happened.'

'With Orville, you mean?'

Chase nodded.

'He sent Emir with some guards to find a room, he asked me about his suit and about the 13th key.'

'Was anyone else there?' Chase asked.

'No,' Noah said.

Chase slapped her lightly on the side of the head.

'What was that for?' Noah said.

'That's for being an idiot,' her friend replied.

'Why am I an idiot?'

'For letting him kiss you!'

'Oh, for Pete's sake, it was just a kiss,' Noah said.

'Really!'

'Yes, really.'

'If it was "just a kiss" why didn't you mention it before?' Chase demanded.

Noah didn't answer her.

'First one, wasn't it,' Chase said.

It was not a question so Noah didn't answer it, but her silence condemned her.

'Knew it,' Chase said.

Noah's contrition evaporated in the heat of the anger that welled up inside her. 'And so what if it was?' she demanded. 'Given that the world could end in less than a fortnight, it could be my only kiss. Ever! Did you think of that? No,' she continued without giving Chase a chance to reply, 'you did not. And considering the way you and Ardis have been carrying on – sneaking off and smooching every chance you get – I don't think you're in any position to be telling me how to behave.'

Chase looked genuinely shocked which Noah found empowering.

'You didn't think I knew about that, did you,' Noah said.

'No,' Chase said, recovering her composure a little, 'but that's irrelevant—'

'Irrelevant?' Noah said. 'So it's okay for you but not for me? Are you listening to yourself? Do you know what a hypocrite you are?'

'The kiss is not my problem,' Chase clarified. 'Although if it was a kiss you wanted, you certainly had better options—'

'You had someone in mind?' Noah said.

'Of course she did,' Brinn snapped. 'You really are an idiot, Noah. I'm sure if you look through her journal, you'll find you were supposed to kiss Emir.'

'You've read my journal?' Chase demanded.

'Don't be stupid,' Brinn said. 'Cats don't read.'

'Emir!' Noah groaned. 'You've got to be kidding, he's beastly – and moody.'

Brinn's tail flicked. 'Well, you'd be the expert on moody,' she said.

'Noah, Brinn's right,' Chase said.

'I am not moody,' Noah insisted.

Chase waved away that comment, 'Not that,' she said. 'She's right about you being an idiot.'

Noah bristled. It was a distinction that didn't make her feel any better.

'Well, idiot or not, I have a lot of work to do at the palace and I don't have time to stand around listening to you two insult me. If you don't have anything constructive to offer me, then go away.'

Noah found that she was shaking. Chase caught her in a bear hug.

'Don't be mad,' she said. 'I really am trying to help.'

The connecting door opened and Emir and Ardis appeared.

'Hello, boys,' Brinn said.

'Hello, cat,' Emir replied.

Brinn gave him a moment to consider his transgression and correct it, but when he didn't, she said, 'I have a name, you know.'

Emir raised an eyebrow. 'So do I, you know,' he said.

Brinn swished her tail but said nothing.

'We need to get going,' Emir said.

Chase looked at him. 'Yes, just a second,' she said. Turning to Noah, she said, 'I'm in research mode. You need to know your enemy, Noah and I will dig up every bit of dirt on Orville that I possibly can. Is there anything else you can tell me?'

Noah looked at her friend. She really did need to know her enemy but she also needed Chase's sewing skills.

'I really need you to help me with my collection,' Noah said. 'Everything is so intricate and elaborate – the beading on the princess's ball gown will take at least a day.'

'I can do both,' Chase said.

'I'll take care of getting information about Orville,' Emir said.

'But I'm good at research,' Chase insisted. 'It's part of what I do.'

Ardis jumped in before Emir could speak. 'You could both do it,' he suggested.

'I don't need her help,' Emir said, 'but Noah does.'

'You don't have to refer to me in the third person,' Chase said. 'I'm right here.'

Emir looked at her. 'I don't need your help but Noah does.'

'He's from Earth,' Noah blurted.

Everyone looked at her. Noah looked at Chase. 'You asked me if I knew anything else,' she said. 'Orville is like me – partly from here and partly from Earth.'

Chase's eyes nearly popped out of her head. 'I take it back,' she breathed. 'You are not an idiot. You're a genius.'

'For the record, I still think she's an idiot,' Brinn said.

'Brinn,' Chase said, 'I need to get out of here and back to Earth.'

'And you're telling me this because …'

'Because you're the only one who could make that happen.'

'I'm not a taxi service, you know,' she sniffed.

'I will buy you cat treats.'

Brinn cocked her head. 'How may bags?'

'Ten,' Chase said.

'Twenty,' Brinn countered.

'Fifteen.'

'Twenty-five.'

'Twenty-five?' Chase said. 'Do you understand how haggling works?'

'Rules don't apply to her, remember?' Noah said.

Chase sighed. 'Right. Twenty-five.'

'Done,' Brinn said. 'Ready to go?'

'Ready,' Chase confirmed.

Emir frowned. 'You need to hurry back, Jemima,' he said sternly. 'This collection needs to be finished.'

Chase saluted before turning to face Noah. 'Before I go,' she said, 'promise me one thing?'

'What's that?'

Chase leaned in close so she could whisper in Noah's ear. 'Do wangle a kiss from Emir if you get the chance,' she said.

Noah shoved her friend. 'As if,' she said.

'God, you two are nauseating,' Brinn said.

'Get over it,' Noah said.

'Is that really your best comeback?'

'It's as good as you deserve,' Noah said.

'At least I'm not an idiot,' Brinn said with a flick of her tail.

Chapter 24

'Well, where is she?' Orville demanded.

Noah was enjoying watching the soldiers squirm. Chase's disappearance had them completely flummoxed.

'You were supposed to bring me six people. Six.'

'I don't know what happened, my Lord,' one of the guards said. 'One minute she was there and the next … just … gone.'

Orville's eyes narrowed but he kept his composure. 'People don't just disappear. Find the writer and bring her back here.'

Four soldiers left the room, leaving the other four to do Orville's next bidding.

'And now, I'll take the 13th key for safekeeping,' Orville said.

Noah's heart felt like stone. She could feel her companion's eyes on her but she kept her gaze on Orville.

'And if I won't hand it over?' she asked.

'Do you want to see Sachin again?' he replied.

'How do I know you haven't killed him already?' Noah asked.

'You don't,' Orville said, 'but is it a risk you're willing to take?'

Noah inhaled slowly and deeply and then exhaled. Reluctantly she took the Dragonsbane's staff from one of her pockets and handed it to Orville.

Orville admired the olluka staff. 'That is beautiful,' he said at last. 'And I assure you, I will keep it safe.'

With a wink at Noah he turned and left the room, taking two guards with him. The two remaining soldiers barricaded the door and positioned themselves in front of it.

'We need to retrieve that staff,' Emir said.

'Patience, Emir,' Ardis said. 'We will find a way but we must be careful.'

Noah turned to survey her new abode. The studio she'd been assigned was huge. There were racks to hang her garments on, pigeon holes to store bits and pieces in, and long sliding shelves to house patterns and cut fabric pieces. Along one wall were separate cutting and sewing tables. In the adjoining room, were five mannequins – one for each member of the royal family and one for Orville. Orville had reminded her that the competition guidelines required all garments to be a perfect fit. She wondered if the other designers had to make him an outfit. Perhaps he was going to choose the one he liked best on the night.

Emir interrupted her thoughts.

'What can I do to help you, Noah?' he asked.

'The competition guidelines,' she said, retrieving them from her pockets. 'I haven't read them properly. If you could have a look through them – that'd be great. I don't need any nasty surprises at the last minute.'

She handed him the papers.

'That's a good plan,' he said, accepting them from her. 'I will study the guidelines. Let me know if there is anything else you need.'

He bowed his head to her before walking away. As he installed himself in a chair at a small coffee table and began reading, Noah shook her head. Emir was so unpredictable. He was such a jerk most of the time but then at times he could be very helpful, even thoughtful. He had bought her the sewing machine, she remembered. And she had to concede that he was brave. He'd risked his life many times in the last few weeks and with a sword there was nothing separating him and Ardis. Perhaps he wasn't quite as bad as she'd made him out to be. But even so, Noah couldn't believe that Chase wanted her to kiss him. The world would certainly end before that happened.

Raven appeared before her. 'Reporting for duty,' he said, saluting with mock formality.

'You said that perfectly,' she said. 'Your speech is really improving.'

He beamed. 'Lots of practice.'

'Don't I know it,' she said, rolling her eyes.

Raven tried to look hurt but failed abysmally. 'Let's get to work,' he said.

Between her, Raven, Ardis and Alan, they had the studio set up in under half an hour. By then, Emir had finished his reading.

'Anything I need to know?' Noah asked.

'Did you know your collection needs to be checked in two days prior to the fashion gala?' Emir said.

'No, I did not know that,' she said taking a deep breath to calm herself. 'That leaves me ten days to get all this finished. Anything else?'

'Well, there is mention of using "fabrics and haberdashery that is appropriate for royal personages" but it doesn't specify what is or isn't "appropriate".'

'Not very helpful, is it,' Noah said.

'It seems like a convenient clause that could be used to eliminate designs that perhaps they don't want in the running.'

Emir lowered his voice to avoid being heard by the guards at the door. 'Have you used anything in your garments that is not from here? Cotton, clips, beads? Anything you brought with you from Earth?'

'I don't think so,' Noah said, thinking hard about the garments she'd made so far. 'Do you think anyone would notice?'

'Depends what it is,' Emir said.

'What if it was something that improved the garment, made it more appropriate for royal personages?'

'I don't know,' Emir admitted. 'I can't say how the clause might be applied. We probably just need to keep it in mind.'

'Yep. Okay,' Noah said.

'Ready to get started?' Alan asked. 'Might I suggest we start on Orville's outfit?'

'I think that's a fabulous idea,' Noah said. She found her sketches and spread them out on the cutting table. 'Originally I'd thought about a double-breasted jacket with tails,' she began, 'but then I thought it wasn't summery enough. I think the Summer Solstice needs something lighter and given that the suit fabric is black, I've opted for a high-buttoned vest instead.'

'I like it,' Alan said. 'What colour shirt?'

'White,' Noah said without hesitation.

'That's very traditional. Do you think Orville is anticipating something more … flashy?'

'Probably,' Noah said, 'but I'm not making something gaudy just because he wants it. It's my name on the label and my reputation on the line. He'll get what he's given.'

'Fair call,' Alan said.

'And see, I'm going for a high collar on the shirt,' she said, pointing to the sketch, 'with a matching cravat.'

'How did you cut yourself?' Alan asked.

Noah looked up in surprise. 'What?'

Alan took her left hand, turned it over and pointed to a fresh scratch. 'There.'

Noah studied her hand. It was about a centimetre long and quite shallow but she couldn't for the life of her think what she'd done.

'No idea,' Noah said. 'It doesn't hurt.'

When Alan didn't release her hand, she said, 'If you don't mind, I'm going to be needing that.'

'Just a minute,' he said, closing his eyes.

For the better part of a minute he stood in silence, still holding her hand.

'Blood magic,' he said at last. 'Your blood has been used in a spell.'

'Who? How? I don't remember being part of any spell,' she said.

Alan's face was serious. 'My guess would be Orville – unless you've run into anyone else recently that dabbles in blood magic?'

Noah shook her head slowly. 'Not that I can think of,' she said. 'Can you tell what kind of spell it is?'

'I'm not familiar enough with blood magic to know,' Alan replied. 'If we could get to Sachin, he might be able to tell us.'

Sachin, Noah thought. Emir and Ardis were working on a way to see him but Noah couldn't see how they'd be able to rescue him from jail without getting caught.

She took a deep breath. 'Right, since we can't sort that out now, let's focus on the suit.'

'Top hat and cane?' Alan said. 'Are they just for the sketch or are you thinking Orville will like the accessories?'

'The outfit doesn't work without them,' Noah said. 'It's an old-style look. The hat and cane complete the outfit.'

'Do you think Orville wants to look old?'

Noah shook her head. 'Absolutely not. But that's what's exciting about this kind of outfit. Even though it's an old-style look, it can look mega-modern and chic on the right person.'

Alan frowned. 'And you think Orville is the "right" person?'

Careful to avoid the words "hot" and "sexy" in her response, Noah said, 'I definitely think he can pull it off.'

Alan's eyes flicked to the guards at the door and then to the sketch on the table. In a low voice, he said, 'I think I can make it so that he can't pull it off, if you get my meaning?'

Butterflies stirred in Noah's stomach. This was what she needed Alan for. She could easily design a suit but to harness and utilise the innate malevolence in the fabric, she needed expert advice from someone trained in raiki. 'Go on,' she said.

'We can use dragonsong to cause the fabric to constrict.'

'So if we use the fabric in the vest, we could force all the air out of his lungs?' Noah said.

Alan nodded. 'And more importantly, he won't be able to suck any air back in.'

♪♫

The early birds were still wiping the sleep from their eyes when Orville arrived in Noah's studio the following morning. Flanked by a dozen guards, he proclaimed his arrival with, 'Secure the premises.'

The guards sealed the doors and seized the occupants. Once her wrists and ankles were shackled, Noah was shoved to the floor next to her brother. Emir, Ardis and Alan suffered the same fate.

'I suppose you all think you are very clever,' Orville said once they were all uncomfortably seated.

'Well, I certainly think we're pretty clever,' said Emir. 'What about you, Ardis?'

'Yes definitely.'

'Me too,' Raven said.

'And me,' agreed Alan.

'I concur,' Noah added, trying to sound intelligent.

Orville gave a sardonic smile. 'Well, in that case, it's lucky I am here to correct your misconceptions.'

He paused, tucking one arm officiously behind his back and then studying the nails on his other hand – his manicure seemingly of more interest than what he was about to say. 'I have had word from the king's army at Mellifont,' he said. 'Apparently, there are a few residents unaccounted for.'

'Unaccounted for?' Noah said. 'How many are "unaccounted for"?'

'As far as the soldiers can tell – all of them,' Orville said.

'All of them are missing? Are you saying that the king's soldiers can't find anyone in Mellifont?' Emir asked. 'Did they look under the beds?'

Orville gave him a sidelong glance but didn't respond.

Ardis chimed in with, 'It's not that surprising that the soldiers can't find anyone, Emir. Let's face it – they couldn't get six of us over here without losing one.'

'Enough!' Orville snapped.

Chase's disappearance was obviously a sore point.

'The next person who speaks will have their tongue cut out,' he added.

That threat brought him the silence he desired.

'Now I know you all had something to do with this little charade and I'm equally sure that you're sitting there feeling quite smug about it. But let me assure you, I will find them and I will sacrifice them before the Solstice Festival. By the king's decree, as a result of their criminal raiki practices, their lives are forfeit. Their blood is now property of the Crown.'

No one spoke.

'Do you want to know how I'll find them?' Orville taunted.

Unwilling to risk having their tongues cut out, Noah and the others didn't answer out loud, choosing instead to shake their heads.

Waving dismissively, he said, 'Well, I'm going to tell you anyway.'

Typical master criminal, Noah thought. *Loves the sound of his own voice.*

'I have more than just the king's army at my disposal,' Orville said. 'I have a host of goblins that won't be deceived. They will round them up – they'll sniff out every last one of them. Adepts will at last make a positive contribution to Talisker.'

Noah shuddered at the thought of goblins. She'd encountered them twice now – once in the forest after they'd sprung Sachin and Montana from jail, and then again at Seychelles. Meeting a goblin in the open was bad enough but Noah imagined meeting a horde of them underground would be utterly terrifying. A picture of Mellifont's residents being routed by swarms of goblins in the tunnels under the city flashed into her mind. According to Orville, they would be taken alive but Noah didn't believe that. Goblins were vicious and wild.

'What makes you think they'll obey your orders to take the prisoners alive?' Noah asked.

'They will,' Orville said. 'We have a deal.'

'You'll never get away with it,' Alan said. 'You are no match for the adepts.'

Orville looked down his nose. 'What are you going to do?' he asked.

'It's not me you need to be worried about,' Alan said. 'There are twelve Majors ready to use their keys against you.'

'Yes, yes,' Orville said, 'and once the goblins have rounded them up, they'll be delivered here to me. I'll then have the twelve Majors, their twelve keys and the 13th key. Thanks to Noah for that one.'

He winked at her. Raven growled.

'Now,' Orville continued, 'since you people are trouble when you're together, I'm going to separate you. Guards!'

Six bear-like soldiers marched towards Orville.

'You know what to do,' Orville said. 'These two'—he pointed to Emir and Ardis—'need to be separated and stay separated.'

The leader saluted. 'Yes, sir.'

Noah watched as the soldiers dragged Emir and Ardis to their feet. Still securely shackled, they were shoved towards the doorway.

'We will get that key back,' Emir said flatly as he passed Orville. 'Your plan will not succeed.'

'My plan,' Orville replied, 'has already succeeded. Raiki is dead. Blood magic is here to stay and the people of Talisker will now enjoy electricity and all the technologies that go with it. The king is opening the first official donation centre this afternoon and the first power plant the day after tomorrow. Everything is just peachy.'

'I thought that was the king's plan,' Emir said, pausing to let the distinction sink in before adding, 'I'm talking about *your* plan.'

'I'm sure I don't know what you're talking about,' Orville said coolly as the guards pushed Emir into motion towards the door.

When they were gone, the room felt eerily empty to Noah. It was now just her, Raven and Alan. She hoped Chase would return soon.

Orville interrupted her thoughts. 'I will be attending the opening of our first donation centre with the king this afternoon,' he said, 'but I would advise you not to get any funny ideas about trying to retrieve your staff in my absence. That would not be good for you or your friends. Besides, you should have plenty to keep you busy.'

In truth Noah was more interested in completing her collection than attempting to reclaim her wand.

'I am going to leave you a present, though,' he said.

'What sort of present?'

To her surprise, Orville laughed. 'Don't be so suspicious, Noah,' he said. 'It's a little something special from Earth.'

'What?'

'A television.'

'What am I supposed to do with a television?'

Noah had never been a great watcher of television, being deaf had significantly lessened its appeal as a source of entertainment.

'You can watch all the interviews,' he said.

'What interviews?'

Orville smiled. 'Each of the designers competing in the fashion gala will be interviewed and all the interviews will be broadcast. As you can imagine, Taliskerans are very excited at the prospect of a new royal tailor being appointed. We thought it would be a great build up to the Solstice festivities for the people to get involved in the process. Broadcasting interviews with each of the designers will give people a chance to get to know the competitors, give them a personal stake in the event.'

Noah was at a loss to know what to say next. Given that Orville was about to destroy Talisker, he seemed to be going to a lot of trouble to make sure people were enjoying themselves to the last.

'So I'm going to be interviewed?' she asked.

'Correct.'

'When?'

'The schedule will be out tomorrow,' he said. 'Obviously we won't be broadcasting anything until after the official opening of the power plant on Thursday. We need electricity before we flick the switches on the televisions. The first interview will be on Saturday.'

'So you're selling all these TVs to people who'll only get a few days use out of them?'

'I'm not selling anything,' Orville said. 'And anyway, the main attraction is the video screen in the palace gardens. Did you happen to see it?'

'I did see it, yes. But—'

'On Thursday evening it will be switched on and we expect a mighty crowd. Because most people won't have access to their own personal television, we'll be encouraging citizens to attend the broadcasts in the palace gardens and at various other parks around the city.'

'How many channels do we get?' Raven asked.

'One,' Orville said, adding, 'you won't have time to watch much anyway – you'll be helping your sister finish her collection. And if you aren't of any use, you can go to a cool-off room too.'

Noah knew that "cool-off room" was a euphemism for jail cell and she certainly didn't want her brother in there.

'Well, if we're going to get started,' Noah said, holding out her shackled wrists, 'I'm going to need these off.'

Orville nodded towards his one of his guards. As her hands were freed, Orville said, 'I will let you know when I will be requiring a fitting for my suit.'

Without awaiting a response, he turned and walked out of the studio.

Chapter 25

Chase returned in the early hours of the morning.

'Man, am I glad to see you,' Noah said, hugging her friend warmly as one of the soldiers at the door scurried off to make a report to Orville. 'What did you find out?'

Chase responded with a question of her own. 'Where are the others?'

'Alan is in the next room … putting the finishing touches on Orville's suit,' Noah said. Choosing her next words carefully for fear of Chase's reaction, she said, 'Orville moved Emir and Ardis to separate rooms.'

'Bastard,' she said, adding, 'You'd better get Alan. I think he needs to hear this too.'

'I'll get him,' Raven offered.

As he raced off, Noah braced herself – unnecessarily as it turned out. Chase avoided mention of Ardis's plight, saying, 'Raven's speech is really good now.'

Noah nodded, relieved. 'He's been practising diligently,' she said.

'You know, it's funny,' Chase said, as they waited for Raven and Alan to join them, 'even though you're both sixteen years old, he's only been talking for a week and you for only a few weeks longer than that.'

'I hadn't thought of it like that,' Noah said. 'It is weird, I suppose.'

Raven returned with Alan close behind.

Keeping her voice low so that the guard by the door could not over-hear, Chase said, 'You are never going to believe what I found out about Orville,' she said. 'My first stop when I got back to Earth was—'

'Chase,' Noah interrupted, 'I know you love to build suspense but can you please just cut to the chase?'

Chase frowned. 'I suppose you think that's funny, do you?'

'Yes, actually I do,' Noah said, smiling.

Chase pulled out an envelope that was tucked inside the back cover of her journal. 'Well, let's see if you find this amusing,' she said as she opened it.

'What is it?' Raven asked.

As she extracted a folded piece of paper from inside the envelope, Chase said, 'Something that deeply offends my sensibilities.'

She handed the paper to Noah, leaving her the job of unfolding it.

'He's a *writer*?' Noah said, studying the image of a book cover.

'He *claims to be* a writer,' Chase corrected her.

'It's not a good book, I take it?' Alan asked, peering over Noah's shoulder.

'I haven't had the misfortune of reading it,' Chase said, 'but the title hardly inspires.'

'*Taliskeran Terror*,' Noah quoted.

'No self-respecting author would use alliteration in a title,' Chase declared.

Ignoring her friend's pique at the literary faux pas, Noah said, 'This book he's written … it's obviously about Talisker?'

'That's correct.'

'And?'

'As I said, I haven't actually read the book,' Chase said. 'It was a self-publishing job – obviously no publisher would touch it! I've had to order a second-hand copy.'

'But you know something,' Noah pressed.

'From the blurb I read, it sounds like this story.'

'This story?'

Chase reconsidered her pronoun choice. '*Your* story,' she said finally.

Noah frowned. 'I'm very short on time and patience, Chase. Can you please just tell me what you know?'

'Okay,' Chase said. Pointing to the copy of the book cover, she said, 'That book appears to be about your quest for the 13th key.'

Noah's frown remained intact and Raven and Alan joined her in her frowning endeavours. 'How can he have already written a book about something that is only just happening now?' she asked.

'I don't know,' Chase said. 'I'll be able to tell you more when the book arrives.'

'Are you cold?' Raven asked her.

Chase shook her head. 'No. It's the thought of reading that book that's giving me the shivers.'

'Okay. What else did you find out?' Noah said.

'Orville Kurz is number seven of thirteen children, smack-bang in the middle, which explains a few things – serious case of middle-child syndrome. He was kicked out of school at the age of seven, eight, nine and finally, eleven – not sure what happened to ten, maybe he was sick for the entire year? According to his biographer, he's an obsessive alpha-male sociopath who enjoys taxidermy and writing poetry. He has an engineering degree and an honorary doctorate in paranormal psychology. *Taliskeran Terror* is his first novel and is dedicated to his paternal grandfather, Bernard Kurz, who apparently taught him how to "break the mould".'

'Quite a catch,' Alan said.

'Indeed,' Chase replied.

Noah absorbed the new information. 'The book's going to be our best bet. The sooner we get that, the better. Good job, Chase.'

'Thanks. So what's been happening here? I see you've got a TV.'

'That is from our host,' Noah said. 'Yesterday we were able to watch the king officially open Talisker's first power plant. Leninstar is the first city with electricity. Power from the people, for the people. It's happening, Chase.'

'How much blood did that take, I wonder?'

Alan answered, 'According to the documentary that aired after the opening, only two litres of blood were needed to start up the plant and supply the electricity for the broadcast.'

'Two litres, huh,' Chase mused.

'There is a collection centre right next door,' Raven added. 'It was opened on Tuesday. People queue for hours to donate.'

'If only they realised that none of their blood will be used anyway,' Noah said.

'Orville has put a blood spell on Noah,' Alan said to Chase.

The fictioneer looked at her friend, wide-eyed. 'What sort of spell?'

Noah squirmed. 'I don't know.'

Chase whistled. 'That can't be good.'

♪♫

While Noah waited for Orville in his office, she mentally checked off all the things she still needed to do. The fashion gala was now only a week away. This time next Saturday she'd be a blithering mess. She had not even started four of her outfits so she was grateful that Chase was back. With her on board there was now a chance her collection might actually be finished in time for the full dress rehearsal on Friday.

Noah found it difficult to concentrate though. The staff lay on Orville's ornately carved desk. He'd no doubt left it there intentionally to taunt her. Something powerful, something that could save her and her friends was only a couple of metres from her but the guards would make sure she didn't get to it.

Orville burst through the door. 'At ease, soldiers,' he said.

A man with the posture of a question mark followed Orville into the room. He carried a full-length mirror under his arm. Without ceremony he set the mirror up against the far wall.

'Will that be all, sir?' he asked.

Orville nodded. 'Yes, Walters, that will be all.'

The man bowed and left.

'Guards, leave us,' Orville commanded.

The soldiers followed his instruction without question or comment. When they were gone, Orville said, 'Shall we begin?'

'Sure,' Noah said, handing him the suit bag. 'If you change into the trousers and shirt first, I'll do the vest last.'

To her surprise, Orville pulled his shirt off over his head and threw it on the desk beside the staff. His torso was more muscular than she'd expected and she was suddenly aware that she was staring. He slipped the new shirt on.

'The sleeves are a bit short,' he said. 'They only come to my elbows.'

'They're supposed to be like that,' Noah replied. 'Just wait until you see the whole outfit.'

When he started unbuttoning his trousers, Noah busied herself with her pin cushion. The man clearly had no inhibitions – but she did.

'Ready,' he announced.

Noah inspected the fit of the shirt. It wasn't going to need much alteration.

'Arms up,' she said.

Orville obliged and Noah ran her hands over the side seams. She felt unexpectedly self-conscious and vulnerable. What would she do if he tried to kiss her again? Her dressmaking pins would be her only weapons – if she had the will to use them against him. She adjusted the left seam, inserting a pin with trembling hands.

'Your hands are shaking,' Orville observed. 'Do I make you nervous?'

'Yes,' Noah said without looking up from her work.

'You needn't be nervous,' he said. 'I won't hurt you. I still need you.'

'Turn around, please.'

As he turned away from her, he said, 'Do you want to know what I need you for?'

'Not right now,' Noah said. 'I'm busy.'

'Okay.'

'What shoes will you wearing to the Gala?'

'Black ones,' Orville answered.

'I'm more interested in the heel height than the colour,' Noah said.

'For the hem of the trousers?'

'Yes.'

'Oh right. *Guards!*'

The door opened and two guards appeared, hands on sword hilts.

'Sir!'

'Have Walters bring my shoes, please,' he said.

One of the guards cocked his head. 'Which shoes, sir?'

'All of them,' Orville said as he walked towards the mirror that Walters had left.

'Yes, sir.'

The guards saluted and left.

Orville turned and picked up the Dragonsbane's staff from the desk. 'Do you know how to use it?' he asked.

'No idea,' Noah said.

'Well, you're going to have to learn,' he said, running his hand over the smooth wood.

Confused, Noah said, '*I'm* going to have to learn how to use it? I thought you wanted it.'

'I do want it,' Orville said, 'but I can't use it. I think you know that already. That's where you come in. *You* are going to use the 13th key to destroy Talisker for me.'

'*What!*'

'I said—'

'I heard what you said – I just can't believe you said it.'

His expectation that she deliver the key to him had been crazy enough, but expecting her to do his dirty work for him as well – that was simply outrageous.

'I have absolute faith in you, Noah,' Orville said, 'and to prove it to you, I'm going to give the key back to you *and* let you visit Sachin so that he can show you how to use it.'

'You're too kind.'

'Yes, it's been said.'

If Orville had been accused of being kind, Noah seriously doubted it had been recently.

'If I learn to use it, I will use it against you,' Noah said.

Orville smiled. 'We'll see.'

'Tell me what you know about my parents,' Noah said.

Caught off-guard by the sudden change in topic, Orville said, 'I beg your pardon?'

'Tell me what you know about my parents,' Noah repeated. 'You said, if I brought you the 13th key, you'd tell me about them. You have the key. Now tell me.'

Orville gestured towards a chair. 'Take a seat.'

Noah sat, butterflies tickling her insides.

Orville perched himself on the edge of the mahogany desk. 'I can't tell you anything about your father but I met your mother once,' he said. 'My grandmother was Taliskeran. Like your mother, she moved to Earth to be with her husband. She knew of your mother's move and went to visit her. I was eight and was staying with my grandparents at the time. My grandmother took me with her. I saw you in your crib, Noah.'

Noah shivered.

'We didn't stay long though,' Orville continued. 'It was obvious your mother was upset by our visit. She said she wanted a fresh start on Earth with her husband – our appearance was a reminder of what she wanted to leave behind. My grandmother was distressed that she'd upset your mother and we didn't visit her again.'

He stopped talking and Noah waited. After several long moments, Noah said, 'But you found out something about her? And about me?'

'I saw your mother's Academy ring,' he said, nodding his head. 'I saw your mark.'

Noah stared at him.

'I knew that you'd be thrilled to know that we have a connection that goes way back,' Orville said.

'Thrilled isn't exactly the word I would use,' Noah said coolly. 'So what? You never visited again but you stalked us from a distance?'

'Stalked is a strong word, Noah,' Orville said. 'Let's just say I kept you in mind over the years. Especially after grandmother told me about the prophecy.'

'That's creepy,' Noah said.

Orville slapped his hands on his thighs and stood up. 'So back to work,' he said. 'Let me see the whole ensemble.'

Fuming, Noah handed him the vest made from Madame Priscilla's special fabric. She picked up the cravat while Orville buttoned the vest. Wrestling her desire to strangle him with the necktie, Noah said, 'Let me show you how to tie it.'

'You have my undivided attention,' he replied as she passed the cravat around the back of his neck.

'I hope so. I'm only going to show you this once. This is a barrel knot,' Noah said. 'When you put the cravat around your neck, make sure you have the right side longer than the left to start. Then create a loop here and pinch the ends of the loop together like so.'

'Okay.'

'Wrap the right side over the left and then pull the left side through the loop. Easy.'

Noah adjusted the knot slightly and smoothed the ends of the tie, arranging them over the top of the vest.

'Now for the accessories,' she said.

Usually Noah enjoyed this part of her hobby. Seeing her creations come to life gave her great satisfaction. It was what she lived for. Creating works of art. But today, she could not divorce herself from the horror of what Orville had in store for her and for Talisker.

'Hat, cane, gloves. You can wear the hat,' Noah said, 'but not the gloves.'

Orville put the top hat on. 'Why can't I wear the gloves?'

'Well, you *can* wear them,' she conceded, 'but you'll look silly. They don't suit the sleeve-length of the shirt.'

'Then why have I got them?'

'Because they're a great accessory,' she said. 'Think of women's handbags. They look great slung over a girl's shoulder but they look dumb hung around their necks. Accessories are great but you have to use them properly.'

'Okay.'

Orville sidled over to the mirror once more and inspected himself from every angle, clearly liking what he saw. When Walters arrived wheeling the rack of shoes, Noah had to help him manoeuvre it into the room. There had to be nearly a hundred pairs. Not bothering to interrupt Orville, Noah chose a pair of shoes for him.

'How about these?' she suggested.

Orville accepted the shoes she'd chosen and put them on. He posed in front of the mirror and looked himself up and down.

'There's something missing,' he declared.

'A pin for the cravat?' Noah suggested.

Orville rubbed his chin while he considered her suggestion. 'I think I'd like a gold fob watch,' he said at last.

Noah winced.

'Problem?'

'I do like the idea of a fob watch but I'd recommend a silver watch with black-etched filigree,' Noah said.

'Why?'

'Silver blends with the black and white. Gold is too flashy. It looks like you're screaming to get people's attention.'

'Silver it is then,' he said. 'I like to be subtle.'

Since when was unleashing Armageddon subtle, Noah wondered.

Chapter 26

Noah's nerves jangled like the large iron keys on the soldier's keyring as he unlocked Sachin's cell. She'd rather have been working on her collection but Orville's orders were clear. She was to learn how to use the 13th key.

'You've got an hour,' the guard growled, 'and we'll be watching you.'

'Got it,' Noah replied as the guard opened the cell door.

Noah stepped into the dingy quarters hoping the guards wouldn't be watching too closely. She wanted to ask Sachin about the blood spell Orville had put on her. The instant she crossed the threshold she knew something was very wrong. Goosebumps sprang up all over her body.

'Noah!' Sachin called.

She could hear the Major but she couldn't see him – her eyes hadn't yet adjusted to the gloom. When they did, the first thing she saw was that the walls were … bleeding. Her feet wouldn't take her any further. She stood rooted to the spot. Blood cascaded down the walls and drained away via a trough around the perimeter of the floor.

'Love what you've done with the place,' she said at last.

'I didn't do that.'

Noah shook her head. She didn't really think he had.

'It's supposed to stop me performing raiki,' Sachin said. 'There is a powerful spell in this room and the blood makes sure it stays intact. So how did you get in here? Where is Emir and the others? Tell me everything.'

Noah forced herself into motion. In the centre of the room she found Sachin sitting on a faded round cushion inside a wooden cage. *A prison inside a prison*, she thought. The cage was unlike anything she'd seen before. Instead of being box-shaped, the cage had a bulbous bottom and curved to a point at the top – the wooden bars shaped like mammoth tusks. Strange carvings marked the wood and Noah reached out to investigate them.

'Don't touch the bars,' Sachin warned. 'There is a blood spell on them. Touching them would be very bad.'

'Right,' she said. 'Well, I am Dragonsbane and I have the 13th key and we're all staying here at the palace – as Orville's guests – until the Solstice Festival.'

Sachin eyes widened. 'Who is "we"?'

'Chase, Raven, Emir, Ardis and Alan are here. Oh, and Raven is human now – not a dog.'

She decided against telling him for now that Emir and Ardis had been locked up too.

Sachin stared at her. 'I almost don't know where to start. I've obviously missed a lot.'

Noah said, 'Well, since Orville has sent me here on a mission, let's start with that. He wants you to show me how to use the 13th key.'

'Why?'

'So I can destroy the world for him.'

Sachin frowned but recovered quickly. 'You have it *here? Now?*' he whispered.

'Yes.'

'What is it?' Sachin said. 'Show me.'

'You're not going to like it,' Noah said.

Sachin was shaking. 'Oh, for goodness' sake, Noah. What is it?'

'It's a wand,' Noah said, pulling the staff from her pocket.

Sachin shook his head in disgust. 'It's *not* a wand,' he said.

'Is so,' Noah said.

'Is not,' Sachin countered.

'Stop that,' Noah said. 'You're being childish.'

Sachin stared at her. 'Maybe so,' he said, 'but I *am* a child. You're being just as childish and you're supposed to be grown up.'

At sixteen, Noah didn't think she had to be completely grown up but she wasn't prepared to debate that with the Major.

Sachin peered through the bars. 'It's exquisite,' he murmured. 'The Dragonsbane's staff. Where did the piece of firestone come from?'

Noah held her ring up for Sachin to see.

'That was firestone?' he asked, incredulous.

Noah nodded. 'The Descera had put a charm on it to hide it.'

'This is actually very good,' Sachin said. 'It makes perfect sense. The Dragonsbane must rise and the music *wield*,' he quoted. 'You don't have to *make* the music; you just have to *direct* it. That is a huge relief.'

'For you maybe,' Noah said.

Sachin ignored her comment.

'You need to tell me everything that's happened while I've been in here,' he said.

Noah related everything she could remember. She told him of her encounter with Madam Priscilla in Jagar.

Sachin interrupted her. '*The Purring Pussy*, you say? What did you think of that, er … establishment?' he asked.

'Fine,' Noah answered. 'Madame Priscilla drives a hard bargain but her fabrics are excellent quality.'

'Indeed,' the Major said, raising his eyebrows.

Sachin was behaving strangely, as Emir had done when they'd gone shopping there. Noah had no time for nonsense right now. If boys didn't like shopping she didn't really care but right now they had work to do.

She told him about their journey to Ironside and her meeting with Madame Priscilla in Dragonhall. Sachin sat in silence as Noah explained how Seth had found and transformed Raven and then shown them what had happened the evening Noah had been branded.

'And then we made the 13th key,' Noah said.

'Who was there?'

Noah launched into her rehearsed lie. 'Seth, Cecil – the phoenix, Madame Priscilla, Raven and I,' she said. 'Dr Grainger turned up after we were done.'

'Dr Grainger?'

'He wanted to be made Dragonsbane but we gave him another assignment. He returned to Mellifont to evacuate the city before the king's army arrived.'

'Good,' Sachin said. 'That is good.'

Noah quickly recounted their return to Leninstar City and her brush with Orville.

'Hold the staff near the stone,' Sachin said. 'I'll use the firestone to see if I can decipher the spell he's put on you.'

Sachin closed his eyes and Noah's skin tingled as he trained the dragonsong on her.

'It's not good news,' he said at last.

'I didn't really think it would be,' Noah replied.

'It's a compliance spell,' Sachin said. 'You'll do whatever he tells you to do.'

'Great,' she said. 'Any way to reverse it?'

'Short of draining all your blood and replacing it, no.'

'Okay, well … not today's crisis,' Noah said. She tapped the staff. 'So how do I use this thing?'

'It's quite simple in theory,' Sachin said. 'You don't have to create any music – you just tap into the dragonsong and direct it.'

'Direct it?' Noah said. 'How do I do that?'

'Use your perception,' Sachin replied. 'The Descera protected your hearing for a reason – you are uniquely attuned to Talisker. You need to listen to the music of this world and use it.'

'But it's equally likely I could use it to destroy the world,' Noah said. 'That's what Orville wants. And if I've got this spell on me …'

'It's going to be tricky,' Sachin conceded. 'I wonder if he really *needs* the power of the 13th key to wake the dragon or is he just trying to be poetic?'

'Chase thinks he's attempting irony,' Noah said.

'Whether it's poetic or ironic is irrelevant,' Sachin replied, 'the real point is whether he *needs* the 13th key or just *wants* it.'

'Why does that make a difference?'

'If he really *needs* you, we have more leverage. If he's just playing with us – we haven't got much to bargain with.'

'If he's toying with us, it shows how arrogant he is. Maybe we can exploit that weakness somehow?' she suggested.

Sachin shrugged. 'Maybe.'

The cell door groaned as it opened. 'Time to go,' the guard said.

Turning her head, Noah said, 'I'm ready.' Looking back at Sachin, she added, 'You behave yourself until I get back.'

'I'll wait right here,' Sachin replied.

Keen to be away from the bleeding walls, Noah hurried out the door.

♪♫

'It's just about to start,' Chase said, fiddling with the volume on the remote control.

Noah gave up on her sewing. She would have to watch the interview and then hopefully she could focus on her collection. It was now Monday – only four days until the full dress rehearsal – and she still had plenty to do. Between fitting Orville's suit, visiting Sachin and then recording her interview, Noah didn't feel she'd gotten a good run at her collection yet.

The picture on the television came into focus. The king's standard scrolled across the screen to some dramatic music.

'Come and sit next to me, Superstar,' Chase said.

'Knock it off,' Noah replied, taking a seat next to her friend.

Orville's face appeared. Raven growled.

'On behalf of the king,' Orville said, 'I welcome you all to the first in this series of interviews with the five designers who are vying for the job of Royal Tailor. Today's interview is with intergalactic designer, Noah Chord. As our only competitor from Earth, there is intense interest around this young lady. So by popular demand, here she is.'

'Intergalactic designer, huh,' Alan said. 'Do you think that's the first time anyone's been assigned that tag?'

'You'd have to think so,' Chase said. 'That is soooo going in my journal.'

When the writer didn't move, Noah said, 'Did you want me to get your journal for you?'

'No, it's okay. I'll do it later,' she said without taking her eyes from the television. 'I don't want to miss anything here.'

'Of course you don't,' Noah said.

The shot panned out to reveal Noah sitting on a stool next to Orville, who was perched on a similar chair and clutching a clipboard. The white room where the interview had been filmed the day before was furnished only with the two stools and a painting on the wall of the late tailor, Valada. Noah was glad that the room was plain. It showcased her outfit nicely.

Her snug-fitting green and yellow tartan overalls would have been lost in the jungle of colours in the ornately decorated rooms that dominated the palace. But against a white background they looked superb. She'd cut the legs of the overalls so they came to just above her knees, a perfect length to wear with white lace-up boots.

'The white T-shirt balances the boots perfectly,' Chase said approvingly. 'Looks great.'

'Why is your belt around your hips and not your waist?' Alan asked.

'It's about balance,' Noah explained. 'Because the shorts are knee-length, my hips are halfway between the shoulders and knees. If I'd had short shorts, I'd have put the belt around the waist because that would've been halfway between the top and bottom of the outfit.'

'Sounds reasonable.'

'Why are you wearing glasses?' Raven asked.

'Orville insisted that I wear them. He said it made me look more hip – more like a designer.'

Chase looked at her sideways. 'They do make you look really hot.'

Noah decided not to dignify her comment with a response, instead turning her attention back to the television.

'So Noah,' Orville said, 'perhaps you could start by telling us a little about your hometown on Earth.'

'I live in a city called Sayle. My brother, Raven and I moved there to live with our Aunt after our parents died in a car accident when I was six.'

Raven beamed at mention of his name.

'And Sayle is known for fashion?' Orville continued.

Noah nodded. 'It's a city of five million people. There is a big demand for fashion.'

'Have you competed in many shows?'

'Quite a few,' Noah lied.

'Won any?'

'Several actually.'

Noah could feel Raven's eyes on her as she watched Orville smile at the camera.

'You so haven't,' he said.

'He told me to say that,' Noah said without making eye contact with her brother. 'I had a script.'

'You had a script to answer questions about yourself?' Alan said.

'Yep.'

'That's insane.'

'That's Orville,' Noah said.

Orville was introducing some video footage.

'We have some footage here of you as a youngster, Noah. Perhaps you could talk us through it.'

A young girl with a dark ponytail strutted along a length of artificial grass laid out in someone's family room. Wearing a lacy ivory dress that was about three sizes too big for her, she had hoisted up the front so as not to trip over it on her journey up the makeshift catwalk. And while necessity compelled her to lift the hemline, one could have been forgiven for thinking her movements were choreographed specifically as part of the performance.

'Where the hell did he get that footage?' Chase breathed.

Noah snorted. 'Relax. It's not even me.'

Her friend looked at her quizzically.

'I told you,' Noah said. 'There was a script. Talisker gets to know what Orville wants them to know.'

'How much of it is true?' Alan asked.

'Very little actually,' Noah admitted.

The picture changed. This time, a girl was accepting an award. Noah's voiceover gave details of the award she hadn't actually won … and then another two after that.

'You're obviously very accomplished,' Orville said when the camera crossed back to the interview room, 'but this is a whole new world for you. Literally.' He paused, smiling.

Noah supplied the obligatory chuckle in acknowledgment of his joke. 'It certainly is,' she said.

'So how do you rate your chances?'

'It's really hard to know,' she said. 'Like you say, this is a totally different environment for me. I feel a bit behind the eight-ball, so to speak. But I've done some background research on the royals and on Valada and I think I have a sense of what they like. I can only hope that they'll like what I'm offering.'

'Do you have anything special from your hometown that you think will give you an edge in the competition?'

Noah winked at him. 'Well, you'll have to wait and see. I'm not giving away any secrets now.'

'Well, how about an easier question. Something I'm sure people want to know … what's your favourite colour?'

'Today it's green,' she said.

'It changes day to day?'

'Sometimes minute to minute,' Noah said.

'Corny,' Raven said.

Noah looked at him. 'That bit wasn't scripted. I ad-libbed that bit.'

'Really?'

'Yes.'

'Oh. Sorry,' he mumbled.

'That's okay,' Noah said. 'Orville wasn't thrilled either. I'm surprised he didn't edit it out actually.'

'Shhhh,' Chase said. 'I'm trying to listen.'

'What'd he just say?' Alan asked.

'I don't know,' Chase replied. 'I missed it.'

Noah groaned. 'He asked if I had a boyfriend.'

'And you said?'

'I don't have time for a boyfriend at the moment,' she recited.

'Well, there you have it, folks,' Orville was saying, 'an insight into our first designer, Noah Chord. Thank you very much for your time today, Noah. I wish you the best of luck on Saturday.'

'Thank you for the opportunity,' Noah said.

Orville turned to face the camera. 'Don't forget to tune in to our next interview tomorrow with Bindi Iis. Until then, good day.'

Chase let out a long breath. 'That was excruciating.'

'You're telling me,' Noah replied. 'Now, with any luck, we can actually get some work done.'

Chase saluted. 'Let's do it.'

Chapter 27

Noah inhaled the delicate chamomile scent that wafted from her teacup. From her privileged position on the palace balcony, she surveyed the antics of the crowd below her. The people of Leninstar were swarming in the king's sprawling gardens despite the early hour. Noah watched as the city's residents made their final preparations for the day's festivities. This year's Solstice Festival would be the most exciting in Talisker's history. This year they were celebrating the arrival of electricity. If Orville got his way though, they wouldn't be celebrating for long. If Orville got his way, this would be the last dawn these people would see.

Noah sipped her tea, which was doing nothing to soothe her abraded nerves. She wished that she could focus solely on the evening's fashion gala but she didn't have that luxury. Orville's plans for Armageddon were a real nuisance. While Chase, Raven and Alan still slept inside, Noah grappled with a plan. She was expected to save the world tonight but still had no idea how she was going to pull it off. She really needed Sachin and Emir and Ardis. Even Brinn would have been welcome.

In the absence of her comrades she reviewed what she knew. She was the 13th key. So what? What did that even mean? What was the point being the 13th key if she didn't know how to use the power she supposedly had? Cradling the warm cup in her hands she took another deep breath and let it out slowly, trying to push the unhelpful thoughts aside. She was the 13th key. Being the 13th key gave her some kind of power

– the power of her mother's firestone ring was part of her. Madame Priscilla had made her promise not to tell anyone she was the 13th key and she'd faithfully kept that promise. Even Sachin hadn't guessed her secret. In effect, she was a secret weapon.

Then there was the Dragonsbane's staff. In spite of the hopelessness of the situation she managed a smile. In company she had taken to calling it a staff but in her own mind it was still a wand. Orville thought it was the 13th key – a fact that she might be able to use against him somehow. Unwilling to dwell on it, Noah moved on to the next item on her mental checklist. Orville's suit.

One of his minions would collect the ensemble this morning but Noah didn't know whether he'd actually wear it or not. He'd made a big deal of commissioning an outfit from her, and she and Alan had laboured long and hard to come up with a crafty way to use Madame Priscilla's fabric. The result was not so much a suit to die *for* but a suit to die *in*. Of course, the plan relied on Alan being able to use raiki to make the material constrict sufficiently to contain the king's adviser. Noah wasn't overly confident that that would be possible.

'A dinah for your thoughts.'

Noah jumped at the sound of Alan's voice, spilling tea over her hands.

'Sorry,' he said. 'I didn't mean to startle you.'

'It's fine. It isn't hot anymore,' she replied. 'I'm just thinking about tonight. Have you had any luck unravelling the spell Orville's put on me?'

His shoulders sagged. 'Not yet. It's in your blood. As Sachin said, unless we drain all your blood to purify it … I can't think of any other way to neutralise the spell.'

Noah frowned. 'Probably not my preferred option.'

'You'll just have to try to resist him,' Alan said. 'Stay as far away from him as you can.'

'Right,' Noah replied with little optimism. Orville had cast a specific spell to achieve a specific end. Noah was under his spell. She would do whatever he told her to do and she doubted that Orville would be thwarted by something as simple as her keeping her distance.

Chase arrived on the balcony still wearing her pyjamas. 'How long have you been out here?' she asked.

'A while,' Noah replied. 'I couldn't sleep.'

'Worried about tonight?'

'Yep. I just wish I knew what Orville has in mind. He's holding all the cards – has everything planned to the finest detail. And what do we have – a vague plan that probably won't work.'

'We have the 13th key,' Chase said, eyeing the staff leaning against the wall.

Noah's stomach tightened. When Chase found out the truth about the 13th key, Noah knew she'd be extremely put out, but now wasn't the time.

'I'm considering hiding it and not taking it to the gala tonight,' Noah said.

'Why? Orville will destroy everything if you don't stop him.'

'Better that he does it rather than me doing it on his behalf.'

'We need Sachin,' Chase said, adding, 'and the others.'

Noah looked at her friend not knowing quite the right thing to say. 'I'm sure Ardis is fine,' she said.

Chase sighed. 'For now at least. I hate to think what's going to happen to him tonight though.'

Noah did too. One thing she was sure of was that Orville intended sacrificing all the adepts and anyone associated with them. 'Pity Orville's book hasn't arrived,' Noah said. 'It would have been great to get an idea of what he has planned.'

Chase shuddered. 'I guess so,' she said, 'but the thought of reading it makes my skin crawl.'

Raven appeared in the doorway, clearly unimpressed. 'You have a visitor, Sis.'

'At this hour? Orville?' she guessed.

Raven nodded. 'He's come to collect his suit.'

Noah picked up the staff before walking back inside with her entourage in tow. Orville smiled at her before his eyes shifted to the implement in her hand.

'You won't forget to bring that with you tonight will you?' he asked.

'I won't forget. I'm going to destroy you with it,' she said with false bravado.

'I don't think so,' he said as he walked towards her.

Raven installed himself protectively in front of his sister and folded his arms across his chest.

'I'm not going to hurt her,' Orville said. 'I still need her. You might consider that I don't need you though. Stand aside.'

Noah stepped around Raven and Orville made a big show of giving her a welcoming kiss on the cheek. 'Give me the key,' he whispered in her ear.

Noah handed over the staff without hesitation.

'It is truly a thing of beauty,' he said, inspecting it as he turned it over in his hands.

Having proven his hold over her, Orville handed it back. The instrument was barely in her grasp when Alan launched himself at Orville. The thud as the two men hit the floor was lost in the *schwing* of swords as they were drawn from the soldiers' scabbards. Before Noah had a chance to react, three guards threw themselves into the melee while three more positioned themselves to dissuade her, Raven and Chase from going to Alan's aid. The corpulent adept landed two solid punches before the guards dragged him to his feet. He continued to struggle as the guards wrestled his arms behind his back. Noah feared he'd dislocate his shoulders if he kept it up.

'Take him away and put him with the others,' Orville said as he got to his feet and smoothed down his clothes.

Noah hoped Alan knew what he was doing. She was counting on him to help her out to activate Orville's suit during the Gala.

'Now,' Orville said, 'my suit?'

Noah shuddered. 'It's in the back room,' she said absently.

Orville motioned to one of the guards. 'Go with her.'

Under escort, Noah went to retrieve the suit. As she walked further away from Orville she felt his pull on her lessen. She concentrated hard, trying to listen to the sound of her blood for any clues that might help her undermine Orville's unnatural spell and to her surprise she found she could identify the irregularities that Alan had spoken about. Although she had no idea how to counteract them, she was buoyed by the fact that she could recognise them.

'There's a hatbox and cane over there that you can take,' Noah said to the guard as she lifted the suit bag down off its peg.

The guard sneered. 'I'm not your slave.'

Noah stared at him coldly. 'Have it your way,' she said. 'It just means you'll have to come back with me for a second trip.'

She walked out without waiting for his reply.

'Here's the suit,' she said, handing the black bag to Orville. 'I just need to go back—'

The soldier appeared at her side with the accessories.

'Never mind,' she said.

Orville smiled. 'Thank you,' he said. 'And just to show you how grateful I am, I want to give you a little token of my appreciation.'

He summoned one of the guards who dutifully carried over a gift-wrapped box. Noah accepted it reluctantly and studied it as a parent might study a long-lost lunchbox they'd just discovered by smell at the back of their child's wardrobe.

'Go ahead – open it,' he said.

Even if she'd wanted to resist she knew she couldn't. She pulled at the azure satin ribbon and lifted the lid cautiously. Inside was a book.

'I'm not much of a reader,' Noah said.

'That's okay,' Orville said. 'You have a very busy day ahead of you. Jemima will read it for you.'

'Why me?' Chase said.

'Because I know you were chasing a copy of my book,' Orville replied, tapping his temple knowingly. 'I've even autographed it for you.'

Chase looked like she'd just licked dog poo off a thistle.

'Noah, give her the book,' Orville said.

Noah did and Chase accepted it with obvious reluctance.

'You could at least have given her a new copy,' Chase said. 'This one has a dirty mark on it.'

'That's blood,' Orville said. 'I've had my wizards put a spell on the book.'

Chase said, 'What kind of spell?'

Orville's face split into a self-satisfied smile. 'One that will stop you jumping straight to the end of the book. Jemima, you will have to read every word on every page.'

'Every word?' she breathed.

Orville nodded. 'Every word. You won't be able to turn the page until you've read everything on the page before.'

Noah looked at the size of the book and wondered if her friend would be able to read it all in one day.

'Chase, I hate to do this to you,' Noah said, 'but you'd better get started.'

As blood deserted Chase's face, Orville chimed in again. 'And so Jemima can keep you updated during the day'—he reached into his breast pocket—'you'll need these.'

'Earpieces?' Noah said, accepting the small package. 'You had these "imported" too?'

'Especially for you, yes,' he said with a broad smile. 'Now, don't forget breakfast starts at 7 am sharp Noah. It wouldn't do to keep the royal family waiting.'

The royal breakfast officially kicked off the Solstice activities and it promised to be quite the soiree. It would be telecast on the giant video screens that had been set up throughout the city. Noah could already hear the crowd at the palace jostling for position.

'I'm sure no one would notice if I wasn't there,' she said.

'If you are not there on time,' Orville said, 'I will send guards to escort you. Do I make myself clear?'

Noah sighed. 'Very clear.'

'Good,' he said, swinging the suit bag over his shoulder. 'I'll see you within the hour.'

Flanked by guards, Orville left without looking back. Raven spoke up first.

'Well, you've got your schedule for today, Sis, and we now know what Chase will be doing … what do you want me to do?'

'He's going with you, Noah,' Chase said. 'I'm not having him hanging around here all day yapping at me.'

273

Raven looked wounded momentarily but moved quickly to his indignant look. 'I have never, and will never, yap,' he declared.

Noah smiled. Despite his transformation, her brother still had "big dog syndrome". Alsatians didn't yap. Alsatians barked. Only little dogs yapped.

'That's not what I meant,' Chase said. 'I just meant I need to be left alone to read.'

Noah sighed again as she opened the parcel and handed an earpiece to Chase and one to Raven. 'It is going to be a very long day,' she said, checking the day's events off on her fingers. 'Breakfast with the royal family and the other designers, then the street parade … after that we're expected to watch the Solstice tournament before heading off to lunch. At two o'clock we need to be at the palace ballroom to prepare for the fashion gala. Then there's time for a quick shower before the official dinner. Then it's the big event …'

'Armageddon?' Raven said as he fitted his ear piece.

'No,' Noah said. 'The fashion gala.'

'Oh yes, the fashion gala,' he said sheepishly. 'Fashion gala first, then Armageddon.'

Noah frowned at her twin. 'Hopefully not Armageddon,' she said. 'That's what we're trying to stop.'

'Yes, of course,' he said. 'That's what I meant.'

Turning her attention back to her friend, Noah said, 'Right – you start reading while we get ready for breakfast. I want a summary of the first two chapters before I go.'

Chase opened the book grudgingly. 'Yes ma'am,' she said as Noah headed for her room.

Noah took her time readying herself for breakfast, partly to give Chase time to read and partly to steady her nerves. By the time she was ready to go Chase had read her allotted two chapters.

'You look pale,' Noah said. 'What's wrong?'

'It's awful,' Chase declared, 'I don't know how I'm going to read every word of this book. Lucky you're my best friend and that the survival of this world depends on it – otherwise there is no way I'd read it.'

'Well, I do appreciate it as I'm sure the rest of Talisker would if they knew of your sacrifice,' Noah said. 'So what have you found out?'

'Okay, the book is written from Orville's point of view. He clearly wants the reader to see him as the protagonist – what a joke that is. So far he is setting up the conflict between the adepts and the State – between raiki and blood magic. Obviously, from his perspective, raiki is bad and blood magic is good. Orville's spies have just reported to him that you have arrived on Talisker to fulfil the prophecy of the evil adepts.'

'Interesting. So the 13th key has been mentioned?'

Chase nodded. 'Yes. In a conversation with the king in chapter two, Orville has recommended finding the key and destroying it along with the other twelve keys.'

'Orville's had opportunity to destroy the key and hasn't done it,' Noah said. 'That doesn't fit with what he's written in the book.'

'Ah, it's early days yet, my friend. This is only the beginning of the story,' Chase said. 'And anyway, you know Orville's not going to be honest with the king. How could he be? He'll tell the king the keys should be destroyed but that's absolutely not what he has in mind.'

'Right,' Noah said. 'We need to go to breakfast. Keep us updated.'

'You bet,' Chase said as she settled back to her task.

Chapter 28

'In twelve hours, I expect this room will look quite different,' Raven said.

'I expect you're right,' Noah replied.

As they waited in line for their turn to greet the royal couple, Noah surveyed the opulently decorated ballroom. The room was awash with vibrant summer colours to honour the Solstice. Set high around the upper tier of the domed ceiling, each of the massive stained-glass windows had been cleaned and polished in honour of the occasion. The morning sun played its part in the ornamentation, streaming in through the glass to create a dazzling spectacle on the white drapes that encircled the tier below.

All the dining tables sported magenta silk tablecloths trimmed with black brocade and were laden with platters of fresh fruits. The crockery was predominantly white but edged with the king's magenta and black. Even the silverware bore the royal crest. Noah was astounded at the place settings. Each table seated twelve people and there had to be at least a hundred tables in the room. She couldn't imagine having twelve hundred dinner plates, side plates, soup bowls, dessert bowls and cups and saucers with the cutlery and crystal drinking vessels to complement them.

The long tables at the sides of the room bore the buffet. Noah wasn't used to such exotic fare for breakfast. Seafood, cured meats, cheeses, nuts, breads, cakes and pastries were on offer and the peach and honey mead – the staple Solstice drink – flowed freely despite the early hour.

Eventually they reached the front of the line where Orville was doling out the introductions.

'And this is Noah Chord, Your Highness … with her brother, Raven,' Orville said.

'I think you were dead last time I saw you,' the king said, extending his hand.

He was obviously trying to be amusing – a very different king to the one she remembered presiding over the improvised court in Mellifont – and Noah knew better than to point out that she'd only been half-dead. Correcting the king would not only be considered poor form, but would certainly be a career-limiting move for someone vying for a position in his employ. She shook his hand while her mind scrambled for the appropriate response.

'Yes, Your Highness,' she said at last, 'but I'm very grateful to have recovered to be here today. It's an honour to be dining with you this morning. Thank you for the invitation.'

'You're welcome,' he replied. 'And I am interested to see what you'll show at the fashion gala tonight,' he added. 'Some out-of-this-world creations, no doubt?'

Noah laughed dutifully if not sincerely. 'I guess only time will tell,' she said.

But the line was still moving and she found herself standing before the queen as she finished her sentence.

'I hope you enjoy the Solstice festivities,' the queen said as she air-kissed Noah's cheeks.

'Thank you, Ma'am. I hope the day passes enjoyably for you also.'

Noah moved on to give Raven his opportunity to greet the queen. Once he was finished they made their way to their assigned dining table. The other designers competing in the fashion gala were already seated at the table. Noah wondered whether the seating arrangements had been by design or by default. Had anyone considered the potential consequences of confining a knot of highly-strung artists to one table?

'Hi Bindi,' Noah said as she planted herself on one of the two empty chairs at the table.

'Good morning, Noah,' the young man beside her replied stiffly.

The ballroom was filling quickly and the noise level rose commensurately. Rather than yelling across the table, Noah nodded her greetings to the others already seated. They barely acknowledged her. She'd been on the outer at the dress rehearsal two days ago and their attitude towards her clearly hadn't changed. Bindi Iis was the least offensive of her rivals – at least he would speak to her, something that Woodstock, Starlight and Vetel wouldn't do.

The place-card in front of her had Starlight's name on it. Obviously Starlight had rearranged the seating to suit herself. Noah decided against making an issue of it. Most likely Starlight was looking for a reaction and Noah had no intention of giving it to her. Starlight had been peeved at the dress rehearsal when an official had mistaken her for Noah. Noah could understand the mistake – there were obvious similarities between them – and she hadn't appreciated it any more than Starlight had. Unlike Starlight, however, Noah had decided to forget about it.

A waiter arrived at the table brandishing a ewer in each hand.

'Peach mead?' he asked.

Noah nodded. 'Yes please.'

The waiter filled her glass and then worked his way around the table. Starlight, unimpressed that Noah had been served first, made her feelings known to the attendant.

With a glance at the place-card, the waiter said, 'I meant no offense, Miss Chord. I'll make sure you're first served next time round.'

Noah smothered a smile as Starlight's eyes widened in horror but before the affronted designer could correct the man, a gong sounded at the far end of the ballroom. The waiter slipped away as everyone's attention turned to the king, who was making a show of testing his microphone. A murmur rippled through the ballroom.

'Good morning, everyone,' King Tambian said, his voice clearly audible throughout the ballroom, 'and welcome to the official start of our Solstice celebrations.'

The diners cheered. They were on their feet – clapping, whooping and whistling. The king waited patiently for the noise to die down and for people to resume their seats. When quiet returned, he continued his speech.

'Every year we have cause to celebrate the arrival of the Summer Solstice,' he said, 'but this year is extra special. This year we celebrate the miracle of electricity. Electricity will make our lives brighter. Electricity will make our lives easier. Electricity will make our lives more prosperous and more enjoyable.'

The crowd applauded again.

'Electricity makes it possible for me to use this microphone to talk to you all at once,' he said, his free arm sweeping across the audience to emphasise his point. 'Electricity makes it possible for all of you to see me better too …'

The king pointed to the large video screen that hung above his table and when his image appeared on the screen, he gave a regal wave. The crowd roared its approval.

'Isn't this wonderful?' he said. 'And this is just the beginning.'

Noah raised her eyebrows. *Just the beginning? If you only knew what Orville had in store,* she thought.

'Today we're not just rejoicing at the *arrival* of electricity,' he continued, 'but also the endless possibilities it presents us. While we marvel at our future, it is also a time to celebrate our success. We've worked hard to get where we are. For many it's been a difficult transition to this new technology. Raiki was the old way. It was ingrained in our culture, in our minds and in our hearts. It was the technology we knew and it worked.

'But I asked you to let go of that – to embrace something new. Something that works better. Blood magic. Power from the people, for the people. Blood magic has given us electricity. The transition – as painful as it was for so many – has been worth it. You can all be very proud of what we have created because you have all had your part to play in this momentous achievement.'

Despite her own feelings about raiki and Orville's unconscionable treatment of Sachin and his fellow adepts, Noah felt her heart swell at the king's words. She was inspired to applaud along with everyone else.

It was little wonder that Orville had gotten his way in supplanting raiki. She clapped dutifully and glanced sideways to make sure Raven was doing the same. They had to appear to support the king's initiative.

Noah took a swig of her peach mead and was surprised to find the bottom of her glass. She caught the eye of the waiter who made a beeline for the table. True to his word he attended Starlight first this time but emptied his ewer in the process.

He smiled apologetically at Noah. 'I'll be right back,' he promised.

Noah gave him the thumbs up as Chase's voice crackled in her ear. 'Hi Noah,' she said. 'Is now a good time for an update?'

Noah and Raven flinched and looked at each other, drawing curious looks from the other diners at their table. Noah leaned over to whisper in her brother's ear. 'We're going to have to do better than that.'

Raven nodded his agreement as Noah said, 'Go ahead.'

'Okay, so I've just read the part where the king holds court in Mellifont,' Chase said. 'It seems Orville didn't get that bit quite right. In the novel, Sachin is arrested for kidnapping.'

Noah dabbed her mouth with her serviette. 'Kidnapping?'

'Yes,' Chase said. 'Orville knew you'd been brought to Talisker but then apparently you'd "disappeared". King Tambian ordered Sachin's arrest and instructed his soldiers to search for you.'

Even Orville wouldn't half kill me, Noah thought. *I'll never forgive Sachin for that.*

'I've also read about the jailbreak from Orville's point of view,' Chase continued. 'Let me read you this little extract from the book. Just to set the scene for you, the king is sitting in the garden and Orville has just arrived with a cup of tea.

The king looked up as Orville arrived. 'Have you heard about the breakout today?' the king said. 'Sachin and Montana have escaped.'

Unfazed, Orville replied, 'Yes, Your Highness and may I say it was a masterstroke on your behalf to allow that to happen.'

A fleeting look of surprise crossed the monarch's brow but he recovered quickly. 'Of course, of course,' he said. He took a few moments to find the right words for his next question. 'Do you think everyone else will see it that way?'

Orville shook his head. 'No. Most people won't appreciate the strategy behind it and nor should they. This is a matter of state security and the masses should not – must not – be privy to it. If I may offer some advice?'

'Your counsel is always welcome,' the king said with obvious relief.

'Publicly our position is that it was an inside job and that those responsible for liberating these criminals will be brought to justice. The inner circle however, should be informed that this is a strategic move on our part to acquire the 13th key so we can ensure that it is destroyed.'

'You think Sachin and Montana know where it is?'

'I don't think any of them know where it is,' Orville said, 'but if I were a betting man, I'd have my money on Sachin. If anyone can find it, he can. I suggest we continue with your plan – give Sachin his head, let our spies keep an eye on him and see what happens.'

The king nodded thoughtfully. 'Yes. We'll continue with my plan and let them find the 13th key for us. Then, we can destroy it once and for all.'

'Very good, Your Highness.'

Chase ceased her narration. 'And so it goes on but you get the idea,' she said. 'From this point on, Orville sees you as working for him.'

Noah and Raven exchanged a look of bemusement.

'Anyway,' Chase said, 'I'll get back to reading and update you again shortly. Enjoy your breakfast.'

A soft click as Chase turned off her microphone signalled the end of her transmission. The king had finished his speech as Chase had been talking and people were now streaming to the buffet tables.

'Want some hot food, Sis?' Raven asked.

Noah glanced at the crowds. 'I think I'll wait for a bit,' she said.

'I can't wait,' he said, smirking. 'I'll be back soon so keep your grubby mitts off my peach mead while I'm gone.'

'Oh, I hadn't thought of that,' Noah said innocently. 'I'll be sure to take good care of it.'

Once her brother had left the table, Noah busied herself with some fruit. She counted five different types of melon and took a piece of each, arranging them by colour on her plate. She tasted the pale yellow one first. It reminded her of mulberries but before she had time to wonder at the unexpected flavour, her plate lurched away from her along with everything else on the table. Noah grabbed instinctively at the receding tablecloth.

'Help!'

Noah looked up to see Starlight sitting bolt upright in her chair, her eyes wide. Her clenched fists held the tablecloth hostage and, as she toppled from her seat – fruit, crockery and cutlery cascaded over the edge of the table and crashed onto the floor. Starlight was in no condition to be calling for assistance so it was left to her attendant to attract attention.

'Help!' she screamed again. 'Somebody please help her!'

Noah tried to make her way around the table to assist but found her path blocked by others with the same intention. Before the cordon closed around the stricken designer, Noah could see her convulsing on the floor. She'd managed to entangle herself in the tablecloth which was making it more difficult for those trying to help.

Four soldiers appeared. A path opened instantly before them and they made quick work of lifting the afflicted girl off the floor. Starlight's attendant scurried behind the soldiers as they whisked the designer from the ballroom.

Raven returned with his plateful of goodies. 'What happened? Did she choke on something?'

'No idea,' Noah replied. 'It all happened so quickly.'

'Maybe she's just trying to get out of the parade,' Raven suggested.

'If that's the case, and it works, she's probably the smartest of us all,' Noah said.

♪♫

Noah was thankful they had their own float. Sharing a breakfast table with the other designers had been trying and she was glad she didn't have to share the confined space of a float with them. At least she and Raven would be able to talk more freely to each other and to Chase when she reported in, assuming they could make themselves heard. The noise on the streets was unbelievable. For the first time since arriving on Talisker, Noah wished to be deaf again.

People were cheering and yelling and singing. Fire crackers boomed constantly. Drums of all shapes and sizes were being hit, tapped and beaten all over the city. Cymbals clashed and horns blasted but there was nothing that resembled music.

Starlight hadn't made it to the parade and Noah wasn't sure if that augured well for her or not. As far as the parade went though, Noah doubted that one float would be missed. Anyone who was anyone in Leninstar had a float in the Solstice parade it seemed. It surprised Noah that there was anyone left to actually watch the parade.

'You get parades like this at home, Miss Chord?' the float driver called back over her shoulder.

Jamille was a veteran Solstice float driver who, judging by her reptilian skin, had seen more than her fair share of the sun.

'Some,' Noah yelled back. 'I've been in the crowd for parades before but I've never been on a float. At home, the crowd is always behind barricades though.'

'We've had barricades before,' Jamille said, 'but crowd numbers are way down this year so we don't really need them.'

Noah looked at the clogged streets. 'There are usually more people than this?'

'Oh, yes.'

'I'm guessing that there are more people in the parade this year rather than watching it?' Noah asked.

The driver laughed like an asthmatic crow. 'No, no,' she said. 'They're all in the parks watching the parade on the big screens that the king has set up. The parks are packed.'

'Do you wish you were watching the parade on one of those screens?' Noah asked.

'Goodness no,' the float-driver said, 'I wouldn't be anywhere but here. This is the best seat in the house. No greater thrill than driving a float in the Solstice parade. And this year is a very special honour for me. There was fierce competition for your float, Miss Chord – you being from Earth and all – and when I got the nod to drive for you ... well, let me tell you that's a moment I will never forget.'

Noah didn't know quite what to say to that but to her surprise, Raven saved her the trouble.

'Well, I think they made the right choice,' he yelled over the cheering as they rounded the corner onto an even more tightly packed street. 'My sister deserves the best float in the parade and she's got it.'

Noah cringed in embarrassment at her brother's words but Raven winked at her as the driver's chest swelled with pride.

'Thank you, Raven,' Jamille said, 'thank you very much.'

'You're welcome,' he said as he waved to the crowd.

Tired of yelling, Noah leaned over so she could talk to Raven at a more sensible volume.

'How long have we been going?' she asked.

'About half an hour.'

Noah groaned. 'You mean there's still an hour to go?'

'Yep. Settle in, Sis – smile and wave. There are worse things you know. At least you're not in jail.'

That was true. Noah thought about Sachin, Emir, Ardis and Alan. She wondered what Emir was thinking right now. For all his beastly arrogance, he often had good ideas. *He probably even had a plan for tonight,* she thought. She'd have given anything to know what it was.

'Hello? Anyone out there?'

'Hi Chase,' Noah said. 'What do you know?'

'Gee, it's noisy. Where are you now?'

'On a float at the parade.'

'Have you been past the palace yet?'

'No.'

'I might go and sit on the balcony so I can wave when you go past.'

'You do that,' Noah said, 'but in the meantime … an update on the story?'

'Okay,' Chase said. 'I've just waded through one of the most self-indulgent monologues I've ever read. Orville is congratulating himself on a job well done by "dispensing" with Valada.'

'He *killed* the king's tailor?' Noah asked.

'Not personally,' Chase said. 'He arranged it though – part of his master plan to host a fashion gala so he could draw you into his net. He knew you wouldn't be able to resist a fashion show.'

Noah sighed. 'And I fell for it so easily.'

'Don't feel bad,' her friend said. 'Orville is a master manipulator. That's what this is all about. He had a plan – he wrote it in a novel – and he's manipulated people and events to achieve his goal. Orville is ridiculously devious.'

Noah thought she caught an undertone of grudging respect in Chase's tone but decided against quizzing her on it.

Chase continued her report. 'Orville knows all about your family tree, Noah,' she said. 'I know you won't want to hear this, but he thinks the two of you have a connection because you're alike.'

Raven, still waving to the crowd, said, 'Alike? Alike how?'

'Because you both are part Taliskeran and part Earthling,' Chase explained. 'Orville's grandmother was Taliskeran and his grandfather was from Earth. That's partly how he got the job as the king's Adviser. He could prove a Taliskeran heritage and he also has a detailed knowledge of Earth and its technologies. King Tambian jumped at the chance to hire him. And once he was here, and had access to state records, he was able to narrow down who might best lead him to the 13th key.'

Noah swore softly. 'Do you have any good news?'

'Unfortunately not,' Chase said. 'Orville knows about the Descera you met at Scratch & Denton too.'

'How?' Noah said.

'Scratch is on Orville's payroll.'

'Seriously?' Noah said, shaking her head. 'Sachin said Scratch was his friend. He trusted him. Sachin is going to be really upset when he finds out his friend is a spy.'

'If he finds out,' Raven said.

A young girl skipped up to the float and threw a flower that landed at Noah's feet. She was followed by a dozen more children all bearing blossoms.

'I hope you win tonight, Noah Chord,' the girl called out.

'Thank you,' Noah called back.

'You're welcome,' Chase said.

'She wasn't talking to you, Chase,' Raven said.

'Who was she talking to then?'

'An adoring fan.'

'Oh, that's cute,' Chase said.

'Chase, how about you keep reading and update us again once we get to the tournament?'

'Sure thing. Talk soon. Over and out.'

'You know what's really bothering me?' Noah said as she caught another small bunch of flowers.

'What's that?' Raven asked.

'That Orville's story matches what's been happening here. Manipulating events is one thing but I really don't understand how he can write about the future – about things that haven't happened yet.'

Raven looked at her seriously. 'Maybe we're not real,' he said.

'What?'

'Maybe we're just characters in Orville's story but other than that – we don't exist.'

Noah stared at her brother. 'You can't be serious.'

'It would explain why everything is happening the way the story says it does.'

Noah continued staring at Raven who was still smiling and waving to the crowd.

'You need to keep waving,' he said.

'And the fact that we might not be real doesn't bother you?' Noah asked as she resumed her smiling and waving duties.

'Hey, I was a dog and now I'm a person. How many people can say that? It doesn't bother me if I'm real or not. I'm having fun.'

Well, if I'm not real, Noah thought, *there isn't much I can do about it right now.*

Chapter 29

'I can't watch,' Noah said, covering her face with her hands.

Raven put his arm around his sister's shoulders but didn't say anything. The same couldn't be said for her rival, Woodstock, who was sitting on the other side of her.

'Don't have the stomach for this, Noah?' he said loftily. 'This is only the joust. You Earthlings must be soft, huh?'

'Don't listen to him, Noah,' Raven said. 'He'll eat his words tonight when you clean up at the fashion gala.'

'I wish we could just get on with the show,' Noah said. 'I don't know how much more of this I can take.'

They only needed to be at the tournament for an hour. Being a celebrity designer had its downsides, Noah decided – attending these events was torture. Starlight hadn't made it to the tournament either. Noah didn't know whether to envy her or not. She suspected she'd have to be dead or close to it to get out of this.

Noah was thankful to have a place in what little shade was afforded by the brightly painted canvas sheets that had been erected over the prime seats in the amphitheatre. Powdery dust, stirred up by feet and hooves, drifted up from the floor of the arena, stinging her eyes and absorbing the sweat that oozed from her pores. She sipped on warm lemonade from an earthenware cup in an effort to settle her stomach.

As if the bloody spectacle wasn't nauseating enough, the smell of horse manure and frying sweetmeats was making Noah even more squeamish.

'Are you there, guys?' Chase said.

'Uh-huh,' Noah said softly.

'You okay?'

'I want to be clean and I want to be cool,' she groaned.

'You at the tournament?'

'Just a minute …'

Noah stood up. 'I'm going for another drink,' she announced. 'Anyone else want one?'

'No thanks,' Raven said.

'That's just an excuse to not watch the show,' Woodstock scoffed. 'You're weak, Chord.'

Noah didn't answer. She excused herself from the seating area and headed for the drink stall, deciding it was easier to talk and walk than to stop anywhere in particular.

'Go ahead, Chase,' she said.

'How's the tournament going?'

'I couldn't tell you.'

'That good, huh?'

'No.'

'Okay, back to the story,' Chase said. 'So I'm up to where Orville has wildly exaggerated your visit to Seychelles to justify his raid on Mellifont and to pass a law banning the use of raiki.'

'I can't believe he knew we would go there,' Noah said.

'Noah, Orville has spies everywhere. According to the novel, *he* was the one who fed information to Montana's warriors to make sure the High Priestess knew about the facility and the slaughter that was happening there. He knew she'd go there and he knew you and Sachin would go with her.'

'Unbelievable,' Noah said.

'And I hate to tell you this,' Chase said, 'but he also knows about the special fabric you bought from Madame Priscilla?'

'*What?* How?'

'The weaver who made the fabric – she works for Orville. She made the fabric on his instruction.'

Noah froze. 'Madame Priscilla?' she whispered. 'Is she working for Orville?

'No!' Chase said. 'She has no idea. She thinks the weaver was working for her. Orville has put one over Madame Priscilla there.'

Noah couldn't decide if that made her feel better or worse. If Orville could fool someone as shrewd as Madame Priscilla, then maybe Noah shouldn't feel so bad about him manipulating her. On the other hand, the fact that Orville had outwitted Madame Priscilla proved how extraordinarily dangerous he was. Noah was relieved at least that Madame Priscilla wasn't working with Orville – she'd much rather have the former Dragonsbane on her side.

Noah rubbed her temples. 'I can't believe he knows about the fabric. That means he won't wear the suit. Bastard!'

'Noah!'

'I can't believe he played me like that. He's been toying with me. What a waste of time that was—'

'Making his suit, you mean?'

'Yes, making his suit. I can't believe he—'

'Noah.'

'—thinks he can manipulate me like that—'

'*Noah.*'

'—and get away with it.'

'*Noah!*' Chase cried.

'What?'

'Settle down. He wants you to get angry. Why do you think he's given us a copy of the book? He wants us to know what he's been doing. He wants us to think he's got everything under control and that it's going to continue to go his way. He wants to make you angry about being manipulated. You need to keep cool. Take a breath.'

Noah did as she was told. Thankfully there weren't many people outside the main arena. Anyone watching her would think she was crazy talking to herself.

'You do realise that Madame Priscilla is a madam, don't you?' Chase said.

Having no idea why Chase thought this important enough to quiz her about it she said, 'Of course I do, it's her title.'

Chase said, 'Not a *Madame*,' she said, 'a madam. You know, some who runs a … house of ill-repute.'

'What?'

'A brothel, Noah. She runs a brothel.'

'No she doesn't,' Noah said. 'She and her sister run an accommodation service.'

Chase chuckled. 'That is really cute,' she said. 'You're a sweet girl, Noah and don't let anyone tell you different.'

'Look, how far through the book are you?'

'About halfway,' Chase said.

Noah looked at her watch. 'You'll be finished before dinner?'

'I should be.'

'You need to be.'

'Right – back to work then. Over and out.'

Noah returned to the bleachers and immediately wished she hadn't. 'That's got to hurt,' she said.

'You don't say,' Raven said.

'And this is supposed to be entertainment?' Noah said. 'People's intestines are supposed to be inside their bodies, not lying in the hot sand.'

Woodstock weighed into the conversation. 'Can you really not appreciate the skill of these brave combatants?' he said.

'I can't see past the blood, I'm afraid,' Noah said.

'You really don't belong here.'

She refrained from agreeing with him – barely.

♪♫

'Finally,' Noah said, 'this is more like it.'

Her dressing quarters were spacious and lavishly decorated. Even though the gala didn't officially start for another few hours, the models were currently getting hair and makeup done, leaving Noah and Raven with the room to themselves for now. Her garments hung on shiny silver racks and all the shoes and accessories were meticulously arranged in square compartments on the shelves that lined the rear wall. The long side walls bore panels of lighted mirrors – courtesy of the miracle of electricity. Talisker didn't have the infrastructure to manufacture the lighting that the dressing room boasted so Noah assumed that Orville had procured them from Earth.

'I think we were safer at the tournament,' Raven said. 'Here, we're likely to meet the same end that Starlight did.'

'No we won't,' Noah said flatly.

Orville had announced the young designer's death only minutes ago and though no details were released about how she died, Raven was rattled.

'Haven't you been listening to Chase?' Noah said. 'We're probably the only ones who *are* safe. Orville isn't going to let anything happen to us.'

'Yet.'

Noah nodded. 'Yet. We're safe until tonight. We've got a collection to show and a competition to win.'

Chase's voice crackled in her ear. 'Are you two setting up for tonight?'

'Yes, we are,' Noah said. 'Where are you up to?'

'Well, I've been reading lots about blood and collection centres and electricity and power stations … lots about what a spectacle this year's Solstice will be and a fair bit about routing the adepts and their sympathisers.'

'Anything that's going to help us defeat Orville?'

'Well, I have just read about the spell he put on you when he kissed you,' Chase said.

'And?'

'Nothing that's going to help us reverse the spell but I can tell you this. When he kissed you he cut your hand with a ring he was wearing, which was laced with something his wizards concocted. Your blood is now contaminated with the substance and that's what makes you susceptible to his commands.'

'Why Orville's commands in particular?' Noah asked. 'How does that work?'

'The potion contains some of Orville's blood. Mixing your blood creates a bond between you,' Chase explained.

'Gross,' Noah said.

'Anyway, Alan's advice is probably the best – just try to stay as far away from Orville as you can.'

'Really? There's no advice on how to counteract the spell?'

'No,' Chase said. 'That kind of detail doesn't make for interesting reading.'

'It would be interesting to me,' Noah said.

'Well, it's not all about you, my friend.'

'Really?' Noah replied. 'I'm only expected to save the world. No big deal.'

'Yeah, get over yourself,' Chase said.

Raven injected himself into the conversation. 'Anything in there about Noah becoming Dragonsbane?'

'Our trip to Ironside is noted in a conversation between Orville and the king,' Chase said, 'but there is little detail. It would appear that Orville didn't have any spies inside Dragonhall. He knows that you come away from there as Dragonsbane and that you have the 13th key, although he's not specific about what it is. Even the great Orville couldn't predict what it would be. That's a good thing. Anyway, I'm anticipating my next couple of hours will be spent reading about the siege at Mellifont and then we should get to our arrival here in Leninstar last week.'

'Well, happy reading,' Noah said, relieved that the true nature of the 13th key had not been revealed. While Orville had seemed to accept that the Dragonsbane's staff was the 13th key, given what Noah had learned about him, she couldn't be sure he didn't know the truth. He was supremely deceitful but at least for now, Chase didn't know Noah's secret.

'Gee, thanks,' Chase said. 'Over and out.'

'So what now?' Raven asked.

'Now it's time for you to have a shower,' Noah said.

'Do I have to?'

'Yes.'

Raven appeared to think hard. 'How about this … if you save the world tonight and we're all still here tomorrow – then, I'll have a shower.'

'This isn't a negotiation,' she replied, throwing her hands in the air. 'Shower. Now.'

'But—'

'But nothing. You're not wearing your new outfit if you don't shower.'

He reached into his bag of tricks and pulled out the sad puppy eyes.

'No, Raven. No shower – no outfit. That's final.'

Noah folded her arms across her chest to emphasise her point.

'Oh, all right,' he said.

He'd barely slunk out of the room when Orville arrived.

'Good afternoon, Noah,' he said. 'I trust everything is to your satisfaction.'

'What happened to Starlight?' she asked.

He smiled at her. 'Chase not up to that part yet?'

'No.'

Orville sighed. 'Well, I guess it won't hurt if I tell you that part. She was poisoned – it was the peach mead.'

'A poisoned chalice?' Noah said. 'I'd have thought someone like you would come up with something more imaginative than that.'

'I'd have thought someone like you would be more grateful than that,' he countered.

'What do you mean?'

'You were actually the target, Noah, and I saved you from that.'

Noah peered at him suspiciously. 'How did you save me from that?'

'Did you think it was coincidence that you two looked so similar?'

'Yes.'

'No. I wrote it that way – to save your life. You might also have noticed that she was sitting in your seat at the breakfast table this morning? I wrote that too.'

'Who was trying to kill me?'

'Just someone who doesn't want an alien to win tonight,' Orville said. 'You have many fans here, Noah – thanks to me – but there are some who want Valada's position to go to one of their own.'

Noah stared at him, unable to think of anything to say. At last she said, 'What do you want?'

Orville walked slowly towards her and stopped only when he couldn't take another step without standing on her toes. He tucked an errant lock of hair behind her ear. 'I just wanted to make sure you have everything you need for tonight,' he said.

'I'd find it easier to get organised if it weren't for all the interruptions,' she said.

'Ah, the joys of public life. I'm afraid your engagements this morning were a necessary evil,' Orville said, glossing over his own interruption. 'Having you all out there promotes this evening's events. We want to drum up as much interest in the gala as possible.'

'Well, I've done my penance and now I'd like some time to collect my thoughts and get my house in order.'

'Certainly. Just as long as you don't forget the 13th key – we're going to need that.'

'At the gala?'

Orville shook his head. 'No, Noah. Not *at* the gala. *After* the gala. I've organised for our special ceremony to take place *after* the gala.'

'Yay,' she said, without enthusiasm.

'Excited about seeing all your friends again?'

'Friends?'

'Sachin and his cronies, Montana, Emir and Ardis … they'll all be at the ceremony.'

'Alive?' Noah asked.

He smiled. 'Initially, yes.'

'And Alan?'

Their plan to use a tonic to trigger the squeeze response in the vest they needed to suffocate Orville relied on Alan being there.

Orville's smile faded. 'No,' he said. 'I'm not having that nauseating whelp in my presence. Now, if there's nothing else?'

Smothering her disappointment, Noah said, 'Actually Orville, there is just one thing before you go …'

'What is it?'

'I don't suppose we could organise for Chase and our outfits to be brought down for tonight?'

Orville took her hand and kissed it. 'Of course, my dear. They'll be here in twenty minutes – you have my word.'

When he released her hand, she inspected it for cuts and was relieved not to find any more. To calm her nerves, she made her way to the clothes racks to do a final inspection of the garments she would show at the gala. In her head she visualised each one and checked that all the shoes and accessories were accounted for. Sixteen outfits. At least the four outfits for the young prince would be modelled on dolls. Those were dressed already.

Raven returned wearing only a towel around his waist and dripping water all over the floor. Noah assumed he was trying to make a point.

'Your outfit will be here shortly,' she said. 'Perhaps in the meantime you could go and have your hair done.'

Raven folded his arms across his chest. 'Have my hair done?' he repeated in disgust. 'I had a shower but I'm *not* getting my hair done.'

'Okay, okay,' Noah said, raising her hands in surrender. 'I'm happy that you showered. Hair styling optional.'

He uncrossed his arms.

'Look, Chase will be here soon with your clothes. I'm going to pop in for a shower. Will you be okay here?'

'Oh yes. I won't let anyone in.'

'Except Chase.'

He nodded obediently. 'Except Chase.'

Noah headed for the shower hoping that there wouldn't be a crowd. She found the amenities block blissfully empty. Choosing the shower at the end of the row she turned on the tap, letting the water run while she stripped off. When the water was steaming she stepped in under the luxuriant spray. She stood for a full minute just letting the water stream over her head and down her body. An array of shampoos, soaps and scrubs sat on a glass shelf on the side of the cubicle. Noah surveyed the collection and decided on the mandarin and ylang-ylang products. She lathered a liberal amount of the shampoo into her hair and the fresh, spicy scent invigorated her.

She took her time; it was possible that this would be her last shower. The soap contained raspberry seed which gently massaged her skin as she bathed. For a few moments she was able to forget about Orville, the 13th key and whether she was real or just a character in a novel but the respite didn't last long. As she rinsed the conditioner from her hair an alarm sounded in the block.

When Noah turned off the shower, she could hear the commotion outside.

Someone was yelling. *Two hours until show time! It's only two hours until show time!'*

Noah rinsed off quickly and towelled herself down before donning the soft, blue robe hanging behind the cubicle door. Collecting her clothes, she hurried back to her dressing quarters to find Raven and Chase helping themselves to a fruit platter. Raven was still wearing his towel and Chase had Orville's novel in hand.

'Did you not hear the announcement?' Noah asked. 'We've only got two hours left. Why are you two just sitting there?'

'Relax – it's two hours, Noah,' Raven said. 'There's plenty of time.'

'No, there isn't,' she retorted. 'Raven, you need to get dressed. Chase, you need to get back to the book.'

Having accompanied her friend to several shows, Chase knew what Noah would be like for the next two hours.

'Raven,' Chase said, 'do as your sister says. Go now.'

'Yes, Ma'am,' he said. 'I think anywhere away from you two right now would be a good place to be.'

When he was out of earshot, Chase said, 'I'll get back to the book. What are you going to do?'

'I'm going to check on my models,' Noah said.

Chapter 30

Noah had asked to stay in the dressing quarters during the show to help dress the models but Orville had denied her request. He had decreed that all the designers sit in the audience – no exceptions. At least this time, unlike the breakfast fiasco, they didn't all have to sit together. Noah sat between Raven and Chase in prime position at the end of the catwalk. The ballroom had been transformed. Eight massive screens hung around the walls to make sure no one missed anything. The extravagant lighting was designed to win over anyone who still had doubts about the introduction of electricity.

Orville appeared from the side of the stage dressed in the outfit that Noah had designed. Her heart leapt at the sight of the suit. It looked fabulous.

'Ladies and gentlemen,' he crooned into his radio mike, 'welcome to tonight's fashion gala. I'm sure we all have mixed feelings about this evening's special event. At the Solstice Festival there are always many things to celebrate. This year we celebrate something very special – electricity. Just look at these lights!'

The audience cheered.

'Tonight we celebrate blood magic – what makes electricity possible. Magic from the people, for the people. It is as it was meant to be. We have the power!'

He punched the air with his fist to emphasise his point and the crowd roared its appreciation.

Noah thought she might be sick.

'Although the Solstice Festival is always a time of celebration,' he continued, 'tonight's is tinged with sadness. Our fashion feast this evening is a result of the death of a great tailor and friend of the king, Valada. Tonight we look for his replacement among some very talented designers.'

He waited while the crowd went 'ooooooooohhhhhh'.

'We had over two hundred applications, which we whittled down to five. Unfortunately, one of those five suffered a tragic accident this morning and won't be with us tonight. Could we have a moment's silence for *Starlight*, please.'

After an appropriate interval, Orville continued his introduction. 'Tonight, you will be wowed by the works of *Woodstock*, dealt a fine showing by *House of Cards*, blinded by *Bindi Iis* and knocked off your feet by *Noah Chord*.'

A drum roll rumbled to its crescendo before ending abruptly on Orville's cue.

'So, without further ado,' Orville said, 'let's have a look at what our designers have in mind for the Ceremonial category.'

Music boomed through the elaborate speaker system. Orville had clearly used his contacts on Earth to import the contraband. The music was unlike anything Taliskerans had heard before but the strong beat and synthesiser were clearly a hit.

'Yours are the best, Sis,' Raven said, raising his voice to be heard over the music.

'Mine are the only ones out there,' Noah replied.

'I know that,' he said, grinning, 'but I don't even need to see the rest to know that yours are the best.'

Noah leaned over to Chase. 'Raven thinks mine are the best. What do you think?' she asked.

Chase looked at her sideways. 'Shush,' she said, 'I'm thinking.'

Noah sighed. As far as she was concerned, there was nothing else to think about. Tonight Orville would win. He hadn't guessed that *she* was the 13th key, but it didn't matter. Orville's imagined ending relied on her finding another piece of firestone after tracking down the Descera and at the end of his story she had used the power of the stone to destroy Talisker.

Blood magic had been only part of the answer to waking the dragon. By itself, blood magic would disrupt the natural music of the world but it wasn't enough to rouse Xan from her slumber. Once the music had been compromised then he needed the 13th key. Orville was particularly proud of his ironic ending – having Talisker's Dragonsbane use firestone to wake the dragon and destroy the world.

Despite Noah's assertion that the situation was hopeless, Chase was still wrestling with a new ending. *What better way to defeat a writer than to have another writer re-write the ending?* she reasoned. Noah had come close to telling Chase the truth about the 13th key but decided against it. Orville's blood spell would make Noah do whatever he wanted. When he told her to use the power of the firestone, she'd do it. Whether the power was inside her or in the stone made no difference. *So why do I still feel bad about not telling her?* Noah wondered.

Pushing her guilt aside, Noah sat back to watch the show. Her work was done. She watched the reactions of the royal couple in the box as the models took to the catwalk. The king and queen conferred on every item and appeared to make notes.

With all the models for the Ceremonial category out on stage, Orville appeared from the wings.

'Aren't they spectacular?' he said. 'How about another round of applause for the Ceremonial garb!'

The crowd obliged with rapturous applause.

'Our next category is Formalwear,' Orville declared.

The music changed as the models showing the *House of Cards* designs took to the catwalk. Noah thought the outfits were traditional, bordering on mundane and *Woodstock's* designs didn't inspire her either. The dress designed for Princess Catriona looked like a failed puce meringue.

'Are these people really designers?' Raven asked.

'Yes, Raven,' Noah replied, 'but keep your voice down. It's not polite to say things like that out loud.'

'Okay.'

Noah settled back again. She was going to win. That's the way Orville had written it. The categories, like the models, came and went in a blur of colour, sequins and frills.

The Lounging category was next. *Bindi Iis'* designs were first to hit the catwalk.

'I like the fitted bodice on the queen's gown,' Noah admitted, 'but the fabric is all wrong.'

'What's wrong with it?' Raven asked.

'The royal couple has satin sheets. A satin nightgown would be too slippery.'

'I thought it was all about the look,' Raven said.

'Mostly it is,' Noah conceded, 'but in this case, if you can make it practical too – it gives you an edge in the competition.'

'But you're going to win anyway,' he declared.

'Shhhh,' she hissed. 'You can't say that out loud. Just watch the show and stop talking.'

He flashed his sad-puppy eyes at her but did as she said.

For the rest of the show, Noah was careful to keep her comments to herself. Even when *Woodstock's* flamboyant Lounging outfits hit the catwalk, Noah managed to contain her thoughts. The royals would have to be heavily sedated to sleep in the outfits he offered.

Despite knowing the outcome, Noah's stomach still knotted in anticipation when Casual Wear was announced. This was her favourite category and the one in which she hoped to blow the others right out of the water. The *House of Cards* offerings were first. The king and queen appeared to approve of their outfits but Princess Catriona looked less than impressed by hers. Noah thought *Woodstock's* designs too traditional and lacking in colour. *Bindi Iis'* nautical designs were surprisingly good. The colours and cuts were fresh and fun and even the teenage princess nodded her approval.

Orville's voice rang out. 'And our last showing for the Casual Wear category and for the evening is from *Noah Chord*.'

As her models strutted onto the catwalk the crowd cheered and whistled. To Noah's delight, Princess Catriona clapped enthusiastically too. Being of similar age to the princess, Noah had hoped to have an edge over the other designers. Of the sixteen outfits she'd designed for the evening, this one was her favourite. She'd gladly have worn it herself – a long-sleeved button-up shirt with green and white checks teamed with short denim shorts. The red braces attached to the shorts matched the red heart-shaped buttons on the shirt and the cuffs of the shorts were trimmed in the same material as the shirt. Noah had rolled up the shirt sleeves to expose a fabulous green bracelet she'd brought with her to Talisker. With the matching green moccasins, the outfit was complete. Exposing so much leg had been a risk but one Noah was glad she'd taken.

'Outrageous!' someone cried.

Noah looked to her left. Vetel, from *House of Cards*, was on his feet and shaking his fist. 'Scandalous. The princess cannot wear something so ... so ...'

He was lost for words but it didn't matter – no one was paying him any attention anyway. The rest of the audience, along with the royal family were applauding and cheering. The show had come to its inevitable conclusion.

Orville sidled out onto the stage. 'Can we have all the designers up on stage please?' he said as the king and queen joined him at the podium.

While the designers made their way to the stage and with the models for the Casual Wear category still on the catwalk, Orville addressed the king. 'How did you enjoy this evening's show, Your Majesty?' he asked.

'Fabulous. Absolutely fabulous,' King Tambian enthused. 'Very colourful indeed. Look at these creations ... they're all amazing.'

'And what did you think, Your Highness?' he asked the queen.

'It's a shame Valada wasn't here to see it,' Queen Rosemary said. 'I think he would have loved what we've seen here tonight.'

Orville nodded. 'I think you're right,' he said. 'But now we come to the moment that the designers have been waiting for. The result. The decision. Who is going to take Valada's place as the Royal Tailor?'

He paused as the crowd cheered again.

'We have four brilliant designers on stage here,' he continued, drawing out the proceedings for as long as he could, 'House of Cards,

Woodstock, Bindi Iis and Noah Chord. I imagine, Your Graces, that you had a hard time choosing just one?'

The king nodded. 'Yes, indeed. It was a very difficult choice but we have chosen.'

'And who have you decided your new tailor will be?' Orville said, smiling.

The speakers crackled out a long drum roll.

'As I said, it was a difficult choice but in the end … I've decided to go with *Noah Chord*.'

The room erupted in applause – although Noah suspected that would have been the case no matter who had won. She floated over to the podium, curtsied before the king before shaking his hand and accepting a bouquet of flowers.

'Congratulations, Noah,' Orville said, shaking her hand warmly and planting a kiss on her cheek.

'Thank you,' she said.

'No doubt you have people you'd like to thank,' he said, handing her the microphone.

Noah accepted the microphone and knowing that she couldn't mention any of her adept acquaintances in present company, proceeded to thank her brother and her friend.

'I couldn't have done this without the support of my friend and seamstress, Jemima Chase and my brother, Raven.' She addressed them directly. 'I love you both dearly and I'll never forget all the sacrifices you've made for me.'

The crowd cheered again.

'I'd also like to thank the king and queen for their vote of confidence tonight and also everyone who has sent me words of encouragement this week – along with flowers and chocolates and perfumes. It's been quite a ride and I'm looking forward to working here full-time. Thank you.'

Another round of applause ensued as Noah handed the microphone back to Orville.

'You forgot to thank me,' he said, smiling and waving to the crowd.

'No, I didn't,' she said.

'Well, you *didn't* thank me.'

'That's correct. What did you expect me to say? And a huge thank you to Orville Kurz for rigging the contest so I could win?'

'Well, not exactly,' he said, frowning.

'And I'd also like to thank him for giving me the opportunity to help him destroy your world.'

'Alright I get the point,' he said, taking up his place again at the podium.

'I sincerely doubt it,' Noah retorted.

'Ladies and gentlemen, this brings the official part of this evening's festivities to a close. There are numerous parties around the palace grounds and throughout the city for you to continue to celebrate this year's Solstice. On behalf of the king and queen, I bid you goodnight.'

Orville turned to Noah and offered her his elbow. 'Ready?'

'Yes,' she replied, linking her arm with his.

'You have the 13th key?'

'Yes,' Noah said. 'It's in my trousers.'

Orville eyed her dress. 'And where are your trousers?'

Noah patted her handbag. 'In here.'

Orville smiled broadly and beckoning to Chase and Raven said, 'Very good. Let's do this.'

While they waited for Chase and Raven to fight their way through the crowd and join them backstage, Orville attempted small talk. 'What did you think of my novel?'

Noah squinted at him in disbelief. 'Not to my taste,' she said at last.

'Shame,' he said. 'It's going to be a best-seller.'

'You self-published! Couldn't convince a publisher of its merit?'

Orville's expression didn't change. 'Publishers like formulaic stories. Boring. This story breaks the mould, establishes a whole new genre.'

'I really can't see the "evil triumphs" angle catching on.'

'It's called a niche market, Noah,' he said. 'I don't really expect you to understand it.'

Chase and Raven arrived both wearing the same dour expression.

'Great, we're all here,' Orville said. 'Let's get this party started.'

'Where are we going?' Raven asked.

'Downstairs.'

'Downstairs?'
'Just follow me,' Orville said, turning Noah around.

Chapter 31

Orville raised his lamp. 'And we'll use the lift here,' he said, extending his free arm towards the open space in the rock wall.

Noah glanced left and right. 'It's not like there's any other choice,' she noted.

'Please,' he said, motioning for her to enter.

'Where are the others?' Chase asked as she followed Noah onto the wooden platform.

Orville ushered Raven through after Chase and then got on board himself. 'Waiting for us,' he said. 'Apart from the king and queen, that is – they'll be along shortly. Before we go … Noah, do you have the staff?'

'In my pocket,' Noah said, patting her Academy trousers.

'Show me,' he replied.

Noah sighed. Though still amazed by the technology that made the trousers possible, she'd hoped to meet her end wearing one of her own creations. Orville's insistence that she change clothes after the evening's festivities irritated her more than she was willing to admit.

Opening a pocket and drawing the Dragonsbane's staff from it, she said, 'Happy now?'

Orville smiled. 'Yes. You can put it away now.'

Noah did as she was told and when Orville pulled the thick iron lever on the wall, the platform lurched. Noah grabbed Raven's forearm for support.

'The worst is over,' Orville assured them. 'Despite the fact that this lift is thousands of years old, it works perfectly well – thanks in part to the restoration *I* instigated when we started work on the electricity network. Chase, would you like to tell your friends what you learned of this lift's history from my novel?'

Chase sniffed. 'Not especially.'

'Do it,' Orville said.

'Or what?' Chase said. 'We'll all be dead soon anyway. What are you going to do to me that's worse than that?'

Orville shrugged. 'Fair point, I guess. Oh well, I guess it falls to me to enlighten your friends then.'

As the platform descended in the rocky shaft, Noah closed her eyes briefly. The lamplight flashing off the stone made her dizzy.

Orville adjusted his cravat before launching into his explanation. 'Each of Talisker's state capitals is built above an ancient Desceran city. This was done intentionally so that the royals could take advantage of the subterranean railcar network that links them. The railcar network allows the kings to visit each other faster and safer than they could travelling overland. But to access the tunnels, which are about four hundred metres down, they needed lift access. The lift relies on relatively simple technology – chains, pulleys, gears and counterweights – but the way it's constructed is really quite amazing.'

'How long is this ride going to take?' Raven asked.

'About three minutes,' Orville said. 'Enjoy it while it lasts.'

'I'd have a better chance of enjoying it if you'd stop yabbering,' Raven said.

Noah glanced at Chase. The writer's furrowed brow told Noah that she was still grappling with a new ending for Orville's story. Noah took her brother's hand and squeezed it gently. Raven broke her grip to put his arm around her shoulder. Pulling her towards him, he kissed her on the top of her head.

'Everything will be okay,' he said.

Not trusting her voice, Noah didn't answer.

Orville put his lamp on the floor. 'We're almost halfway,' he announced. 'Very soon, we won't need the lamp anymore. This shaft will open out and you'll be able to see the underground city from up high.'

When the rear rock wall eventually gave way, Noah gasped.

'Oh, my goodness,' Chase whispered.

Raven said, 'Surely you're not surprised by the view, Chase. This is what you'd have pictured from the vivid description in the novel, isn't it?'

Orville rolled his eyes at the sarcastic remark but said nothing.

'It's an underground valley,' Chase murmured without taking her eyes from the view.

Noah nodded. Ornate buildings and houses had been carved into the mountainsides and more stone buildings protruded from the floor. Though narrow, the floor of the valley extended for several hundred metres in both directions from the lift shaft. Three deep, lava-filled chasms cut across the valley, dividing the city into four sections. Noah could imagine the great dragon, Xan raking her giant claws through the earth and leaving the gaping wounds. The exposed lava flowing in the gorges gave the city its warm, ambient glow. Arched bridges spanned the chasms, giving the illusion that a serpentine creature had been frozen in time as it slithered through the underground, its humped form giving rise to the crossings.

Noah studied the section of valley floor directly beneath the lift. A large sandstone building like a stepped pyramid straddled the width of the valley. In the otherwise empty courtyard at the front of the structure stood an olluka tree, its dark wood unmistakable. A railcar sat idle at the rear of the building.

'There – behind the palace – is one of the railcars I was telling you about,' Orville said with a nod. 'You can see the tracks leading into the tunnel in the far wall. That tunnel leads north to Seychelles – where the six underground highways meet. That's why the electricity generator was built there. The other Taliskeran kings were only willing to contribute to the funding of the network if they could get access to it. All the wiring runs from the generator through the tunnel to here.'

'Except that you never intended for them to get it,' Chase said.

'True,' Orville admitted with a shrug. Changing the subject, he added, 'See the olluka tree?'

'It looks like it's dead,' Raven said. 'It doesn't have any leaves.'

'It doesn't have any leaves because it's underground,' Orville said curtly. 'There is no sunlight – no photosynthesis – therefore no leaves required. The olluka tree gets its nutrients from the blood of Xan – from the lava deep in the earth. What you see there is just the very *end* bits of a very big branch.'

Chase frowned. 'Or perhaps,' she said, 'what we see here is the "delicate tendrils adorning the end of a gargantuan branching structure that is buried deep within the earth"?'

Raven nodded. 'That's certainly more poetic than the "very end bits of a very big branch".'

As the lift slowed and stopped, eight of Orville's scarlet-robed minions assembled.

'I'm so glad you're enjoying some poetry in your final hours, Raven,' Orville said, 'but given that you are running out of time, allow me to speak plainly. *Get ... off ... the ... lift.*'

Raven glared at him but stepped off the wooden platform. Noah followed him with Chase at her side. She leaned in close to Chase and whispered in her ear. 'Any ideas for a new ending?'

'Not yet,' Chase said, chewing at her lip. 'I'm still working on it. It's hard. I know what ending I'd have for the story *I'd* have written, but Orville's story is different and it's hard to come up with an ending that fits with what's gone before.'

'Lock those two up with the others,' Orville said, pointing to Chase and Raven, 'and if they resist, start cutting bits off them.'

'Cutting bits off won't stop me,' Raven growled as he resisted the wizards who tried to grab his arms.

Orville drew a dagger from the scabbard of a surprised wizard. Holding the point of the blade to Noah's ear, he said, 'I need your sister for a bit longer yet, Raven, but I don't need *all* of her.'

Raven ceased struggling and Orville returned the wizard's dagger.

'Oh, Chase,' Orville said, 'I'll be having the novel back before you go. It was a gift to Noah – not to you.'

Chase reached into her handbag and took out the book. She handed it to Orville, wiping her hand on her trousers once she'd done so.

'Thank you,' Orville said.

'The pleasure's all mine,' Chase said.

Noah watched as Raven and Chase were marched away towards the bridge. Her blood felt hot in her veins. *What's the use of being the 13th key if I can't even help them?* she thought.

'Where are you taking them?' she asked.

'Prison,' Orville said. 'After I send the lift back up for the king and queen, I will take you over there so you can have one last visit with all your friends. After that, you have a world to destroy.'

With his novel tucked under one arm, Orville reset the counterweights and set the lift in motion again. Noah winced at the clattering of the ratchets as the wooden platform soared upwards to collect its royal cargo.

'Okay,' Orville said, 'let's go.'

Noah's heart beat faster as they walked towards the courtyard in front of the Desceran palace. She stepped from stone to stone, trying to avoid the joins. A momentary flash of homesickness struck her. She pictured herself back in Sayle, pounding the pavement on her way to a fashion show. For as long as she could remember she'd been superstitious about standing on the joins. *Stupid,* she thought. *This world's about to end and I'm still worrying about stepping on joins.*

Another thought occurred to her. Had any of the Descera she'd met ever walked here? Archie or Edwina? Or Benji or Saul? Or Seth? Even though they'd passed on she felt a measure of comfort at the thought that they might have trod on the same stones she walked on now. But she also felt the weight of responsibility. They'd clung to life through the centuries to ensure the 13th key was made. She owed them.

As they neared the olluka tree, Noah stopped.

'Don't even think about it,' Orville warned.

'I'm not the coward you are,' she retorted. 'I wouldn't abandon my friends to run back to Earth and save my own skin.'

'Neither would I,' he said.

Noah nodded. 'I believe you. I don't reckon you'd have any friends.'

It was Orville's turn to nod. 'That's true. Friends just drag you down. I have no ties – I am completely free. You'll never understand how that feels.'

'For which I am very grateful actually,' Noah said.

'*Anyway* ... do you want to see your friends or not?'

'Of course I do.'

'Then let's get moving.'

Orville turned and walked towards the bridge. Noah followed, quickening her pace so she could walk alongside him.

'See that switch?' he asked as they stepped onto the bridge.

'Yes.'

'The bridge is electrified. There's a switch on each side. This bridge ... is the heart of my plan,' he gloated.

'Good for you,' Noah said as she looked over the railing of the stone bridge, thankful that this bridge was sturdier than the rickety wooden one she'd used to get to Dragonhall. The lava flowed only a few metres from the top of the chasm and its heat assaulted her. As she passed the halfway point on the bridge, Noah focused her attention on the double-storey building on the other side.

The prison block was set back from the edge of the chasm. It was close enough that it could be monitored from the palace but the crevasse provided a natural barrier. And the prisoners could be easily monitored. The metal bars on the front and rear walls of the block meant anyone outside could see what the prisoners within were up to.

Even from this distance, Noah could easily identify the twelve Majors from Mellifont on the left side of the lower level. Across the passageway Emir, Montana and Ardis took up the first three cells on the other side of the block. Next to them, Orville's wizards were locking the gates on Raven's and Chase's cells.

Once the wizards' task was done, all the scarlet robes formed up in rows. Noah counted ten rows of six. As she neared the prison, Noah looked at the instruments on the ground outside the respective Majors' cells. Lyre, violin, harp, bugle, trombone, tuba, drums, bells, xylophone, flute, clarinet and bagpipes... Orville had them all. The Majors stood, peering through the bars at her. Noah's eyes met Sachin's. Grim-faced, he nodded at her. A bead of sweat trickled down Noah's back as she nodded in return.

'Not long to wait now, people,' Orville said. 'The king and queen will be here shortly and then we can commence. We will be rid of raiki and the Academy for good.'

The wizards applauded.

'Along with Talisker and everyone on it if you destroy all the keys!' Sachin cried. 'Everyone is going to die! *Everyone!*'

One of the wizards snorted. 'Not everyone!' he said. '*We're* all going to live on Earth with our master.'

Noah's stomach tightened as the other wizards cheered and Orville bowed.

Major Maggie put her arm between the bars and shook her fist in Orville's direction. 'You will all be punished for your evil ways!'

'Silence!' Orville snapped. 'It is *you* who will be punished for *your* evil ways. We warned you that any use of the keys to compromise the electricity network would result in forfeiture of all the keys. Major Sachin, *you* broke into the facility at Seychelles with a key in your possession. It is *you* who has brought this consequence on you and your fellow Majors. The decree of the Sovereign States Alliance has been put into effect.'

'I did nothing to compromise the network,' Sachin protested.

'I am not here to argue,' Orville said. 'The court has tried your case; you have been found guilty. For using a key against the Crown, the penalty is forfeiture of *all* the keys. For breaking into a Crown facility – an act of treason – the penalty is death for you, Major Sachin.'

'You won't get away with this,' Major Maggie said.

Orville chuckled. 'I will get away with it,' he assured her. 'Just relax and enjoy the show.'

He took his fob watch from the pocket of his vest, looked at it and smiled. As he tucked it away again, Noah found herself wishing Alan was amongst the prisoners. The tonic he'd composed to activate the vest would have put Orville in his place.

As if he could read her mind, Orville unbuttoned the vest Noah had designed for him. 'You did a wonderful job on this, Noah,' he said. 'It's a shame you won't see if your plan for it would have worked.'

He took off the vest and tossed it to the wizard closest to him.

Noah shook her head.

'Are you impressed that I was able to manipulate Madame Priscilla?' he asked.

'No,' Noah said. '*I* manipulated her into giving me her job. And don't try to tell me you had anything to do with that!'

'It's true,' he said, 'that I had no influence inside Dragonhall, but then I didn't need it. I had everything else in place. I must say, it did feel good to trick the old hag though.'

'Well, she's not in charge anymore. I am Dragonsbane now,' Noah said. 'You're going to have to get past me.'

Orville chuckled. 'Brave words, but hollow. No one here believes you can beat me – not even you.'

Noah turned away.

'You have no idea what you're up against, Noah,' he continued. 'I have planned and plotted for years – *years* – for this moment. You can't win here. This is *my* night. *My* time to triumph.'

'We'll see.'

'You wouldn't even be here if it wasn't for me,' he said.

'Really?'

'Really,' he said with a nod. 'I was ten when I figured out you'd be the one to find the 13th key – thanks to my grandmother, her book and our visit to your mother. It was one of my spies in Mellifont who led Sachin to you. It's always been me, Noah. I have orchestrated everything here. Everything.'

A knot of helplessness burned in Noah's stomach. 'You can't possibly control everything,' she said. 'Nobody can do that.'

He smiled and rubbed his chin. 'I don't need to control *everything*,' he replied. 'Details don't matter – only the events. Everything I needed to happen, has happened. I have an electricity network based on blood magic, I am about to destroy the twelve keys and you have found the 13th key for me. It's perfect – brilliant actually.'

Noah looked at him and shook her head. 'You're unbelievable.'

'Yes,' he agreed. 'I am.'

'I didn't mean that as a compliment.'

'Sure you did,' he said. 'Now … I am going back to the lift so I can greet the king and queen when they arrive. *You're* going to stay here like a good girl until I get back. My wizards will keep you company while I'm gone.'

'Great,' Noah said without enthusiasm.

She watched Orville stride towards the bridge. *Bastard,* she thought, and though she was appalled at what he was about to do, she continued to watch him – anything to avoid the expectant stares of her imprisoned friends. In his absence, she wrestled with how she might use the Dragonsbane's staff to defeat him since she had no idea how to use the power of the firestone within her. By the time the lift appeared, all she'd come up with was hitting him over the head with it, hardly a sophisticated plan.

Orville bowed as the king stepped off the lift. Noah sighed as Tambian then took his wife's hand and led her from the platform. The subterranean city was silent as the trio made their way across the courtyard and over the bridge.

'Noah?' King Tambian said when he reached her. 'What are you doing here?'

'An excellent question, my liege,' Orville cut in, 'and one that will be answered very soon. I ask that you just bear with me for now.'

The king frowned but nodded. 'Okay. Proceed.'

Orville turned to Noah. 'Time to get started?'

'Don't ask me,' Noah said. 'Read your book if you've forgotten where we're up to.'

He winked at her and turned back to the royal couple.

'Let us begin,' Orville said sombrely. 'Welcome Your Royal Highnesses, to tonight's ceremony.'

The royal couple nodded their acknowledgment.

Orville bowed his head. 'Tonight we carry out the sentence imposed by the court on these criminals. First, we will deal with the twelve keys. Wizards, you know what to do.'

The front dozen wizards walked to where the instruments lay and each picked up one.

'*NO!*' the Majors screamed.

As Mellifont's adepts continued howling their displeasure, the wizards walked towards the chasm. At the edge of the crevasse they stopped and held the instruments above their heads. The Majors fell silent.

'Now!' Orville commanded.

The wizards dropped the twelve keys into the lava. Steam shot towards the ceiling and the ground trembled.

'Should it be doing that?' the king asked as he put his arm around his queen to support her.

'Yes,' Orville said. 'But hold on – this ride's going to get a great deal bumpier yet.'

The king's lips disappeared into a thin white line. 'What do you mean?' he asked. 'What's going on here?'

'What's going on here?' Orville repeated. 'History is being made here tonight, Your Highness. The end of your world heralds the birth of an exciting new genre of fiction writing on Earth. It's quite an honour.'

'What are you talking about?' the king demanded. 'What do you mean the end of the world?'

Orville nodded to the wizards that had taken their positions behind the royal couple. 'Secure them.'

Six wizards pounced, removing the king's sword and shackling his wrists before he could defend himself.

'Release us!' King Tambian demanded as he struggled against his captors. 'This is treason. You can't do this.'

Orville smiled. 'I can do this,' he said. 'But coming back to your question about the end of the world – your world is going to end tonight because I'm going to wake the dragon.'

The wizards pushed the royals to their knees.

'How are you going to do that?' the king said, his eyes blazing and beard twitching.

'Well,' Orville said, 'the widespread use of blood magic to power the electricity network weakens Talisker's dragonsong. And now that we've destroyed the twelve keys, there's no way to repair that damage.'

'You can't just destroy Talisker,' the queen said.

'I can,' Orville countered.

The royal couple stared at Orville, incredulous.

'You can feel the beginning of it already,' Orville said.

The king's face flushed red with the anger of Orville's betrayal. Noah looked away.

The queen spoke again. 'Why are you doing this?'

'Just a moment please, Queen Rosemary,' Orville said. He handed his book to Noah and whispered, 'Page 386. We're starting from the top of the page.'

Noah thumbed through the book.

'Ready?' Orville asked.

'No,' Noah said, despite having found the page he'd specified.

'Too bad,' he said. 'We're on.'

Orville cleared his throat before addressing the assembly. 'I am doing this because I *can*,' he said smugly. He looked at Noah, prompting her to recite her lines.

'I'm not buying it,' Noah said, reading from the book. 'People eat chocolate for breakfast when they move out of home "just because they can". People max out their credit cards buying jewellery they can't afford "just because they can". But people don't set out to destroy another world "just because they can". There must be more to it.'

Reading the lines made Noah feel unclean but she consoled herself with the knowledge that the self-indulgent monologue coming up would give Chase more time to devise a plan. Noah looked up at the stonework above her, wondering how long it would be before the rumbling underfoot shook something loose.

'Well, I'm a writer,' he declared.

Chase guffawed loudly and Orville shot her a withering look.

'My grandmother, Alina Kurz, had a book about Talisker and this prophecy,' he said. 'It was a non-fiction text and I was fascinated by it. I would spend hours reading through it, looking at the pictures, dreaming about what it would be like to go to Talisker … and then I had an epiphany.'

He seemed to drift off, lost in his memories.

'I thought to myself, *I could be the evil of which the prophecy speaks.* And then, as I got older it occurred to me that fiction needed a whole new genre. A genre where evil triumphs, where the "bad guy" comes out on top. I got sick of reading stories with "happy endings" and where the "good guys" win. *Boring!* Life isn't like that; so why do we write like that?'

'Because it's *fantasy* fiction,' Raven called from his cell. 'Fantasy fiction *must* be different from reality.'

Orville ignored Raven's interjection. 'Anyway, as I was saying,' he continued, 'a new genre is required. I am pioneering it. Right here, right now. The novel is written'—he pointed to the book in Noah's hands—'and in the end of the story, this world is destroyed. That's where we're up to now.' He turned to Noah. 'Come.'

He turned and walked towards the bridge. Noah followed. When he reached the bridge, he turned back to his audience. Pointing to the tunnel across the chasm, he said, 'The cabling for the electricity network runs from Seychelles to here through that tunnel. And then you can probably see the cable that runs from there and connects to this bridge.' He patted the bridge's railing to emphasise his point. 'Oh, and look – there's a switch here. So I flick this'—Orville flicked the switch with a dramatic flourish—'and combine electricity produced by blood magic with the firestone from twelve keys and I'm well on my way to waking up that lazy dragon.'

The bridge crackled as electricity flowed through the cabling on the railing.

The queen looked to Montana whose face was wedged between the metal bars on her cell. 'What about the prophecy?' Queen Rosemary asked. 'The prophecy says the 13th key is supposed to save us!'

Orville didn't give the High Priestess a chance to respond. 'I'm so glad you brought that up, Your Highness.' He recited the prophecy, obviously enjoying the sound of his own voice. '*The thirteenth key the world shall need, for evil to be brought to heel – One of two, the Dragon's bane must rise; and the music wield.* You'll be pleased to know that I have the 13th key.'

The king and queen both stared at him as the tremors underfoot intensified.

'What is it?' the king asked.

'Noah,' Orville said, 'show them the 13th key would you, dear?'

Noah reached for a pocket on her trousers as everyone's attention shifted to her. Heat flushed her cheeks, though it was more from frustration than embarrassment. Again she wished she could counter the blood spell that compelled her to obey Orville's commands.

'Behold the Dragonsbane's staff – the 13th key,' Orville declared.

Noah held up the staff for all to see, the firestone glinting in the light from the lava.

'Noah, you have to save us,' the queen implored.

Noah opened her mouth to speak but Orville cut her off.

'Unfortunately she can't do that,' he said. 'It's not how I've written it. In line with the prophecy, she will wield the music of this world – but she will do so to destroy the world, not save it.'

'But why?' the king said to Noah. 'Why would you do that?'

'She's going to do it,' Orville declared, 'because she's in love with me.'

Steam blasted from the lava pit but all eyes in the room turned to Noah.

'Tell them, Noah,' Orville goaded. 'Tell them that you're in love with me.'

Powerless to resist his command, Noah said, 'I'm in love with him.'

'No she isn't!' Raven yelled.

Orville extended his hand to Noah. 'Come, my dear.'

Noah resisted the urge to scream. Things were going to Orville's plan and, despite the power she supposedly had, she didn't know how to stop him. She held her breath and looked at Chase. The further this spell went, the harder it would be for Chase to conjure up a new ending.

With Chase and Raven the only exceptions, everyone else looked at her with resentment and disbelief. They didn't know about the spell Orville had put on her; didn't understand her compulsion to follow his orders. To them it appeared she was willingly betraying them. She could feel Emir glaring at her so she didn't look at him.

Chase squealed. Noah looked up and followed where Chase was looking. Brinn sauntered around from behind the prison block before stopping suddenly to indulge in an emergency paw clean.

'Where did that cat come from? There's no cat in this story!' Orville bellowed. *'Wizards! Get rid of that cat!'*

Noah's heart pounded. While Orville was temporarily distracted, she waved to Chase to get her attention. When her friend looked in her direction Noah started signing. 'Your doing?' she signed.

Chase put her hands between the bars to sign her reply. 'No, but she's given me an idea!'

'What is it?'

'He obviously wasn't expecting Brinn,' Chase signed hurriedly, 'and now that I think about it – she's not mentioned in his novel. She's not part of his story. If he doesn't know about *her* – what else doesn't he know about?'

Orville doesn't know I'm *the 13th key,* Noah thought, but her hands wouldn't make the signs. She didn't know how to be the 13th key so there was no point giving Chase false hope. They didn't have time for that. They needed a real solution.

As Noah battled to think of something else that might give them an advantage, Chase smiled. Goosebumps prickled Noah's skin.

Chase signed excitedly. 'I've got it!'

'What?' Noah signed.

'You and Emir,' she signed back.

Noah shrugged. 'What?'

'Oh come on, Noah. It's perfect,' Chase signed. 'If *you* can't figure out that you're in love with Emir, how would Orville ever know? Answer? He couldn't. He'd have no idea. That's something we can use!'

Noah shook her head. Even if it *were* true, which it clearly *wasn't*, she didn't see how that would help.

Orville screamed again. *'Catch that damn cat and lock those prisoners back up!'*

Noah turned her attention from Chase to Brinn. Emir and Ardis were free and the cat, with a key in her mouth, squeezed between the bars of Montana's cell. In a heartbeat, the cell door opened and the High Priestess ran out. 'I'll release the others,' she said to Brinn.

The cat nodded and launched herself at the face of one of the wizards as Montana opened the door of Raven's cell. Emir and Ardis, with the swords they'd acquired, shielded Montana so she could release the rest of their comrades.

As Noah took off to help her friends, Orville grabbed her arm. He pulled her towards him until her face was close to his. 'You stay right there,' he said, eyes blazing. He turned off the switch on the bridge before pointing to her feet. '*Don't* move off that spot.'

Chapter 32

Orville ran towards his wizards, yelling orders as he went. Even though the scarlet robes outnumbered the prisoners three to one and the rumbling underfoot had subsided now the switch was off, the battle was intense. Swords clanged, some men shouted orders while others screamed in agony. Once Major Maggie had unshackled the king, he punched a wizard, sending him sprawling on the rocky ground. Collecting the dropped sword from the ground, Tambian cut his wife's bonds before kicking and slicing another wizard.

'*Raven!*' Noah called.

When he looked her way, she beckoned for him to come to her. He darted between two wizards, pushed another over – stealing his sword in the process – and ran towards his sister. Three scarlet robes chased him towards the bridge where Noah waited. She bobbed up and down on the spot, willing her brother to run faster. Brinn ran alongside him.

'*I* can't move off this spot,' she explained hurriedly when Raven reached her, 'but *you* can move me.'

'Got it,' Raven said as he put his shoulder against her hip.

'Watch out behind you,' she said as she folded herself over his shoulder.

'Right,' he said as he stood up and turned.

Sword raised, he yelled a challenge to the wizards that bore down on them. To Noah's surprise, they ran by them and onto the bridge.

'Cowards,' Raven muttered as he took off towards the cell block.

Noah looked down at Brinn as they passed. 'Can you stop them?'

'Easy,' Brinn said. 'Watch this.'

The cat stood up, wiggled her rear end and leapt into the air. Though Raven's shoulder dug painfully into her abdomen as he ran, Noah kept her eyes on the feline. Brinn sailed over the canyon beside the bridge. She landed nimbly on the other side and strolled across to the foot of the bridge to greet the renegade wizards. As they approached, she hissed ferociously. The scarlet robes skittered to a halt. They looked at her, then back across the crevasse.

'How the hell did she make it over that?' one of the wizards said. 'That's impossible!'

She defies all rules, Noah thought with a smile. *All rules. Even rules of nature.*

Satisfied Brinn had secured the bridge, Noah looked for Orville and found him scrambling backwards on his buttocks trying to avoid being impaled on Sachin's sword. Major Dolon was closing in on him too. If the bearded bagpipe player got a hold of him, Orville was going to have a lot more to worry about than the torn shirt and swollen eye he had now.

When Raven stopped and deposited her on the ground, Noah found herself standing before Emir and Chase near the prison block.

Emir engaged another wizard as Chase hugged her.

'So glad you're back,' Chase whispered in her ear.

'Good to be back,' Noah said.

Chase released her. 'You need a sword,' she said.

Noah brandished the Dragonsbane's staff. 'I think I'll be right.'

Chase grinned.

'Noah!' Orville called. 'Get back here!'

Noah immediately took two steps in his direction. Emir grabbed her arm. Breathing hard, he said, 'What are you doing?'

'It's a spell,' Chase explained hurriedly. 'She's compelled to do what he says.'

Noah slipped from his grasp and took another two steps before a searing pain ripped along her left arm. Blood streamed down her arm. She looked at Emir whose sword tip now rested under her chin.

'Take another step and I'll cut your throat,' he said.

Noah glanced sideways towards Orville, who was now crawling between the legs of the wizards trying to shield him from Sachin and Dolon.

'Ouch!' she said.

'*Emir!*' Chase said. 'Stop it!'

'No listen,' Noah said. 'It feels better. I don't feel as much like following Orville's commands.'

'Yes, but you know what Sachin said,' Chase replied curtly, 'we'd have to bleed you completely to fix it. We're not doing that.' She turned to Emir. 'You need to kiss her.'

'*What?*'

'Emir, kiss her,' Chase said.

'Why should I kiss her?'

'Because you're in love with her.'

'Says who?' Emir challenged.

'Says *me*,' Chase said, 'and I know about these things.'

'No,' Emir said flatly.

Chase threw her arms in the air. 'Look, we don't have time for this – you're going to do it to save the world and that's final!' she declared. 'And I'm not having any more nonsense from either of you. Got it?'

'Orville's coming back,' Raven put in as he raised his sword to fend off another wizard. 'Whatever you're going to do, you'd better do it fast.'

Noah looked around to see Orville pushing wizards out of the way as he approached.

'Now?' Emir asked.

Chase folded her arms across her chest like an old school ma'am. 'Now.'

As the chaos continued around them, Emir lowered his sword but didn't release it. He put his free hand behind Noah's neck, cradling her head gently as he leaned down to kiss her. It was much better than Noah had expected. To her surprise she found herself enjoying it. If Orville managed to get his plan back on track and destroy the world, to have this as her last memory wouldn't be so bad.

'What are you two *doing*?!' Orville screamed as he ducked his way through the mayhem. 'You're not supposed to be doing that! Emir you don't even like her! What about all those things you said about her? Shallow. Fickle. Selfish. Conceited. This ringing any bells for you?'

'Don't listen to him,' Chase said.

'And she doesn't like you either,' Orville continued, almost apoplectic. 'She thinks you're heartless, arrogant, dismissive and untrusting. Stop that!'

Emir pulled away from her. 'Arrogant? You think I'm arrogant?'

'You think I'm shallow?' Noah countered.

'Oh, cut it out, you two,' Chase snapped. 'We've made him *really* angry. *Now* we need to capitalise on the chaos before he gets his house in order.'

'Yes,' Emir said.

He hooked his hand under Noah's armpit and shoved her into the cell behind them. Unbalanced, she fell to her hands and knees on the stone and the Dragonsbane's staff skidded across the floor. The door slammed shut behind her. Noah reached out and grabbed the staff, clutching it protectively against her as she turned around again. Getting gingerly to her feet, she looked through the bars at Emir's back.

'If you want her, Orville,' Emir said, his sword raised in challenge, 'come and get her.'

Sachin's voice cut through the commotion. '*LET ME GO!*'

Orville raised his hands in the air. '*Finally!*' he said.

The fighting stopped. Silence returned.

Noah craned her neck to see what was happening. A warm flush rolled through her. Two wizards held Sachin at the edge of the crevasse.

'Now,' Orville said, smoothing his rumpled clothing, 'there is the matter of your death penalty, Major Sachin. I'd thought I might just leave you imprisoned with the rest of your friends so you could all witness the end of your world together. But since you have been so troublesome, I've changed my mind. You can take a swim in the lava.'

'Stop!' King Tambian growled. 'This is madness. Release him!'

'It's the will of the court,' Orville said. 'The death penalty stands.'

'I can pardon him,' the king countered.

'Yes, you can,' Orville agreed, 'but in case you hadn't noticed – I'm not following your orders anymore.'

As the pair continued their banter, Noah waved the Dragonsbane's staff to get Brinn's attention. Across the other side of the crevasse, the cat jumped up onto the bridge's railing and cocked her head to one side. Noah raised her index finger and then pointed down. *Flick the switch on,* she thought. Brinn gave no indication that she'd understood the gesture but she jumped down from the bridge. Noah touched the firestone in the staff against the barred door, releasing the catch. She counted her heartbeats while she waited to see if Brinn would do her bidding.

When Brinn screeched, it was like a hundred tomcats fighting. Without exception, everyone clamped their hands over their ears. Noah looked to Sachin. He dived away from his captors as the crackle and hum of the electricity through the bridge railing started. Noah kicked the cell door open and bolted through. As Emir turned, she whacked him behind the knees with the Dragonsbane's staff as the floor began trembling. When he fell backwards, she ran towards the bridge.

With the flurry of bodies writhing on the floor, things were a blur. Noah scanned the room but couldn't see Orville.

'Orville, where are you?' she called.

'Over here,' he called, his voice nearly a full octave higher than it had been earlier. 'I *need* that staff. Bring it to me *now!*'

Noah glimpsed his grimy shirt as he pushed a corpulent wizard off him. She ran towards him as best she could over the bucking floor. Hand to hand combat started again. As Noah threaded her way through the fracas, avoiding active fighting, as well as bodies on the floor, proved difficult. She slipped in a pool of blood on the floor as she reached Orville. He yanked on her arm to keep her from falling.

'Keep *moving*,' he said.

'Oh, I intend to,' Noah assured him.

Blood dripped from a laceration on his cheek and his bloodshot eyes reminded her of her Aunt Polly during one of their many heated arguments.

'I *am* going to win,' he assured her. 'Just you—'

Ardis leapt in front of them, sword raised. 'Let her go,' he said.

'Kill him,' Orville hissed in Noah's ear.

Though blood still oozed from the gash on her arm and her compulsion to follow Orville's orders had lessened, she still wasn't free. Noah swung her staff at Ardis's head. As she'd expected, he blocked the blow easily and pushed her back. She swung again. He sidestepped neatly. She thrust. He parried.

'Stop messing about, Noah!' Orville yelled. *'Finish him!'*

Noah spun, dropped and then launched herself at Ardis, ramming his ribs with her shoulder. As they both crashed to the ground, Ardis grunted.

'That was dirty, Noah,' he wheezed.

With her mouth near his ear, she whispered, 'You're going to punch me – not too hard – I need to be able to get up.'

'Noah—'

'*Don't* argue!' she hissed. 'Just do it.'

Noah pushed herself up. Ardis closed his eyes and swung his fist, collecting her on the chin. Noah reeled then fell to her right.

'Noah, get up,' Orville commanded.

Noah squeezed her eyes shut as dizziness rocked her. *I'm sure I said "not too hard".* She felt cold steel against her throat.

'Everyone stand down,' Orville said, pulling Noah against him as he shuffled back towards the bridge.

Noah gripped the staff as best she could but slippery hands made it difficult.

'Wizards,' Orville said, 'take your leave.' He looked at Brinn. 'You move, I'll finish her.'

The scarlet robes didn't hesitate. They ran across the bridge as rocks and pieces of the buildings on the slopes above crashed down.

'You're getting soft,' Noah said, 'letting your *friends* go first.'

Orville snorted. 'Don't be daft, Noah. They only *think* they're going to Earth. Actually, they won't survive the olluka tree. I made sure of that.'

'And I'm going to make sure *you* don't make it either,' Noah said as her friends closed in around her. 'If Xan wakes up, you're going to die here alongside us.'

She looked at who was left. Emir, Chase, Raven, Ardis and Montana stood together. King Tambian and Queen Rosemary flanked the seven Majors who remained. Every one of them was bleeding but each still brandished a sword.

'That's close enough,' Orville warned.

'You're outnumbered,' Tambian said. 'Let her go.'

'No chance,' Orville said. 'Noah – throw the staff into the lava!'

Noah obeyed.

A chorus of 'NO!' was drowned out by the hiss of steam as the firestone met the lava. The floor bucked violently and cracks appeared in the bridge as the stones shifted. Orville let her go and Noah collapsed against the bridge pillar.

As Raven tackled Orville, Emir crawled towards her.

'Get out of the way, Noah,' Emir said, reaching around her to turn off the switch.

'Don't turn it off yet,' Noah said, summoning all her strength to push him away. 'Trust me, I know what I'm doing.'

Emir looked her in the eye. 'You're under Orville's spell – I'm trying to help you. Why won't you let me?'

'I know what I'm doing,' Noah insisted.

'You just destroyed the 13th key, Noah!'

'I didn't destroy the 13th key. You have to trust me.'

'No. I don't.'

Noah knew he wouldn't be fobbed off, the bloody gash down her left arm proved that. If he was going to trust her, she would have to trust him. She leaned forward. 'I didn't destroy the 13th key. That was a decoy.'

'Fake firestone?' he asked.

Pillars of steam spewed into the air and the ground heaved again as the blood magic and firestone mixed in the lava.

'No,' Noah said, feeling even more lightheaded, 'real firestone.'

'Then where's the 13th key?' he said.

Noah took a deep breath. 'You're looking at her,' she said.

Emir stared at her. 'That's not possible.'

'It *is* possible,' she said, 'and it's also true.'

'*Noah!*' Raven yelled. 'Orville is loose.'

Noah turned and saw Orville running across the bridge.

'Finally,' she muttered to herself. 'Raven stop!' she called. To Emir, she said, 'Get back.'

Chunks of stone fell from the bridge and into the lava as Orville ran. Throwing his sword aside he pumped his arms harder.

'*No! No! No!*' he screamed. 'You will *not* win! I did not write it that way!'

Noah closed her eyes and concentrated on the lava. Fighting the giddiness that threatened to steal her consciousness, she identified the thirteen pieces of firestone being churned around in the lava. *I need your music,* she said in her mind, *I need you to do what I ask.* Suddenly, she knew that the stones would obey her because they were connected to her. Firestone was in her blood – part of her. Talisker's dragonsong was hers to wield.

'*The olluka tree – burn!*' she cried.

Noah opened her eyes and even though she'd commanded it, she gasped at what she saw. Ribbons of lava streamed out of the pit towards the tree. Thirteen firestones, like tiny comets, sailed through the air.

'I don't believe it,' Emir said as Noah flicked off the switch.

Orville glanced back over his shoulder as he cleared the bridge. The ground trembled again and he pitched forward, flailing his arms in an effort to recover his balance. But he slammed into the ground shoulder first. '*I* am the master,' he cried. 'I *will* make it.' He scrambled to his feet and lurched towards the olluka tree again. 'I *will*—'

He was almost at the tree when the stones hit and Noah lost sight of him in the fireball that erupted as they landed. Wild tentacles of flame reached upwards and outwards. Emir dived across Noah, shielding her from the heat.

'You're squishing me,' she wheezed.

'You're welcome,' he replied as he shifted his weight.

Raven and Chase appeared and each took one of Noah's wrists. Heaving her to her feet, they hugged her simultaneously. She embraced them tightly. Almost afraid to ask, she said, 'How is everyone else? Are they alright?'

King Tambian answered her. 'We have lost five Majors.'

'But they died with honour,' Sachin said. 'They fought to preserve our world and with their help, we have succeeded.'

'Where's Brinn?' Noah said.

'Wherever she needs to be,' Montana said.

'But not here?'

Montana shook her head. 'Not here.'

'Is she alright?'

'I'm sure she's just fine.'

'She could have said goodbye,' Noah said, 'just so we knew for sure.'

'Trust me,' Montana said, 'if she wasn't fine – we'd all know about it.'

Everyone smiled.

'Well, the keys are gone but we can retrieve the firestone,' Noah said, nodding towards the flaming olluka tree. She looked at King Tambian. 'I know I'm just a tailor, but can I suggest that we get rid of blood magic?'

The seven adepts who remained gathered around her.

The king put up his hands in surrender. 'From what I've seen here, Noah, you are not "just a tailor". But to answer your question, I have seen the danger of blood magic and you can all rest assured that I will work to undo the damage that has been done.'

Chapter 33

'You can't do that!' Noah protested. 'You can't just throw it right to me. You're supposed to turn around and throw it back over your head.'

'I'm the bride so I can do what I like,' Chase replied loftily. 'And that includes how I throw my bouquet.'

Noah risked a furtive glance over her shoulder.

'Princess Catriona doesn't look amused,' she whispered. 'I'm pretty sure she wanted to catch it.'

'I don't care,' Chase said. 'She's a spoilt brat and she needs to learn that just because she's a princess doesn't mean she can always get her own way.'

Noah glared at her friend playfully. 'Steady on,' she said. 'Keep your voice down. Her dad is my boss, remember?'

Chase laughed. 'I think I'd be more worried about Alan. He looks equally miffed that he didn't catch it.'

It was Noah's turn to laugh as Ardis came up behind Chase, wrapping his arms around his bride's waist.

'Ready to go?' he asked.

'Absolutely,' Chase smiled.

To Noah's surprise, Ardis took her hand and kissed it solemnly.

'Thank you for everything,' he said. 'I owe you a great deal.'

'Don't be silly,' Noah said, embarrassed by the attention. 'It was my honour to make Chase's dress. That's what I do, you know.'

'I don't mean the dress,' he said. 'If it wasn't for you, none of us would be here. You kept Chase safe and you delivered us a great victory here. These things are not easily forgotten.'

'Don't mention it,' Noah said, really meaning it.

She hugged them both one more time before heading off to get a drink.

'Punch?' Raven asked upon her arrival at what would better be described as a punch trough than a punch bowl.

'The liquid kind, yes please,' Noah said as he gesticulated wildly with the ladle. 'Who died and made you minister-in-charge of the punchbowl anyway?'

'No one,' he answered jovially, 'but Princess Catriona says I'm a natural with punch.'

'I'm sure she did,' Noah said, sipping the delicious concoction.

There were definitely benefits to working for the king. He'd been very generous in offering his home and catering service for Chase and Ardis's wedding. In the wake of events at the Solstice Festival, the king had been falling over himself looking for ways to thank Noah for her efforts. She hadn't accepted anything for herself but had been more than willing to milk his generosity for her friend.

'I'm going to dance with the princess,' Raven said.

'Have fun,' Noah called to his retreating back.

The two weeks since the Festival had been a whirlwind time. Noah had been officially appointed to the position of Royal Tailor at the palace in Leninstar. In the rush to repeal all the legislation outlawing raiki since Orville's spectacular demise, most of the Majors had stayed in Leninstar for the past fortnight. As Ardis and a contingent of his soldiers had also been required to oversee matters relating to the dismantling of the Blood Magic Board in Leninstar, it had been decided that his wedding would best be held in the royal city. With wedding bells in the air, all the usual suspects had been in town – Chase's mother had even come for the nuptials – but now it was all coming to an end.

Tomorrow, all Mellifont personnel would return home. Sachin and his fellow Majors would escort the twelve pieces of firestone Noah had rescued from the lava to fashion into new keys. Noah had avoided thinking much about it until now but in the morning, her friends would be heading out. Chase was going with Ardis and Raven was leaving too. She'd be the only one left in Leninstar. Everyone else would be a thousand leagues away. There'd been absolutely no thought of returning to Earth. There was nothing for her to go back to. Her real family and friends were here. She'd visited Aunt Polly to try as best she could to explain the situation. It hadn't gone well but Noah hadn't expected it to.

Alan arrived as Noah sipped on her punch.

'Would you care to dance?' he asked, offering her his hand.

Though she'd warmed to Alan over the past few weeks, Noah was still reluctant to get too close to him. However, it would be rude to refuse. 'I'd love to dance,' she said, placing her glass on the table.

'I see you've got the stone back in your ring,' he said. 'Do you think it's wise to advertise that you have a piece of firestone?'

'No,' Noah admitted. 'Sachin says I can't keep it this way but I'm allowed to have it until I return to Mellifont for formal training.'

'I can't wait for you to come to the Academy,' Alan said, eyes gleaming.

Noah laughed. 'Steady on,' she said. 'I'm going to be pretty busy – King's Tailor, Dragonsbane and sorting out the family farm so I won't be there any time soon.'

'Well, I'll be waiting for you,' he said. Glancing at her shoes, he asked, 'How do you dance in those things?'

Noah looked down. 'They're very stylish I'll have you know.'

'If you're wearing them, then I don't doubt it, but my question is how do you dance in them?'

'Just like walking,' she answered, 'one foot after the other.'

Alan was a surprisingly good dancer and Noah found herself enjoying a jig on the dance floor.

'Seen Brinn?' she asked as she ducked under his arm.

'I'm right here,' Brinn said.

Noah turned to see Sachin at her side, with the haughty feline lying limply in his arms.

'Are you hurt?' Noah asked with concern.

'Don't be stupid,' Brinn admonished. 'I'm dancing with Sachin. Can't you tell?'

'Of course you are,' Noah said. 'My mistake.'

'I don't know how she managed to save the world,' Brinn muttered, 'dumb as a spanner, I swear ... Are you sure it wasn't someone dressed up as her? A cat in disguise maybe?'

Sachin smiled apologetically. 'We'll catch you later,' he said as he sashayed away with the cat in his arms.

Noah laughed as Emir tapped Alan on the shoulder.

'May I?' he asked.

'Of course,' Alan said. 'I'll see you later, Noah.'

Noah nodded. 'Where've you been?' she said to Emir as she took his hand.

'Talking to the king,' he replied. 'He's offered me a job.'

'Oh?'

'Orville's old job actually,' he said.

'Really?' she said. 'I didn't know you were a bad fiction writer with an insatiable desire for world domination.'

Emir shook his head. 'Not that job,' he said. 'The one he was supposed to be doing – advising the king.'

'Oh, that one,' said Noah. 'I think you'd be much better at that one.'

'Yes,' Emir agreed. 'I think so too.'

An awkward silence followed.

'So is that okay with you?' he said.

'What?'

'Is it okay with you if I take the job?' he replied.

Why was he asking her permission? Things had been really weird between them since the Solstice Festival. Dealing with Emir had always been awkward but now talking to him was like exfoliating with a cheese grater – you could get the desired result but it was a painful journey.

'Would it make you uncomfortable if I took the job? You have a job in the palace already. If I took this job I'd be in the palace too ... I just thought it might make you uncomfortable,' he said.

'You haven't accepted the job?'

He shook his head. 'I told the king I'd think about it.'

'You told the king you'd think about it?' she said, incredulous. Was he crazy? 'Let me get this straight,' she said, 'the king offered you a job and you said you'd get back to him?'

'Something like that,' he said.

'Gutsy,' she said.

'Well?'

'Do you want the job?' Noah asked.

'Yes, I think it would be good,' he replied.

'Then do it,' she said. 'As long as you're not advising him in matters of fashion, I don't think we'll have a problem.'

'Okay. Good,' he said. 'I have to go back to Mellifont to tidy up a few things so I won't be starting for a couple of weeks. You'll have some time to get settled before I get back.'

She nodded. 'Yep, everyone's pretty much heading off tomorrow.'

'You going to be alright?' he asked.

'Of course,' Noah said. 'I'll be really busy designing and thankfully I like my own company.'

'Yeah, well … I have something for you … before I go …'

'What is it?'

'I can't tell you what it is. I have to show you. Come on,' he said, taking her hand and leading her off the dance floor.

'Oh, please tell me what it is.'

'I told you, I'm not telling you. You'll have to wait and see.'

She gave up. She knew how stubborn he was. If he said he wasn't going to tell her, then he wasn't going to tell her. She'd just have to wait until they got to wherever it was he was taking her.

The palace grounds were huge and she wondered if she should remove her shoes as a precaution. It could be a long walk. Emir took her outside to a fenced-off area. They walked up to the fence.

'You're giving me a garden?' she asked.

Emir whistled and a small ball of fur barrelled out from behind a shrub and came scampering towards the fence.

'A puppy? For me?'

Emir nodded. 'I thought you might get lonely after everyone left.'

Suddenly Noah was panic-stricken. 'What if the king won't let me keep him?' she said.

'He's fine with it.'

'You've checked?'

'Of course.'

'Can we go in there?'

'The gate's unlocked.'

Noah raced along the fence to the gate, flung it open and caught the fur-ball as it catapulted itself into her arms. She had quite a time of it trying to avoid its slobbering tongue but she didn't care. Nor did she care that she was dressed in very expensive clothes; she hugged her Alsatian puppy tightly. Too excited to stay still for long, the pup struggled to get down and then leapt around her legs. Noah was overwhelmed.

'This is the best present,' she said as she tried to pat the pup. 'Thank you. You're very thoughtful.'

'So not heartless, arrogant, dismissive and untrusting?' he said.

'That's what Orville *wrote* that I thought,' she said. 'It's not really what I thought.'

He raised an eyebrow.

'Okay, I might have thought you were a bit stuffy,' she admitted. 'Do you still think I'm shallow, fickle, selfish and conceited?'

'Not any more, no,' he said.

Noah's eyes widened and she slapped him playfully on the arm.

Emir smiled and looked at the puppy that was still bouncing around at their feet. 'What are you going to call him?'

Noah really had to think about it. 'Kane,' she said eventually.

'Any particular reason?'

Noah smiled. 'Because that's what we gave Orville – a caning.'

'I like it,' Emir said, putting his arms around her and kissing her tenderly.

Titles by Sarah Fisher

Dragonscale series

The 13th Key
Firestone
Redemption

For the latest news on new releases, sign up to Sarah's website:
https://www.sarahfisherauthor.com/

Or follow Sarah on Facebook or Instagram:
@sarahfisherauthor